OBEDIENCE

Obedience
Copyright © 2025 by James Kennedy

All rights reserved.

No part of this publication may be reproduced, distributed, or transmitted in any form or by any means, including photocopying, recording, or other electronic or mechanical methods, without the prior written permission of the publisher, except as permitted by U.S. copyright law. For permission requests, contact jtkennedyauthor.com.

The story, all names, characters, and incidents portrayed in this production are fictitious. No identification with actual persons (living or deceased), places, buildings, and products is intended or should be inferred.

ISBN: 979-8-9932472-1-2 (paperback)
ISBN: 979-8-9932472-8-1 (hardback)
ISBN: 979-8-9932472-5-0 (e-book)

Cover Design by LLewellenDesigns.com

First Edition 2025

To God, who I am forever obedient to.

"Do not be conformed to this world, but be transformed by the renewal of your mind, that by testing you may discern what is the will of God, what is good and acceptable and perfect."

Romans 12:2 (ESV)

Dear Reader:

You are about to embark on a journey that has been a labor of love for nearly twelve years. *Obedience* first began for me in November 2013, shortly after I saw the *Catching Fire* movie in theaters. As a teenager, I was an avid fan of *The Hunger Games* series. Going into the movie, I had high expectations for how the events of the book would play out on screen — particularly Katniss's climactic act of defiance, when she shoots her arrow at the force field.

I remember sitting on the edge of my seat, waiting for the cinematic explosion. In my mind, I'd already envisioned it a hundred times: a blinding flash of light, a storm of energy shattering the arena. But instead, the force field broke into hexagonal plates that rained down around Katniss. With each piece that crumbled, so did my vision.

That day, I made a promise to myself: One day, I would write a story with a force field, and it would look the way I'd always envisioned. Not a dome made of metal plates or geometric tiles, but something spectacular. A transparent shield, clear as glass but hard as stone. A barrier that pulsed with energy, powerful enough to cover an entire city.

And so, the Barrier was born.

New York City's One World Trade Center quickly became the anchor point for the story. As the tallest building in North America, it made sense that the Barrier would radiate from its spire and seal Lower Manhattan beneath it. From there, John Madoc's story began to unfold — a story that has changed nearly a dozen times, rewritten again and again for more than a decade.

I never would've imagined all this story would come to mean to me. And I hope, if nothing else, it sticks with you the same way it has stuck with me.

To me, John's story is more than just fiction — it carries a piece of my own testimony. When I was John's age, I wrestled with the pressure to appease others and to be someone I wasn't. I lost sight of my true self, and for a time, I became someone I hardly recognized.

Like John, I learned to overcome. But it wasn't in my own strength — it was through Christ. His redeeming love and grace freed me from the craving for the world's approval, from the sorrow that made me question my worth, and from the chains that bound me. In Him, I discovered my true identity, and the truth of His gospel set me free.

It's with that heart that I hand *Obedience* to you. My hope is that within these pages, you find room to laugh, to cry, and to feel deeply. But most of all, I want you to feel hope. Reassurance. Strength. The trials you've faced aren't barriers meant to break you or restrain you. They're a testimony to your resilience and God's sovereign hand over your life. And because of that, through faith in Christ, you can endure all things — so long as you refuse to give up.

May you see that same momentum carrying John to the very last word.

Happy reading,
James

OBEDIENCE

JAMES KENNEDY

One

THERE'S A SPLIT SECOND before the sun rises when an iridescent glow covers the city. It's so fleeting that at first, you might think your eyes are playing tricks on you. But it repeats each morning, just long enough to reveal a curve in the sky that wasn't there before. Almost as quickly as it appears, the sun breaks over the horizon and renders the curve invisible. That split second is the only time you'd ever know you were under anything but the sky.

It serves as a reminder that we're trapped here. That the world we're living in is real, and the Barrier still stands. I've never known a day without it, and I've never known a life on the other side of it.

Mother used to tell stories of life before the war, before the Barrier. But they always felt more like dreams than memories. "Things haven't always been this way," she'd tell me. "And they won't be forever."

But as I open my eyes to the technicolor hues dancing across my bedroom walls, dread sinks to the pit of my stomach. For eighteen years, I've hoped *this* day would be different. That long before today ever came, we'd be delivered from this, and I'd be spared from who I'm expected to become. But for eighteen years, nothing's changed. Eighteen years today.

As soon as the sky transitions to the soft, warm glow of a natural sunrise, I hear shuffling in the hall outside my door. Lifting my head, I see light sifting through the crack beneath it. There's a shadow there that sways back and forth, and soon, tiny toes poke through. They can only belong to one person — my little brother, Liam.

He bursts through the door like a bull out of its pen, charging straight for the bed. He gains momentum with every step until he reaches the footboard, then lunges onto the mattress. I barely move my legs in time to avoid being crushed under his weight, but he doesn't stop there. He practically somersaults up the mattress until he's hovering over me. His small hazel eyes — our mother's eyes — lock on mine as he grabs my shoulders and shakes me.

"John!" he shouts. "Wake up, wake up, wake up!"

I groan. "Liam, I'm clearly awake. What's the matter with you?"

The shaking ceases. He releases my shoulders and plops on my chest, knocking the breath out of me.

"Mother sent me to get you up, chump. The Market opens in fifteen minutes, and if you're not there early, you'll be lucky to make it home before dark."

"Why can't *you* go?" I argue.

"Just 'cause it's your birthday doesn't mean you get a free pass," he winks.

I sigh and pretend to start getting up, which causes Liam to roll off the bed. Before I can fully sit up, he's already halfway to the door.

"Fifteen minutes!" he shouts over his shoulder. "Or I'm coming back up here!"

I trace his footsteps down the hall, then listen closely as he fumbles downstairs until he hits the ground level. At that point, the floor between us blocks out any other noise, and I'm safe from him.

My head falls reluctantly against my pillow, and I let out a heavy sigh. The last thing I want to do is get out of bed. Doing so means the day has started, and every second of this day puts me closer to being drafted.

The draft. The thing I've feared my whole life. It comes for every eighteen-year-old boy on the first day of a new year. All the boys who turned eighteen the previous year are rounded up and shipped to a military base in Lower Manhattan for a sixteen-week training term. Afterwards, they're enlisted into different roles in the military. Some are responsible for food supply, while others go on to train the next wave of draftees. All are trained to fight — no one is exempt from that. The draft has been required by law ever since day one under the Barrier. It exists to keep our military employed and our community safe in case the Barrier ever falls.

It's comforting, really, to know the massive dome designed to keep us safe may not actually do so in the long run. And, as a result, boys like me are predestined to be our last line of defense.

Today means a lot of things for me — my birthday, the end of another year. But none of it matters with the draft hanging over my head. It's always felt distant, but now, it's pounding at my door.

I feel myself start to slip away and flinch at the sound of something clattering against the floor downstairs. I realize if I don't move now, Liam will march back up here and drag me out of bed himself.

I close my eyes and try to silence my thoughts, take a deep breath, and slide my feet over the side of the bed. As soon as they press into the carpet below, I know there's no going back.

I feel my way to the bathroom and flip the switch. Instantly, a harsh white light flickers to life, blinding me. I squeeze my eyes shut and slowly reopen them as they adjust. When they do, I come face-to-face with my reflection in the mirror above the vanity. Hollow ice-blue eyes stare back at me. Unkempt blonde hair drapes across my forehead. Dark circles burrow beneath my eyelids. Weak, paper-thin arms hang out of a one-size-too-big T-shirt, and a pair of gray sweatpants barely cling to my waist.

These are the men we trust to fight for us. Men like me — weak, tired, and afraid. Forced to grow up and become a hero for the rest of the community. I give myself a pitiful look and reach over to run the shower.

I shower quickly for the fear that Liam might be waiting in my room if I take too long. Wrapping an overused towel around my waist, I tiptoe back into the bedroom. I step into a pair of dark corduroys, button up a white long-sleeve shirt, then tug a coarse sweater vest over it, flicking the shirt collar neatly over the neckline. Once I'm comfortable, I spin around and catch one more glimpse of myself in the bathroom mirror through the open door.

"Happy birthday, Johnny," I mock myself, shooting pointer fingers out at my reflection.

I almost laugh at the irony of it all. I don't look like a soldier. I'm certainly not dressed the part. I don't have the strong build you'd envision when you think of the men fighting to protect our nation. I don't have the endurance, the perseverance, much less the courage. And yet, this is who I'm supposed to be. I don't know how.

Even more, I don't know why they'd ever choose us.

Without wasting any more time, I step into the hall and ease my way toward the stairs with caution. I don't want to give myself away just yet, even though Liam's probably counting down the seconds. I don't want to see the look on Mother's face — not today. Not with the draft looming. Any last moments we have together are already tainted by what's coming tomorrow. If I can just make it out the door fast enough, it won't matter how long I'm stuck at The Market. The longer I'm gone, the better it'll be. For everyone.

Our home is quaint: bay windows at the front of the house that overlook the street. A small living room with a beige sectional. Chestnut furniture that predates us. Bare walls, no pictures, not even a single keepsake to make it feel like our own.

None of it is actually ours, anyway. When the Barrier touched down, men and women from all over the East Coast were brought into the city and sheltered in selected housing. The military arranged it all, from the number of people allowed under the Barrier to the location of our neighborhoods to the homes we live in now. My parents were some of the fortunate ones housed in an upper district, arguably one of the nicer areas of the city. Red-brick townhomes and apartment buildings line the streets, and much of the city is still intact here. The deeper you go, the worse it gets.

As I round the landing, I teeter off balance. My foot slaps against the hardwood, giving me away. Liam jerks around mid-sentence. I halt like a deer in headlights.

"John!" he hollers. I wince at his voice. Before I can disappear, he's running at me, arms wide.

"You're right on time," he affirms as his little body collides with mine. His adoration would be flattering to anyone else, but to me, it's painstakingly annoying.

I pat him on the back, then gently push him away, trying to create space between us. Mother watches thoughtfully from a distance. Her eyes find mine as she sweeps across the threshold between the kitchen and living room.

"Happy birthday to you . . ." she sings.

"No, no, no," I plead. "Please don't."

She chuckles and pulls me into a hug. Her apron crunches against my shirt, and I glance down to find a dried stain that won't wash out easily. She smells of vanilla and eucalyptus, sweet but earthy. It smells like home.

I return her embrace because I know it's what she wants. But the longer she holds me, the more pressure builds in my chest. She pulls away and anchors me in front of her, arms-length away, examining every detail of my face.

"John," she exhales. "You look so handsome . . ." I grin bashfully, but it instantly fades because I know what comes next. ". . . so much like your father."

It almost comes out as a whisper. *Father*. Even the word feels foreign. Father has always been more of a shadow than a part of our family. He wasn't always gone, but I have more memories of his absence than I do of him being here.

It's been said that the war, the thing that sent us into exile, began in the west. When it started moving east, men were incentivized to work as free laborers on the Barrier in return for a spot in the city for their families. One of these men was my father. He and Mother tried to adapt and start fresh under the Barrier, and the best way they knew how was to start a family. They had me, and Father was around for the earliest parts of my life. Until he wasn't.

Not long after the inaugural draft, he signed on to train draftees and help lead the efforts supporting the draft. Whenever Draft Day rolled around each year, he'd disappear for the duration of the term. Then, like clockwork, he'd be right back here with Mother and me. A decade later, Mother became pregnant with Liam, and things began to change.

I was never sure what it was for him. Maybe it was the pressure of having another child or his obsession with the draft. But that year, Liam came early before the term had ended. Weeks passed, and Mother waited for Father to return home to meet his new baby boy. Then months. Then years. We could only assume the worst, but the military never confirmed his death. He just never came back.

I look away from Mother and try to focus my gaze elsewhere, but she persists. Her eyes burn into my profile as I desperately try to escape the moment. It's frustrating being constantly compared to someone I hardly knew, let alone someone who walked out on his family at a time when we needed him the most. If that's all anyone sees when they look at me, how could I see myself any differently?

Mother lowers her eyes and clears her throat. "Right," she mutters. She pauses briefly as the gears spin in her head, working to change the subject. "I assume Liam already told you about your errand?"

From over her shoulder, I watch Liam swipe a stack of compartmentalized trays off the counter. He waddles out of the kitchen, the trays wobbling with each step, barely balanced in his grubby hands. When he reaches us, he dumps them into a worn leather messenger bag hanging from a coat hook beside the front door.

"Ready to go, chump!" he beams, dusting off his hands.

My eyes drift back to Mother, and I give her a subtle nod.

"You sure you don't mind?" she asks gingerly.

I shake my head. "Not at all."

Obediently, I remove the bag from its hook and sling the strap over my shoulder. Its gravity threatens to pull me down, but I resist. I slip on a pair of sneakers and tighten the laces with shaky hands. My heart races, urging me to move quickly. I need to get out. Before Mother can say anything more — or anything about the draft.

But before I can, she stops me at the door. "Try to at least enjoy yourself for one more day, John," she begs. "Don't punish yourself for what's out of your control."

I shrug. "I'll do my best, I guess."

Turning the brass knob, a cool winter breeze blows in from outside. I know there's more Mother wants to say, and there's more I wish I had the guts to say too. But I can't stand to be here any longer, and she knows it.

As I step through the doorway, I glance up at the sky. A clear blue pallet illuminated by natural sunlight, seamless and unending. But it's merely a reflection. Though I can't see it, I know the Barrier is there, sealing me and everyone else inside the city. There's no stopping what's coming. Not even another day I could escape to. Even if I tried to run, there's nowhere I could go.

"John!" Mother calls out to me. I turn to face her with my hand still gripping the knob, one foot in, the other out the door.

My chest tightens. *Don't say it*, I think. *Please, just let me go.*

But to my relief, a tender smile softens her face. "Happy birthday." She looks at me as if I'm still a little boy, not a young man crushed by the weight of his destiny. "Tomorrow we know what happens, but today — today is *your* day. They don't get to take that from you."

For a moment, I believe her. Before the Barrier, I'm sure boys my age dreamed of turning eighteen. It was probably a rite of passage, of sorts. They could be anyone or do anything. They had their whole lives ahead of them. I try to hold onto that feeling as if I do too.

As Mother looks at me longingly, I return her smile. This time, it's genuine.

Two

Everyone is outside today. Children rambunctiously chase each other through crowds of civilians. They're all out for the same reason I am. Each week, the military provides each household with enough food to last the week. It comes in pre-packaged plastic trays that we return to The Market to receive our rations for the following week. If you don't, you won't eat. There's no second round. And when the whole city relies on one day to make it happen, it's never a quick process.

I clutch the messenger bag close to my chest and shrink into the crowd. I do everything I can to blend in and not draw any attention to myself. It's likely someone would recognize me. After all, when you live under a bubble, everyone's a familiar face.

Just when I think I'm in the clear, one face in particular stands out among the rest. Deep in conversation with an older man across the street — and clearly blocking the flow of traffic — is Ethan Greene, possibly the closest thing I have to a best friend. Aside from Mother and Liam, he's the only other person who knows what today is. So when his wide green eyes find mine, I know there's no avoiding it.

And Ethan Greene is never discreet about anything.

Anxiety swirls in the pit of my stomach. It's not that I'm not happy to see him, but I know he'll only want to talk about one thing. Ethan turned eighteen months ago, and he's waited eagerly for the day I'd finally catch up. He's had all this time to prepare, while I've barely had a morning.

I want so badly to turn in the opposite direction. To disappear into the crowd. After all, there are enough people. But it's no use. He's already wrapping up his conversation and crossing the street toward me.

Ethan weaves through the crowd with his trays in hand — one set for him, and another for his mother. His shaggy brown hair bounces in step with his feet. He cradles the trays in the nook of his arm and waves with the other, trying to get my attention. In doing so, he manages to drop a few. He bends to pick them up in the middle of the street, resulting in frustrated remarks from the people around him. Several shoot a glance in my direction after noticing him waving. Heat rushes to my cheeks. So much for trying to blend in.

I keep walking forward while Ethan collects himself. Before I can stop, my body slams into an object in front of me. I grunt and stagger backward. "Oh, I'm sorry," I blurt out.

Looking up, I see a man staring down at me. He's as still as a statue in the middle of everyone else. His neck is beaded with sweat, and his gray quarter-zip is soaked through. His body reeks of cigarette smoke and days without a shower. Black teardrops are tattooed under his eyelids, making his eyes look dark and otherworldly. In his hand, I notice he's holding a wooden rod. And connected to it is a once-white poster that reads:

**DRAFT DAY ISN'T COMING.
THE END TIMES ARE NEAR.**

My heart pounds as I read the words over again. I know they're not true — they couldn't be, right? But something about them strikes me. Is this really what people think? I try to move away, but I'm frozen in place.

Suddenly, a hand drops on my shoulder, startling me. Clearly my face shows it too, because when I turn to see Ethan standing beside me, his eyes stretch as wide as they can go.

"Geez, Johnny, don't give yourself a heart attack," Ethan remarks. He glances up at the man holding the poster and squints to read it.

"The end times are near, *wooo*!" He twiddles his fingers and leans in close to my face, then laughs, mocking the protester.

The man spits at Ethan and barks obscenities at him, but Ethan shakes it off. "Nice try, hot shot! Next time, make a better poster. You're not fooling anyone."

Ethan slings his arm around my shoulder and guides me away from the man before he can bite back. Looking around, I notice other men like him standing among the crowd. Still as a rock, raising their posters high above the crowd. All saying the exact same thing.

"What's with these guys?" I ask, though I don't expect Ethan to know the answer.

He keeps his gaze ahead as he says, "They're extremists, John. They're out here every year before Draft Day. You'd know this if you went outside more often."

"This is *exactly* why I don't go outside," I scoff.

"But they sure do look mighty stupid when the birthday boy himself is—"

I slap my hand over Ethan's mouth. He halts where he stands and furrows his brows. A few people shuffle past us.

"Keep walking, kid!" one of them hisses impatiently.

"Ethan, please . . . just don't say anything about it, okay? Not here." I beg him, throwing a nervous glance at a nearby protester.

Ethan rolls his eyes and peels my hand off his face. "John, you can't hide from the truth forever. Besides, it's not like it's criminal to have a birthday the day before Draft Day. Just . . . a bit unlucky, yeah?"

"Yeah, well, you know who would disagree? Those *extremists* who believe the draft isn't coming this year." I throw his own word back at him.

Ethan crosses his arms. "Psh. As if the draft wouldn't happen. Everyone knows it's coming, John. Especially now that you're of age, there'd be no reason for it not to. You're the last one."

I can't deny he's right, but I don't want to admit it.

"Anyway, should we get going?" Ethan suggests, signaling in the direction of The Market.

I nod and secure the messenger bag back over my shoulder.

Ethan and his mother live near the edge of our neighborhood. His father also worked on the Barrier, same as mine, which is how they met. Like my father, Ethan's was recruited to help oversee training for the draft. He eventually became my father's second in command. After each term, Ethan's parents would frequently visit our home for dinners and drop-ins, and Ethan was always with them. Given we're the same age, we quickly became friends, though Ethan didn't give me much of a choice. Ethan could make friends with anyone, and he made it his personal mission to become mine. Lucky for him, it worked.

His father died tragically of a heart attack during the same term my father disappeared. The military confirmed it. They were on the Greene family's doorstep that same afternoon to collect his belongings. Ethan says his mother never got over it, but I don't think Ethan did either. He just has a better way of hiding it.

And now, here we are, nearly a decade later. The Madoc and Greene boys, destined to be drafted together. It's sickening to know we'll surely be the talk of the draft once it starts. Even worse, our fathers aren't even here to see us off. They were supposed to train us themselves — now all we have is each other.

"Your mom really sent you to do this today? On your birthday?" Ethan asks.

"It's not like I had to move around any plans. Besides, I wanted to get out of the house."

"That's fair," he says. "That makes two of us then. I usually make the run for my mom, though, anyway."

"Yeah, how's she doing?"

Ethan shrugs. "Well, she's not out here with one of those posters declaring the end times are near, but she sure is acting like it at home. She's nervous for me, I think."

His words seem to drift off. I can tell he has more on his mind, but he's quick to rush into a new topic.

"Hey, have I told you about tonight yet?"

"What about tonight?" I ask, a little harsher than I intend.

"Some of the guys our age are getting together at the pub on the corner of 14th and 8th to ring in the new year." He pauses for a moment before adding, "And, you know, to let loose for one more night of freedom."

I know the place he's referring to. Right on the edge of our neighborhood is an old pub. It's completely abandoned. Much of the interior hasn't been touched since the Barrier came down. It's nothing but a bunch of dusty chairs and barstools, but it's been popularized as the go-to drinking spot. Its entire collection of booze from when it was in operation is still mostly shelved. I take it that's what he's referring to when he says *let loose*.

Ethan can tell I'm already uncomfortable by the invitation. "Oh, come on, Johnny. Live a little! Don't be so close-minded."

I don't respond, and I don't alter my composure. Having a few drinks, letting my guard down, all on the last night before the rest of our lives change sounds completely irresponsible. It's what the military wants. They want us to be disoriented and defenseless when they come for us. Going to the pub tonight with a group our age in the wake of the draft feels suicidal.

"How'd you hear about this?" I question.

"Word gets around, and I hear about it. I'm pretty popular, you know."

I let out a laugh. He and I both know that's *not* true.

"All I'm saying is, you should come, man," he persuades. "The party is super exclusive. Invitation only. You're lucky I'm even telling you about it."

"Oh, and I'm supposed to be honored?" I chuckle. "Exclusive as in, it's the only party happening in the entire city tonight?"

Ethan laughs with me. "No, but really. I heard some guys talking about it the other day and figured you and I could pop in. You don't have to stay long. Don't even feel like you have to drink. It'd be a good way to connect with some of the guys we'll be bunk buddies with, is all."

I stuff my hands in my pockets, still resistant to the idea.

"Birthday. Boy." Ethan jabs his finger into my shoulder with each word. I push him aside playfully.

"I'll consider it," I say, even though I don't mean it. But it's enough to get him off my case.

Up ahead, the Freedom Tower comes into view. It looms proud and mighty over the rest of the city. Not a single inch of it is warped or damaged in any way. It's still as pristine as the day it was built. It holds the Barrier from the tip of its antenna. From there, the dome falls over Lower Manhattan, hugging the rim of the peninsula.

With so much of the skyline in ruins, the tower is even more prominent, rising from the ashes that surround it. It serves as a beacon of hope for our community and a symbol of the freedom that unites us under the Barrier. Or at least that's how some people view it.

Ethan and I press on until The Market tents appear in the distance. As we get closer, the streets narrow and give way to heavy overgrowth. Weeds burst through cracks in the concrete and cling to the sides of buildings like spiderwebs. Thick mossy grass blankets the ground beneath us, making it difficult to walk.

We stay close together as people begin to form a line in front of The Market. We're close enough now to hear voices urging the crowd forward to receive their rations. I peer over a few heads and spot men dressed head to toe in skin-tight armor as black as night. Some wear helmets that shield their faces, while others are exposed. Soldiers stand guard around the perimeter and keep watch over the crowd. They clutch weapons strapped to their shoulders, fingers tapping the triggers. Ready to fire at the first sign of disloyalty.

"There's a look at our future, eh, Johnny?" Ethan nudges me.

I swallow hard and stay silent, letting that reality sink in.

Ethan and I step forward as more people are ushered inside. Up ahead, a break in the trees reveals the massive silky white tents of The Market stretched tight across the clearing, their tops pinched into twin peaks. Thick coiled wires are secured around the rim of the park, anchoring the tents in place. The whole thing sits in the middle of a ring of dead grass that used to be a park.

Soldiers shuffle in and out of the tents, lugging heavy wooden crates between them. They load them onto the backs of military transports stationed near the edge of the park. Their engines idle with a low mechanical growl that sends a tremor through the ground. As they lurch forward, their tires kick up clouds of dust, leaving a thick haze hanging in the air.

At the front of the tents, the drape is pulled back to form an entryway. Soldiers stand on either side, carefully inspecting each person who approaches them. Their arms are crossed over padded vests, rifles slung across their backs. From the looks of it, they only allow two people to enter at a time.

As soon as the pair in front of us goes in, Ethan and I step up to the soldiers. Their faces are hidden behind reflective visors built into their helmets. Their necks tilt downward, giving the impression they're looking at us, but all I see is my own timid reflection staring back at me.

"How's it going, fellas?" Ethan greets them casually.

As expected, the soldiers don't respond. They remain stiff as stone.

"Tough crowd," Ethan whispers out of the corner of his mouth.

I disregard his comment and drop my gaze. Even though I can't see their eyes, I can feel the soldiers examining me. It's possible they recognize me. They might recognize Ethan too. After all, we're both spitting images of our fathers. I shrink into myself, trying to hide any trace of resemblance. Ethan, on the other hand, doesn't seem to care.

The soldiers split up. One pats me down from head to toe, and the other does the same to Ethan.

"Clear," they mutter in unison. One of them swats the drape aside, allowing us to enter. I nod timidly as a courtesy but keep my face lowered.

Sawdust and plastic hit my nose as we slip through the opening. Inside, The Market unfolds in a wide circular space enclosed beneath the towering tents. Massive wooden crates are stacked in the center. The lid of one has been pried open, revealing hundreds of plastic packs containing our rations, each stamped with a military emblem and labeled by meal type.

Next to the open crate stand two more soldiers. Their visors are lifted, revealing their faces. Both look young, maybe only a few years older than Ethan and me, but their expressions are worn and stern. Their roles in the military have clearly stripped away any youth they had left.

Accompanying them is an older woman. Her salt-and-pepper hair is pulled back in a tight bun, stretching her facial features. Her eyes are smoky, and her lips press into a flat line against a lit cigarette. Smoke trails from her mouth, mingling with the cool mist rising from the open crate. Judging by the sculpted calves bulging against her cargo pants, she's more fit for the draft than Ethan or me.

"Name?" one of the soldiers barks. His eyes narrow at Ethan first.

"Ethan Greene," Ethan states proudly. He even strikes a pose, placing his fists at his hips and lifting his chin up to the soldier.

The soldier rolls his eyes. "How many in your household?"

"Two," Ethan replies.

The soldier opposite the woman begins digging through the open crate. He pulls out a handful of packs and cradles them in the nook of his elbow.

"Age?" the soldier asks next.

"Eighteen."

The soldier retrieving the packs stops, then returns half of what he's picked up to the crate. Ethan barely seems to notice, but I do. My heart skips a beat. They know the draft is coming — and they know Ethan's rations will be served to him separately.

The soldier dumps the allotment into Ethan's hands. Ethan shows no sign of weakness, even though his flimsy biceps quiver beneath the weight.

"Keep loading me up, sarg," Ethan jokes. "I can take it." But the soldier isn't amused. The woman next to him pulls out a device and begins jabbing her finger into the screen.

The soldier turns to me now. "Name?"

I cringe. "John Madoc."

The woman's eyes shoot up from her screen. She tears the cigarette from her mouth and holds it between her index and middle fingers. Her eyes ricochet between Ethan and me, connecting the dots in her mind.

"Madoc?" she croaks.

My breath catches in my throat. I don't acknowledge her. I don't even flinch, pretending I didn't hear her. I glance nervously back up at the soldier and wait for him to continue.

"How many in your household?"

"Three, sir."

As if on cue, the soldier behind him begins digging through the crate again. The woman continues to stare curiously at the two of us. My eyes dart all over the room, everywhere except where she stands, never lingering in one place for too long.

"As in Anthony's boy?" she asks. She's not backing down.

Anthony. My father's name. A name that doesn't feel like it belongs to anyone anymore. A name that shouldn't even be spoken because it hasn't been said in so long. My stomach twists into a knot when she says it. The soldier interrogating me raises his brow. *He knows.*

"Age?" he asks next — and I wish he wouldn't.

I freeze. I don't want to say it. The soldier tilts his head, waiting for me to respond, but something tells me he already knows the answer.

"Eightee—" Ethan butts in. I punch him hard in the shoulder, and he gives me a wounded look.

"Somebody had to say something," he mutters.

"Well then?" the soldier asks, raising his voice. He clearly heard what Ethan started to say, but he fixes his gaze on me. He wants to hear it from me.

"Eighteen, sir," I relent.

The other soldier swings a stack of packs in my direction, but I intercept him with the messenger bag. He deposits them inside, and I seal the bag with its clasps as soon as he's finished.

The woman clicks a button to power off her device and slides it into her back pocket.

"Well, it was nice chatting," Ethan says, his voice rising in pitch. I glance over to see his arms still quivering and his foot tapping the dirt impatiently. "But we better get going."

"Madoc, you wait just a second," the woman intervenes. Ethan's eyes grow frantic, his lips parted just enough to show he has the next words locked and loaded. But the woman steps forward and holds her palm to his face, silencing him.

"You're free to go, Greene," she dismisses him. Pointing a firm finger at me, she says, "You stay."

Ethan throws me a pitied look. I know he doesn't want to leave me here, but he has no choice. He attempts to stand his ground, but one quick, insistent glare from the woman is enough to send him on his way.

"Don't forget about tonight, Johnny. If you do, I know where you live," he whispers as he goes. He lifts his eyes to the soldiers once more, then adds, "I'll be seeing you boys soon, I suppose."

They find no humor in his words. They only continue to glare back, visibly annoyed that he hadn't gone when he was first told to leave.

Ethan rushes out through the open drape behind us. My stomach twists even tighter as the woman steps closer. She returns the cigarette to her lips and lets out a puff of smoke. I hold my breath to keep from breathing it in.

"Gentlemen, hold down the fort for me, would you?" the woman demands. Both soldiers glance at each other, then one starts to argue her request. But before he can fully form his statement, she turns and narrows her eyes at him.

"I just want to have a word with the boy. I knew his father." Her remark is enough to silence the soldier. I'm not sure where she gets her authority, but it's clear they take orders from her — not the other way around.

She grabs ahold of my arm and raises her lips to my ear, smoke and stale perfume clinging to her like a second skin. "Come," she whispers. "There's something I want to tell you."

Before I can protest, she yanks me away from the soldiers and toward the edge of the room. She lifts the bottom of the tent just enough for me to slip through. Sunlight hits me like a spotlight, a harsh contrast to the muted light beneath the tents. She follows close behind, drops the flap back into place, then grabs my arm again.

To our right, civilians continue lining up to receive their rations. The woman walks with me in the opposite direction toward the remnants of a massive arch. Its twin pillars tower above the ground. White marble slabs lie in ruins at the base, torn away from the rest of the structure. At the top of the rubble, the bridge of the arch clings to what's left. I gaze up at it in horrible awe, stunned by its size but even more so by its condition. I've never been this close to the destruction before — and this is only a gateway to the rest of it.

"Name's Mae," the woman blurts out as she pulls me up to the arch.

Nice to meet you, Mae, feels inappropriate at a time like this. I don't reply, and she doesn't seem to mind.

From a distance, I observe the soldiers patrolling the perimeter of the park. They haven't noticed us, or maybe they don't care to.

Mae squeezes my arm, stopping me at the base of the arch. We're so close now that I can see every detail and fracture in full definition. High above, I spot an inscription etched into the bridge of the arch: LET US RAISE A STANDARD TO WHICH THE WISE AND THE HONEST CAN REPAIR — THE EVENT IS IN THE HAND OF GOD — WASHINGTON. I shudder at the irony and quickly look away.

The smell of smoke trails by my nose again, and I turn to see Mae relighting her cigarette. She plops down on one of the slabs at the base of the arch and exhales.

Looking up at me, she says, "You want one?"

I almost laugh. "No, ma'am. I've never smoked before."

This gets a rise out of Mae. "Now's as good a time to start as any. You might wish you'd taken me up on my offer once you're drafted."

I wince at her words. She knows it's coming, and it's coming for me — there's no denying it now.

"You know," she continues, "I've seen just about every wave of you boys over the years. Since the very beginning. I watch you all grow up and get shipped off, then some of you come back to work for me after they're through with you. It all repeats year after year."

Lovely, I think. What are Mae's intentions here? Does she want to nag me about the draft, or could this really be about my father? After all, it was his name that sparked her interest in talking to me.

"I'm sorry, kid," Mae sighs.

I feel my cheeks get hot. I can't tell if she's apologizing because I'm clearly uncomfortable, or if it's something more.

"For what?" I ask timidly.

She clears her throat. "For all of it. I'm sorry you have to grow up in a world like this. Back in my day, boys your age dreamed of turning eighteen. It meant freedom, leaving the nest, maybe even settling down with a partner. You ever thought about that?"

"No, ma'am," I admit. Thinking about any sort of reality other than the draft has never crossed my mind.

My eyes catch on a soldier stationed near the perimeter. He's angled slightly more toward us now. His face is covered by his helmet, the closed visor glinting in the sunlight. I can't tell if he sees us or not. But I convince myself he can.

"I knew your father," Mae starts. "That wasn't just some sort of trick to get you out here."

I turn my attention back to her and block out the soldier in my peripheral.

"Oh yeah?" is all I manage to say.

"Madoc. That name carries weight in the draft," she nods. "Your father was a powerful man, and he did a lot of good for our community. Of course, they like to leave that part out, though."

She puts her cigarette out on the slab and stands. Without warning, she rushes up to me, so close we're merely inches apart.

"I've always thought that someday, we'd be delivered from this," she says. Her voice is hushed and hurried. Over her shoulder, I see the soldier now fully turned in our direction — and I swear he's a few feet closer than he was before.

Mae continues. "I've thought, there's got to be *someone* who knows something and has the power to change things for us. That someone used to be your father, until they banished him."

Banished? She lifts her eyes and sees me looking past her. She quickly glances over her shoulder at the soldier behind her, noticing him too. Our eyes meet again, and she presses in even closer.

"If you see anything or hear anything while you're there, don't take it all at face value. Pay attention, and don't trust anyone too much. There's more to this than we all know. All it takes is one person asking the right questions for the whole system to break. But you have to be careful," she warns.

Heavy footsteps crunch against the dirt behind her. My heart beats wildly. I can feel it pulsing in my throat, nearly choking the air out of me.

Before I can respond, Mae pulls me into a tight hug, catching me off guard. She draws her lips right up to my ear. I feel them brush against my skin.

"I'm counting on you, Madoc. Finish what your father started." She releases me slowly, and her once-stern expression is now soft and innocent. She smiles as if she's never been happier to see me. I try to play along, but I'm too distracted by what she's said. And what it all means.

A deep muffled voice calls out from a few feet behind Mae. My body seizes slightly, startled by it.

"Everything alright over here?" the soldier asks, a hint of suspicion in his voice.

Mae continues to smile at me and nods. "Oh, yes! Just catching up with my boy here. He's a dear family friend," she lies.

I don't shift my eyes from Mae. *Finish what your father started*, I repeat in my head. What does she mean? What did he do?

"You need to return to your post, miss," the soldier demands coldly.

Mae nods in submission. "Of course."

She gives me one last pat on the shoulder before walking back toward The Market. She flicks her dull cigarette onto the ground to smolder. My eyes flicker over to the soldier, and I catch my reflection in his visor. Evidence of what Mae said is written all over my face.

"Have you collected your rations?" the soldier asks me.

"Y-yes, sir," I stammer.

The soldier throws a gloved thumb over his shoulder. "Then get back to your home."

His command lights a fire under me, snapping me out of my trance. I take off past him and head toward the streets beyond the park, clutching the messenger bag close. I sense him watching me as I go.

Mae's words echo through my mind. I barely knew my father, let alone anything he was working on or planning. How could I finish something I know nothing about? And why should it matter so much to Mae?

Maybe there's a reason he never came home. *Banished.* That's the word she used. Mother always said the military is full of powerful men. They control every facet of our lives under the Barrier, and nothing falls under their radar. Whatever my father started, maybe they found out — and they didn't like it. So they banished him for it and made sure he'd never be found.

I can't stop what's coming tomorrow, but I can choose what I do when it does. And if I choose to get involved — to finish what my father started — I'm afraid of what it might do to me. Choosing to stay out of it might never give me closure. But choosing to get involved might be the thing that kills me.

Three

A FEW HOURS PASS before I decide to go to the pub. The streets are mostly deserted, except for a few wandering people. We exchange the same wary glance, silently wondering what the other is doing out at this hour. Most people are tucked inside their homes for the night — and part of me knows I should be too. But I need to find Ethan. I can't shake what Mae said. Every time I think I've forgotten, her words ring louder than all the other noise in my head: *Finish what your father started.*

I think about turning back at least a dozen times before I reach the old pub. It sits wedged between the cracked asphalt below and the decaying shell of a high-rise above it. Thick wooden planks cover the front windows, colored with graffiti. The glass door is spray-painted black, concealing what's inside. It's easily an eyesore — unless you know to look for it.

I backtrack to the alley and slip into the shadows. Muffled voices seep through the wall. I follow them to an unmarked side door, where the noise grows louder. *This is so stupid*, I think as I reach for the handle. I shouldn't be this hesitant, but I am. If I can just find Ethan, tell him what Mae said, and avoid most of the other guys, I'll be fine. Then I'll be on my way and back home before midnight. Before tomorrow comes and everything is taken from me.

Reluctantly, I pull back the door and step inside. Soft light spills out, chasing back the shadows, and the chatter swells around me. To my right, three boys chant and down drinks from glass mugs faster than they can keep up with. One of them stands on a table, while the other two cheer him on. When he empties his glass, he hurls it at the cement floor. I wince as it makes impact, shattering with a sharp crack. For a moment, the room goes silent. Then another group of boys hollers with delight. One of them is Ethan.

He notices me as his eyes shift toward the crash. Immediately, a smug smile creeps across his face. I nearly turn and slip back out the door, but it's too late. He's already making his way over.

"Well, well, well," he says with a pleased look. "Look who showed up after all."

"Did I have much of a choice?"

"No, no you didn't. I would've come and dragged you out of bed myself if you hadn't."

"Exactly," I state, proving my point.

I try to get a lay of the land before Ethan can rope me into any unwanted introductions. A few wooden tables line the nearest wall — one of which is dripping with beer foam. Black chairs are placed haphazardly at each one. Across the room, Ethan's entourage crowds around a corner booth. One of the boys leans against the table, which wobbles slightly on uneven legs.

Directly in front of me, the bar stretches from the back wall to the midpoint of the pub, then curves toward the booth. Shelves brim with liquor bottles of every shape, size, and distinction. Gold backsplash glistens in the dim overhead lighting, giving the bar a sort of timeless elegance.

To my left, a boy sits alone at the bar, swirling the last bit of his drink in his glass. A half-empty bottle lingers nearby on the bar top. He doesn't finish the last sip. He just watches as it swishes at the bottom, eyes fixed. He doesn't seem particularly interested in what the other boys are doing, and they don't seem to notice him. Before I can stare any longer, Ethan tugs at my arm and pulls me toward the booth.

"Ladies and gentlemen," he announces dramatically. *Ladies* earns a chuckle from the boys, who have all clearly had more to drink than they'd admit. "I present to you, John Madoc!"

I wave shyly, eager to break away. But they've already taken an interest.

One of them — a pale boy with ink-black hair swooping across his forehead and a stocky build — approaches me and slings his arm around my shoulder. "Welcome to Hell, John! We've been expecting you."

Ethan bursts out laughing along with the other boy, who steps forward to introduce himself too.

"Don't mind him," he says. "I'm Drew Fitzgerald, and that's Carson O'Hair."

Drew extends his hand, and I shake it loosely. His dark skin contrasts with the whites of his eyes, making them pop. His black hair is neatly buzzed close to his scalp, the short stubble still visible. He smiles kindly as he pulls back his hand and clasps his drink.

"Ethan tells us you've been pals for quite some time, yeah?" Drew asks.

I nod. "Ever since I can remember."

"Isn't it romantic?" Ethan jokes. "He loves me, but he'd never admit it."

Drew laughs. "Well, why don't you fix him up something to drink? Drinks are on the house," he winks at me.

Ethan guides me over to the bar, where I slide onto one of the barstools. Instead of doing the same, Ethan leaps over the counter, drops down on the other side, and spins around like he's just stepped into character.

"So, what'll it be, eh?" he asks, mimicking a thick New York accent.

I stare at the assortment of bottles cluelessly. I'm not even sure I want anything, but Ethan is insistent. And I need the excuse to talk to him privately, anyway. I scan the labels, hoping something will stand out, but nothing does.

My eyes drift back to the lone boy at the other end of the bar. He's just finished the last swig from his glass and is already pouring a second round.

"I don't have all day, kid. Whadda ya want?" Ethan's voice snaps me back.

"Your choice."

Ethan smirks. "How strong d'ya like it? You wanna loosen up a bit, or d'ya wanna forget until the mornin'?"

I laugh at his poor accent but commend him for committing to the bit. "Forgetting until the morning is tempting, but I've got a big day tomorrow. Just something to take the edge off will do," I play along.

Ethan throws two finger guns out at me and says, "I know just the thing! You stay right there, stay a while!"

He spins on his heels and reaches for a bottle about halfway up the wall. As he does, his shoulder bumps a few glasses hanging from a low rack beneath the shelf. He teeters on his tiptoes, and I tense up, bracing for everything to come crashing down around him. But he sticks the landing.

Ethan slams the bottle down on the counter and slides a dusty glass in front of me. Judging by the look of it, there's only a little bit left at the bottom of the bottle. He doesn't hesitate to empty it into my cup.

He presents the drink to me, and I stare at it, hesitant to take the first sip. But Ethan's already reaching for his own glass to drink with me.

"Cheers!" he exclaims. He clinks his cup against mine and forces the harsh liquid down his throat.

I plug my nose and tip the glass to my lips. As soon as the liquor hits my tongue, its bitter taste sizzles across my taste buds. My shoulders clench as it sears my throat, spreading warmth through my chest. Ethan gives me an approving nod while I smack my lips, trying to shake the taste.

"How are you guys drinking this stuff?" I spit out.

"It's not so much about what it is you're drinking, but the act of drinking itself." Ethan replies, trying to be profound.

I chuckle at how ridiculous he sounds. Ethan laughs too, perpetuated by the alcohol.

"Did you come up with that just now?" I tease him.

"What can I say, I'm full of wisdom." He takes another swig from his glass, then rests his elbows on the counter and leans in. "Anyway, what did that lady want with you after I left The Market?"

"She . . ." I start, unsure how to say it. But this is my chance. "She knew my father."

Ethan's cheeks puff up with air, and his eyes widen. He nudges my drink closer to me as if I'm going to need it once I get to talking about my father.

I push it aside and keep going. "She said the military banished him for something he was involved in. Something he started that he never got to finish. And she wants me to be the one to finish it."

His eyes grow even wider. He leans in closer, intrigued. "So obviously we have to do it."

I shake my head. "No, it's not that simple. Whatever it was, she thinks it had the power to change things — for all of us. But the military clearly didn't want anyone finding out."

Ethan's composure doesn't change. He's intoxicated by the mission, but he hasn't considered the consequences.

"It could be dangerous," I add. "We don't know what we'd be getting ourselves into. And we *don't* need to be making any enemies."

"I wouldn't mind making a few enemies."

I swat at his drink and center him. "Dude, I'm being serious. You're not in your right mind."

"I'm being serious too," he fires back, his tone firmer. "So what if it's dangerous? The draft is dangerous. Every day of our lives under the Barrier is dangerous. Besides, aren't you the least bit curious to know what your father was working on?"

"Of course I am," I say, lowering my voice. "I just . . . don't know if it's worth it, is all."

Ethan's eyes lock on mine for a moment. "John, this could be your destiny!" Then they slightly glaze over, and I sense the alcohol starting to kick in. "To find out what happened to your father and avenge him. To finish what he started. If she told you all that, she probably had a good reason."

It would've been simpler if Ethan had just confirmed my fears about it being too dangerous, but he's right. Mae wouldn't have said anything unless it mattered. Unless she truly believed I could finish what my father couldn't.

Ethan notices me cracking and grins. "You have to at least try. She said they *banished* him, right? That's the word she used?"

I nod.

"Banished doesn't mean dead, John. What if he's still out there?"

"Out where? Beyond the Barrier?" I ask. "Even if he were, it's been nearly a decade. There's no way he could've survived out there that long."

Ethan shrugs. "You don't know that."

There's more to this than we all know. Mae's words echo in my mind. Could my father really have survived outside the Barrier all this time? It's been said that everything beyond the city is uninhabitable. But it's also been said that my father is dead. If that's not true — and he really *is* alive and out there — what does that say about the outside world?

"We have to be careful," I say. "And I mean it. We can't let anyone else in on this."

Ethan places his hand over his heart. "You have my word."

"And I mean absolutely *no one*. We don't know these guys." I signal to the other boys in the pub. "And they don't know us. Best not to let them in on something like this before we know if we can trust them."

Ethan nods. "Roger that."

All at once, he downs the rest of his drink, flattens his palms on the counter, and springs over it in one swift motion. His feet clumsily land next to where I sit, and he grabs my shoulders to steady himself.

"Now, if you excuse me, I'm going to do some more mingling with the locals. But not *too* much mingling," he clarifies. He holds two fingers up to his eyes and moves them back and forth between his and mine. I push him away playfully, and he stumbles to the booth where Drew and Carson sit.

Before I can turn back to the bar, an unfamiliar voice cuts in. "Sounds like a riveting conversation."

My heart plummets. I spin around to find the lone boy now seated at the open barstool beside me. The smell of liquor clings to his breath, but his gaze is steady, showing no signs of intoxication. I stare back stunned, unsure if he's just overheard my entire conversation with Ethan.

"Didn't mean to scare you there, mate," he chuckles. His accent is foreign. His words all seem to flow together — still English, but somehow more refined.

"Did you—" I start, but I stop myself. If he didn't overhear us, I don't want to give myself away.

"Just get here? Yeah," he answers before I can finish, though it's not what I was asking. "Not sure what you and that bloke were talking about, but looked like you could use some saving. I'm not really one for parties either."

My lips press into a thin line, embarrassed that he's probably been watching me this whole time.

"My name's Leo. Leo Patton." He extends his hand, and I shake it.

"John," I say. And I leave it at that. "And that was Ethan. He's a friend."

We turn in tandem to see Ethan hollering with Drew and Carson as they play a drinking game they've likely just made up. Their banter fills the entire pub.

"Quite the opposite of you," Leo observes.

"Yeah," I scoff. "That's for sure."

Leo takes a long sip of his drink and exhales. "You from around these parts of the city?"

"Just a few blocks from here, actually," I tell him. "What about you?"

"I'm from the east side. My parents came over from the UK on holiday when everything started to fall apart. They were just visiting the city, and they weren't able to get back." He lowers his eyes and swirls the liquor in his glass, slipping back into the same contemplative state as before.

"They're lucky they even made the cut to stay under the Barrier. Eventually they came to terms with it all. They had me, and well, the rest is history."

"I'm sorry to hear that," I say, softer than before. I can't imagine how he must feel knowing he could've had a completely different life than this. One that a cruel twist of fate stole from him.

"Don't be," Leo shrugs. "I suppose things weren't much better across the pond now, were they? Who's to say?"

I'd never considered that before. All I've ever known is what happened here, in *our* country. As for the rest of the world, Leo's right. No one knows for sure.

"So, you've been of age for a while then, yeah?" he asks.

My palms start to sweat. "Yeah, long enough," I lie, though it's not entirely untrue. One day of being eighteen has already felt like a lifetime.

"Believe it or not, I was one of the first to turn of age," Leo raises his brow. "I've had to wait the whole year for everything to go down."

"That must've been torture."

"You're telling me," he sighs. "I envy the blokes who turn of age and only have to wait a day or so."

You're looking at one, I think. But I don't dare say it out loud.

"Just gives you some time to think, y'know?" Leo continues. "I've always wondered why they drag it out so long. Especially now, it's like, why wait until the morning? If we're all of age, let's get on with it then, shall we?"

Behind us, a few of the other boys gather around an old clock mounted to the back wall. To my surprise, it still seems to work. The small hand is fixed at twelve while the longer one is just shy of covering it — almost midnight.

"Ten, nine, eight..." the boys begin to chant. Ethan, Drew, and Carson pause their game and join in. "Six, five..."

"Anyway, just a curious thought. Cheers to a new year?" Leo raises his glass and tilts it toward mine, all the while the rest of the pub rings in the new year.

"Three, two, one..."

My heart sinks to my gut. Suddenly, every detail sharpens — from the shouts of the other boys to the clink of Leo's glass against mine to the distinct thud just outside the pub door. The boys' voices fade, and a few hush each other, as if listening for something they think they've heard.

Without warning, the front door shatters. The boys closest to the blast dive out of the way. I topple off the barstool and shield my face from the fall. My head slams against the floor, causing my vision to blur. Glass shards spray my face, tearing at my skin. From the ground, I watch as a dozen pairs of black boots march through the opening where the door once was. As everything refocuses, I trace them up to the sleek black uniforms and carbon fiber helmets that could only belong to one group of people.

Soldiers swarm the pub. Several boys cower in the corner as the soldiers aim their weapons at them, shouting orders. Leo tugs at my arm to help me up. As soon as I'm standing, a soldier rushes toward me and presses the barrel of his gun into my chest. I stumble backward against the bar and lift my hands in surrender.

"Nobody move!" a soldier barks from across the pub.

Fear washes over me, followed by a crashing wave of sadness. I think of Mother and Liam back home. They have no idea this is happening right now. They were expecting me home tonight. Liam will likely come into my room tomorrow morning to wake me, only to find the bed empty. Mother was counting on one last moment together, but now, she won't get it. They've ripped away any hope we had of saying goodbye.

"Walk," the soldier in front of me snarls. I wince as he digs the tip of his gun further into my chest.

Slowly, I peel myself from the bar and walk toward the front of the pub. The soldier repositions his gun and jabs it into my spine to keep me moving.

As I walk, I catch a glimpse of Ethan. All the color has drained from his face. He stares back at me, eyes full of guilt. I know he regrets pressuring me to come tonight, but it's not his fault. The soldiers knew we'd be here. They've known all along this is exactly how it'd go down. I feel sick imagining them posted up outside the pub, waiting for the perfect moment to strike. Any freedom we thought we had for one last night was never ours, and now it never will be. We belong to them now.

We march out of the pub and into the bleak night. Outside, nearly three times as many soldiers are lined up in the street, facing us. A few are holding flame-lit torches. The fire dances against the backdrop of the decrepit city, casting eerie shadows on the horror unfolding around us. As the soldiers usher us forward, the warmth coming off the flames licks my face, stinging my wounds. The entire temperature of the night has shifted from a frigid winter to a blazing heat.

The soldiers shove us into position, filling the gaps between those in the street. Looking ahead, I see other boys emerging from different parts of the city, being escorted in a similar manner. Once we're all in line, the soldiers take their places — one in front, the other at our backs, boxing us in. Then everything falls silent.

My heart hammers against my ribs. To my left, the painted glass from the pub door litters the sidewalk. Everything else is clouded by soldiers towering on either side of me.

Before long, the sound of heavy footsteps crunching against the asphalt grows closer. I refrain from turning my head, afraid that if I make even the slightest movement, the soldier behind me will slam his gun into the back of my skull. The footsteps come to a stop next to me. My blood runs cold. I still don't turn, but I can tell whoever it is, they're waiting for me to acknowledge them.

I glance to the side and see a pair of piercing green eyes staring back at me. This soldier isn't wearing a helmet, but he's clearly military. He clears his throat and narrows his reptilian eyes.

"John Madoc?" he asks. I nod my head regrettably.

The soldier begins to fumble with something around his belt. Before I can look, he lifts the barrel of what appears to be a gun to my eyes. Instinctively, I leap away from him, but the two soldiers beside me grip my arms and force me forward. I squeeze my eyes shut, too afraid to watch, every molecule in my body resisting what comes next.

The soldier lets out a howl in amusement. "Relax, kid. This won't hurt. It's just a necessary precaution."

As I peel my eyes open, a fluorescent beam of green light shoots out of the device. It lands right between my eyes, blinding me for a moment. Then it moves down to my chin, then onto the rest of my body. The soldier and I both trace its path until it hits my feet. The light flickers three times, then retreats back to where it came from.

The soldier deposits it back into his belt and nods. Judging by his reaction, if this was some sort of test, I must've passed. Next, he removes a translucent tablet no larger than a sheet of paper from a pouch on his chest. *How many things does this guy have on him?* I think and immediately make a mental note to mention it to Ethan. He'll surely get a kick out of this when it's his turn.

The tablet illuminates the soldier's face as it powers on. He moves his eyes from mine to the screen. From where I stand, I can make out some text, but it's hardly legible — at least from my angle.

"Full name: John Anthony Madoc," he reads from the screen.

I nod.

"Age: Eighteen."

Another nod.

"Son of Lilian Penelope Madoc and Anthony Liam Madoc."

I nod again. This time, more reluctantly.

"Brother to Liam Marshall Madoc. Age: Eight."

My chest stings at the thought of Liam again. By now, he and Mother have surely been woken up by the noise outside. Other civilians have already emerged from their homes. Some only poke their heads out, while others step out into the street. All looking on with pity.

"No other living relatives," the soldier states. I nod, though I'm starting to doubt that's true.

He runs through my demographic information next — height, weight, eye color, hair color — until he's checked off every box on his list. Each piece of information he reads off is met with an affirmative nod from me.

It dawns on me that they have all this information on record. Everything down to the most up-to-date statistics. It shouldn't surprise me, but it sends a chill down my spine.

"All clear," the soldier says once he's finished running through his roster. He powers off the tablet and slides it facedown into his chest pouch. "You are who you say you are."

As if I'd be anyone different, I think.

The soldier steps closer, so close that I can smell stale coffee on his breath. He jerks his right hand up to the corner of his forehead in a salute.

"Please do as I do and repeat after me," he orders.

My hand trembles as I raise it to my forehead. The soldier stares back, unblinking.

"I, John Madoc . . ." he bellows.

"I, John Madoc . . ." I repeat.

". . . vow to obey, preserve, and protect my nation, in whatever capacity necessary, from this day forward."

". . . vow to obey, preserve, and protect my nation," I swallow hard before reciting the next part, "in whatever capacity necessary, from this day forward."

"I vow to undergo the necessary training to ensure I am in the optimal physical and mental condition to defend my nation . . ."

My mind feels like it's drifting in a hundred different directions, but I try to focus on his words. "I vow to undergo the necessary training to ensure I am in the optimal physical and mental condition to defend my nation . . ."

". . . in the event the Barrier were to fail to do so."

Gulp. ". . . in the event the Barrier were to fail to do so."

"From this day forward," he pauses.

"From this day forward . . ."

"I vow to be ready at all times to go to war against the forces that plague our nation . . ."

This isn't happening. This can't be happening. "I vow to be ready at all times to go to war against the forces that plague our nation . . ." Sweat drips from my palm. The heat coming off the soldier's torch next to me feels increasingly hotter.

". . . to wholly fight without hesitation or remorse — even to the point of death so that others may live."

I can't do this. There's got to be a way out of this. But there isn't. ". . . to wholly fight without hesitation or remorse — even to the—" the words catch in my throat. The soldier raises his brow, waiting for me to finish.

"... even to the point of death so that others may live." I don't even recognize my own voice as the words come out.

The soldier doesn't miss a beat. "It is by this pledge that I, John Madoc..."

This is it. "It is by this pledge that I, John Madoc..."

"... will be held accountable, in the event I fall out of line or fail to do my part."

This is the only way. "... will be held accountable, in the event I fall out of line or fail to do my part."

I imagine my father saying these same words decades ago when he gave his life to the draft. He fell out of line — by their standards, at least. And just as this pledge warns, he was held accountable. Banished for believing in something different. Whatever happened, I have no doubt they're responsible. That *they* did something to him.

I have to find out the truth. I won't be able to rest until I do.

"Blessed be the United States of America, what's left of it and what's to come..."

What's to come? "Blessed be the United States of America, what's left of it and what's to come," I recite back.

"... and may the draft continue to serve our nation and pave the way for our future."

I feel like I'm about to be sick. "... and may the draft continue to serve our nation and pave the way for our future."

The soldier lowers his hand. "Thank you," he says. "Wait here until you're told otherwise."

I stand frozen with my hand still inches from my forehead, trying to comprehend what just happened. And what I've agreed to.

The soldier makes his way down the line, reciting the same pledge to each of us. It feels like hours pass before he's finished, but once he is, the soldier behind me shoves me forward. The whole group moves in unison. As we march, the soft weeping of civilians follows us, mourning another batch of draftees. Reminding us all that the draft is still necessary, and the war still rages on outside the Barrier.

For the first time, I cry too. I give in to the flood of emotions I've bottled up for eighteen years. My vision blurs with tears, smearing the torchlight guiding our path. As we drift away from the old pub, I don't get one last clear look at my neighborhood before it's lost behind us. The only thing that lies ahead is the Freedom Tower and the unshakable feeling that my life, from this day forward, is no longer in my hands.

Four

We march until we're swallowed by the city. With every step, the buildings rise higher, and their deterioration becomes more grotesque. None of us have ever ventured this far before, so the damage — even in the low light — is staggering.

Up ahead, the soldiers veer left between two skyscrapers. As we round the corner, I notice them descending a set of stairs leading beneath the ground. A shadow hangs over the opening, making it look like a black hole sunken into the city. My whole body recoils in retaliation, but with the soldier hot on my heels, I have no choice but to sink into it.

As we descend, the soldiers put out their torches one by one. I stumble down the stairs in complete darkness. My only source of stability is the stone wall beside me, slick with icy moisture. A violent shiver runs down my spine, and I fold my arms tight across my chest, trying to keep warm.

Relief rushes over me when my feet hit level ground. Despite not being able to see anything, I can sense the vastness of the space around me. Curious, I reach out my hand — and to my surprise, the soldier ahead of me is gone. But a sharp kick to my back confirms the one behind me isn't. He grabs my arm and yanks me aside. Another soldier restrains my other arm, and together they pin me against the wall. I bite my tongue to keep from crying out as their fingers dig into my biceps.

My eyes fail to adjust. I whip my head from side to side, desperate to latch onto something, *anything*. But there's nothing. Only darkness.

The sound of our marching fades, and a hush falls over everything. My heart rattles against my chest. There's no telling what comes next. For a moment, I wonder if this is what death feels like — being consumed by a darkness so great, it's as if my mind and body could split apart.

Just then, an orb of light pierces through the darkness. From where I stand, it looks like it could be miles away, but it's bright enough to reveal where we stand. Soldiers are dispersed across a wide concrete platform. Each draftee is flanked by two soldiers. All their heads are turned toward the light, watching as it grows. As if it's moving.

My eyes burn the longer I stare at it. Turning away, I spot Leo nearby. His hands are clasped behind his back. His face is ghostly pale, though it might be partially from the light. I glance around for Ethan, but I don't see him. He's lost among everyone else.

Without warning, a deafening roar blares throughout the platform. I fight the urge to rip my arms free from the soldiers' grip to cover my ears. The sound reverberates off the walls of a hollow curved tunnel with nowhere to escape. The sheer volume rattles me to my core. Metal grinds against metal at an ear-splitting pitch, and it's only getting louder.

I jerk my head around and squint at the light, which has now expanded from a tiny, distant orb to a searchlight illuminating the whole tunnel. Vines crawl all over the walls, coiling around pipes fastened to the low rounded ceiling. Directly below the light, I catch a glimpse of a set of copper rails. The light seems to be riding along them.

The entire platform shakes as the sound escalates. Dust rains down from the ceiling. None of the soldiers show any signs of concern, but every draftee wears the same look of terror. The light sweeps across the platform wall. Just when it looks like it might crash into us, it veers right, revealing its true form.

A rusted metal train bursts into view, speeding alongside the platform. It rushes past with such force, it nearly blows me off my feet. Gradually, it slows to a halt. The wheels screech against the rails, filling the air with the bitter scent of burnt metal and oil.

As soon as it stops, the doors swing open automatically. Inside, sleek silver seats line a walkway that spans the full length of the car. Floor-to-ceiling poles stand parallel to the doors. At the back, a screen display hangs from an upper corner. The soldiers closest to the edge shove their draftees forward, forcing them to step on board.

I watch in awe from the back of the platform. How is this even possible? I had no idea something like this existed beneath the city — or that it *could* even exist. As I approach the train, I glance past it into the tunnel beyond the platform. I can only imagine how far it stretches and how much of the city it connects. But I don't have time to wonder for long.

The soldier behind me shoves me through the doorway, and I stumble forward into the car. My eyes squint against the harsh overhead lights. He pushes me again, and I collapse into a nearby seat. The soldier takes the vacant seat to my right, while another settles into the one on my left.

I rub my fists over my eyes to reorient myself. When I reopen them, a smile spreads across my face. Seated directly across from me is Ethan. He doesn't notice me at first, but as soon as he does, his eyes light up.

"John, thank God!" he exclaims.

The soldier beside him elbows him hard in the shoulder. "Shut up," he orders, and Ethan cowers.

I don't respond. I gently lift the corners of my mouth to show I'm glad to see him.

Once we're all seated, the doors slide shut. The train lurches forward abruptly. As it accelerates, the overhead lights transition from a stark white to a cool, soft blue. I grip the ice-cold armrests on either side of my chair, bracing against the force. Meanwhile, the soldiers occupying every other seat remain unfazed.

The screen mounted to the back wall lights up, and a feminine voice comes over an intercom. "Next stop: Battery Station," it says in a smooth, robotic tone. The screen seems to display a map. It's nothing more than a gray two-dimensional landscape of thin lines and unmarked shapes. But even in its obscurity, I recognize it as the city above us. Every few seconds, a blue dot blinks along a thick red line tracing our path, pinpointing our location.

Exhaustion tugs at my eyelids. It's well past midnight by now. Every time I start to drift off, I jolt myself awake, reminding myself where I am. Other than the pitter-patter of Ethan's sneakers tapping anxiously against the floor, the only other sound is the engine's steady whir beneath us.

Within minutes, the train begins to slow. As it does, the lights brighten back to white, and the woman's voice returns over the intercom. "Arriving at Battery Station," it says. Almost as if on cue, the soldiers rise from their seats. The two next to me grab my arms and lift me to my feet.

I teeter off balance as the train screeches to a full stop. Outside the windows above the seats, a new platform comes into view — only this one is much smaller compared to the one we came from. Instead of a staircase leading up to the surface, it dead-ends with a massive vault door. Near the top, a small rectangular slot is sunken into the metal. And at the center is a large wheel with prongs that extend outward, connecting to the frame.

My breath catches. As I stare out at the platform, a wave of claustrophobia hits me. We're trapped here, somewhere beneath the city, with no way out. Even though the train ride lasted only minutes, we're likely miles from home. Far from the only part of the city we've ever known. There's no telling what waits for us on the other side of that door, but there's only one direction we can go — through it.

The soldiers shove us onto the platform and keep tight at our sides as they drag us toward the door. Ethan files out after me, and though I can't see him, I can feel his shaky breath on the back of my neck. Once we're all out, the train doors slide shut with a mechanical clunk, followed by a forceful hiss. The train roars to life and barrels into the tunnel ahead. I catch one last glimpse of the rear car as it rounds a sharp corner and disappears out of sight.

One of the soldiers near the front of the group approaches the vault door. He lifts a gloved hand and bangs on the metal three times. The sound echoes around the platform before it's choked out by silence. Almost instantly, the slot near the top slides open, revealing a pair of eyes. They scan the soldier, then us, then vanish as the slot snaps shut.

From the other side of the door, a lock clicks out of place, and the door peels away from its frame. A man stands in the opening. He's dressed like the other soldiers, except he isn't wearing a helmet. His jet-black hair is combed neatly to one side, and his eyes are just as dark. Pale skin clings tightly to his bones. His arms are crossed over his chest, feet planted wide, exuding dominance.

"Bring them in," he commands the soldier who knocked, then turns away. I watch his silhouette move through an inner chamber bathed in misty blue light. He waves his hand in a gesture, and a second door slides open from deeper inside. Almost as soon as he passes through, it shuts behind him.

The first draftee is led into the chamber by the soldiers accompanying him. As soon as all three step inside, the door slams shut with a vicious thud that makes me wince.

Panic bubbles inside me. My breath quickens, and my whole body trembles. What are they doing to him? Why not bring us all in at once?

Some of the other boys start to murmur, but they're immediately silenced by the soldiers. Up ahead, I hear the crackle of a radio and a static voice that says, "Clear." Upon that cue, the next pair of soldiers pulls open the vault door. But the first draftee is no longer there — the chamber is empty. A few draftees gasp, but already the next victim is being dragged inside.

The cycle repeats until it's my turn. "Clear," a static voice crackles again, this time from a radio clipped to the soldier on my right. He rips open the vault door, revealing the empty chamber on the other side. The hum of the blue lights fills my ears, beckoning me toward my own demise. My heart races. The soldiers pull me inside without hesitation, but my feet drag. My body fights to resist, but they're stronger. They throw me inside like a limp doll. Adrenaline surges through my veins. As the door closes, my eyes catch Ethan standing at the front of the line. His face mirrors mine — pure fear.

As soon as the door locks into place, the blue lights shut off. For a split second, it's pitch dark. Somehow even darker than the first platform, which is nauseating. I squeeze my eyes shut, too afraid to see what comes next.

A puff of smoke hits me from both sides, covering me in a thick mist. I let out a startled yelp. With my arms free, I try to swat it away, but it fills my nostrils until it suffocates me. I hunch over, coughing as my lungs contract, desperate for oxygen. Maybe those extremists were right. Maybe there's no draft this year. Maybe we've become so useless to society, they decided to gas us to death. I fall to my knees and let the smoke consume me, feeling my body surrender.

But before it takes me, the smoke is pulled from the chamber. A bright green light floods the room as fresh air reenters my lungs. At the same time, a beeping tone sounds, activating the second door. It slides open to a sterile hallway. To my relief, about halfway down the hall are all the draftees who went before me, perfectly alive and lined up against the wall. They haven't killed us — not yet, at least. And whatever the smoke and lights were for, at least I made it through.

The soldiers hoist me to my feet and usher me toward the other draftees. The walls are clad in polished sheet metal while the floors appear to be carved from stone, almost as if we're walking on bedrock. The hallway stretches endlessly. The only doors are the one we came through and an identical one mirrored at the opposite end. The ceiling is low, and even though I can stand upright, I still feel the need to duck my head.

Once we reach the others, the soldiers shove me into place, shoulder to shoulder with the draftee before me. Nobody says a word. We stand still, most of us either still drunk or too afraid to move, or somewhere in between. The soldiers form their own line across from us, staring back through their faceless helmets. They remain so motionless, I almost forget beneath all that gear, they're real men. Men who once stood where we are now.

Within seconds, the chamber door opens again and spits out Ethan. His hair is unkempt, tousled by the force of the smoke, and his eyes are bloodshot. The chamber's affirming green light casts a halo behind him.

Another pair of soldiers stow him next to me and take their places across from him. He exhales loudly, then glances over at me.

"Nothing subtle about that," he whispers. "Who knew it'd be such a grand entrance?"

Out of the corner of my eye, one of the soldiers snaps his head in our direction. I quickly straighten myself and ignore Ethan's comment.

The rest of the draftees file in behind Ethan, with Leo taking up the rear. A few moments of silence pass before the dark-haired man from earlier steps forward.

"You're dismissed," he says to the soldiers.

Together, they lift their hands in a salute and pivot in the direction we just came from. I watch as they march about halfway down the hall, then turn toward the blank wall. One soldier extends a badge clipped to his belt and scans it against a small black strip protruding from the wall. To my surprise, the wall panels slide away, as if granting him access to a hidden room. The soldiers dutifully file inside. Once they're in, the wall slides back into place, restoring the hallway to its original state.

Silence returns, and the dark-haired man stares coldly back at us. His mouth curls into a crooked smile. "Alright, follow me," he orders.

He turns toward the door at the other end of the hall. Fixed to the wall beside the door, I notice another black strip. He tugs at a badge tethered to his own belt and swipes it across the scanner's surface. A single eye of green light blinks at the top, followed by a thunderous click that echoes down the hall. He pushes the door forward, allowing us to step through.

On the other side of the door is a second hallway, but it's a far cry from the one we came from. The floor and walls are carved entirely from rugged rock. It feels unfinished — like it was excavated from the foundation of wherever we are and left untouched. A few exposed light bulbs jut from the ceiling, barely illuminating the dim corridor. They buzz faintly overhead, the sound prickling my ears as we pass beneath them.

The dark-haired man storms ahead of us and throws open a second door on our left. He steps aside and gives a curt nod, ordering us to enter.

We step into a room no bigger than my bedroom. Here, the polished stone floor returns, and the cinderblock walls are painted white. The lighting is much harsher and unforgiving, exposing every detail. My tired eyes squint against it as I fight to keep them open.

Scanning the room, I count six bunk beds — one pressed against the left wall, four across from each other in the center, and another along the far wall. Their metal frames are sturdy but rusted in places, and the mattresses look as stiff as the floor. Across from the door, the back wall splits in two, revealing a conjoined bathroom. I spot a long trough lined with faucets and a rectangular mirror spanning the length above it. In the reflection, I catch sight of the open shower stalls across from the sinks. I take it these are our sleeping quarters.

"Draftees," the dark-haired man bellows. We freeze and turn toward him. "Welcome to The Battery. This will be your home for the next sixteen weeks. My name is David, and I'm your facilities officer."

A dozen pairs of glazed, half-drunk eyes stare back at him. My stomach twists in a knot.

"In just a moment, I'll leave you to locate your belongings. Sheets have been provided for each of your beds as well as towels and toiletries for showering. You can find these in the drawers located at the base of each bunk. An extra set of clothes has been provided for your comfort as well, which you're welcome to wear any time you're in your barracks.

"Each of you has a uniform with your first initial and last name labeled on the front. Uniforms are already laid out on each bed, as you can see. Please ensure you're wearing your uniforms at all times when you leave the barracks, otherwise you'll be penalized. Do you understand?"

A few draftees mumble in response, but most have tuned him out. I cling onto every word.

"Very well," he says. "For now, take some time to get settled, then it's in all of your best interests to get some sleep. I'll be by in the morning to wake you for breakfast, followed by a few opening remarks from the general. Any questions?"

Nobody makes a peep.

"So be it." He nods and clasps his hands properly behind his back. As he turns to head out the door, his eyes fall on me.

"Madoc," he mutters under his breath, then exits the room. My heart plummets to my stomach. He's already well aware of who I am. There's no escaping it.

Ethan punches my arm. "I call the top bunk," he snickers.

As soon as David is gone, everyone scatters. Laid out on each mattress is a black long-sleeve tactical shirt paired with black cargo pants. A thick belt is neatly folded where the pants and shirt meet. Laced combat boots sit ready at the foot of each bunk with long socks draped overtop.

We all scan over the uniforms, searching for our names. I meander between the bunks, glancing back and forth. Others seem to be finding theirs quickly. As they do, they claim a bunk and stow their uniform in the drawer beneath it. When I turn, I notice Ethan has found his uniform on the top bunk nearest the door. He teeters on the edge of the ladder, holding the shirt out in front of him, E. GREENE stitched across the chest. Another draftee I don't recognize reaches for the uniform on the bottom bunk. As soon as he reads the name etched into the fabric, he turns, and his eyes lock on mine.

"Madoc," he grunts. My cheeks flush, instantly giving myself away.

The draftee's light eyes hold mine as he clutches the uniform. He's well above my height, with a muscular build that makes him look much older than eighteen. His thick black hair and bushy eyebrows are a stark contrast to his bronze skin. A long pointed nose dominates most of his face, and his lips are pressed into a scowl that sharpens his jawline. I timidly approach him and extend my hand, reaching for the uniform.

"That's me," I admit. I take the uniform from his hand and glance down at the name stitched in metallic gray lettering across the left breastplate: J. MADOC. I tip my head and offer a soft smile in appreciation. His lips press firmer together.

"I'm Apollo," he introduces himself. "I don't think we've had the chance to meet yet."

"I don't think we have," I confirm. "I'm John. And that's Ethan." I point up at Ethan, who's now climbing down from his bunk to join in.

"I know Greene already," Apollo smirks.

Ethan slings his uniform over his shoulder and places his hands on his hips. "Do you, now?"

"Sure do. I know both of you, actually."

Something in his demeanor sends my pulse racing. He's not here to make friends. He's here to assert his dominance.

"Our fathers worked together in the military," he continues. "Seems to be that mine was the only one smart enough to make it out alive."

Ethan lets out a laugh — the kind that only comes out when he's gearing up to fight. I shrink away from him and Apollo.

"Yeah, well, we'll see if you can live up to his legacy then," Ethan scoffs.

"You think that's funny?" Apollo takes a step forward. His accent sharpens the more assertive he gets. It reminds me of the native New York accent Ethan mimicked at the pub.

Ethan takes a step forward too. "No, what's funny is that you think you know us just because your daddy had something to do with the draft."

"Alright," I intervene. Glancing nervously over my shoulder, I notice a few other draftees starting to eavesdrop. All the while panic sears through my chest. "Thanks for the uniform, Apollo. We're not looking for trouble."

"Your name's already got trouble written all over it, pal," he snarls. The sound of a bunk creaking behind me indicates another draftee has now tuned in.

Lowering my head, I lean in close and whisper, "Now's not the time for this."

A sinister grin grows on Apollo's face. "You're a coward, Madoc. Your father left a stain on the draft, and I'm going to make sure you don't do the same. My father warned me about you two," he jabs a finger at Ethan and me, "so don't think I won't have my eye on you. You're bred from the same rebellious blood that could've gotten us all killed, *especially* you," he directs at me.

The whole room is listening now. I turn again and see everyone staring like deer in headlights. Leo stands at the back of the room, leaning against his bunk. His eyes meet mine, and he furrows his brows, trying to understand.

"You better watch it, Madoc," Apollo warns. "We may be fighting the same war, but we're not on the same team."

He holds eye contact for a few seconds longer to make sure his words cement, then pushes past me toward his bunk. I stand stunned, still clutching my uniform, looking around at the perplexed stares of the other draftees all around me. The majority of them lose interest quickly, but not Leo. He stares back longer than the rest.

I tuck my uniform into the drawer below my bunk and pull out the sheets. Quickly, I make the bed and undress out of my old clothes, then slip beneath the covers. As soon as my head hits the pillow, all my exhaustion hits me. Sleep tugs at my eyes, but my mind is racing.

I flip over on my side and watch a draftee fumble with the light switch. Before the room goes dark, I see Apollo crouched on the edge of his mattress. His eyes flick over to mine, and in the last glimmer of light, his face contorts into a devilish grin. The lights go out, and darkness fills the room. Yet somehow, I can still sense Apollo staring at me. Watching me through the shadows. Taunting me.

Making sure I know if I have any intention of finishing what my father started, he'll stop at nothing to make sure I don't succeed.

Five

THE FIRST THING THEY take from us is our hair. Early in the morning, David returns with an entourage of soldiers. One by one, they take us into the conjoined bathroom and shave our heads. The stiff razor grazes over my scalp, buzzing in my ear like a bully, mocking me as it uproots every follicle of my dignity. With my head down, I blink blonde hair out of my eyes and watch helplessly as it falls to the floor.

After they're finished, another soldier grabs me by my bare scalp and forces me into the shower. My whole body trembles as I rinse in lukewarm water, embarrassed and exposed. Once I'm clean, the soldier hands me a towel and orders me out into the barracks to dress in my uniform. As I cross the threshold, the next draftee steps forward, and the cycle begins again.

I slip on my uniform, though it doesn't feel like mine. The shirt clings to every rib, molding around my skin. The collar coils around my neck just below my Adam's apple, nearly choking me. My feet squeeze into the pair of boots assigned to me. I fasten the laces tightly and stand, wiggling my toes until they can't go any further.

Every draftee leaves the bathroom looking entirely different than when they went in. All that's left to tell us apart now is the color of our skin and the names stitched across our chests.

Ethan exits the bathroom proudly, rubbing his hands over his head like a crystal ball. His once-shaggy hair is now completely gone, leaving behind a shadow of stubble. I almost don't recognize him. He squats down to fetch his uniform out of the drawer and glances up at me.

"It's not too bad of a look," he shrugs. "I don't know about you, but I feel lighter."

I wedge my hands under my arms and look away. I can't muster the same optimism he can. Everything that made me who I am has been stripped away — my family, my hair, even the clothes on my back. All of it erased and morphed to fit the mold of who I'm expected to be.

As the last draftee pulls on his uniform, David steps into the room. He claps thunderously to get our attention. The sound cuts through the chatter but doesn't linger. It's instantly swallowed up, as if we're inside a vacuum where nothing echoes.

"Good morning, draftees," he begins. "We hope you found it easy to settle in last night."

A dozen pairs of bloodshot eyes stare back at him, hollow and burning with exhaustion. My eyes flash across the room to Apollo. Even without hair, he's unmistakable. He rises to his feet, towering over the other draftees, then folds his arms across his chest and widens his stance.

"Today is your first full day at The Battery," David announces. He smiles at the end of his sentence as if expecting some enthusiasm from us, but he gets nothing.

"We're going to take you up for breakfast before we head to the Assembly Hall for your induction ceremony. There, you'll receive your training assignments, and your training officers will provide further instructions. Any questions?"

Our half-hearted attentiveness and tired groans are enough of an answer for him.

He leads us out of the barracks and into the hallway. With no natural light or windows down here, it's impossible to tell what time of day it is. It almost feels like no time has passed since we arrived last night. Though the hunger gnawing at my stomach says otherwise.

We march about halfway down the hall before David tugs at his badge. He presses it to the scanner on the wall — the same one the soldier used last night. Green light flashes at the top, and the wall panels slide away, revealing an empty elevator pod on the other side.

"Everyone inside," he orders. I retreat to the back corner while the other draftees pack in shoulder to shoulder.

David presses a circular button engraved with an M on the button panel. As soon as he does, the doors slide shut, sealing us inside. Claustrophobia sets in, and my chest tightens.

The elevator jolts and begins moving upward. A low whir hums beneath our feet, rising in pitch as we accelerate. Pressure builds in my ears. I work my jaw to try and release it, but it only temporarily relieves me.

Within seconds, the pressure subsides, and the elevator slows to a stop. A melodic bell chimes from a speaker above us, and the doors slide open. Relief washes over me, and instantly it feels easier to breathe. The draftees begin pushing out of the elevator. Through the crowd, I can't make out what's on the other side, but I suspect it's no different than the lower level we came from. It isn't until I'm able to shove past a few draftees and make my way to the front that I realize I'm wrong. And what I see nearly sends my jaw to the floor.

We step into a grand atrium, similar in length and shape to the lower level, but much more spacious. The ceiling soars nearly three times as high. Morning sunlight bathes the otherwise dull room in luminous gold, making everything come alive. Two sets of double doors mark the front entrance, framed by towering panes of glass that reveal the city outside. From where I stand, I spot the Freedom Tower looming in the distance, closer than I've ever seen it before. Patches of dead trees dot the courtyard in front of the facility, obscuring some of the view. But the tower dominates over it all.

Both corners of the atrium jut out from the front wall like turrets, forming round towers on either side. Each one contains a wide spiral staircase that hugs the wall, curving up to a landing that's hidden from view. But most eye-catching of all is the emblem engraved into the stone floor in the center of the room. It forms an outline of the Freedom Tower encased in a circle. The circle stretches from the tower's base to the tip of its antenna, mirroring the Barrier. Where the antenna meets the edge, a series of intersecting lines come together in a star formation. The star extends high past the emblem's border, as if shining above it all. Gold fills the divots of the outline. The sunlight pouring in through the front catches on it, causing the emblem to shimmer.

David ushers us toward the staircase on our left. As we ascend, the glass wall at the front of the facility stretches higher, sharpening our view of the city. And with it, the upper level starts to take shape.

On the upper level, a plexiglass barrier borders the edge overlooking the atrium. Opposite that, the wall is entirely made of glass, offering a panoramic view of a manicured lawn outside. The facility's circular frame wraps around the lawn, enclosing it like a ring. Sleek cafeteria-style tables are scattered throughout the landing. Many are already occupied by soldiers eating from trays similar to the ones used for our rations.

A grand oval buffet sits in the corner of the room. Heat lamps hang overhead, emanating a red light over covered bins of food. Stacks of trays are positioned at the end of the line, along with utensils segregated into bins. Soldiers move down the buffet line and fill their trays, then take their seats at one of the tables nearby.

I turn back toward the view of the city. From this level, the tower is even more breathtaking. Everything around it pales in comparison. Buildings sag, their charred remains nothing more than skeletons of what they once were. But the tower is flawless — completely preserved.

"Help yourselves to the buffet," David says, snapping me out of my daze. "If you don't, you won't have another chance to eat till dinner. You'll eat when you're told to eat — no exceptions. I'll come by to gather you once everyone's finished. Until then, you're free to seat yourselves."

Other draftees begin splitting off in pairs or small groups. Ethan grabs my arm, claiming me.

"C'mon, Johnny. I'm starving," he whimpers.

Together, we walk to the edge of the buffet and join the line. When it's our turn, we take a tray from the stack, along with a set of silverware. I slide the tray along the smooth countertop and scoop a generous helping of oatmeal out of a bubbling pot, wincing as it plops against the plastic.

I grab a few more items and separate them neatly on my tray until I'm satisfied. Ethan grabs a mug of instant coffee, and I fill a reusable cup with water from a filtration machine at the end of the buffet. Once we're finished, we head toward a table at the back of the room, where Drew and Carson are already seated.

Ethan and I slide onto the bench across from them. Looking around, I notice a handful of draftees are seated at the table next to us. Leo sits with Apollo and two others whose names I don't know yet at a table further away.

"So this is it, huh?" Drew says as I'm turning toward my meal.

"What do you mean?" Ethan asks, his mouth stuffed full of food. It smacks against his lips, loud and wet, making my skin crawl.

"This is our life now. *You eat when we tell you to eat, or else*," Drew lowers his voice, mimicking David.

Ethan and Carson chuckle. Timidly, I pick at my food and pull away from the conversation.

"Anyway," Drew exhales as his laughter fades, "how'd you guys sleep?"

"Not long enough," Carson groans.

It's clear we're all exhausted. After the shock of the draft, not to mention the discomfort of sleeping in the barracks, we could all use some more rest. But something tells me rest is not on the agenda for today.

"I feel like I hardly slept at all," I reply to contribute something. "Still feels like I'm in a daze from last night."

"Feels like one long, never-ending night," Drew sympathizes. "Speaking of, what was the deal with Apollo last night? Something about your father?"

His question catches me off guard. But Drew wouldn't know anything about my father, unless Ethan happened to bring it up at the pub. He has a right to ask, considering it caused quite the scene in the barracks.

"Yeah, uh," I stutter, trying not to say too much. "It's nothing, really. It's no secret my father and Ethan's have some history with the draft."

"It's news to me," Drew replies without missing a beat. "Anything we should know about?"

Ethan slurps down the last of his food with a belch, which pulls Drew's attention away for a moment. "Nothing that concerns you or anyone else," Ethan says politely. "Or that even concerns me or Johnny, for that matter. We hardly knew our fathers."

Drew raises his brows in surprise. I'm relieved Ethan said something. But as he slouches back on the bench, it's clear he has nothing more to add. Which puts the spotlight back on me.

"It's true," I confirm. "So whatever it is Apollo has against me or my father, I know nothing about it. It's his grudge, and I want no part in it."

"Got it," Drew states. "Well, if it ever becomes a problem, you can talk to us. We're on your side."

I smile softly in appreciation.

But he's not finished. "In fact, I say we make a pact right now. The four of us, we're a good group. And before we get too deep into this, I think it's important to pick your people. What do you say we all stick together?"

"Count me in," Ethan gives a thumbs-up.

I exchange a glance with Carson, who's forcing down the last of his instant coffee. With a sour look on his face, he swallows and nods. "Works for me."

I nod too, and without a word, Drew takes it as a yes from me. It feels good knowing even though I've already seemed to make an enemy, I have people in my corner. It's only day one, and a lot could change. But for right now, it means everything.

David comes by and rounds up each table. He instructs us to return our trays to a conveyor belt behind the buffet, which carries our dirty dishes into the kitchen. Once we're all accounted for, he leads us down to the main level. A sea of black uniforms floods the atrium as soldiers crowd toward the elevator, all headed to the same place.

"It's mandatory for all military staff to attend the induction ceremony at the start of each term," David shouts over the noise. "There's a lot of foot traffic, so please stay together."

We press in behind the crowd and wait our turn for the elevator. Once it returns, we cram in as many people as it'll hold. This time, David presses a button engraved with an *L*, most likely for the lower level.

The elevator floor feels like it drops out beneath us, and for a split second, we're free-floating. Then gravity kicks in, and our boots slam against the floor. We spiral downward at a dizzying rate. Pressure builds in my ears again the deeper we go. Finally, it slows, and the soft chime overhead signals our arrival.

We pour out of the elevator as soon as the doors open. Soldiers fill the corridor, all moving toward the same destination. To my surprise, the doors leading into the Assembly Hall are already wide open. David leads us toward one of the entrances, and we squeeze inside with the rest of the group.

Inside is a large circular auditorium, roughly the same size as the lawn above us. We enter at the top of a sloped ramp leading down to a stage. Folding seats are bolted to the floor in rows on either side and stair-step all the way to the bottom, where the ground levels out. Most are already filled with soldiers. David guides us down the aisle to a row on the left, about three rows from the front.

We shuffle into the row and take our seats. The whole room buzzes with noise. As I glance around, it's shocking to see just how many people make up the military — and how few of us there are in comparison. David takes the aisle seat at the end of our row, and two other soldiers cap it off at the other end, blocking us in.

There's a moment of stillness before anything happens. All the commotion dies down, and the lights dim, silencing us.

One of the entry doors at the back of the room clicks open. Nobody turns — everyone faces forward, eyes glued to the darkened stage. In the silence, I can hear footsteps drawing closer, moving down the aisle beside our row. I crane my neck to get a glimpse at who they belong to, but I can hardly make out more than a silhouette.

A man passes by our row and moves toward the side of the stage. He ascends a small set of stairs and steps into a spotlight beaming down on the center. He's dressed in a forest green uniform with gold buttons that gleam in the light. His thin salt-and-pepper hair is slicked back against his scalp. A neatly trimmed mustache covers his upper lip, but the rest of his face is clean shaven, revealing cracks in his skin from age. His eyes are lowered, focused on his feet as he glides to the edge of the stage. As he takes his position, his face slowly lifts, the beginnings of a smile forming on his lips.

"Draftees," he roars. The power in his voice reverberates through the room. His eyes scan our row, examining us closely.

"Welcome to The Battery. My name is General Louis Conrad, and I'm very much looking forward to getting to know each of you — some of you more than others."

As he finishes his sentence, his eyes land directly on me, and the smile fully forms across his face.

The spotlight illuminating him shuts off without warning. His smile fades into the darkness, but somehow, I can still visualize it.

In the same moment, an even brighter light bursts from the back of the room, stretching over our heads. It projects a blank white screen onto the bare canvas behind the stage. The general reappears, his shadow looming in the glow. He shifts out of the way until he's no longer blocking the screen.

"As you may already know, you're here for a very important purpose. All of you." His eyes sweep across the room, addressing every soldier. "And it's important that you understand your time here is not just a civic duty. It's a privilege."

Ethan scoffs next to me. I throw him a frantic look, worried the general might hear him. He doesn't seem concerned — but I am.

The general continues. "One that can be taken away from you, if you fall out of line. Your purpose here, as a draftee—" his eyes shift back to our row, "is to undergo the necessary training to become a soldier. And as a soldier—" he directs his attention to the other side of the room, "your purpose here is to protect the city from a great evil that lurks beyond its borders."

He begins pacing back and forth in slow, sanctioned movements. Each time he turns, his boots scrape against the slick stage floor. I grit my teeth at the sound.

"Seated around you are hundreds of other men who've given their lives to the same cause. A cause that's worth fighting for, wouldn't you agree?"

"Yes, sir!" soldiers around the room shout in unison, startling me.

"Very good," the general smiles, pleased. "Now, don't get me wrong. This fight is not for the faint of heart. We're up against a very real enemy — one that is murderous, relentless, and will stop at nothing until it's infiltrated our Barrier. But we're not going to let that happen, are we?"

"No, sir!" the soldiers shout again. My stomach twists.

"But it's a fight we must endure, every single one of us!" he declares. "Because of who we're fighting for. Think of your families back home. The communities you were raised in. The parents who raised you. Their ability to walk down the street at night without fear of what may be lurking around the corner. To sleep in a bed with a roof over their heads every night, knowing the next day is guaranteed. That's what we're trying to protect here. Order, peace, and community. It's what we all want, is it not? And anything that threatens that *must* be stopped."

But at what cost? I think. The whole reason the draft exists is to protect us if the Barrier were to fall. If order, peace, and community are the goal, why not build a stronghold that lasts? Instead of putting our lives at risk?

"We all share a common enemy." He pauses for effect and squints, then lifts a finger to his chin as if pondering. "Yes, we do. The Truth, as you know it, has taken our once-great nation and flipped it on its head."

I know the general isn't talking about honesty. The Truth, what we've named the entity that wiped out nearly our entire nation, is hardly ever spoken of. The military did everything they could to cover it up and help people forget. When people came under the Barrier, all anyone wanted was a fresh start. To forget about the horrors of what happened. So we don't talk about it, and we give it a nickname so that those of us — like me — who were born under the Barrier will never know its true identity.

"It's forced us into exile beneath our Barrier while it prowls outside our borders. It preys on our vulnerability. It feeds on our fear. It wants to enslave us. It wants us to feel as though it has the upper hand."

The general slams his boot into the stage with a thud that shakes the whole auditorium.

"But we're here to prove that it does *not* have the upper hand. This is how we show we have the upper hand — that we've *always* had the upper hand. By training our men to be stronger than The Truth. To exceed the bounds of what it thinks we're capable of and rise above the odds. If our Barrier were to fall, it's not us who should be afraid. It's our enemy! It will quake when it sees just how strong we've become. We will give it no choice but to retreat back to the depths of Hell it crawled out of."

Every soldier in the room applauds. My heart pounds violently in my chest. I can tell he's trying to rile us up, to feel empowered by his words. But it only elicits more fear. The truth is, we have no idea what we're up against. We're not stronger than it. If that were true, there'd be no need for the Barrier. No fight for survival. No draft. Yet here we are.

The general resumes his original position in front of the screen, standing in the light of the projector. His face looks ghostly and his eyes lethal, like a snake ready to strike.

"So, never forget you're here for a purpose," his voice softens. "You're part of something much bigger than yourselves. And the longevity of humanity depends on you performing at your fullest potential. But to understand how we need to move forward, we must first remember where we came from."

A black outline begins to materialize on the screen behind him. The lighting in the room changes, dimming to a soft blue tone, similar to the subway. The outline forms a sphere, and within the sphere, different hues of deep blues and greens fill in the shape. This continues until it forms Earth. The rest of the screen dims fully to black, darkening the room. The globe rotates slightly, and as it does, the projector zooms in, focusing on one green landmass in particular.

"This is the United States of America, as it used to be," the general says. The projector slows until the United States is the only visible part of the globe. It spans across the entirety of the back wall. The general's shadow cuts straight through the center, making him appear as large as the country itself.

I lean in to examine the image more closely. I've heard the story told many times — that before the Barrier, our country used to span thousands of miles over different states. But seeing it laid out like this puts a whole new weight to it. Everything we lost is so much more than I realized.

"As you all know, nearly two decades ago, our country was as you see it before you now: vast, flourishing, and rich with life."

Millions of little blue dots begin to populate across the map. Thick clusters form in more densely populated areas. The dots cover nearly the entire map until the shape of the country is hardly identifiable anymore.

"Each dot represents a life, totaling the population of our country at the time — before The Truth," the general explains.

My eyes widen in amazement. But it's quickly swept away by dread from what comes next.

"One day, this was who we were. And the next, this is what we became."

On cue, the blue dots begin to dissipate one by one, beginning on the leftmost side of the map and spanning east until every dot west of the midpoint is gone. The only dots remaining are now sprinkled across the eastern coastline, and they're few and far between. Before long, even those dots start to vanish until there's nothing left but one cluster in the top right-hand corner.

"It began on the West Coast in Los Angeles, California. Previously one of the most populous cities in America, it was a deadly target for our enemy. People naturally began to flee east, attempting to outrun death, but death caught up to them. By the time the United States government realized the caliber of the threat, more than half the population was gone."

The horrifying pieces start to fall into place. If The Truth could eradicate more than half a population that quickly, it'd take seconds for it to wipe out our community, if given the chance.

"The government exhausted all its resources to euthanize the threat. Specialists and foreign military personnel were called in from around the world in an attempt to discover its origin. We hoped that by uncovering its roots, we could find a way to reverse it. But it was too late. Things were quickly spiraling out of control, and it was clear we needed a solution before there was no one left. That solution was our Barrier."

The map shifts, and the projector zooms in on the cluster in the upper right-hand corner. As it enlarges, the individual dots join together like magnets to form one massive dot. It stretches until it becomes three-dimensional. The map shifts again to an aerial shot of New York City, and the dot takes the shape of the Barrier.

"People were reluctant to accept the idea of the Barrier at first. Our once-great nation was known as the land of the free, and people struggled to accept this . . . newfound freedom," he chuckles, as if it's comical to compare what we once had to what we have now. "People refused to believe the Barrier was our only option. They demonstrated this by tarnishing the city we'd selected as our Barrier site. Riots filled the streets, buildings burned, and lives were lost. But no matter how badly they burned the city, no one touched the Freedom Tower. Even the most radical, rebellious bunch knew it needed to remain intact. They knew — whether they cared to admit it — there would be no other option. And we needed the tower for our Barrier.

"Despite their protests, we proceeded with the Barrier. And it made our city beautiful again." He pauses to take in the image behind him. Even with his face turned toward the screen, I can see his mouth widen into a grin. He looks upon the encased city with pride, almost as if he prefers it this way.

He pulls himself out of his admiration and continues. "You heard me mention freedom just moments earlier. That's what we offered people — freedom under the Barrier in return for their work on the Barrier's construction. Men and women from all over the East Coast came for a chance at a new life under the Barrier. We allowed them to be part of something bigger than themselves, to contribute to their community and their future. And that gave people a whole new appreciation for the life they had under the Barrier."

He steps to the edge of the stage and gazes out at the audience. "And now, we've enlisted the first generation of Barrier-born draftees — young men who were born under the Barrier and raised here all their lives. Not our largest bunch, but still, a historical moment, nonetheless."

The soldiers turn toward us and fill the room with applause. David smiles proudly from the end of the row, as if we should be honored to have spent our whole lives under the Barrier.

Should we be? The fanfare from the soldiers, General Conrad's speech about freedom, should it move me in the same way it moves them? Should I feel grateful to have spent my entire life here?

Worst of all, should I feel guilty for wishing I hadn't? For wishing my life would've been different? It's not that I'm ungrateful for the protection we have under the Barrier. But part of me doesn't care to take ownership of it the way all the men before me have. Is that so wrong?

"So, draftees," the general says, facing us, "it's time for you to step up. To do your part in protecting the city you've called home all your lives. After all, that's what this is all about. Because if our Barrier were to fall, who would we have to count on but ourselves? We're fools to think the Barrier will stand the test of time, but it will buy us time to build up an army large enough to vanquish our enemy. And every single one of you is a part of that victory."

The soldiers continue to cheer, this time with more passion. A few even holler and whistle. I notice something starting to stir in the other draftees. Even Ethan, who's always been impartial to the draft, starts to smile, entranced by the general's speech.

I close my eyes and replay General Conrad's words in my mind. I drown out all the noise, trying to find my own source of motivation. Regardless of how I feel, I have to force myself to be a part of this. I have to play the part. If I don't, who knows what will become of me?

One foot in won't win the war against The Truth. And it won't get me any closer to finding out what happened to my father. I have to believe I can do this. Because if I don't, we'll lose — and he'll stay lost forever.

The projector beam is sucked to the back of the room, taking the image of the city with it. The lights slowly lift back on. Everyone stirs, and I sense the ceremony coming to an end.

"To commemorate this year's batch of draftees, I'd like to invite them to join me on stage," General Conrad declares. On command, David rises out of his seat and steps aside, then signals for us to get up. A few draftees jump up immediately. Others hesitate. But within seconds, we're all making our way to the end of the row.

We march down the aisle toward the stage. The general waits for us patiently, his figure magnifying as we get closer. When we reach the stage, we form a line along the back wall, facing the crowd. One glance at the audience causes my stomach to lurch, and I instantly drop my eyes to my feet.

Once we're all in line, the general begins pacing. He pauses in front of each of us, inspecting us like we're fresh meat. When he stops in front of me, my whole body tenses. I keep my eyes downcast, fixed on his boots as they pivot toward me. I don't meet his gaze. I know when he looks at me, he sees my father. It's all anyone sees. He knows who my father was and what became of him. What *they* did to him. He lingers for a moment longer before turning away, moving on to the next draftee.

As soon as he reaches the end of the line, he spins around. His boots scrape against the stage in another sharp squeal.

"Training officers, please join us on stage," he commands.

From the end of our row, two soldiers rise and make their way toward the stage. One is slightly shorter than the other, but both have the same strong build and steely demeanor.

"These will be your training officers for the next sixteen weeks," the general states. "You'll all follow the same training regimen, but you'll be divided into smaller units so your training officers can observe you more closely."

The training officers position themselves in the corner of the stage. They keep a generous distance between each other with their hands tucked firmly behind their backs, chins raised, eyes fixed on the crowd as the general speaks.

"We'll start with Lieutenant Jude Kelley," General Conrad announces.

"Sir, yes, sir!" shouts the taller of the two. His hair is buzzed down to his scalp — no different than the rest of us now — and his jawline is razor sharp. The bone structure in his face makes him look skeletal, with sunken eyes and a sharp, pointed nose. But the dense, muscular build of the rest of his body gives him some appeal.

"With Lieutenant Kelley, we'll have Drew Fitzgerald, Carson O'Hair, Ethan Greene . . ." David ushers each draftee over to Lieutenant Kelley as their names are called. Ethan holds eye contact with me from across the stage, hoping my name is called next.

". . . Rory Taylor, Adrian Hart, and John Madoc."

All the tension in my body releases. I march over to where Ethan stands, trying to hold back a relieved grin. All the while Lieutenant Kelley keeps his gaze forward, not bothering to greet us or so much as look at us.

"Next up, Lieutenant Nathaniel Tillman."

"Sir, yes, sir!" the other training officer hollers back. The stubble on his head is a bright shade of orange. Freckles dot his face, and his brows are the same vibrant color as the shadow of his hair. His face is much fuller than Lieutenant Kelley's, and his short stature makes his strong build feel much more impressive. He mimics Lieutenant Kelley's posture with his hands tucked behind his back, eyes forward, and ears attentive to the general.

"With Lieutenant Tillman, we'll have Leo Patton, Dom D'Angelo, Danny Guerra, Luca Ross, Joey Callahan, and Apollo Andres."

The rest of the draftees disperse one by one and form a group next to us. Apollo throws a smug look in our direction as he passes by.

"Clearly the more superior group," he mumbles, taking his place beside Lieutenant Tillman. Ethan growls at him, but Apollo doesn't notice.

With us sorted into our training groups, General Conrad turns toward the audience once more. "Before we end today, I'd like to familiarize our draftees with a little saying we have around here. A pledge of allegiance, of sorts. But it only consists of three simple words: Obey, Preserve, and Protect."

He pauses for a moment to dramatize the phrase. The words feel powerful, and I can tell they hold significance for the soldiers. I suspect they should come to mean the same to me one day.

"Each word represents something," the general explains, "and each word holds equally as much weight as the other. Before you join us in reciting the pledge, you need to understand what each word means.

"First: Obey. A soldier is marked by his obedience. Before our Barrier came down, our nation was in disarray. There was no order, and any attempt to create order was met with rebellion. Now that we've established order, it's crucial that you obey the rules we have in place — the same ones every individual seated before you abides by. The system works for a reason, and it's necessary that you obey it."

All it takes is one person asking the right questions for the whole system to break. Mae's words flash through my mind unexpectedly. If what the general's saying is true, that the system works for a reason, why would she want me to break it?

He continues. "Next: Preserve. It's our duty to preserve the state of our community under the Barrier. Outside the Barrier, the world is sick. Desolate and uninhabitable. A healthy community cannot function in those conditions. But here, within the Barrier, there's life. There's hope. There's a chance at rebuilding what we lost, and it's pivotal that we preserve what's left so we don't lose any more."

He flows seamlessly into the next word of the pledge. "And finally: Protect. We end with Protect because it's our call to action. With obeying the rules of society and preserving what's left of our nation, there's a responsibility to protect it. As draftees and soldiers alike, your purpose is to protect the citizens who've sought sanctuary under the Barrier. There's no greater purpose in the world we find ourselves in than to protect those around us — no matter the cost. And each of you should feel honored and empowered to do so."

The general raises his arms with his palms up, motioning for every soldier in the room to stand.

"Now, if you believe in these words, I want you to declare them with me," the general shouts. "Obey, Preserve, Protect!"

Everyone in the room beats their fists against their chests and lifts up a shout. "Obey, Preserve, Protect!"

For a moment, hearing everyone repeat the words in unison moves me. I feel a flicker of the purpose General Conrad spoke of beginning to take root inside me. The pledge is only a small spark of the immense amount of hope we need to survive, but it's enough to keep us going.

Drew grabs my arm in the uproar of soldiers chanting the pledge. I glance at him and notice he's gotten Ethan and Carson's attention too.

"Remember what we agreed on," he hollers, still low enough that only we can hear him. "The pact we made. The four of us, we're in this together."

We all nod in agreement. As I turn away from him, my eyes drift over to the other training group. Apollo stares at me, zeroing in on me while the rest of the draftees join in the pledge. Reminding me even though it feels like we're all unified in this moment, there are still other sides to take in this war.

But standing next to Ethan, Drew, and Carson, knowing they're on my side, having an enemy doesn't feel so intimidating — whether it's Apollo or The Truth. If there's a way we can survive this, we'll figure it out. Together.

Six

ONCE THE NOISE SUBSIDES, the training officers lead us out of the auditorium. We line up in the hall as soldiers pour out around us. They split off toward the elevator, but we hang back, awaiting further instructions now that we're in the hands of the training officers.

As soon as the lower level clears, Lieutenant Kelley steps forward. "Congratulations, kids. You're stuck with us," he chuckles wickedly.

No one laughs. We stare back timidly, unsure if he's someone we can trust yet.

"Ah, you all need to lighten up," he frowns. "Lieutenant Tillman will take his group to the lawn for their fitness evaluation while my group tours the training facilities. Once we're finished, we'll swap. Then you can return to your barracks for a shower — because let's face it, you'll need one after we're finished with you."

He chuckles again, but he's only amusing himself. I get the impression he enjoys having authority. More specifically, he enjoys taunting us.

"Any questions?" he offers.

We all mumble back in response — a chorus of *mmhmm*s and hesitant nods. Lieutenant Kelley stands dumbfounded. His eyes widen dramatically, and he takes a step back as if we've offended him.

"That's the first thing you need to work on," he says. This time, his voice comes back harsher. "When Lieutenant Tillman or I ask you a question or give you an order, you're to respond with *yes, sir* or *no, sir*. Not *yeah* or *okay* or whatever pathetic noises just came out of your mouths. It's *yes, sir*," he demonstrates in a loud, definitive tone that echoes down the now-empty hallway.

He waits a moment for his words to stick, then crosses his arms over his chest. "So, let's try that again. Any questions?"

"No, sir," we all reply in a monotone chorus. But it's not enough for him.

"I said, any questions, soldiers?" he screams. The sheer intensity of his voice flattens me against the wall.

"No, sir!" we call out, matching his volume.

A devious grin spreads across his face. "See, was that so hard?"

"No, sir!" we shout again, afraid if we don't, he might lose it again.

"I didn't need a response that time, but I like it," he says, clicking his tongue.

He glances over at Lieutenant Tillman. "Take your group. Radio me when you're done."

Lieutenant Tillman lifts his hand in a salute. "Yes, sir," he replies. "You six, follow me."

He points a finger at the draftees in his group. They peel themselves from the wall and march down the corridor, glancing at us as they go.

"Best of luck to you, losers," Apollo sneers as he follows Lieutenant Tillman.

"Go on, set the bar low for us," Ethan snaps back.

Lieutenant Kelley lets out a huff, and Ethan quickly straightens himself. Apollo snickers, having evaded Lieutenant Kelley's wrath. But the same can't be said for Ethan.

"Soldier!" Lieutenant Kelley shouts. He steps forward and leans in mere inches from Ethan's face. Ethan's eyes fall to the ground, unwilling to meet his glare.

"Seems to me like you need to learn how to hold your tongue," he hisses. "I don't want to see any more of that out of you, understood?"

"I'm not the one you need to be—"

"I said, is that understood, soldier?" Lieutenant Kelley screams. Ethan trembles, pressed against the wall as far as he can go.

"Yes, sir!" he shouts, his eyes still glued to the floor.

Lieutenant Kelley slams his palm into the wall above Ethan's head, causing him to flinch. He backs away slowly but holds his stare the entire time. I don't bother to glance over. I keep my eyes pointed ahead, mouth shut, and almost forget to breathe.

"Follow me," Lieutenant Kelley snarls.

We head down the corridor in the same direction as the last group, bypassing the elevator. Drew and Carson walk ahead of us, and I hang back to take up the rear with Ethan.

"Close call back there," I whisper.

"I swear I saw my life flash before my eyes," Ethan says, letting a slight chuckle escape his mouth.

"Apollo will get what he deserves," I mutter. "It's only a matter of time before he says something that'll get Lieutenant Kelley to snap at him like that."

"I'd love to be there when that happens," he admits.

Lieutenant Kelley stops at another blank wall near the end of the hall. Similar to the other rooms, there's a small scanner mounted to the wall. Lieutenant Kelley lifts his badge to it, and the panel dislodges, folding inward like a door. The training officer pushes it forward with his palm and moves aside, waiting until all six of us are inside.

The room on the other side is completely dark. The sound of our boots echoes like footsteps down a hollow shaft, reminding me of the subway tunnels. Lieutenant Kelley steps inside. As soon as the door clicks shut behind him, overhead lights flicker on one by one.

"This is our shooting range," Lieutenant Kelley says. His voice bounces off the walls, chasing the lights as they illuminate the length of the room.

To our left, the room is sectioned into three shooting stalls, each one bordered by a thick concrete wall. At the far end of each lane, humanoid dummies hang from the ceiling, wrapped in chains. Crimson red targets are painted over their chests and faces. Dark, gritty sand fills the floor like a dugout, lining each lane from the dummy to the half-wall divider at the end closest to us.

"There are three aspects of your training," Lieutenant Kelley explains. "Strength, strategy, and skill. Here, you'll learn the skill of operating a gun. Weapons are only one part of your training, though, and arguably the least important. It's one thing to know how to shoot a gun, but another to know what to do when the ammo runs out."

He strides over to the corner of the room, facing toward the wall opposite the stalls. He reaches for his badge again and slides it against a scanner I can't see. A trio of beeps indicates he's activated something, followed by the sound of a lock clicking open. At once, the entire wall glows with white light, revealing a wall of copper lockers that were seemingly hidden before. Their grid-patterned doors make it easy to see the array of weapons stored on the other side. Guns of all shapes and sizes sit on racks, neatly organized according to their kind.

Lieutenant Kelley pulls open a few lockers. By the looks of it, there have to be nearly a hundred guns stored here. At the base of each locker is a small extendable cubby, like a drawer. Lieutenant Kelley opens one, and inside, copper bullets glisten in the bright lighting overhead.

"These are the weapons you'll train with over the next sixteen weeks," he continues. "Proper munitions are stored in the cubby below each locker, as you can see. We'll be starting you off small," he runs his hand along a rack containing handheld guns, "and moving our way up as your skills develop."

He moves his hand from the handguns to another rack a few rows down, where the guns are much bulkier.

My stomach twists as I think of holding one. Even more so at the thought of using one. I can't imagine myself in that position. Wielding something that holds the power between life and death. It feels wrong. But I know at some point, I'll have to. I'll have to learn how to harness that power, otherwise it'll be my life on the line.

I shudder at the realization that even though it feels bizarre now, one day, it'll feel natural. Almost like second nature.

"Don't worry, you'll be pros in no time," Lieutenant Kelley says with a wry smile as he snaps the lockers back in place. "Each week, we'll reconvene with Lieutenant Tillman's group and have a few of you practice at a time. The goal is not to be better than your peers, but to learn how to be precise. Every time. Lack of precision will get you killed, and I take it none of you want that."

He leans in close, his eyes scanning us. We all stare back stunned, too intimidated to speak.

But before he can say any more, white noise crackles from a radio clipped to his belt. Through the static, I hear Lieutenant Tillman's voice on the other end.

"We're finished," he says. "Headed down, over."

"Roger that," Lieutenant Kelley replies into the radio. "Well then, it's your time to shine," he says to us. "You'll grow more familiar with these facilities as we begin training. For now, we'll head up to the main level for your fitness evaluation."

We start to head toward the door, but before we make it, Lieutenant Kelley holds out his palm. His brows furrow, like he's remembered something he'd forgotten.

"Actually, before we go," he starts, "I'll go ahead and distribute your badges."

He fumbles his hand in his pocket, and when he pulls it out, he's holding six plain plastic badges, each with a black clip and coil on the end. He holds them out to us like a deck of cards, inviting us to pick one.

Each of us grabs one from his hand and holds it tentatively. Once they're all gone, Lieutenant Kelley explains what they're for.

"These badges will grant you access to your barracks as well as the elevator between both levels of the facility. Everywhere else requires an all-access badge, which only myself and Lieutenant Tillman have, as far as you should be concerned. The subway, the training facilities, none of it is accessible to you unless you're under our supervision. Understood?"

"Yes, sir!" we holler without missing a beat.

A grin spreads across his face. "That's better. Any time you're away from your barracks, your badge should be on you. There's no crying to me or Lieutenant Tillman if you've lost it or forgotten it in your barracks. You'll sleep on the floor of the atrium, if that's the case," he laughs, but he's not humoring us. He's completely serious.

With our badges clipped to our belts, we exit the room and march back down the hallway toward the elevator. When we reach the scanner, Lieutenant Kelley stands still. He doesn't reach for his badge. Instead, he eyes us and waits for someone to take initiative.

"I didn't just give you your badges as a prop. You, soldier," he says, nodding his head at Drew. "Summon the elevator."

"Yes, sir," Drew mumbles. He steps forward and swipes his badge against the scanner. From within the wall, I hear its steady whir as it lowers down to our level. The familiar chime signals its arrival, and the panels split apart.

On the other side, Lieutenant Tillman and his group are standing there. Lieutenant Tillman steps out first, stone-faced and unbothered. Meanwhile the draftees behind him are dripping with sweat. Their faces are flushed — even Apollo's — and none of them meet our gaze. They lazily slump out of the elevator and follow Lieutenant Tillman down the hall, trading places with us.

I gulp and glance over at Ethan.

"Looks like they had a great time," he mumbles.

"Inside," Lieutenant Kelley growls, pointing his finger toward the vacant pod.

We gather inside and wait for the elevator to lift off. Within seconds, it carries us to the main level. The doors open, and we spill out into the atrium. Lieutenant Kelley immediately guides us over to one of the open archways carved into the wall, leading out to the training lawn.

A cool breeze wraps around us as we step outside. The sun hides behind a cloud, making everything a bit more gray than it was earlier. Around the exterior veranda, a few soldiers shuffle about. They pay no mind to us as we stride to the center of the lawn.

Lieutenant Kelley comes to a screeching halt and spins around. I can only imagine what we must look like to him. A group of ragtag teenage boys, unprepared for what happens next. Intimidation and fear smeared across our faces, especially after seeing what the last group looked like.

It must give him a thrill. It can't have been more than a decade ago that he was in our position. Now he's forgotten what it was like, his ego boosted by his authority. He has the power to do whatever he wants to us — and he knows it. We're completely at his mercy.

It makes me wonder, are we destined to become like him? Will the draft harden us and make us crave that same power? Or is it possible to still come out of this with some semblance of who I am and not lose myself in the process?

"Alright, listen up," Lieutenant Kelley orders, pulling me out of my thoughts. By now, the lingering soldiers have disappeared inside the facility, leaving us alone on the lawn.

"Today, you'll undergo an initial fitness evaluation to assess your level of strength, strategy, and skill coming into the draft," he explains. "You'll be evaluated on these same things at the end of each quarter to measure your progress. You'll be ranked based on your progress, and the top five ranked draftees will be granted special permissions throughout the term. The assessment will not look the same each quarter — and that's intentional. The objective is not to get good at the same test, but to become a master at all the skills you need to possess as a soldier.

"For this assessment, we'll run through a series of circuit exercises to test your physical and mental stamina. There's no need to impress us," he stops and smirks. "We're not expecting anything impressive in the slightest. For most of you, this is the first time in your lives you'll have worked your body in this way. The objective is to push yourself to the limit, and once you feel like you're there, keep pushing. Show me what you're capable of, even when it feels like you have nothing left to give."

By proximity, he steps up to Carson's face. Carson immediately recoils. "After all, you don't get to tap out in war. You either keep pushing, or you die."

He shoves Carson back playfully, but it's only playful to him. Carson stumbles backward. Drew grabs his shoulder to stabilize him. Lieutenant Kelley cackles wildly and patrols the rest of the line.

"Some of you will rise above the ranks . . ." He pauses in front of Ethan. Instantly, Ethan tenses, bracing himself for Lieutenant Kelley to snap again. "Others won't have what it takes." He turns on his heels and, this time, pauses in front of me. His eyes narrow on mine. I stare straight ahead, not meeting his eyes but also unable to escape them.

"And others will surprise us, and even surprise themselves," he finishes. "Starting now, it's up to you to decide what kind of soldier you want to be. What kind of man you want to be. Do you want to be the kind of man who cracks under pressure?"

None of us say anything, but we quickly realize he's expecting a response.

"No, sir!" we shout out of sync.

"Do you want to be the kind of man who can't protect his nation? Or his own family?"

"No, sir!"

He pauses for dramatic effect. Seconds go by, but it feels like minutes before he speaks again. "Then prove it," he hisses. "All of you drop where you're standing!"

There's a shared hesitation where no one does anything. I look at Ethan to my left, then Carson to my right, and they glance back at me. All of us waiting for the other to act.

"Now!" Lieutenant Kelley growls.

We fall on our stomachs. The stiff low-cut grass crunches beneath my uniform. I turn my head to keep it from scratching my chin, but no matter which way I face, I find another reason to be uncomfortable.

"Fifteen push-ups, now!" Lieutenant Kelley demands.

I don't think I've ever done a push-up before. But somehow, my body falls naturally into position.

I push with all my might and feel my biceps burn, my uniform tightening around every muscle. Veins bulge from my neck, and before I know it, I'm struggling to breathe. Ethan's not much better than me, and Carson can barely even support himself through the first few. My arms tremble as my elbows bend. I lower my body close to the ground, then push back up again. This cycle repeats fifteen times before I finally collapse to the ground.

Ethan finishes before me, but I'm only a few reps behind him. Glancing down the line, Drew seems to be finished too, but Carson still has a ways to go.

Lieutenant Kelley squats down in front of Carson, twisting his neck until their foreheads meet.

"Keep pushing, soldier!" he screams.

Carson's face flushes bright red. Saliva pools around his mouth as he grits his teeth through each push-up. His whole body shivers, and for a moment, I wonder if he might be sick. It's evident he's more out of shape than the rest of us, but to my surprise, he finishes all fifteen without giving up.

But this is only the beginning. And something tells me it only gets worse from here.

Lieutenant Kelley continues running through the rest of the circuit. He increases the amount of reps each time, or adds in some variable that makes it arguably harder than the time before. My body grows weaker with every rep. I've never known pain like this. I've never pushed myself like this before. Every muscle in my body feels like it's been lit on fire. Sweat pricks at my forehead and burns my eyes, and my palms rub raw against the blades of grass.

At any hint of reluctance or any slowed movement, Lieutenant Kelley is right there to bark at us.

"Give me more than that!" he shouts, looming over us. He paces down the line with his hands tucked behind his back as we squirm beneath him.

He presses in until we've reached our breaking point, just like he said he would. And right when we're about to burst, right when it feels like I can't take any more, that's when he pushes us the most.

Next up, we run drills around the training lawn. He orders us to do loops around the veranda, circling the lawn in an endless cycle. From there, he introduces a variety of other ways to torture us — having us lunge across the lawn, or bear crawl, or sprint from side to side as fast as we can. My body springs into action at Lieutenant Kelley's commands, but I feel limp, like a puppet tugged along by his strings.

Once we've completed the circuit, we drag ourselves back to the starting point, all of us red-faced and a shell of who we were when we first started.

Lieutenant Kelley's body language indicates we might be nearing the end. Relief soothes my muscles, but it's temporary.

"Nice work," Lieutenant Kelley says. But it feels half-hearted.

His brows lower, and the corners of his mouth curl into a grin. "Now do it all again."

Every single draftee groans — including me. We drop back to the ground helplessly and begin the cycle of pushing ourselves down and up again. Everyone moves much slower the second time around, which only heightens Lieutenant Kelley's harassment.

I focus on Ethan and Drew to my left, watching as they go down and up, down and up, trying to mimic their pace. I work up the strength to push up as they do and hold my breath as we lower back down to the ground.

Without realizing it, I become so focused on them that I lose track of which rep I'm on. I don't even hear it when Lieutenant Kelley squats down in front of me.

"Soldier," he snaps. My head jerks upward. His face is inches from mine. He holds my gaze as I push myself down and up again. "What are you looking at?"

"N-nothing, sir," I stutter, forcing my way through each movement.

My lower lip sags until my whole mouth hangs open. My eyes remain fixed on Lieutenant Kelley's face, but my vision starts to blur.

Lieutenant Kelley stands back up with a deep exhale. He lifts his boot, and I feel it press into my spine. The pressure is light at first, then as I bend my elbows, it grows heavier. I attempt to push myself back up, but it's impossible. The weight of Lieutenant Kelley's foot is crushing.

My elbows buckle, and my arms give out. I collapse to the ground with a thud, wincing as my jaw makes contact with the lawn. He takes his foot off, and both grease-black boots step back into my line of vision.

"You're weak, Madoc," he insults me. My lungs heave as I sink into the grass. It feels like I'll never be able to get up again. Even the thought of doing so is exhausting.

"Just like your father was," he finishes.

Lieutenant Kelley spits down at me. Through the blur, I watch his boots turn and walk away, leaving me crushed under the weight of his words.

Seven

The next morning marks the official start of training. All the introductions and formalities are over, and that's clearly demonstrated by the training officers barging into the barracks at an ungodly hour.

Even without any windows, I can tell it's early. My body surges with pain the minute my eyes open. My muscles ache, still worn down from the fitness evaluation yesterday, and I doubt they'll recover any time soon.

"Rise and shine, draftees!" Lieutenant Tillman shouts with a bolt of enthusiasm.

A chorus of groans spreads around the room. Instinctively, I flip over onto my side and bury my face in my pillow. My eyes blink shut, and it takes seconds before I'm drifting back to sleep again.

But it's short-lived. Lieutenant Kelley rips the covers from my body. A cold breeze slaps my bare chest, and I instantly shrivel up.

"On your feet!" he barks at me. "All of you, on your feet!"

We all roll clumsily out of our bunks. The cold stone floor stings my blistering feet. I tuck my hands beneath my arms for warmth. Ethan scurries down from the top bunk and stands next to me. He lets out a huge yawn, stretching his arms toward the ceiling. To my surprise, his fingertips almost touch it.

"Report to breakfast in ten minutes," Lieutenant Kelley orders. "We'll brief you from there on how the rest of the day will go. Understood?"

"Yes, sir!" we reply.

The training officers give each other a nod, then turn to leave the room. Lieutenant Tillman files out first, and Lieutenant Kelley is almost out the door before he stops. Looking back at us, he repeats, "Ten minutes," with a menacing glare.

With that, he slams the door shut. I wince as it makes contact with the frame and clicks into place.

"Kill me now, please," Ethan begs, turning toward me. With his eyes barely open, he falls forward limp, like a rag doll.

I shove him back, and he catches himself with the frame of the bunk. "I don't think you need me to do that for you," I say. "Lieutenant Kelley will kill you himself if we're not upstairs in ten minutes."

"In that case, I'm going back to bed." Ethan begins climbing back up the ladder. I grip the back of his T-shirt and yank him down.

"If I have to go, so do you."

His shoulders sag in defeat. "Fine," he sighs. "But if they make me do another push-up, I'm making a run for it."

Reluctantly, we dress in our uniforms. I slip on my boots and clip my badge to my belt. A few draftees head out of the room, while others — like Ethan and me — take more time to get ready.

Apollo glares at me as he passes by our bunk. He doesn't say anything, but he doesn't have to. I hold his stare until he rounds the corner and disappears through the doorway.

"Don't worry about him," Leo's voice says.

I turn away from the door to find Leo standing in front of me. He seems rested, or just really good at hiding how tired he is. Ethan glances at him while sliding his head through his tactical shirt.

"It's him who should be worried," Ethan chimes in.

"He's got an agenda, is all," Leo reasons. "But don't we all, right? We've all got something to prove."

Ethan scoffs. "I have nothing to prove. What you see is what you get."

Leo laughs, but I know Ethan isn't joking.

"It's alright," I say to ease the tension. "Apollo can say or do whatever he wants. There are more important things to focus on, anyway."

"That's the spirit, mate," Leo replies, tipping his head toward me.

Drew and Carson make their way over to our bunk. Soon enough, it's only the five of us left in the room. Once Ethan has his uniform on, we don't waste any more time. We slip out of the barracks and down the hall toward the elevator. Drew, Carson, and Leo walk a few steps ahead, while Ethan holds my pace at the back.

"*He's got an agenda, is all*," Ethan mutters, mocking Leo's accent.

"Relax, man," I nudge him. "He's just trying to keep the peace. He didn't mean anything by it."

"He plays for both sides," Ethan scoffs. "He's in Apollo's training group. It won't be long before he's one of his minions."

As we near the elevator, Leo scans his badge to summon the elevator. Instantly, I hear it making its descent toward us from within the wall.

Before we catch up to the rest of the group, Ethan tugs at my arm and pulls me aside.

"You heard Lieutenant Kelley yesterday," he whispers. "The top five ranked draftees will be granted special permissions. Just . . ." he pauses, glancing over at Drew, Carson, and Leo. The wall splits apart, revealing the pod on the other side, and they step inside.

"Just don't get too friendly with him, alright? Special permissions might give you an advantage to learn something about your father. And as far as I'm concerned, him and Apollo — they're your competition. Leo might be on your good side, but I don't trust him to not stand in your way."

Leo sticks his head out of the elevator. "You lads coming?" he hollers with a wave of his arm.

"Remember what I said too? We don't need to be making any enemies," I remind him. "I haven't lost sight of the mission, dude. But I appreciate you looking out for me."

Ethan tries to say more, but we're out of time. Together, we step into the elevator and squeeze in beside the others. Drew jabs a finger into the button marked *M*, and the elevator jolts. Pressure builds from the floor up, gluing our feet to the ground as we're propelled upward.

I can't deny Ethan's right. From this day forward, every moment counts. Every moment will either put me closer to the truth about my father or further from it. I'm not here to make friends, and I'm not looking to make any more enemies either, but I can't afford to lose. I can't afford to let anyone get in my way. If rising through the ranks is what it takes, I have to try. It's up to me to make it happen — no one else.

The elevator doors open into the atrium. Leo jogs ahead to meet up with his training group, while Ethan and I follow behind Drew and Carson. As we crest the staircase, I spot Lieutenant Kelley and Lieutenant Tillman eating with another group of soldiers. Lieutenant Kelley's eyes lift, mentally marking our attendance, then shift back to his meal.

We maneuver through the buffet line and take a seat at the same table as yesterday. It feels like only a few minutes go by before the training officers rally us up.

"They don't waste a second, do they?" Ethan complains, shoveling the last of his food into his mouth.

Lieutenant Kelley stops in front of our table and folds his arms. "Return your trays to the kitchen, then meet us outside at the front of the facility," he orders.

It takes me a moment to realize what he *didn't* say, but Drew catches on quicker.

"Not the training lawn?" he asks timidly.

"At the front of the facility," Lieutenant Kelley repeats, then moves on to the next table.

We all stare wide-eyed at each other, gripping our trays. But nobody makes the first move.

"Well, boys," Drew exhales, "here goes nothing."

We stand in unison and walk our trays to the conveyor belt behind the buffet. A few other draftees from Lieutenant Tillman's group aren't far behind us. We descend the stairs down to the main level and make a sharp turn toward the front doors.

Pushing through the doors, the morning wraps us in its icy embrace. The sun is still dragging itself over the horizon, coloring the sky with vibrant streaks of pink and gold that feel misplaced against the dreary city. Lieutenant Kelley and Lieutenant Tillman stand no more than twenty feet from the facility, their black uniforms a stark contrast against the glow of the sunrise behind them.

My hands tingle from the cold. The wind feels like it blows straight through my uniform. I slip my fingers into my pockets and clench my jaw, trying to hold still. Afraid if I loosen up, my teeth will chatter uncontrollably.

All the draftees shuffle into place and form a line in front of the training officers. Once we're all accounted for, Lieutenant Kelley steps forward. I take in a sharp breath, bracing myself for what he's about to say. But nothing can prepare me for it.

"Good morning, soldiers," he greets us. "Your first assignment today will be to run the city."

A couple murmurs spread down the line. Every ache in my body sinks to my feet, and suddenly, I'm painfully aware of how sore they are. The thought of doing anything more today feels unbearable, and judging by the quiet groans around me, I'm not the only one who feels that way. For a moment, forgetting what my father started and leaving it to fate is tempting compared to pushing through the pain.

He continues. "There's a two-mile stretch between here and the Holland Tunnel that's been marked for you. The Holland Tunnel is northwest of the tower and is the furthest you're allowed to go in the city during your term."

My eyes lift from Lieutenant Kelley to the tower looming in the distance. I peer past it, trying to envision the path we'll take, but it's hidden by the other buildings.

"The path will take you right along the Hudson. Once you get to the tunnel, the path will veer right, taking you along the border between our side of the city and the civilian side. From there, you'll continue down the path until you reach the barricade."

Barricade? I don't recognize what he's talking about. Most of the other draftees don't either. Even through their exhaustion, their furrowed brows are aimed at Lieutenant Kelley.

"Then, there's a straightaway that'll take you back to The Battery. All in all, it's about a five-mile route," he concludes.

My whole body sags. I don't think I've ever ran more than a block in my life. Or if I did, it was playful, thoughtless, not intentional in the slightest. Ethan lets out a sigh next to me. No matter how little we want to do this, there's no way out of it. *You either keep pushing, or you die.* Those were Lieutenant Kelley's words.

This is what's expected of us, so it's what we'll do — even though death feels like the better option.

Lieutenant Kelley's voice comes back with more force behind it. "Under no circumstances are you to venture off the path. The rest of the city is unsuitable for anyone to be in. And you are *not*, for any reason at all, permitted to go near the tower. Do you understand?"

"Yes, sir!" we chant back.

He leans back slowly, eyeing us to make sure his words cement. My heart quickens, and I glance nervously back at the tower. Its antenna pierces the sky, which is now deepening into a natural blue. The tower holds all things together — the Barrier, which protects the city and, in turn, protects us. Is it possible that any minor disturbance could jeopardize that balance? Maybe that's why it's so crucial we don't go near it.

They're worried if any one of us does, we could shut the whole thing down.

To my surprise, Lieutenant Tillman steps forward now. "Unlike yesterday, where you were purely being observed, your performance during this run will be ranked. Everything you do from here on out will determine your rank at the end of the quarter." His voice comes out smoother and higher-pitched than Lieutenant Kelley's, eliminating some of the intimidation factor.

My eyes shift down the line to Apollo. He's locked in, his body leaned forward, drooling over the challenge. Meanwhile my heart threatens to burst from my chest. The longer they keep us here, the more my anxiety festers.

"Lieutenant Kelley and I will be keeping track of your time during the run," he continues. "How quickly you complete the course will determine your initial ranks."

A moment of silence passes, then Lieutenant Tillman steps back. Lieutenant Kelley's mouth curls into a devilish grin as he adds, "In other words, run fast. And don't make us have to drag you back here ourselves."

This is it, I think. This run will set the tone for training. I only have to be quicker than seven other draftees to make it into the top five. Surely I can do that, right?

Lieutenant Kelley reaches into his pocket and pulls out a small silver whistle, along with a stopwatch dangling from a thin wire. He places the whistle between his lips and blows. The shrill sound tears through the air. Every draftee stirs, some even bend their knees, ready to take off.

"Good luck," he winks.

As the training officers step out of the way, a narrow paved path comes into view. It branches away from the facility and winds through a small cluster of dead trees between us and the city. Apollo is the first to take action. Ethan and Leo are next, followed by the others.

I freeze. The sound of my heart racing morphs with the sound of their boots trotting against the pavement. My eyes dart to the training officers, who stare back at me, expecting me to move.

"Time's ticking, Madoc," Lieutenant Kelley snarls.

I don't think. I don't try to come to terms with the distance. I just run.

My feet carry me down the path behind the other draftees. Before long, the trees close in on both sides. Their bare, thorny branches claw at the sky and blot out most of the sunlight, casting a twisted shadow over the path.

I manage to catch up to Ethan. Leo is already a few strides ahead, but Drew and Carson are close by. The four of us fall into step with each other almost instinctively. The path starts to descend, quickening our pace, and the trees fall away — revealing the gateway to the city.

Along the outer rim of the facility, where the trees meet the city's edge, is a huge curved cement wall. It seems to loop behind us and form a protective wall around the plot of land the facility sits on. Barbed wire curls into sharp coils along the top of the wall, making it look menacing. The path runs straight through a passageway carved into the wall. On either side are two soldiers standing guard. Their faces are masked by helmets, both carrying rifles slung across their bodies.

I slow for a moment as we run past them, glancing to see if they notice us. Or if underneath all that gear, they're even real men. They stand as still as statues, facing toward the facility. They don't even flinch as we pass by.

We cross through to the other side of the wall. Turning my head, I notice two more guards positioned on the opposite side. They stare out at the bleak city, keeping watch over who comes in and out. I pity them, imagining how dull it must be to stand there, waiting for something to happen. Praying nothing would.

The path widens, but the ground becomes more rugged. Even through my boots, I can feel each imperfection in the pavement. Looking down, I notice the path is coated with grass and thick weeds. Small debris litters the path, which adds to the texture.

As I run, my foot lands in a shallow hole, and my ankle rolls slightly. I suck in a sharp breath, trying to hide the pain. But Ethan notices. His eyes flick back to me, brows furrowed with concern.

"You okay?" he asks through staggered breaths.

"Fine," I let out. "Good enough to keep going." I keep my eyes glued to my feet, afraid if I look up, I'll injure myself further. All the while the ground changes with each step, becoming more layered the deeper we go into the city.

On either side of us, the path is bordered by a small retaining wall. It creates a foundation for a chain link fence that stretches nearly double our height. It runs right up against the skyscrapers towering on the other side. The fence continues on for miles ahead, clearly defining the path, just as Lieutenant Kelley said.

Up ahead, the Freedom Tower grows against the pale morning sky. I have to strain my neck just to look up at it. From this angle, the antenna isn't visible. It's far too high and tucked behind the top of the building. As we run past it, I stare up at it in awe, hypnotized by it. It isn't until my ankle rolls again that I'm able to focus back on the run.

We can't be more than a mile in before my side starts to cramp. I dig my fingers into the spot, trying to rub out the knot. But it hardly works. My lungs rise and fall heavily, burning against my ribcage. The bitter cold bites at my face, but it doesn't feel as cool anymore. The burn in my muscles is enough to make it feel warm.

To my left, the ink-black waters of the Hudson come into view. If it weren't for the fence and a few scattered buildings, we could veer off and dive right in. By now, Carson has fallen out of sync with us. He trots a few strides behind me, and Ethan and Drew hold a steady pace just a few feet ahead.

"Everyone holding up okay?" Drew hollers back.

I hear Carson let out a huff, but he doesn't reply. Ethan glances back, checking to make sure we're both still within view.

"We're alright," I say. "No other choice but to keep going, right?"

They accept this and turn back. We all keep our focus ahead as we push through the rest of the first stretch.

Half an hour must go by before we reach what Lieutenant Kelley referred to as the Holland Tunnel. The path ahead abruptly comes to an end, and beyond the fence to our left is the gaping mouth of a tunnel. It swallows the road and disappears past the edge of the city, burrowing beneath the banks of the Hudson.

We follow the path to the right and put the tunnel at our backs. Ethan lets out a victorious holler in honor of making it to our first landmark, but it sounds more like a cry for relief. My legs sear with pain, and my feet ache. Even though my body begs me to stop, I keep pushing forward. No ounce of physical energy left. It's all mental now.

The next mile is completely absorbed by the horrific remains of the city. My eyes shift from left to right, taking it all in. Vines creep up from cracks in the pavement and wrap around dilapidated buildings, pulling them further down toward the earth. Buildings bend at unnerving angles and groan in the wind, prompting me to run a bit quicker, afraid that one forceful gust might send them toppling over. These are the depths of the city we were never allowed to venture into. The parts that were too unstable for us. And now that we're in the midst of them, I can see why.

We reach the end of the next straightaway. The path veers abruptly to the right, but something to the left catches my eye, stopping me in my tracks. My boots skid against the ground as I come to a screeching halt.

Just beyond the fence, wedged between two buildings and stacked just as high, is a massive impassable pile of junk. Street lamps jut out from the center, broken and bent at odd angles. At the base, a flattened subway car acts as a support beam, anchoring the weight of everything above it. At the top of the heap sits a hulking metal box. Each of its four sides looks like a screen, but they're all busted in. Thick wires spill from the bottom like veins torn from a body. Further down, a few more oversized screens are crushed beneath the debris, each one as big as a billboard.

The sides of both neighboring buildings are blown out. Their inner contents spill onto the heap, adding to the mix. Desks, office chairs, appliances, and rusted scaffolding all culminate into one gargantuan, horrifying sculpture, barricading us from the civilian side of the city — *our* side. Our community.

My jaw drops. I stand completely frozen in the center of the path. A few draftees run past and glance up at the towering pile, but they don't stop. Even Carson catches up to me. He does a double take, pausing for a moment in disbelief. Then just as quickly as he stops, he continues on with the rest of the group.

This must be the barricade Lieutenant Kelley mentioned — the next landmark on our run. Grass has already begun to grow over it, giving it the look of an ancient ruin. Something lost in time but preserved by nature. It's clear it was put here intentionally, but the longer I stare at it, the more it feels like it belongs here. Like it's always *been* here. Everything has grown around it and adapted to it being there. And now, it's just as much a part of the city as the skyscrapers are. The thought of that makes my stomach twist.

"John!" I hear Ethan call out, his voice distant. I spin around to see him and Drew glancing back at me from at least a hundred feet ahead. "C'mon, man!"

I snap out of my trance, and my legs spring into action. I take off down the straightaway away from the barricade. The further I run from it, the more it shrinks into the background, molding into the skyline.

Still, I can't shake the image from my mind. All the items displaced and intricately placed there. Stacked and wedged together to form a blockade between this side of the city and the one we inhabited. I imagine my father was one of the men who helped build it. With each object he hammered into the barricade, he drove the nail further into the coffin between *his* city and *our* city.

Between that, the fences on either side of us, and the outer wall surrounding the facility, one thing's clear: We're not really free. We're contained. We rely on the Barrier to keep us safe, but we don't actually trust it. So instead, we've built up barriers of our own because we don't believe one stronghold is enough. And that's our newfound freedom, as General Conrad put it — having enough safety nets that if one fails, another will be there to catch us. Keeping us from ever knowing what it feels like to hit the ground.

Just when it feels like I have nothing left to give, The Battery comes into view. I can make out the curve of the outer wall and the soldiers standing guard, still positioned on either side. The majority of the draftees are already passing through the gate. As soon as they're through, they disappear into the dead forest between the city and the facility.

Something in me comes alive. My feet quicken their pace, and my whole body begins to fight, pushing toward the finish line. Ethan and Drew cross through first, and I follow after them a few seconds later.

The trees close in around us, and the path narrows as it slopes upward toward The Battery. The slight incline sets my calves on fire, but I keep pushing. By now, I can see Lieutenant Kelley and Lieutenant Tillman waiting for us. The other draftees have already finished, most of them sprawled out on the ground, stretching their legs.

I close my eyes, breathe deep, then exhale. My arms swing rapidly at my sides and propel me forward. I break into a dead sprint, surpassing Ethan and Drew. As soon as I break through the trees, my body collapses onto the pavement at the training officers' feet.

Pain surges through my whole body. All the ache I felt during the run comes to a head. My ankle throbs, and my lungs gasp for a steady stream of air. Sweat and drool drip from my chin onto the pavement. I press my palms against the ground to lift myself up, leaving behind dark, wet handprints.

I hobble over to Ethan, who's in a similar state. Carson lies flat on his back, hands clasped over his forehead. Drew slumps against the side of the facility. Ethan offers me a hand and helps me down to his level. I drop next to him with a heavy sigh.

Lieutenant Kelley strides over to us. I pull my knees up to my chest and bury my head. The last thing I need is some snarky comment from him before I can even catch my breath.

"Congratulations, soldiers," he says flatly. "You did it."

Silently, I pray they'll dismiss us back to our barracks. *Surely they won't make us do anything else*, I think. But mercy isn't in Lieutenant Kelley's vocabulary.

A devious grin spreads across his face. I wish so badly I could smack it off with what little strength I have left. That run was only the beginning of what's in store. Because in war, there's no relief. There's no time to compose yourself. There's only fight or die.

"Now, you know the drill," he shouts. I shove my head further between my knees, trying to hide from what comes next. "Everyone drop and give me twenty!"

Eight

We're spared from another dreadful wake-up call the next morning. We take our time getting up and shower off the ache from yesterday's training session. Pressing my feet to the floor, my legs wobble beneath me. It feels as if they've aged twenty years since the last time I stood on them. I practically limp my way to the bathroom, wincing with each step.

I throw all my weight against the sink and grip the sides. Looking into the mirror, my eyes are sunken with exhaustion. My features are worn, and sleep wrinkles streak across my face. I cup cold water in my hands and splash it against my face, trying to wake myself up. But it barely does the trick. I blink the water out of my eyes, and when my reflection comes into focus again, the same tired eyes stare back at me. Wishing to shut again. Longing for this day to be over before it's even started.

Once we're ready, we head to breakfast. Drew and Carson follow me out, fully dressed and ready to go, while Ethan tumbles out of bed. With his eyes still snapped shut, he throws up a hand and mutters, "Don't worry, I'll catch up with you guys."

Muscle memory carries us down the hallway to the elevator. Already, the whole process feels routine. The elevator delivers us to the atrium. The doors slide open to reveal a gloomy haze outside that's turned the whole facility gray. Through the glass doors, the sky seems to be holding back a storm. Dark clouds swirl above the Barrier, and thunder rumbles in the distance.

We round the staircase to the upper level and make our way to the buffet. We shuffle down the line and find our seats at the same table we've occupied for the past couple days now. I leave the space open next to me for Ethan, while Drew and Carson sit across from me.

"Ready for another run today?" Carson asks through a mouthful of food.

Drew releases a deep groan as he swallows his bite. "I sure hope not."

"Oh, c'mon," I chime in. "You and Ethan were holding a pretty good pace the whole time. You didn't seem to mind it."

"Glad to know that's how it looked from the outside, because that's not how it felt," he scoffs.

"I just knew if I didn't keep running, Lieutenant Kelley would drag me by my ears back to the facility. That was motivation enough to keep running," Carson admits.

Drew pats him on the back. "Don't worry, buddy. You'll get there."

Without warning, Ethan slides into the spot next to me until he's pressed up against me. He gives me a nudge, almost knocking the spoon from my hand. His shoulders sag, and his head droops down at his tray.

"Good morning," he drones miserably.

"Good morning, sunshine," Drew chuckles.

Ethan flashes a full-teeth smile at him, then shoves the first spoonful of oatmeal into his mouth with a scowl.

"I don't know," Drew continues, circling back to the prior topic. "Part of me wants to try. For most of us, that's the first time we've ever ran a distance like that. I think I could get better over time."

Carson lets out a laugh. "For some of us, that's the first time we've *ever* ran."

I laugh too, remembering how breathless Carson looked by the time we made it back to the facility. Picturing him always several strides behind us, huffing and puffing down the path.

"I'll be happy if I make it out the other side of this alive," I let out. "And that's really all I care about right now."

"You might surprise yourself," Drew says, catching me off guard. "You never know what you're capable of."

"I know what I'm capable of," Ethan interrupts. "And it's not this. I'm in the same camp as John. I'll be lucky to make it out alive."

Drew shrugs and presses his lips into a firm line. It's clear he has more to say, but he's holding back. Trying to discern whether it's right, or how it'll go over with us.

He takes another bite of his breakfast and exhales, then lifts his eyes with a sternness that wasn't there before. "All I'm saying is, like it or not, we have to perform well, to a certain degree. They're counting on us." He throws a look over his shoulder, indicating the figurative people outside the facility. The ones back home.

"Now you're starting to sound like the general," Ethan garbles with his mouth full, making his voice sound warped.

To my relief, Drew gets a kick out of this. He and Ethan laugh with each other light-heartedly. I exhale, allowing my shoulders to relax. I didn't expect that to go over so well with Drew, but I'm glad it did. The stiffness in his eyes fades as he starts to loosen up.

Ethan abruptly cuts off their laughter and jerks his chin toward something behind Drew. I glance past him and spot Lieutenant Kelley and Lieutenant Tillman ascending the stairs. When they reach the landing, they stop and survey the tables of draftees and soldiers alike.

"Draftees," Lieutenant Kelley bellows, his voice echoing around the room.

Every draftee's head lifts toward him in sync. The other soldiers carry on, unfazed.

"We'll meet in the shooting range today for skills training." He lowers his chin and hardens his stare before delivering his next words. "You have five minutes. Don't be late."

He holds his stare for a second longer, then turns away. The training officers disappear back down the stairs, off to prepare our daily dose of torture.

Drew turns back to face us. "Shall we?"

Ethan quickly slurps down the last of his breakfast. "Like you said, they're counting on us," he says with mock enthusiasm.

We return our trays and manage to catch up with the rest of the group at the elevator. Together, we head down to the lower level. Once we arrive, Lieutenant Kelley and Lieutenant Tillman are waiting for us at the end of the hall. When they see us, Lieutenant Tillman scans his badge and opens the door to the shooting range. He steps inside while Lieutenant Kelley ushers us in from the hall.

We line up along the back wall, pressing our backs to the weapons lockers. The overhead lights buzz, filling the otherwise silent space with white noise. Once we're all inside, Lieutenant Kelley closes the door and joins Lieutenant Tillman at the front of the room.

"Today, we'll begin phase one of skills training," he announces. "The objective is to familiarize you with the proper handling of a firearm so, should you need to use one, you don't crack under pressure — or accidentally shoot one of your peers."

This gets a crack out of a few draftees. Looking down the line, I realize none of us have probably ever held a gun before. The thought of holding one myself feels wrong. But judging by the looks on some of the draftees' faces, it's exhilarating to them.

Lieutenant Kelley removes a tablet from a clip on his belt and powers it on. The screen casts a bright blue glow across his face, highlighting his skeletal features. He clicks something unseen, and suddenly, the image jumps off the screen and projects beside him in midair. A couple draftees gasp, some let out a *whoa* in awe. The hologram displays a list of our names, arranged in a specific order. Judging by the layout, I take it this is the training scoreboard so far.

"This is where your ranks currently stand," Lieutenant Kelley confirms. I scan the list for the first five, eager to see if I've made the cut. But it's not until the seventh spot that I find my name. Ethan's name falls just below mine, followed by Drew. A few others come next, and Carson takes the very bottom.

"Figures," Carson mutters under his breath, but he doesn't seem too disappointed.

Leo, on the other hand, sits at number five. My eyes drift from his name to the top, where the obvious candidate sits at number one.

"As you can see, Andres currently holds the highest rank," Lieutenant Kelley reports. "Your rank is based on your ability to perform at a level that either meets or exceeds our expectations. Every time you fall short, you'll be docked. And every time you improve, you'll move up."

He powers off the device, pulling the image back into the screen. It fizzles out of thin air and disappears entirely. Lieutenant Kelley clips the tablet back to his belt and crosses his arms over his chest.

"Today, some of you will have the ability to change your rank," he says confidently. Apollo snickers down the line and throws me a sly glance. I read the words *good luck* on his lips and roll my eyes.

A few draftees stir. There's clearly a competitive spirit in the air now. I take it that was Lieutenant Kelley's intention in showing us our ranks so early on — to motivate us to do better.

To show us who has a chance and who's already falling behind.

Lieutenant Kelley continues. "We'll take turns, starting with a group of three from Lieutenant Tillman's group, followed by a group of three from mine. Then we'll finish with the remaining three from each group. Understood?"

"Yes, sir!" we chant back.

"Good," he states. "First, Lieutenant Tillman will demonstrate how to properly handle the gear. Then it's up to you to prove you know how to use it. But remember, the goal is not just to shoot — it's excellence. Shoot as if your life depends on it, because someday, it might."

I swallow a harsh lump in my throat. No matter how hard I try, I still can't envision myself holding a gun. I feel a slight twinge of sadness that I even have to.

"Nathan, you do the honors," Lieutenant Kelley signals to Lieutenant Tillman.

Lieutenant Tillman breaks away and strides over to the leftmost stall. As he approaches it, the overhead lights flicker on until they reach the humanoid dummy hanging at the opposite end.

Placed atop each divider is a handgun, a handful of ammo, clear plastic safety glasses, and a set of orange ear plugs. My eyes move to the right and find the same gear positioned at the other two stations. Lieutenant Tillman balls the ear plugs and ammo into his fist. With his other hand, he gathers the handgun and safety glasses. Then he returns to Lieutenant Kelley's side.

"All eyes up here," Lieutenant Kelley snaps. We shift our eyes from elsewhere around the room and focus on him. Step by step, he begins his demonstration of how to shoot a gun, one he's probably recited a dozen times.

"First things first, place the glasses over your eyes, and plug your ears."

At his words, Lieutenant Tillman slides the glasses onto his face. He removes the ear plugs from his fist and pushes them into his ears. They seem to mold around the shape of his inner ear once they're in.

A little louder, Lieutenant Kelley continues. "Next, make sure your clip is loaded. It's up to you — and only you — to make sure you're well stocked on ammo. Lucky for you, we've provided the ammo for you, but in war, you're responsible for your own ammo. If you run out . . ." Lieutenant Tillman unhooks the magazine and drops three copper bullets into the clip. With a click, he deposits it back into the body of the gun. ". . . well, you might as well be dead," he smirks.

Lieutenant Tillman places both hands around the grip and moves back toward the stall. He positions himself so that his elbows hover inches above the divider, the gun aimed straight ahead.

"Always keep your gun pointed downrange, in case you trigger something by accident," Lieutenant Kelley explains. "Don't be the idiot who shoots himself in the foot."

A couple draftees snicker, but Lieutenant Kelley silences them with a look. He's not kidding.

"Now, maintain your position and be aware of anything and everything downrange. You should be aiming at your target, and nothing should be standing in the way of it. Nothing you don't want to send six millimeters of lead through, that is."

All our eyes fixate on Lieutenant Tillman. Like clockwork, as Lieutenant Kelley speaks, Lieutenant Tillman demonstrates. I watch his knees bend, his balance stabilize, and his arms lift and lock in place slightly below his chin. The room goes silent, and it's as if time stands still while we wait for what comes next — because we all know what's next.

Lieutenant Kelley continues. "Make sure you have a good handle on the weapon before putting your finger anywhere near the trigger."

Lieutenant Tillman's fingers recoil, then coil back around the grip. His biceps bulge through his shirt, and his eyes squint, honing in on the dummy at the end of the lane.

"Once you're locked in on your target, hover your index finger over the trigger."

Lieutenant Tillman's finger lifts and stops no more than a centimeter shy of the trigger. My palms drip with sweat. In the stillness between Lieutenant Kelley's words, all I can hear is the slight hum of the lights and my heart beating rapidly in my chest.

"On my command," Lieutenant Kelley orders, followed by a nod from Lieutenant Tillman. I shrug my shoulders up to my ears and squeeze my abdomen, bracing for the sound. I see the corners of Lieutenant Kelley's mouth curl into an intoxicated grin. Even though he's done this countless times, this part must never get old.

"Ready," he shouts. "Aim, fire!"

Before I can comprehend it, three thunderous claps sound off one by one. Each time, my body flinches in perfect rhythm. I cower back against the lockers. My ears ring so loudly, it drowns out all the other noise. Even my own heartbeat sounds muffled.

I lift my eyes timidly and glance downrange. The barrel of Lieutenant Tillman's gun smokes. He steps back from the divider and sets the gun down on top of it. At the end of the lane, three fresh holes are now singed into the dummy's forehead. Looking at them, my blood runs cold.

Lieutenant Kelley turns and opens his arms wide, inviting the first draftee to step forward.

"Who's next?" he winks.

Lieutenant Tillman calls up the first three draftees from his group at random.

"Andres, D'Angelo, and Patton, you're up," he orders.

All three step forward. Lieutenant Tillman positions Apollo at the far-right stall, Dom at the opposite end, and Leo in the middle. One at a time, they put on the safety glasses and squeeze the ear plugs into their ears. Before Leo and Dom can even load their guns, Apollo has run through the entire procedure like he's done it a hundred times before. Maybe he has — but there's no way. Guns were never allowed in our community. The only people trusted to carry weapons are military personnel. In theory, he's never laid a finger on a gun until today.

Unless his father managed to pull some strings.

Leo's arms shake nervously under the weight of the handgun. He glances over his shoulder at me while Lieutenant Tillman assists Dom. I stare back at him in disbelief, trying to wrap my mind around what's happening.

From down the line, Ethan intercepts my stare and silently mouths *minions*. I roll my eyes dismissively. But looking at Apollo, Dom, and Leo — three of the five draftees holding the top five spots — I get what Ethan means. Leo might mean well, but he's just as much an obstacle as Apollo.

Once all three draftees are set, Lieutenant Tillman steps back to give them space.

"Draftees, ready!" he shouts.

Apollo's heel digs into the floor. Leo awkwardly tries to get a proper handle on the gun, but he can't quite figure it out. Dom lunges back and forth on both feet, eager to fire.

"Aim!"

I press my palms against my ears, but it's no use. It only barely muffles the noise.

"Fire!"

Clap! Clap! Clap! Apollo sends all three of his bullets flying out of the gun at once. One strikes the dummy in the shoulder, the other close to where its collarbone would be, and the third in the upper chest. He lowers the gun in a slow gesture, and I can tell he's pleased with himself.

The results are underwhelming for both Leo and Dom. Leo's first shot misses the dummy by several feet. Another hits the dummy in its hip, and the third where its appendix would be. Dom fires two rounds back to back, both striking the dummy in the throat, but the third soars over the dummy's shoulder and ricochets off the wall behind it.

Lieutenant Tillman removes a tablet from his belt and records the results. All three draftees place their guns back on the divider, slide off their glasses, and pocket their ear plugs to throw away later.

Lieutenant Kelley steps forward now, trading places with Lieutenant Tillman.

"Madoc, Greene, Fitzgerald," he beckons. "You're up next."

I nearly jump out of my skin when he says my name.

Ethan places a hand on my shoulder as he steps out of line. "We've got this," he mutters to me. Drew smiles optimistically beside him. My whole body shudders in response.

I approach the center stall and stare down at the handgun lying in wait. As I get closer, my chest tightens. My hand hovers over it as if it's venomous, and one touch might lead to a fatal strike.

Carson claps his hands in support behind us, which startles me. "Let's go, boys!" he cheers. Lieutenant Kelley rolls his eyes.

Ethan and Drew have already put on their gear and loaded their clips with ammo before I've even made contact with the gun. Lieutenant Kelley notices and stomps toward me.

"What's the hold up, Madoc?" I hear Apollo shout before Lieutenant Kelley can reach me. "Afraid it's going to bite you?"

A couple draftees snicker and tease, but Carson's quick to defend me.

"Cut him some slack, man," I hear him say. He's met with a string of quips from Apollo and Dom, but I tune it all out as Lieutenant Kelley's voice whispers close to my ear.

"Boom!" he exhales, causing me to jump. His breath hits the back of my neck and draws goosebumps to the surface of my skin. "Any hesitation could cost you your life in battle, Madoc. Just like that."

My heart pounds. I stare wide-eyed down at the gun, willing myself to pick it up. To at least touch it. But my arms don't move. They remain glued to my sides like magnets incapable of being pulled apart.

Lieutenant Kelley leans in closer. "Now's not the time to be a coward," he mocks me.

He slams his shoulder into my back. I stumble forward, teetering off balance. I reach out my hands to catch myself, and my fingers make contact with the cool metal frame of the gun. A shiver shoots down my spine, but there's no going back now. *Grab it*, I think. *Just grab it.*

I let out a deep breath and wrap my fingers around the grip. Just as Lieutenant Tillman demonstrated, I slide the magazine out from the body of the gun and deposit three copper bullets inside. Once it's locked into place, I use my free hand to put on the safety glasses. I force the ear plugs into my ears, and the more I push them, the more they resist. Any further and they might get stuck. I feel them expand and mold around the shape of my ear. As they do, the noise around me muffles, and the banter from the other draftees turns into a low hum in the background.

With shaky hands, I lift the gun out in front of me. My vision blurs through the glasses, and it takes several blinks before it focuses. The humanoid dummy stares at me from the other end, faceless and lifeless. Fresh punctures in its midsection from Leo's bullets, and a clean canvas everywhere else for me to deface.

It's one thing when it's a dummy, but it's another thing entirely when there's a real threat on the other end of the gun. I close my eyes and imagine myself standing in the city, somewhere between here and my community. Gunfire cracks through the air. Civilians scatter in every direction. Chaos ensues. In front of me is no longer a dummy, but a man dressed in full-body armor. Slung over his shoulder is a weapon much larger than mine. Something about his figure is alien, but his features are masked behind his helmet. He hasn't noticed me yet, but he's about to.

"Ready!" I hear Lieutenant Kelley say, but his voice is nothing but a distant echo in my mind.

The man turns, and as soon as he notices me, he raises his weapon.

"Aim!"

Lieutenant Kelley's cue seems to breathe life into him. He takes off in a sprint, running toward me with his weapon aimed at my chest.

I take my left hand and wrap it around my wrist for stability. I lift the handgun out in front of me, which only causes the man I'm envisioning to run quicker. He holds his weapon with one hand, and his free arm swings violently at his side. I feel myself start to panic, but I can't move. My feet feel glued to the ground, and my neck is stiff. The only thing I have control over is my index finger trembling inches away from the trigger.

When he's no more than a few feet away from me, the man's feet propel him off the ground in slow motion. He lifts off the pavement, towering over me. Involuntarily, I feel my arm start to lift in sync with his body, raising my gun with it.

"Fire!"

My mouth rips open with a cry. It forces its way up from my throat, over to my shoulder, and burns through my right arm and out the barrel of the gun. My whole body convulses, but I stay firm, frozen in place.

Clap! Clap! Clap! My finger drills against the trigger three times. Each bullet breaks through the man's gear, shattering his helmet into millions of pieces. He dissolves in front of my eyes, taking the city and everything else around me with him. And when I open my eyes, the man is gone, the city nonexistent, and I'm back in the shooting range. And every eye in the room is on me.

At the end of the lane, three new bullet holes are smoking from the dummy's body — every single one in the center of its head.

Nine

"Dude, I still can't believe you actually did that!" Ethan exclaims the next morning at breakfast.

I stare down at my meal through tired eyes. Ever since skills training, all Ethan's been talking about is my performance. Looking over at Carson and Drew, I say, "He's never going to live it down."

"I can't blame him," Drew remarks. "It was impressive, man."

But there's some reluctance to his words. I can tell he's envious, worried that his rank is in jeopardy since he didn't perform as well.

Ethan's eyes grow wide. "Impressive is an understatement. You should've seen the look on Apollo's face!"

Apollo, on the other hand, has been talking about anything *but* my performance. Even though I appreciate Ethan's fanfare, I don't feel like I've done anything to deserve it. My memory of standing in the range feels more like a fever dream than reality — and that's how it felt in the moment. Still, I can only hope it had some sort of positive impact on my rank.

"If that doesn't take you to the top of the ranks, I don't know what will," Carson grins. "Can't say the same for the rest of us."

"When one of us wins, we all win," Ethan declares triumphantly, slinging his arm around my shoulder.

"Keep in mind, though, that our individual ranks *do* matter," Drew reminds us. Ethan releases me and slides back over to his side of the bench. Guilt twists like a knot in my stomach.

I start to apologize, but I stop myself. What do I have to apologize for? I may have performed better at skills training, but it's not to say Drew won't do better than me at another activity. And besides, even though we've formed an alliance with Drew and Carson, they're just as capable of surpassing me. I should be grateful for this small victory — and what it could mean for me.

"You're right," Ethan admits. "But it's better to have John rising up in the ranks than some other people."

"I can't argue with that," Drew says to keep the peace.

Once we're finished eating, we return our trays and head downstairs to meet the training officers. The rest of the draftees aren't too far behind us. Outside, we line up in the courtyard and wait for instructions.

From down the line, I glance at Apollo. His hands are tucked behind his back. His chin is lowered, and his eyes are glued to his boots. He never lifts his head, not even when Lieutenant Kelley begins his introduction.

"Good morning, soldiers," Lieutenant Kelley greets us. "We'll begin today by running the city, the same course we introduced you to earlier this week."

This stirs up a groan out of a few draftees. Apollo raises his chin and tilts his head back. Out of the corner of his eye, he notices me staring. His cold, dark eyes cut through me. He purses his lips and shakes his head subtly, warning me not to mess with him.

Lieutenant Kelley continues. "I want all of you back in fifty minutes — nothing less. Otherwise you can kiss your ranks goodbye."

Lieutenant Tillman steps forward and removes a stopwatch from his pocket. He makes a presentation out of clicking a button on the side, then flashes the watch face at us to show that time is ticking.

Ethan places a heavy hand on my shoulder. "Time to run like the wind, Johnny," he says before picking up his feet.

My whole body sags with dread.

We take off down the path leading away from The Battery. As soon as we pass through the outer wall, the path widens, and we all disperse.

As we run, the Freedom Tower molds seamlessly into the baby blue sky. Sunlight glints off its exterior, giving it a wonderful glow it didn't have before.

Still, it provides no hint of the Barrier, but I picture it anyway. I imagine it cascading from the tip of the antenna, fitting all of Lower Manhattan perfectly inside. And within it, we traverse the wreckage of the ruined city while the tower shines down on us.

We follow along the harbor until we reach the tunnel. Almost instinctively, I throw a cautious glance into its nightmarish mouth. Even with the fence and a few feet of distance between us, the sound of our boots echoes off the hollow opening.

My feet seem to move seconds ahead of the rest of my body. It takes no effort at all to keep placing them one in front of the other. Before long, it feels mindless. The tightness in my side disappears. My lungs expand and oxygenate, and I feel weightless. Free-floating through the city as my feet glide over the ground. I completely lose sight of Ethan and Drew, and Carson is barely a speck in the distance. He's just now rounding the corner near the tunnel by the time I look back.

It feels like I could run for miles, and for a moment, I crave it. I long for the path to never end, for the city to reveal new pathways for me to venture down. I feel insane for wanting it to last, but it's a high unlike anything I've ever felt before.

I let that feeling carry me all the way to the barricade, where I veer right and enter the final straightaway. Before I know it, I pass through the opening in the outer wall, and the path narrows. My feet hit the gradual ascent toward the facility and trample up the path. Lieutenant Kelley and Lieutenant Tillman come into view, and I notice only one other draftee has made it back — Apollo.

My feet come to a screeching halt. As soon as I break through the trees, Lieutenant Tillman clicks his stopwatch, marking my time. Apollo lets out a grunt. I look just in time to see him roll his eyes and turn his body away while he stretches.

I ride the high all the way down until my lungs gasp for air and my knees cry out. All the pain stifled by the feeling hits me at once. I hunch forward and place my hands against my knees, spitting thick gunk out of my throat to clear my airway.

"Nice work, Madoc," Lieutenant Kelley states.

I don't show it, but I'm thrown by how exhilarating the run felt. It doesn't intimidate me anymore. For the first time, I feel like I could improve — or that I *am* improving. Not just because I'm motivated to uncover the truth about my father, but because I know I'm capable.

Maybe it's not enough to just survive the draft. Maybe I want more, after all.

Leo is next to finish. He emerges from the trees with a huff. Looking around, he notices no one else has made it back, no one but Apollo and me. His heavy breathing quickly turns to laughter.

"Unbelievable," he lets out.

Apollo lifts his head, but it's clear Leo's remark was directed toward me. This only makes Apollo more flustered.

"What'd you do, take a shortcut?" he asks.

I shake my head. "I can't explain it. It felt good after a while."

Leo and I take a seat away from Apollo. He places his hands behind his back and lets out a hysterical laugh. "You're a mad man, Madoc! Nothing about that is remotely enjoyable, mate."

I can't help but laugh too. It's insane, really. Even hearing the words come out of my mouth feels ludicrous. But it's true. Something shifted, and the last half of the run seemed to have no toll on my body whatsoever until it was over.

A few other draftees start to come in more consistently. Ethan and Drew appear within seconds of each other. Leo leaps up from his spot and shuffles over to his training group as Ethan and Drew migrate toward me.

Drew's face turns sour for a moment, and I can read his expression so clearly. But he swallows his pride and pats my shoulder as he sits.

"You've done it again, John," he says with a sigh.

Ethan lays flat on his chest, which gets a rise out of us. "Make it stop," he pleads. "My head is pounding."

"Great job, Drew," I acknowledge. He smiles softly, but that's all he gives me. And I don't push it any more.

Every draftee except Carson seems to make it back by the time Lieutenant Tillman's stopwatch reaches the fifty-minute mark. Right as he stops the time, Carson comes hobbling up the path. His eyes are barely open, and his feet shuffle lazily against the concrete.

"We're not getting any younger here, O'Hair!" Lieutenant Kelley shouts. A couple draftees snicker. Carson finishes the ascent and collapses to his knees. His cheeks are cherry red, and he inhales as if he could suck all the oxygen right out of the atmosphere.

He crawls over to where we sit, but Lieutenant Kelley intercepts his path.

"On your feet, soldier," he orders.

Carson reluctantly rises to his feet. His limbs hang limp at his sides, as if there's no life left in them.

Lieutenant Kelley crosses his arms and widens his stance. "Start doing jumping jacks, right where you are. And don't stop until I tell you to."

"But—" Carson interjects, but he doesn't get another word out.

"I *said* start doing jumping jacks, soldier, and that's an order!" Lieutenant Kelley shouts. "You had fifty minutes to complete the run. Fifty minutes and seventeen seconds isn't going to cut it. That extra seventeen seconds could cost you your life."

Carson sighs in defeat. He glances from Lieutenant Kelley to us, then back to Lieutenant Kelley, looking for an escape. But there's no way around him.

"Jump, soldier," Lieutenant Kelley snarls.

Carson lifts his arms weakly over his head and begins jumping, moving his arms and legs in sync. His whole face twists in pain with each repetition, but Lieutenant Kelley's not letting up on him any time soon.

Lieutenant Kelley puts his back to Carson and turns to the rest of us. "Strong start today, soldiers," he says, though I can't tell if he actually means it. Carson grunts in the background with each move he makes. "Today, we'll begin strategy training. Lieutenant Tillman will lead you to the combat ring while your friend here finishes out the rest of his punishment. Understood?"

"Yes, sir!" we shout back.

He motions for Lieutenant Tillman to take us inside, then turns back to Carson with no ounce of mercy in his eyes. We all rise to our feet and follow Lieutenant Tillman toward the facility.

As we go, Drew, Ethan, and I throw Carson a pitied look. He continues flailing his arms over his head, jumping, and repeating the movement, all the while gritting his teeth through the pain. My body aches just from watching him.

We pass through the atrium and step out onto the training lawn. Sunlight beats down on us, making the otherwise crisp winter air feel warm. We cross the lawn to a circular pit dug into the corner, filled with dark, powdery dirt. A thin strip of concrete borders the ring, acting as a step leading down into it.

Lieutenant Tillman stops just shy of the edge and turns toward us. We gather around him, awaiting his instructions.

Peering over his shoulder, I stare down into the ring with dread. Just hearing the words *combat ring*, I know exactly what they're expecting from us — they want us to fight. Adrenaline surges through my veins. Suddenly, I envy Carson, wishing I was doing jumping jacks instead of what we're about to do here.

"Draftees, as Lieutenant Kelley said, today marks the start of strategy training," Lieutenant Tillman announces. "Today, you'll learn the art of hand-to-hand combat."

Gulp.

"Let me make myself perfectly clear: This is not the time to give your least favorite draftee a shiner. It's intended for you to sharpen your reflexes, develop strategies, and learn to predict your opponent's moves. Lieutenant Kelley and I are not going to tell you what to do, but we'll instruct you as we see fit.

"We do have a few ground rules, though," he continues. "Number one: Bail at the first sign of blood. It's safe to say each of you can handle a bit of a beating — even if you disagree — and anything that happens to you in the ring is meant to build grit. But we don't need anyone carried off on a stretcher."

His eyes fall on Apollo and his posse, who are clearly the most aggressive bunch. Lieutenant Tillman knows it too.

"Number two: No outside resources. Lieutenant Kelley and I will redirect you if your performance is faulty, or if we see an opportunity for you to take. Other than that, the only thing that should be helping you in the ring is your own intuition. Do not, under *any* circumstances, bring anything into the ring with you aside from the clothes on your back. Understood?"

"Yes, sir!" we shout back.

"Again, this is a training exercise, not a bloodbath," he reiterates. "Number three, and for the love of God, don't make me say this again: Don't kill each other. Your peers are not your enemy. They will role-play as such in the ring, but they're not your enemy in real life. You may have daddy issues—" this time, his eyes fall on me, "but this isn't the time to hash any of that out. Strategize, observe closely, and fight back so you can fight better together outside the ring. But do not kill each other. Please, we need as many of you as we can get," he adds under his breath.

It seems extreme to have a rule against killing each other. At least from the outside looking in, it's easy to believe it'd never happen. But when you're staring down your opponent, taking blow after blow, who knows what you'll do. Or who you'll become.

That's what terrifies me the most.

"This is how we're going to do this," Lieutenant Tillman begins. "One member from my training group and one member from Lieutenant Kelley's will face off in the ring. The rest of you will observe from the lawn. If it's not your turn, I want you at least three feet back from the edge. Is that clear?"

"Yes, sir!" we reply.

"D'Angelo, you're up first," he orders.

Dom steps forward a little too eagerly. He jumps down into the pit, kicking up a cloud of dirt.

"Greene," Lieutenant Tillman says next, "you'll join him."

My stomach drops. I turn to Ethan, whose face has gone pale.

"I'm a dead man," he mutters. "I'm dead."

"You've got this," I assure him. "Remember rule number three: Nobody kills each other. You'll be fine."

"You ever heard of somebody breaking the rules? Happens all the time," he snaps.

"Not on my watch." I let out a soft chuckle and give him a friendly push forward.

Ethan's whole body shudders. He slowly steps down into the ring, standing opposite Dom. They lock eyes, waiting for Lieutenant Tillman to commence the fight.

"Remember, your objective is not to hurt each other," Lieutenant Tillman stresses again.

"Yeah, well, our objective isn't to hold hands and hug it out either," Ethan mutters.

"Observe your opponent, devise a strategy, and stick to it," Lieutenant Tillman instructs. "Greene, step forward."

Ethan balls his fists and raises them to his chin. He takes one step forward, and Dom springs into action.

Dom tucks his head against his chest and dives. He wraps his arms around Ethan's waist and lifts him off the ground. They both collapse hard against the dirt, with Dom crushing Ethan under his weight. I practically see the breath leave Ethan's mouth in the cool morning air.

Before Ethan can come to his senses, Dom grabs ahold of Ethan's wrists and pins them down, disarming him from being able to take a shot at him.

"Nice work, D'Angelo," Lieutenant Tillman calls out. Dom keeps his eyes fixed on Ethan. Veins bulge from his forearms as he exerts as much force as possible to keep Ethan pinned down.

"What do you do next, Greene?" Lieutenant Tillman barks at him. Ethan's eyes swim desperately between Dom, Lieutenant Tillman, and the crowd of draftees circled around him.

"I— I don't know," he mumbles.

"Uncertainty gets you killed," Lieutenant Tillman says. "You have to make a decision, even if it's not the right one."

Ethan glares back at Dom. I can tell he's racking his brain, trying to think through his options. Dom grins back victoriously.

In a split second, Ethan wraps his legs around Dom's midsection and rolls over, sending Dom onto his back and putting Ethan on top. It's enough force to momentarily loosen Dom's grip on Ethan's wrists. With his hands free, Ethan pushes himself off the ground and backs away. Dom takes little to no time to recover. He jumps back onto his feet and circles

Ethan like a lion circling its prey. Before long, he closes the gap and knocks Ethan's legs out from under him, causing him to fall to his knees.

Ethan ducks just in time to miss a punch from Dom that easily could've taken out a tooth. Ethan's eyes widen, and I can tell he's relieved. But he's not out of the woods yet. Dom pushes his foot against Ethan's chest, sending him onto his back. Ethan's body thuds against the dirt. Dom jumps behind him and crouches down. His left hand pins down Ethan's shoulder, and his right hand stops just inches from his throat.

"Are we done here, sir?" Dom asks, glancing up at Lieutenant Tillman. Lieutenant Tillman nods. "Good enough."

Dom releases Ethan's shoulder, leaving him breathless on the ground. He starts to chuckle, and his eyes grow more alert, as if he's just now gaining awareness of what happened. Dom politely offers him a helping hand, but Ethan pushes it away.

"Oh no, not falling for that," Ethan says, but Dom's offer was genuine. Ethan rolls over and scrambles to his feet. Dirt clings to his uniform. He brushes it off as he steps out of the ring and rejoins us.

At the same time Ethan takes his place beside me, Carson appears on the other side of me. His face is an even darker shade of red than before. Sweat trickles down his neck, wetting the collar of his shirt.

"What'd I miss?" he asks, breathless.

"You missed me getting my butt kicked, that's all," Ethan sighs.

"Better luck next time," Dom winks from down the line.

Lieutenant Kelley joins Lieutenant Tillman at the edge of the ring. They briefly exchange a few words about the first round, logging the results on their tablets. Then Lieutenant Tillman steps aside, allowing Lieutenant Kelley to take over.

"Madoc, you're next," Lieutenant Kelley demands.

Ethan gives me a slight push forward, reminiscent of the same thing I did to him.

"Break a leg," he whispers. "But not actually, please."

Hesitantly, I approach the ring with trembling hands. My mind screams at me to turn back, but I know I can't. There's no escaping this. With Lieutenant Kelley staring down my neck, I step into the ring, my boots sinking into the soft dirt that won't feel soft for long.

From over my shoulder, I hear Lieutenant Tillman name my opponent. "Andres, you'll join him."

I freeze. My whole body tenses. Apollo lifts his eyes from the ground and meets mine. Something in his demeanor shifts, and it's as if his entire life has been leading to this moment.

"Gladly," he growls menacingly.

Apollo strides confidently into the ring. His dark eyes stare back at me, sharp as daggers. Raised and ready to pierce me.

"This shouldn't take too long," he mutters, the corners of his mouth flicking into a grin. I bend my knees and pull my fists up to my chin, pulsing back and forth on my heels.

Apollo doesn't wait for Lieutenant Kelley's cue. He launches toward me like a bullet. I immediately dive out of the way and fall flat against the ground. A cloud of dirt covers my face, blinding me. I swat at it with my hand and scramble to my feet before Apollo can see I'm down.

"You wanna dance, Madoc?" he shouts as he circles me, eager to strike again.

He moves quicker than I can comprehend. His boots glide across the dirt so fast, it's as if they don't even make contact with the ground. My first instinct is to curl into a ball and make myself small, but I don't.

Instead, once Apollo is close enough, I deliver a knuckle punch straight to his jaw.

His head spins on its axis, throwing him off balance. It's clear he wasn't expecting me to fight back. He massages his cheek and spits a thick wad of gunk onto the ground.

"What's your deal, man?" I say as he composes himself. My fist swells with pain, but I don't show it. I don't want Apollo to think I'm weak — any more than he already thinks it. I want him to see I'm capable of fighting him, and that he might not stand a chance against me.

A sinister grin spreads across his face. We circle each other slowly with knees bent, arms out, waiting for the other to attack.

"My father was second in command to the general when your father was a lieutenant," he whispers in a low growl.

In the blink of an eye, he charges at me. I manage to dive out of the way, but this time, I don't have enough time to get back on my feet. His hand wraps around my ankle and yanks me backward. My chin drags against the dirt. I gag and cough as it collects in my mouth. As soon as he lets go, I roll onto my back in time to see his fist closing in on my face. I roll again, this time to the side, and feel the earth shake as his fist crashes down next to me.

"So what?" I whisper back harshly.

I manage to get back on my feet, and we resume the same position as before, circling each other. Waiting for the next move.

"Your father was unpredictable," Apollo says. "Not only did he threaten the draft, but he endangered the lives of many men — including my father."

He charges again. Before I can dart away, he thrusts his palms hard into my chest, sending me stumbling backward. I lose my footing but don't fall, but I'm not steady either. Apollo uses this to his advantage and shoves me again. This time, I fall onto the stone step along the edge of the ring. I cry out as my tailbone strikes against it. In the same moment, Apollo twists my shoulder, and I cry even louder as pain rips across my collarbone. Out of the corner of my eye, I see his opposing hand gear up to deliver a punch.

Before he can, I duck underneath his arm and jab my fist into his gut. I use my other hand to shove him aside. As quickly as I can, I crawl away and scurry back to the other side of the ring. It takes only a few seconds for him to notice, and then we're back in the same position.

His eyes burst with rage, and his expression shifts from anger to almost canine. He stares at me like a hungry animal, desperate to sink his teeth into me.

"My father made sure to warn me about you before the draft," he continues. "He said the best thing that happened to our community was Anthony Madoc's death. He said as long as he lived, no one was safe. He jeopardized everything. And he told me if anyone would try to finish what he started, it'd be his son."

His words baffle me. I stare back amazed that anyone could be so cold. That anyone could hold a grudge so tightly without knowing the full story. Because the truth is, my father isn't dead. Somewhere, beyond the Barrier, he could still be alive. I don't know what he was involved in. All I know is Mae — a woman who's dedicated her life to serving our community — *begged* me to finish what he started. If what Apollo's saying is true, that he jeopardized everything, why would she want that?

Did he really put people in jeopardy, or did he just challenge the system, and the military saw that as a threat?

I don't even see Apollo coming until his fist makes contact with my chin. The blow reverberates through my skull, rattling my brain. I clutch both sides of my head, trying to stop the shaking, but it's no use. My vision blurs, and I lose sight of Apollo. Then he's behind me. He kicks out my legs, causing my knees to buckle. I collapse onto the dirt and pull my elbows up to my head, trying to make everything stop. The fight. The questions about my father. All of it.

"You're a threat to me, Madoc," Apollo spits. "You're a threat to me, the other draftees, and to everyone who believes in the draft."

Apollo presses his boot into my spine, squashing me against the ground. I suck in a breath, but it's all dirt and saliva, and I choke. My eyes water.

Apollo grabs me by my shoulder, and I wince from the pain that's still fresh from an earlier hit. He flips me onto my back and towers over me, feet planted on either side, caging me in.

I look left, right, trying to find a blind spot. But anywhere my eyes go, Apollo's go too. His burly hands clasp around my throat, tight and vicious. He lifts me off the ground and holds me out in front of him like a doll. My eyes bulge as my airway closes. I think I hear Lieutenant Kelley's voice, but it's muffled. All I can hear is the croaking coming from my own throat.

Apollo's mouth curls into a grin as my vision tunnels. My lungs burn, shriveling as every ounce of oxygen is drained from my body. Tears leak from the corners of my eyes, and for the first time, I contemplate death. I imagine myself slipping into total blackness, all in the name of a father I hardly knew. Atoning for his sins at the hand of Apollo. I start to hate him. I hate my father for what he did. I hate him for abandoning Mother, Liam, and me. I shouldn't have to carry all this weight he left behind. I shouldn't have to pay for his crimes.

But now, I'm going to die for them.

Right as I feel myself dissociating, Apollo releases me, and I fall limp against the dirt. In a rush of sound, all the voices of the training officers and draftees around us flood back in at a normal volume.

But it's not their voices. Not really, at least. Staring up at Apollo, the sun blazes behind him, framing him in a halo of light. Only the blurred outline of his silhouette is visible. But still, I know it's him.

What's wrong, John? I hear him say, but his lips don't move — his words just an echo in my mind. *Daddy's not here to fight for you.*

Apollo! a woman's voice calls out. *Mother?* No, it's not her. Someone rushes up to Apollo and tries to pull him away. But who?

What's happening to me? I think. The draftees' voices morph into the frantic shouts of children. I press my palms into the ground and find its surface hard, like concrete, no longer soft like the dirt in the ring. I turn my head as another faceless figure rushes toward me, blonde hair tracing the outline of its face, glinting like gold in the sunlight.

This will only sting for a moment, it says, the voice feminine and sweet. Different from the woman before. Trustworthy. *Then you won't feel any pain.*

I gasp as something pricks the crease of my elbow. In a flash, the vision is sucked away, and I'm back in the ring. The ground is soft again, dirt clenched in my fists. Lieutenant Tillman drags Apollo out of the ring by his shirt. As everything refocuses, I notice his entire demeanor has changed. He looks mortified — genuinely mortified. He stares at his hands as if they belong to someone else. His eyes find mine in the most confusing way, guilt-ridden and innocent, while Lieutenant Tillman shoves him onto the lawn.

Lieutenant Kelley slides down into the ring. He lifts me gently under my arms and brushes the dirt off my uniform.

"You alright, Madoc?" he asks, his tone sincere.

I start to speak, but the words feel like a flame licking my throat. Instead, I nod my head and let that be enough.

Lieutenant Tillman tears into Apollo, screaming vulgarities at him. Apollo doesn't meet his eyes. He can't stop looking at his hands. The only time he does is when my feet reach the lawn, then his gaze switches to me.

"John, I'm so—"

All my rage spikes when he says my name. No matter how much it burns, I force the words out in one dry, hoarse croak. "You were completely out of line."

"I know, I just—"

Daddy's not here to fight for you.

Before he can finish his sentence, his voice contorts, becoming more childlike. But the words don't make sense.

I stumble backward and fall against Lieutenant Kelley. Everything blurs, like I'm slipping in and out of consciousness, losing my grip on where I am. Unable to separate what's real from what's memory.

But this memory... whose is it? It doesn't feel like mine. I can tell Apollo wants to say more, to plead a case for himself, but I don't let him. I need to get away from him. I need him to stop taunting me — whatever version of him *this* is.

"Stay away from me," I snap at him.

Ethan pulls me in and ushers me toward the rest of the group. Apollo's eyes lower in shame and return to his hands. In the most peculiar way, he examines his palms, then flips them, and repeats this. Does he not remember? Does he not understand what *he* did?

As I walk away, I hear Lieutenant Tillman scream, "What do you have to say for yourself, soldier?"

"I— I don't know..." Apollo's voice breaks, almost like he's afraid. "I don't know what came over me. It didn't feel like me."

Despite the rage burning in my chest, something in his voice chills me. I don't know what he experienced. But I can't shake the feeling that somehow, it's connected to what's unraveling inside me. Like we're both caught in the same invisible current, unable to control it.

I can't explain it, but I believe him.

Ten

The weeks following our first week of training fly by. Before we know it, we've reached the end of the first quarter. Today, I wake up earlier than everyone else. Maybe it's jitters or my body adjusting to the severe lack of sleep, but I have no trouble pulling myself out of bed. Once my feet hit the floor, I'm wide awake.

I step into the bathroom, triggering all the overhead lights to come on. I shower in private and, once I'm clean, wrap my towel around my waist. The mirror fastened above the sink is fogged from the humidity. I approach it and swipe my hand across it in a diagonal motion, revealing a sliver of my reflection. It strikes me, almost as if I'm seeing myself for the first time. It takes me back to the morning of my birthday — the morning before everything changed.

The same blue eyes stare back at me, but there's a confidence in them that wasn't there before. My skin clings more tightly to my cheekbones. My shoulders are broader, and abs poke through my midsection in a prominent cluster. There's clear definition in my muscles, making my body look strong and formidable. And though they're not impressive in size, it makes me feel powerful. Capable. More like the soldier I'm supposed to be.

Back in the barracks, I slide on my uniform. Once I'm dressed, I crawl into my bunk and rest my head against my pillow. I stare up at the bottom of the top bunk where Ethan lays asleep. The sound of his breathing rattles the measly frame. I've grown used to it over time. I know it'll be a while before he or anyone else wakes up, and I like that. It makes this time feel sacred, similar to the glow of the Barrier. Momentary. Just for me.

I never imagined I would feel any different toward the draft. All my life, it's done nothing but take from me. But now, it's given me so much.

Ethan, Drew, Carson. The friendships I have with them have gotten me this far.

Leo. Though I've kept him at a distance, he comes around every so often, always eager to check in.

Apollo has never missed an opportunity to patronize me, but I'm tough enough to withstand it now. I'm not as breakable as I was four weeks ago — and he knows that.

I've been beaten and pushed past my limits. But I've learned how to mend, to rise above the challenges and keep pushing, even when it's painful. Even when it feels like the odds are against me.

And now, it'll all be put to the test during our first quarterly assessment.

Whatever happens today will determine the top five. Even though there will be plenty of chances to improve in the weeks ahead, I can't afford to blow this first assessment. Everything has been leading to this moment. And now, right when it matters most, I can't back down.

A few draftees stir and begin waking up. Even as they move through the motions of the day, there's a collective sense of unity among us that hasn't always been there. It took nearly the entirety of four weeks, but we've learned how to be a team. How to work together for something bigger than ourselves, even if we don't see eye to eye as individuals. Our training officers have drilled the importance of that into our minds. If we lose sight of that, we'll never win the war.

It took having the right understanding of the draft to understand our place in it. As soldiers, as men, and as part of the last living legacy of our nation.

Ethan plops down from his bunk with a harsh slap of his feet against the floor.

"You nervous about today?" he asks through a yawn.

I shake my head. "Not one bit." And I mean it.

"Me neither," he says. "I feel ready."

Before he can move from his spot, the barracks door opens. Lieutenant Kelley and Lieutenant Tillman step in, and a hush falls over the room.

"Draftees, congratulations," Lieutenant Kelley bellows. "You've made it to the end of the first quarter."

He pauses for a moment, but we all remain silent.

"The only thing left now is for you to complete your quarterly assessment," he explains. "While your first assessment was used to assess your fitness coming into the draft, this assessment will be more advanced. It'll combine all three aspects of your training — strength, strategy, and skill — and put them equally to the test. You'll go one at a time, and you'll each have an hour to complete the assessment. Is that understood?"

"Yes, sir!" we shout.

"If there aren't any questions, we'll go ahead and get started."

Every draftee clings to the moment, eager to know who will go first. My heart races, thinking it could be me.

"O'Hair," Lieutenant Kelley declares, "come forward."

"Oh, brother," Carson groans. He drags himself across the room until he's standing at Lieutenant Kelley's side. He stiffens, trying to conceal his nerves.

"The rest of you will wait here until it's your turn," Lieutenant Kelley orders.

Carson glances over his shoulder and drags his finger across his throat as he follows the training officers out of the room. Ethan snickers, and I give him a smile to show that everything will be fine. All the while wondering what's really waiting for him in the assessment.

Time seems to stand still. It feels like nearly the entirety of one hour goes by before Carson returns. When he does, every draftee jumps to their feet, wide-eyed and eager for any hint at what to expect.

Carson freezes in the doorway. His face is flushed red, and the collar of his shirt is soaked with sweat. He looks no different than how he'd look after a run. But there's an intensity in his eyes, as if he's witnessed something he's still trying to process.

"Oh no," he snaps. "Nope. You're not getting anything out of me."

He shakes off the initial shock and charges into the barracks. Behind him, Lieutenant Tillman lingers in the doorway.

Carson crosses the room to his bunk and grabs a towel from his drawer. He slings it over his shoulder and heads for the showers.

"If I had to go in blind, so do you," he hollers. His voice echoes from the bathroom, then trails off as soon as the water starts running.

"Andres," Lieutenant Tillman says. "You're up next."

"Excellent," Apollo smirks.

He strides confidently from his bunk to the doorway without batting an eye. From the hallway, I hear him say, "Let's show these boys how it's done."

The door swings shut behind them, and silent anticipation creeps back into the room.

When Carson exits the bathroom, Drew and I lock eyes, and we rush toward him. Ethan sits upright in his bed, not bothering to come down, but tuning into everything we say.

"C'mon, man," Drew pleads. He lowers his voice a bit, pretending every other draftee in the barracks can't hear him. "You're really not going to tell us anything?"

Carson shakes his head definitively. "Not a peep. What's it to you, anyway? Both of you will be just fine." He lifts his eyes to Ethan, who's now crouched on all fours, leaning over the edge of the bunk. "You too, Greene. Seriously, you all have nothing to worry about."

My shoulders settle. Drew and I let him off the hook and move out of his way. Once he's dressed, Carson plops down in his bunk with a disgruntled huff. Within seconds, he's already fast asleep.

I sit on the edge of my bed and wait for Apollo to return. I stare at the thin-framed clock mounted on the back wall, watching closely as the seconds tick by, waiting for the hands to strike the next hour. It reminds me of that night in the pub, as some of the boys gathered around the clock to ring in the new year. Their voices echo in my mind, counting down the seconds till our demise: *Five, four, three, two—*

Almost as if on cue, the door to the barracks clicks open. Every draftee jumps to their feet again — all except Carson, who couldn't be woken by anything. Apollo walks in just as confidently as he left. All eyes are on him, which only inflates his ego. Judging by the way he struts over to his bunk, it's clear he's proud of his results.

Same as Carson, he doesn't say a word. He scoffs at Dom, who stares doe-eyed at him from the top bunk. He kicks off his boots, rips the towel from his drawer, and heads for the showers.

As he passes by, he stops in front of me. "Good luck," he sneers. "You're gonna need it."

Turning my head, I notice Lieutenant Kelley standing in the doorway now, ready to take his next victim. All the other noise fades away as he says my name.

"Madoc," he hisses sharply.

I swallow hard against the anticipation burning in my chest. Doubt creeps in, overshadowing any confidence I had earlier. Maybe I'm not ready for this. Maybe I haven't improved as much as I think I have, and I don't have what it takes.

But I know that's not true. Deep down, I know I can do this. I have to. Every step forward could bring me closer to the truth about my father. Failure isn't an option — not this time.

I rise to my feet and slip through the doorway. Lieutenant Kelley ushers me down the corridor away from the barracks. When we reach the elevator, he summons it with his badge, and the doors slide open to reveal the empty pod.

We step in, and out of habit, I retreat to the back corner. Lieutenant Kelley stands near the button panel with his back to me. He presses his finger into a button I haven't noticed before marked *S*. My eyes scan the other options, trying to see how I might've missed it before. But I guess I never had a reason to notice it.

The elevator doors shut, and the floor jolts beneath us. My eyes remain locked on the glowing button engraved with an *S*. What could it stand for? *Secret? Secure?* I switch my gaze up to the digitized panel above the door. The letter *M* blinks across it, quickly followed by the letter *U* for *Upper*, as in the upper level. But the elevator keeps rising — and it doesn't seem to be slowing any time soon.

"W-what does—" I stutter, but I stop myself. I realize how pitiful I must sound and instantly regret saying anything.

"Speak up, soldier," Lieutenant Kelley barks.

"Uh, where are you taking me?" I manage.

Lieutenant Kelley's head slowly turns until I'm in his peripheral. The letter *S* blinks across the panel, followed by the soft chime signaling our arrival.

"You're about to find out," he replies.

The doors slide open to reveal a luminous room. The floor, walls, and ceiling all merge into one seamless grid of reflective white panels. Fluorescent lights trace the outline of the panels on the walls and ceiling, giving the room a high-tech glow. The whole space gleams like a mirror. Its reflective surfaces send ripples of light across the floor with each step we take. I glance down at my feet and see my distorted reflection staring up at me.

Directly across from the elevator, the wall is black — a stark contrast to the rest of the room. It's framed by a continuous band of polished tile, creating a border that separates it from the white space. Lieutenant Tillman waits there, clutching a tablet and an array of other items. He gestures for us to come forward. Lieutenant Kelley nudges me, breaking my hesitation, and I stumble over the threshold where the two spaces meet.

"Lieutenant Tillman will run through how the assessment will work," Lieutenant Kelley says. To my surprise, his voice doesn't echo. It falls flat the minute the words leave his lips. "I'll stand by in case there are any concerns."

Lieutenant Kelley steps aside, allowing Lieutenant Tillman to approach me.

"Alright, listen closely, Madoc, because I'm not repeating this twice. I already had to do that for the first guy," he mutters. Immediately, I feel a twinge of pity for Carson.

"There are three pieces of equipment you'll have on you," he explains. "The first is the vest." He removes a padded vest from over his shoulder and drops it into my hand. My arm jolts from its weight.

I slip my arms through the openings on both sides, and it sags against my shoulders. Once it's on, Lieutenant Tillman moves behind me to zip it. As he slides the zipper up to the ball of my neck, the vest tightens, squeezing the breath out of me.

"There are sensors located in six different areas on the vest. The first is in the back." He slaps a firm hand against the backside of the vest, and I feel a thin plate within the fabric collide with my spine.

Lieutenant Tillman swings around to the front. "Each sensor is strategically placed to provide a sensory experience for you while also transmitting information over to us. That way, if you get hit or knocked down, we'll know."

My eyes shoot across his face. "I'm sorry, *hit*?"

"Right," he states plainly, as if there's nothing to question. "Moving on, the other five sensors are located in the front of the vest: two on your shoulders, one in the center of your chest, and two just above your hips on either side."

He demonstrates this by tapping each sensor spot. All the while my mind spirals. What does he mean by getting hit? What would hit me — or who?

"The next piece of equipment is your gloves," he continues. He pulls a pair of lightweight black gloves out of his back pocket and deposits them into my hands. Small blue scales cover the fabric in a pattern, and all five fingertips are hooded with a silver microfiber material. As I slide them onto both hands, I'm amazed at how minimal they feel.

"Each finger contains a micro-sensor," Lieutenant Tillman explains. I flip my palms and examine the silver material more closely. Squinting my eyes, I notice a small fingerprint design etched into the fabric, perfectly shaped for each finger.

"These sensors are more for us than they are for you. With them, we can read how many times your hands make contact with something, and how many times you pull the trigger of your gun."

I open my mouth to say something, but the words catch in my throat. *My gun?* I think. *What would I have to shoot at?*

"The last piece of gear — and arguably the most important — is the headset," he says. Clutched in the nook of his arm is a sleek rounded helmet. The front has a translucent visor that shields the face. On the left side, there's a small microphone built into the frame. The mic hovers over a vent in the chin guard where my jaw would be. It's linked by a tight wire pinned to the side of the helmet, threaded between two black spots: one where my ear would be, and the other at the back.

Lieutenant Tillman does the honors of sliding the helmet over my head. It instantly muffles all other noise, except the sound of my breathing. I can hear each breath shudder out of my mouth and filter through the vent, almost as if I'm breathing underwater.

Through the visor, I see Lieutenant Tillman's mouth moving, but his voice is suppressed. He holds up a finger and reaches into his pocket. He pulls out a small black earpiece and slides it over his ear. Connected to it is a microphone that rests just below his cheekbone.

"Can you hear me now?" His static voice comes through the helmet, startling me.

"Yes, sir," I hear my own muffled voice reply.

"Very good," he says. "Now, let me explain. Behind this door," he signals to the black wall behind him, which doesn't appear to have a door, "you're going to enter into a virtual reality. The program is designed to simulate a war zone, in which you'll encounter a few enemies. Your objective is to defeat as many of them as possible while sustaining the least amount of damage. These enemies cannot hurt you in real life, but they can hurt your score in the simulation. Do you understand?"

"Yes, sir," I say timidly, though I'm not sure I do.

"As soon as I activate the simulation on my device, you'll be able to see everything through the headset. Lieutenant Kelley and I will be able to communicate with you the entire time, and you with us. If you need to stop for any reason, all you have to do is ask. Just know, choosing to leave the simulation early will severely affect your rank. The longer you're in, the more enemies you take down, the better you score. Clear?"

I gulp.

His voice goes flat for a second, then resumes. "Which . . . reminds me . . ." he unclips something from his waist, and the familiar touch of a handgun meets my gloved fingers. I tilt my head down to gaze at the weapon.

"This is what you'll use to defend yourself," he finishes.

"Is it loaded?" I spit out before he can say anything more.

Lieutenant Tillman scoffs. "Of course not. The gun isn't a live weapon. It's linked to the program, so you'll notice when you pull the trigger, it'll have the same effect as a real gun — but only in the simulation. Not in reality."

That somewhat relieves me. If nothing in the simulation can have any real effect on me, then I have nothing to worry about. After all, Carson and Apollo didn't come back with bullet wounds. It wouldn't benefit them to harm us — they need us alive.

"Do you have any questions before we begin?" he offers.

"No, sir," I reply.

Lieutenant Tillman turns around and places his hand against one of the panels in the wall. Just like on the lower level, it pushes back like a door, revealing an opening on the other side.

"Whenever you're ready, soldier," Lieutenant Tillman says through the headset.

My eyes flicker over to Lieutenant Kelley, who stands with his back pressed against the wall. He gives me a nod in the direction of the door, prompting me to go through.

Turning toward the opening, I close my eyes, grip the gun at my side, and step forward.

With my eyes still clenched shut, I hear the muffled clap of the door closing behind me. This time, the sound lingers, reverberating through the room before fading into a hollow, distant echo — almost as if I'm standing in a tunnel. My eyes flutter open, but the room around me is pitch dark. I lower my head, searching for the faintest outline of my hands, but they're not visible.

My head swivels, desperate for some sort of tether to reality, but there's nothing. Nothing but pure darkness. I extend my hands out in front of me and walk forward until I hit a wall. My fingers glide over the surface and trace the familiar outline of the door, sealing me on the other side.

"What happens now?" I blurt out. For a moment, I wonder if Lieutenant Tillman was lying about being able to communicate with me while I'm in here. For all I know, he can't hear me, and I'm calling out to someone who isn't there.

But to my relief, his static voice comes through the headset a moment later.

"Like I said, as soon as I activate the simulation, you'll be able to see everything through the headset."

"I can't see anything," I mutter. "I can't see anything at all."

"Calm down, Madoc," Lieutenant Tillman snaps. "That's how it's supposed to be. It'll all come into view in a minute."

"What am I supposed to be looking for?" I ask frantically. "Will I know, once it starts?"

"You'll know," he says. "Wait for the simulation to take shape around you, then let your mind take care of the rest."

I don't know what that's supposed to mean.

Pressing my hands against the wall, I close my eyes again. My breath quickens, each one constricted by the vest. I try to conjure a mental image of what I might see, or what the room might look like, but it's useless.

"Okay," I say out loud, though I'm talking to myself now. "Just relax. You can do this."

Once my breathing steadies, I exhale, open my eyes, and watch through the visor as the room begins to transform.

A distant, faint orange glow breaks through the darkness, partially illuminating the room. As it magnifies, it reveals the contours of a curved corridor. The glow traces the curvature of the room, making its rounded shape undeniable. Meanwhile the floors and walls remain formless and void, darker than a starless sky.

I step away from the wall hesitantly and move toward the light. The space around me seems to swell. Through the visor, I notice the glow is coming from a small orange ember floating in midair. Within seconds, it expands into a thin beam of light that soon resolves into the outline of a building. From there, the light jumps, and the same thing happens on the other side of the room.

My breath catches as an entire cityscape unravels around me. The exterior of the buildings remains as black as the rest of the room, but their luminous outlines make it clear what the simulation is trying to project. It's replicating the city — or *a* city. The light spreads throughout the room, weaving together a labyrinth of glowing digitized skyscrapers. They rise higher and higher, defying the limits of the room, towering over me just as real city buildings do.

Once the room is completely transformed, a small ember of light materializes again in the center of my path. Only this time, it morphs into a different shape, tracing the silhouette of a human figure. First, its head forms, followed by the slope of its shoulders, the droop of its arms, and finally its lower half. Rather than flesh, its body is clad in an intricate pattern of three-dimensional cubes, giving it depth. Its outline burns with the same fiery glow as the rest of the city. Once it's fully formed, its head cocks to the side, and though it has no face, I know it's looking directly at me.

And something deep in my subconscious tells me it's not a friendly look.

The figure slices through the space between us in a sprint. My stomach somersaults. For a moment, I'm paralyzed. I glance around, desperate for a hiding place, but the towering buildings are nothing more than hollow facades that offer no real refuge.

My gloved fingers tighten around the grip of the gun in my hand, reminding me that it's there. There's nowhere to run. Nowhere to escape to. No shadow deep enough to hide in. All I can do is stand here and face the enemy hurtling toward me.

And shoot.

I lift the gun and aim at the center of the figure's head. My index finger slams against the trigger, and to my surprise, a searing blue beam erupts from the barrel of the gun. Instinctively, I step back in shock. The beam cuts clean through the figure's skull. As it does, all the microscopic cubes that make up its body begin to break apart and dissolve until the figure fizzles into thin air.

I slowly lower the gun with trembling hands. I tilt it slightly, peering down into the barrel, trying to understand where the beam came from. I wave my palm over the opening, feeling for any heat remaining from the shot, but it's just as cool and dull as before.

I remind myself it's not a live weapon — it's just an illusion. But still, it looked so real.

My shoulders sag in relief. As I survey the room, my mind buzzes on high alert. I may have survived the first test, but the assessment is far from over. It's only just beginning.

I venture further into the digitized cityscape. The glowing buildings follow the curve of the room. The deeper I go, the more boundless the city feels, growing larger and more advanced with each step I take. Soon, I reach a fork in the road. The outline of a building stands at the junction, splitting the path in two.

Curiosity takes over me. Timidly, I approach the building and lay my palm against its shadowy surface. To my surprise, it's solid. My gut lurches, and I jerk my hand away, shaken by the feeling. But as soon as the shock fades, curiosity kicks back in. I ball my hand into a fist and beat it against the structure. Pain shoots through my knuckles, and the orange beams framing the building vibrate from the impact.

I glance down at my glove and flex my now-aching fingers. Lieutenant Tillman's words echo in my mind, reminding me the simulation is designed to be a sensory experience. *It's all in my head*, I think. *It's designed to feel real, but it isn't.*

But somehow, the ache in my fist still lingers.

Without any reason, I choose to follow the path to the left. As I go, the floor starts to slope steadily beneath my feet, propelling me forward. The buildings seem to grow taller the further I drift beneath them. Here, their outlines expand, jutting into the walkway and constricting the path.

The path tightens until it's no more than a thin ribbon of empty space. Up ahead, I notice a break between two buildings, reminiscent of an alleyway. I make that my target and squeeze through the last stretch of the confined path. Relief washes over me as I round the corner and the path widens. But it's quickly overshadowed by dread — because I'm not alone in the alley.

Hunched in the corner are two more humanoid figures, blazing with the same orange glow as the last. At first, I don't recognize them. They blend in with the glow emanating off the neighboring buildings.

But as soon as I step into the alley, their heads twist over their shoulders, as if looking back at me. Their posture stiffens, and their knees bend, ready to pounce.

This time, I run.

I burst out of the alley and sprint back up the way I came. The humanoid figures are hot on my heels, clawing at me with their shadowy hands. As soon as I have a sliver of distance, I whip around and level my gun, locking in on them. They surge forward in a chaotic frenzy that makes my blood run cold, practically climbing over each other just to get to me.

My finger presses into the trigger and releases the same blue beam from the gun. It soars through the air between us and slices through one figure's shoulder. But almost as soon as it does, its geometric skin regenerates, making its shoulder whole again.

I think back to the first figure I encountered. *The head*, I realize. *I need to aim for the head.*

With both figures no more than a few feet away, I drive my finger into the trigger twice, sending two beams straight through their skulls. Instantly, both figures dissolve into a virtual mist. Pixelated shards of their cubed skin rain down on me, but I don't feel them. I keep my weapon raised until the last trace of them vanishes, then lower it.

I turn around, intending to head in the opposite direction. Toward the parts of the city I haven't ventured into yet. But my plan is cut short. From around the corner ahead, another group of figures emerges — at least five of them. My pulse spikes. Without hesitation, I bolt back toward the fork in the road. Instead of going left, I veer right.

A quick glance over my shoulder confirms they've noticed me, and they're gaining on me quicker than the others before them. Their difficulty must be increasing the longer I remain in the simulation. Just as I turn my attention forward again, three more figures materialize ahead of me, blocking my path. My heels screech against the pitch-black floor as I skid to a stop.

I'm trapped.

The illusive buildings around me offer no sort of escape plan. It's inevitable — I either continue forward and face the three while the rest gain on me, or I turn to face the larger group while the others attack from behind. This must've been the final straw for the draftees before me. Outnumbered eight to one with nowhere to run. Nowhere to go but headfirst into the battle.

After all, isn't that what we're expected to do? To stand our ground and fight?

I realize no matter where I go, there will always be more of them. They'll keep regenerating and piling up until there's so many, I'm forced to surrender.

I can't give up. Not now. Not when I'm so close to proving myself.

I have to fight.

Weighing my odds, I flip around and send a blue beam through the skull of the figure leading the larger charge. It dissolves in an instant, but the others press on, unfazed. I aim again and strike down another one. But before I can aim for another, a sudden vibration courses through me, rattling my bones. I feel the sensation of weight on my back. But slinging my arms behind me, I don't feel anything.

It takes a second vibration before it dawns on me — the sensor. The sensor in the back of my vest is reacting.

The figure. It's on my back.

I wiggle my body and manage to break free. Spinning around, the figure looms inches from my face. It lunges toward me, and on instinct, I send my fist into its jaw. To my surprise, this works. The figure's form blurs briefly, weakened by the impact, but not dead.

Wasting no time, I raise my weapon and fire. The blue beam sears through its skull, and the figure disintegrates into nothingness.

I kick out my leg, and it collides with one of the five remaining figures, sending it flying backward. At the same time, I raise my gun at the one closest to me and fire. The blue beam cuts through its skull, and it dissolves. As I pivot around, the other four figures advancing from behind are already upon me. They're too close now, and I don't have time to react.

I panic.

I stumble backward and scramble into a narrow gap between two buildings. My shoulders brush against their illusive surfaces. The remaining figures surge into the alley, piling over one another like rabid animals. They claw and gnash their way toward me, their digitized bodies contorting in an unnatural way.

A scream rips out of my throat. Any ounce of courage I had before is gone, shattered by the horrifying scene unfolding before me.

"Focus, Madoc," Lieutenant Tillman's steady voice comes through the headset, taking me out for a moment. Reminding me where I am and who's really in control.

This isn't real, I remind myself. *I have the power. I have control.*

This spurs me to action. I continue scrambling backward until my spine hits the wall at the end of the alley. I slide my back against it until I'm standing upright, facing the figures barreling toward me head-on.

Ready.

My hands tremble as I raise my gun.

Aim.

I steady my breathing and ease my nerves. Once I'm ready, I lock in on the figure at the head of the pack.

Fire!

The beam tears through its skull, and it dissolves in an instant. Three more remain. I fire again, taking down another, but the last two close in on me quicker than I expect. Their shadowy forms loom over me, forcing me back against the wall. I slide down the wall until I hit the ground and try to steady my gun.

I pull the trigger, but my aim is off. The beam ricochets off the building, disappearing into the void beyond the figures. Gritting my teeth, I try again. This time, the beam drives into the figure's skull, leaving just one remaining.

The last figure leaps onto me. Its weight sends a jarring vibration through my vest. I wrestle for control, but the figure is relentless. Somehow, I manage to wedge the gun between us. The grip digs into my ribs, and I can barely wrap my finger around the trigger. But I do. I press the trigger three times in rapid succession. Each beam slams into the center of the figure's chest, forcing it back. As it stumbles, I jump back to my feet. Without hesitation, I level the gun, lock in on its head, and fire one final shot. The beam pierces through its skull with innate precision, and the figure dissolves into a mist.

The alley falls silent, and the cityscape becomes vacant again — all except for me.

I lower my gun and sigh in disbelief. Even though I'm backed into the alley, I turn around, scanning my surroundings for any more figures.

Suddenly, the wall behind me becomes reflective. Through its polished surface, I see a spitting image of myself. My sleek black uniform clinging to my frame. The sensory vest snug across my chest. The helmet obscuring my face.

But something is wrong. The reflection begins to move out of sync with me. Its arms rise while my own remain at my sides. It reaches up to remove the helmet, gripping the chin guard and lifting it to reveal the face underneath.

A sharp, involuntary breath escapes me. This isn't my reflection. It can't be. It has to be some twisted trick of the simulation — because staring back at me is a version of myself I don't recognize.

It wears my face, but the resemblance is grotesque. Its skin is ashen and riddled with gaping rotten pores that ooze vile fluid. Patches of blonde stubble cling to its thinning scalp, reminiscent of my own hair, but it's wilting away. The blue in its eyes is gone, and instead, its eyes are pure white. Its lips are stale and dry, splitting open as they twist into a ghastly grin. Ruby-red blood drips from the fissures, tainting its lips, making them look vicious. Behind its smile, its teeth decay, almost on the verge of crumbling to dust.

It's like something out of a nightmare, but still, it's *me*. When I tilt my head, it tilts its own. It mimics every movement I make as if we are one. I think about raising my weapon, but I'm too stunned, caught in its gaze.

Cautiously, I lift a trembling hand, compelled to reach for it. As I do, I wonder if I'll make contact with the wall or the decaying skin of the figure standing before me. My fingertips hover closer, afraid to get too close, but needing to know — is this real? Or is this in my head too?

But before I can find out, a blinding light floods the room, washing away the image.

In its place, my true reflection stares back at me through a wall of mirrors — the helmet still covering my face, my hand still outstretched, caught in a motion that's incomplete.

I jerk my hand away at the sound of a door opening behind me. Turning my head, I see Lieutenant Tillman standing in the doorway, framed by the glow of the room on the other side. As I glance around, the shape of the room is apparent now: a narrow corridor curving in both directions, binding together like an infinite ring. The room is completely bare and made entirely of reflective glass. There are no buildings, not even any objects or pillars to mimic the shapes of buildings. Stunned, I look down at my gloved hands. I flex my fingers, remembering what I felt, marveling at how real it all was. Or how real the simulation made it feel. But it was all imaginary.

Lieutenant Tillman ushers me out of the room. We return to the other side, where Lieutenant Kelley stands occupied. His fingers type vigorously on his tablet like he's taking notes. He doesn't even notice when I come out.

"That's all," Lieutenant Tillman says, closing the door behind us.

"But what about—" I start, but I stop myself. The monstrous reflection flashes through my mind again. Was that not part of the simulation? A final enemy I needed to face? And if not, what was it?

I decide not to say anything. Still, I can't shake the image, but I figure it's best to keep it to myself. Instead, I glance at both training officers and ask, "How'd I do?"

Lieutenant Kelley's eyes lift from his screen. Though I can't quite read his expression, his words confirm it's somewhere between disbelief and pride.

"Soldier," he says, "you might've just earned yourself a place at the top of the ranks."

Eleven

That evening, we gather in the Assembly Hall. The room buzzes with the thrill of finding out our results. Most of the draftees are exhausted from the assessment, but still, the anticipation keeps us energized. We follow our training officers to the same row we sat in four weeks earlier, when General Conrad first welcomed us to the facility.

Once we're seated, General Conrad strides onto the stage. Silence falls on the room. He plants himself in the center of the stage and tucks his hands behind his back. Lifting his chin, he surveys the audience, leaving us in suspense.

"Soldiers," he greets us, "I'd like to begin by congratulating our draftees on completing their first quarter of training."

The room erupts in applause. Both Lieutenant Kelley and Lieutenant Tillman applaud too, glancing down the row at us, grinning in support.

As soon as the applause subsides, General Conrad continues. "Our training officers have been monitoring their progress over the past four weeks. And now that each draftee has completed his quarterly assessment, the results are in. I'd like to invite our training officers up to present their ranks."

Lieutenant Kelley and Lieutenant Tillman rise from their seats. I grip my armrests as they march down the aisle and join the general on stage. When they reach him, they click their feet together and lift their hands in a unified salute. The general returns the gesture.

General Conrad outstretches his hands with his palms upward. Lieutenant Kelley unclips the tablet from his waist and hands it off to the general. Taking hold of it, General Conrad dismisses both training officers, who obediently return to their seats.

The tablet comes to life, highlighting the general's face. His eyes scan over the screen, hard and unchanging, then widen in surprise.

He must be looking at the results, I think. And he must not have expected what he sees.

Every single draftee inches to the edge of their seat. None of us move, or so much as breathe, the entire time the tablet is in his hands. My mind scrambles to prepare for the outcome. If what Lieutenant Kelley said earlier is true, that I earned myself a spot at the top of the ranks, I worry it's my name General Conrad is surprised by. Was my father ranked number one, and General Conrad is reliving the moment Anthony Madoc was crowned top of his class?

But I worry if I *am* number one, it'll do more harm than good. Fourth would do, or even fifth. As long as I'm in the top five. But at number one, I'd become a target. The obstacle between everyone and their shot at the top. The one everyone wants to beat. With all eyes on me, it'd be impossible to find out anything about my father.

As General Conrad lifts his eyes, every draftee holds a collective breath. The screen behind him flickers on, and every light in the auditorium dims. Behind the general, in large blinking blue letters, are each of our names, numbered in ranking order from one to twelve.

"Draftees, as it stands now, here are your ranks," he says.

1. JOHN MADOC
2. APOLLO ANDRES

3. DOM D'ANGELO
4. LEO PATTON
5. ETHAN GREENE
6. DREW FITZGERALD
7. DANNY GUERRA
8. LUCA ROSS
9. RORY TAYLOR
10. CARSON O'HAIR
11. ADRIAN HART
12. JOEY CALLAHAN

My eyes immediately skip to the bottom out of fear. I find Carson's name at number ten, and moving up, I don't see my name.

But I know where it is before my eyes reach the top. Lieutenant Kelley was right — and now everyone else knows it.

"Congratulations, John Madoc," General Conrad declares. "Our top-ranked draftee. Keep up the good work, soldier."

His eyes find me in the crowd, and a grin spreads across his face. Dread sinks to the pit of my stomach. Ethan's hand clasps down on my shoulder, shaking me in disbelief. Every eye in the room is on me, burning into my profile.

"We actually did it," Ethan remarks. "Top five, baby!"

My emotions betray me. I can't deny the fact this doesn't bode well for me, and it's written all over my face. Apollo's glare from the end of the row confirms what I feared — this doesn't mean victory. It means the real competition is just now getting started.

As the applause subsides, the projector sucks the list of names off the screen. The lights around the room lift, but General Conrad isn't finished yet. He dangles the tablet at his side, clutching it in his hand as he steps to the edge of the stage.

"As your training officers shared at the beginning of training, the top five ranked draftees will be granted special permissions. Because of your hard work and diligence, we've decided to put you up for a task."

My spine straightens against the seat. My whole body leans in, anticipating his next words.

"Tomorrow morning, at dawn, we're sending you on a supply run," he announces. "Supply runs are routine operations that serve to salvage miscellaneous items and supplies that can be useful for our community. We're fortunate to have plenty of resources under the Barrier, but we'd be foolish to think there aren't more resources we could take advantage of outside the Barrier."

Outside the Barrier? I don't follow at first. Surely I misheard him. We can't — we couldn't, could we?

"Your mission will be to retrieve specific items of value from a designated location beyond the Barrier and bring them back to the city. Your training officers will give you further instructions in the morning. But for now, rest. Get some sleep. Because tomorrow, a whole new world awaits — one that's not as forgiving as ours."

My heart quakes inside my chest. I cling to the edge of my seat, forgetting to breathe. I recall the word Mae used — *banished* — implying my father could be somewhere out there, beyond the Barrier.

I replay General Conrad's words in my head to make sure I didn't misunderstand.

But the look on Ethan's face confirms I heard him right. And just like that, four weeks of brutal training blur into nothing — worth every bruise and breathless run just to hear those words.

Tomorrow, we're being sent outside the city. We're going beyond the Barrier.

Twelve

Obey, Preserve, Protect. The words echo in my mind long after we're finished chanting them in the Assembly Hall. They play like a soundtrack over my dreams as I picture the world beyond the Barrier. I think back to General Conrad's presentation from our first day — the map of an entire nation ravaged by The Truth. Then, it felt real enough. But it can hardly compare to how real it's about to be.

I can't believe we're going to see it for ourselves.

My eyes shoot open at the sound of the training officers bursting into the barracks. Several draftees groan, but those of us headed out on today's mission don't miss a beat. Quickly, I roll out of bed, pull on my uniform, and lace up my boots. Ethan scrambles down from the top bunk, half-dressed and barely awake by the time I'm standing in front of Lieutenant Kelley, ready to go.

Apollo, Dom, and Leo join us once they're dressed. Across the room, Drew gives a friendly salute to Ethan and me.

"Good luck today, boys," he hollers, a hint of envy in his voice.

"Ready for the craziest day of our lives?" Ethan says breathlessly as he steps into line next to me.

"Never been more ready," I grin.

We shuffle down the corridor behind the training officers toward Battery Station. The vault door is already wide open, but instead of going through it, Lieutenant Kelley stops a few feet away. He presses his badge to a nearby scanner, and the door to the shooting range pops open. "In," he growls, and we pass through under his arm.

Lieutenant Tillman rests his back against the door, propping it open. Within seconds, a swarm of other soldiers flood the room. One of them approaches me and hands me a vest. "Put it on," he demands. His face is covered by a carbon fiber helmet with a smoky visor striped across the front, large enough to only reveal his eyes.

The weight of the vest sags against my shoulders. It's heavier than the vest I wore during the assessment. Instead of sensors, it's stuffed with thick padding. But I tighten it around my chest all the same.

"Listen up!" Lieutenant Kelly shouts as more soldiers enter the room, tending to the other draftees. "These men are going to give you what you need for today's supply run. You will do what they say, wear the gear they give you, and keep your mouth shut. Understood?"

"Yes, sir!" we respond in unison.

The soldier places a coarse black belt in my hand. "Fasten this around your waist," he orders. I reach behind myself and weave it through my belt loops. With a gentle tug, I tighten it and clip it at the front.

While I'm focused on the belt, I almost miss the soldier sliding a helmet over my head. I feel the weight of it come down on my scalp and flinch on instinct.

"Stay still," the soldier hisses impatiently.

I straighten myself and allow him to finish. He forces the helmet down over my ears until it's snug. Similar to his own helmet, there's a visor stretched across the front. The tint clouds my vision, but it's clear enough to see through.

The last piece of gear the soldier hands me is a thin pair of gloves, similar to the ones from the assessment. Only this time, the fingertips aren't sheathed with sensors. I squeeze each finger into its designated slot and gulp. There's nothing simulated about what's happening today — this is real.

The side of my belt sags. Peering down, I notice the soldier clipping a holster to my waist. The grip of a handgun pokes out of it. This time, I don't have to question whether it's a live weapon. A chill runs down my spine as the soldier applies weight to it, making sure it's secure.

"This gear is not optional," Lieutenant Kelley says. "So long as we're outside the Barrier, you should always be wearing it. Each of you has been given a handgun and a pager, both of which are secured to your belt. The gun is just a safety precaution, but it's loaded in case you need to use it. The pager is to alert you when the train arrives."

I pat my hand against my waist, feeling for the pager. I don't recall the soldier giving it to me. I must've been too distracted by the gun to notice it. Right at my hip, my fingers trace the outline of a smooth circular device, no larger than the palm of my hand.

"When the train is close, the pager will light up and vibrate," Lieutenant Kelley explains. "When this happens, you'll have precisely five minutes to make it to the nearest station and board the train before it departs. I've already scouted the area we'll be in today to ensure we're within a reasonable distance of the station. That way, we should all have no issue making it back on time."

The soldiers finish strapping us with gear. Once we're set, Lieutenant Kelley signals for Lieutenant Tillman to escort us out of the room. We file back into the hall and continue toward Battery Station.

The platform is bustling with activity. The subway is already stationary. Its doors are peeled back, with soldiers flowing on and off, carrying out their assigned duties. Two soldiers rush toward us with a set of gear packs pulled tight by a single drawstring strap. They hand one off to each of us.

"Each pack contains a water canteen and basic first-aid kit," one of them explains. I slip the strap across my body and let it rest at my hip.

Once we receive the all-clear from the other soldiers, Lieutenant Tillman leads us toward the subway. But before we can board, Lieutenant Kelley throws out an arm, blocking us from stepping on.

"I want each of you to listen to me very closely before getting on that train," he shouts.

We lean in close, trying to make sure we can hear him. The padding in our helmets and the noise of the subway behind him make it difficult.

"What you're doing today is a privilege," he says. "You've been given this opportunity because you've proven over the past four weeks you're capable of it. Do *not* prove me wrong."

"Yes, sir!" we reply.

Lieutenant Kelley's eyes scan over us one last time before he lowers his arm. One by one, we file into the rear car. I take my seat and watch the other draftees board. It feels like just yesterday we were sitting here, tired and half-drunk, surrounded by soldiers dressed head to toe in gear. Now here we are again — only this time, we're the ones dressed for battle.

A draftee takes a seat next to me. He presses a button sunken into the side of his helmet, and his visor flips up, revealing Ethan's wide green eyes.

"Oh, pleasure seeing you here," he says, acting surprised. He extends his hand to shake mine, and I play along.

"I can't believe we're actually doing this," I mutter in disbelief.

Leo is the last to board. As he's stepping into the car, I hear him say, "Are you not coming with us?"

"That's none of your concern, soldier," Lieutenant Tillman snaps. "Someone needs to stay back with the rest of the unit."

Leo shrugs in acceptance, then takes an available seat near the door. Lieutenant Kelley hops on behind him, and with a salute, the training officers split up. My eyes trace Lieutenant Tillman's path back to the vault door, where he disappears inside the facility.

As soon as we're all on board, the doors shut. The subway hums beneath us before it lurches forward, nearly jolting me out of my seat. I dig the heel of my boot into the floor, resisting against its force.

Within seconds, the acceleration gradually transitions to a steady pace. I peer out the window behind me just in time to see Battery Station fade out of view.

The muffled sound of a bell rings from the other end of the car, followed by the feminine voice over the intercom system. "Next stop: Philadelphia," it says. It draws my attention to the screen mounted to the back wall, displaying a map of our location. It offers three different views: one zoomed in on our blinking dot, another zoomed out to show Lower Manhattan, and a third zoomed out further to show the entire northeast corner of our nation.

On the map, our dot moves along a thick blue line that connects to a location south of the city, which I assume is Philadelphia. From Philadelphia, there's a purple line drawing a parallel path to a point back in Lower Manhattan, just north of the facility. Finally, there's a third line — a red line — leading back to Battery Station.

My fingers find the same button Ethan pressed on the side of my own helmet. It lifts my visor so I can get a clearer look at the screen. Our dot begins to creep closer to the edge of the Hudson. I know as soon as it crosses that boundary, we'll have passed under the Barrier. I watch closely as it blinks, still on the peninsula, then blinks again — this time, in the middle of the Hudson. On the other side.

Adrenaline surges through my veins. Just like that, we're beyond the Barrier. The dot continues blinking along the blue line and makes landfall on the other side of the river. Everything from this moment on is unfamiliar territory. We're completely untethered. No more walls. No Barrier. It should feel liberating, and yet, it terrifies me.

I can't help but think of my father. It'd be naive to think he's there, in Philadelphia. Waiting for the day I'd slip beyond the Barrier to find him. But part of me hopes if he's really out there, he's left something behind — like a message, or a sign, just to prove he's alive. After all, he'd surely be familiar with these supply run routes from his time in the military. If he knew I might go looking for him somewhere, this would be the place.

Suddenly, everything brightens. Sunlight seeps through the windows, washing out the dim blue lighting on the subway. The train ascends out of the tunnel until it's riding above ground. My stomach lurches. I spin around and kneel against my seat, eager to get my first look at the outside world.

Endless miles of barren land pass by in a blur. There are no skyscrapers. No streets. No forms of shelter. Any buildings are nothing more than mounds of rubble coated in weeds. A thin layer of snow blankets everything, glistening in the morning light. Mocking the ruins buried beneath it.

Nothing. There's absolutely nothing. General Conrad was right: The world beyond the Barrier is desolate and uninhabitable.

Ethan must sense what I'm feeling as our eyes meet. "It's alright, Johnny," he whispers. "He's gotta be out there, somewhere."

But I'm not so sure anymore.

The subway continues zipping through the passing landscape with ease. No more than an hour goes by before it starts to decelerate. It emits a hum that wakes any draftees who dozed off. The subway dives underground, and the blue interior lights return as walls of black absorb the outside view.

"Everyone up!" Lieutenant Kelley shouts. He pulls on his helmet and stands, gripping the vertical poles for support. Without warning, a buzzing sensation rattles against my hip. Looking at the other draftees, all our pagers are alive with green light. "Arriving at Philadelphia," the voice confirms over the intercom.

Through the window, a narrow platform comes into view. Unlike Battery Station, it's not a wide loading platform — it's a small slit of concrete bordering a staircase that leads up to an opening. Crumpled papers and old clothing litter the ground. Dark cement pillars hold everything together, covered in graffiti and vines. Exposed pipes run along the ceiling and drip with moisture. The handrail bordering the stairs barely hangs on. It's bent backward and dangling loosely over the platform, creaking in the rush of wind from the subway.

"When the doors open, I want all of you off as quickly as possible," Lieutenant Kelley orders. "No hesitation. Wait on the platform for my command. Understood?"

"Yes, sir!" we holler back.

As soon as the subway comes to a full stop, the doors swing open to release us, and the pager's vibration ceases. A gust of thick air slaps against my visor, fogging the plexiglass. I use my glove to wipe it away and clear my vision. Everything about this platform feels wrong, like somewhere we don't belong. Even though there's an opening above us, the sunlight barely reaches down here, making it look dark and sinister.

We step off the subway and onto foreign soil for the first time. Lieutenant Kelley leads us to the base of the stairs, where he does a quick headcount. Within minutes, the subway peels out of the station, sweeping up a cloud of dust and loose particles all around us.

I watch with dread as it disappears into the tunnel, leaving us here. Alone on the platform. A hundred miles from home.

"Eyes up here," Lieutenant Kelley barks. Even through the helmet, his voice resonates throughout the vacant station, filling the silence as the whir of the subway fades.

"The train will circle back to get us in a couple hours," he says. "Until then, the rules are simple: Only retrieve items that are salvageable.

Today, we're looking for any protective gear, weapons, loose ammo, or communication devices. You can use these to collect your items."

He tosses each of us a flimsy canvas sack that's nothing more than a battered pillowcase. Its coarse fabric is frayed and worn thin from years of use. One wrong tug and the whole thing looks ready to tear apart. I fold mine into a narrow strip and drape it over my shoulder.

"We'll stockpile them near the station and load everything onto the train when it returns. Remember: Stay close, stay alert, and do *not* disobey my commands. If one of you gets left behind, you better hope The Truth gets to you before I do."

Every draftee stares back with sober eyes. His statement would be somewhat witty if it weren't for the fact that out here, The Truth is a very real threat.

On his command, we follow him up the stairs toward the opening. My heart races as we breach the surface, but I keep my head down, too afraid to look up. As soon as my feet leave the last step, I slowly lift my eyes — and nothing prepares me for what I see.

The first thing that strikes me is the silence. An eerie quiet fills the entire city. I quickly remind myself we're the only living things out here. Everything else is dead and has been for nearly two decades now. Large heaps of rubble and twisted metal lay all around us. A thick orange haze hovers over it all, making the air look toxic. Any buildings that still stand are completely gutted and stripped down to their structural bones. It hardly looks like a city at all — it's one massive nightmarish landfill.

My blood runs cold. The damage is evident in New York, but this is something else. Something much worse. I don't know how anything could be salvaged from a place like this.

We advance further into the city. The deeper we go, the more severe the damage gets. Old cars are sunken into the ground. Their tires are melted, sticking to the asphalt like chewed gum. Huge slabs of concrete are ripped up from the earth, cluttering the path. The five of us zigzag behind Lieutenant Kelley, who constantly shifts our course to avoid them.

We march on for several minutes before Lieutenant Kelley stops. To our left is a high-rise that seems to be in decent condition. It sits wedged between two other buildings that sag and hold it in place. At the front of the building, a couple mannequins stand in a fractured display case. Their white plastic exteriors are peeling in places, distorting their shape. One of them is missing its head. Lowering my eyes, I find it lying at the foot of another with a bullet-sized hole between its eyes.

Lieutenant Kelley puts his back to the entrance and lifts his visor. "This is where we'll be today," he states. "Pay attention to your pagers, and don't wander off. You have exactly two hours to see what you can find and return with it to me. I'll be right outside the whole time."

"Yes, sir," we murmur. All of us stiff with fear.

Ethan grabs my shoulder and pulls me toward the building. We file in close behind the other draftees. Inside, the space widens into what used to be a department store. There are several racks of clothing that look untouched, but others that have been stripped bare. I notice the display case is busted open from the inside. Jagged edges of broken glass bordering its frame catch in the sunlight. A layer of dust covers the tiled floors, thick enough that my boots leave clear prints. I wonder how long it's been since someone stepped foot in here.

Lieutenant Kelley stands guard outside. His head turns on a swivel, looking left and right, scanning the street. His weapon is drawn and clutched closely at his side, but it doesn't make me feel protected. If anything, it heightens my awareness that out here, we're vulnerable to The Truth.

Apollo and Dom split off to the right. They begin sifting through a few drawers behind an old cash register. Leo goes left, leading his own charge.

Ethan pauses in front of a lifeless escalator in the center of the room, leading to an upper level.

"Want to head upstairs?" he suggests.

I scan the main level, watching as Leo vanishes into a side room while Apollo and Dom deposit a few small items into their bags.

"Sure," I say half-heartedly.

Ethan steps onto the escalator first. As he shifts his weight, the entire mechanism releases a loud groan that pierces through the silence.

Both Ethan and I freeze. Instinctively, I reach for my holster, ready to draw my gun.

"Cut it out!" Apollo hisses.

"Sorry," I whisper, shooting Ethan a cautious glance. "We're going to head up here. You know, cover more ground."

Apollo narrows his eyes, then lets out a sharp huff through his nose. He turns back to Dom, and the two of them continue surveying the area.

Ethan ascends the escalator in slow, calculated movements. I follow behind him, keeping my hand on my holster.

At the top, we reach a landing that wraps around the escalator bay. Looking around, there's an assortment of furniture on display, staged to model different rooms. Each item is wrapped in plastic wrap and coated with dust.

The store seems to flow into a much larger space. I walk ahead of Ethan and peer out at the opening. There are no exterior windows, so the majority of the space is shrouded in darkness. But from what I can tell, there are other storefronts lined along an interior foyer. Barred metal doors are pulled down over their entrances and bolted to the ground, preventing anyone from getting in. Vines creep along the walls and twist around pillars, making the shopping center look like a jungle.

Out of nowhere, a bright light hits the side of my face. I yelp and lift my hands to shield myself from it. The beam moves, and there's Ethan — grinning as the culprit.

"W-what are you doing?" I stammer.

The light shuts off. In his hand, Ethan holds a long black flashlight. "Can you believe this still works?"

I lift my visor to examine it. "Where did you find that?"

Ethan nods vaguely to the left. "Buried back there, along with some other stuff."

He peers past my shoulder and out into the foyer. He reactivates the flashlight, casting the beam across the open space. As the light sweeps over the walls, my eyes catch on a message spray-painted in red: Defend the City. Ethan notices it too. He grits his teeth and turns back to me, the flashlight still illuminating the words.

"Hate to say it, but they failed," he says grimly.

His arm twitches, and the light moves to an unlit exit sign above a push door. As soon as he sees it, his eyes widen. "C'mon," he urges me. "Let's go see what else we can find."

He motions for me to follow him. The door opens without any effort, revealing a stairwell on the other side. Ethan throws a curious look over his shoulder and raises his brow. He steps through the door, making the decision for us both to head upstairs. I groan, hesitant to follow him. But I know I have to. I can't let him go on his own, and I don't want to be left alone here either. With one last look around the foyer, I step through and follow him up the stairs.

The stairwell dead-ends at the top. Bolted to the wall is a rusted ladder leading to a hatch in the ceiling. Ethan shines the flashlight on it, and I notice the hatch door is slightly warped. He clicks off the light and slides it into his pocket, then reaches for the first rung.

I grab his shoulder before both feet leave the ground. "Ethan, wait," I caution.

He furrows his brows. "How come?"

I glance down the stairwell, which is nothing more than a shadowy void, then back up at the hatch. I think back to the other buildings we passed on our way here. How unstable they were. How it seemed like at any moment, they could come crashing down. All it'd take is one wrong move.

"What if it doesn't hold?" I throw my eyes up the ladder. "The roof, I mean."

"Are you calling me fat?" he snaps, then breaks into laughter. He lets go of the ladder and jumps down. The landing beneath our feet shudders, and both our eyes grow wide in concern.

"See?" I start. "The building could cave in at any moment. How do we know if it'll hold?"

Ethan considers this for a moment, then shrugs. "There's only one way to find out."

With his mind made up, he scurries up the ladder. When he reaches the hatch, he pounds his fist against it, sending the door flying off its hinges. I hear it thud against the surface above us.

Sunlight pours in through the opening, casting a spotlight down on the stairwell. Ethan pulls himself through to the other side and disappears, then returns with a thrill in his eyes.

"Come on up, Johnny!" he hollers down at me. "It's safe!"

I guess I don't have much of a choice. I reach for the ladder and pull myself up. Once my hands find the roof, I press my palms flat and push through the opening. My body rolls across the gravel rooftop, the padding in my vest absorbing most of the impact.

Ethan stands a few feet away with his back to me. His hands are clutched at his hips, and his neck is strained up toward the sky.

Rising to my feet, I take in the aerial view of the dilapidated city. The buildings seem to fall into each other like dominoes. The haze covers the streets below us like a layer of polluted clouds. The devastation stretches on for miles, all the way to the banks of a river. Trash and other debris bob in the browning water. From this angle, I can make out the metal frame of a collapsed bridge jutting out from the surface. The ramps it used to connect to hang over the edge on both sides, never to meet again.

"Does the sky feel bigger to you out here?" Ethan asks.

Lifting my eyes, I don't notice a difference. "It's hard to tell," I admit.

Ethan grabs the sides of his helmet and pops it off his head. In a panic, I rush toward him. "Ethan, don't!" I yell.

His eyes widen in shock. His face contorts, and he sucks in a sharp breath. His fingers claw at his throat. For a moment, I think he's suffocating, the toxicity in the air poisoning him.

But before I can reach him, his face softens, and he howls with laughter. "You should've seen the look on your face!"

"Dude, c'mon," I shove him. "That wasn't funny."

"No, it was *very* funny," he chuckles. "The air is just fine."

"Lieutenant Kelley said we need to keep our gear on at all times," I remind him.

"Psh," Ethan scoffs. "Lieutenant Kelley isn't up here, is he? Take off your helmet, man. Stay a while."

Reluctantly, I remove my helmet and set it beside Ethan's. We find a spot to settle for a while near the hatch. Reaching into my pack, I pull out the water canteen and take a sip. Below us, everything is still. Almost as if Ethan and I are the only ones left in the city.

After some time, we slide on our helmets and descend the ladder. Once we reach the landing, we make our way back down the stairs.

With two flights left, something stops us dead in our tracks — the sound of a door opening. Peering over the railing, I see a lower door fly open. It slams against the wall with a thud, sending a thunderous echo throughout the stairwell. Ethan reaches for his holster and looks back at me. Both of us hold our breath, waiting to see what happens next.

"Don't move," I whisper.

Footsteps rush down the stairs a few levels below us. All of a sudden, something hits the ground. Hard. The noise ricochets off the walls as if something were rolling down the stairs, ending with one final thud. I hear someone grunt, then the stairwell falls silent.

Ethan's eyes don't leave mine. His hand hovers an inch above his gun. With his other hand, he lifts his visor.

"Leo?" he calls out.

I punch him hard in the shoulder and retreat a few steps up in a panic.

"What's your deal, man?" Ethan whispers. "It could be one of us."

"Or it could be something else," I snap. I lift my own visor and narrow my eyes at him.

Ethan considers this, then peeks over the railing. "Apollo?" he calls out again. "Dom?" But he's met with silence. Neither of us moves.

"We have to go down there," he decides.

"No, we don't."

"It was clearly a person, John. They must've fallen. They could be hurt."

"I don't care," I spit out. *No, that's not true*, I think. "I don't . . . I didn't mean that. I just—" my mind spirals. We're two flights away from where we need to go, and whoever came bursting through that door is at least another two flights down. In the amount of time it'd take us to reach the door, whoever it was could easily intercept our path.

"What if something was chasing them? Why else would they have come through the door like that?" I add. My mind reels with every worst-case scenario.

Ethan doesn't budge. He's braver than I am. When it comes to people — even if they're not his favorite people — he'll do whatever it takes to get to them.

It's one thing when it's a simulation or a dummy in the shooting range, but this is outside the bounds of what I'm comfortable with. This is not what I'm trained for.

Actually, it's exactly what I'm trained for.

I stare back at Ethan for another minute. With a shudder, I suppress my fear. I lower my visor and draw my gun, holding it steady as we go.

We creep down the stairs with caution, wincing at every preventable noise. As we pass the second-level door, I stare at it longingly. This could be our escape. We've made it here, now all we have to do is push through the door, hobble down the escalator, and we're safe. The rest of our unit will be there, and we can call on them for backup.

But Lieutenant Kelley trained us to fight for each other. And Ethan's right — if it's one of us down there, we can't leave them behind. The longer we do, the more susceptible they are to The Truth.

I round the corner of the lower landing first, and Ethan follows behind me, gun in one hand and flashlight in the other. I grip my weapon with both hands as we approach the last flight of steps, ready to fire.

But there, at the bottom of the stairs, lying in a heap on the ground, is a girl. Her blonde hair is pulled back into a ponytail, and her shirt is tattered. Blood drips from a gash on her forehead, pooling around her neck. Her arms are sprawled out in front of her, and just inches from her fingers lies a large hunting knife.

Ethan clicks off the flashlight and grips my shoulder, stopping me. But something takes over me. I push out of his grasp and rush to the girl's side. Dropping to my knees, I slide the gun back into my holster and pull her onto her back. I can't believe what I'm seeing. I don't even know what exactly I'm seeing, or what it means, but one thing's clear — she's not one of us. She's another person. And she's here.

"Oh no," Ethan stammers. "No, no, no." He drops his gun, and it clatters to the floor. The sound is ear-splitting, but the girl doesn't flinch. She's clearly unconscious, but she's breathing. She's alive.

"Ethan, we have to help her," I say. Scanning her body, it seems the only blow was to her head, most likely from the fall.

"Where was this chivalry a few minutes ago?" Ethan shouts. "When we thought it might be one of us?"

"I don't know, man. This is different." My body kicks into overdrive. Nothing else matters anymore. The hesitation I felt before, Lieutenant Kelley, the rest of our unit. None of it. Because if she's here, and she's alive, then maybe . . .

"This is not good," Ethan interjects. He pulls off his helmet and sets it at his feet, rubbing his head in disbelief.

"Do you know what this means?" I ask, raising my voice. "She's alive, Ethan. She's here. There's someone else out here."

His expression hardens. "I know what you're thinking. But it's not— we can't, *she* can't—"

A sudden vibration cuts him off. Glancing down, I see both our pagers buzzing with green light. Panic sears across his face.

I rip off my helmet and toss it aside. Carefully, I wrap my arms around the girl's back and hoist her up into a seated position. Her body sags against mine, lifeless, though I can still feel the rhythm of her lungs fighting to breathe.

"Ethan, please," I beg. "We don't know what this could mean. And besides, we can't just leave her here."

"John," his voice tenses, and for maybe the first time in his life, he's dead serious. "There's nothing we can do here. We have to get back to our unit right now." He tears the blinking pager from his belt and thrusts it in front of my face.

From two levels above us, I hear a voice call out, "Madoc! Greene!" Lieutenant Kelley's voice.

"We're down here!" I scream.

Ethan slaps his hand over my mouth, silencing me. "Are you out of your mind?"

I shove him off me. "What do you mean? She needs help!"

"John, we have to go," Ethan shrieks. "Right now!"

I hold his stare, silently pleading. "I'm not going anywhere without her."

Ethan drags his hands down his face. He stands and begins pacing, trying to think of how he can reason with me. But I'm not budging.

After a moment, he stops, picks up his gun, and extends a hand to me. "Fine, then she's coming with us. But we need to get moving. Now."

I take his hand and jump to my feet. Together, we peel the girl off the ground. We drape one of her arms over Ethan's shoulder and the other over mine, both of us wrapping our arms around her back for support. Her bloodied head droops to the side, and her feet drag limp beneath her. When we reach the second level, we kick through the door and scramble toward the escalator. As soon as we're down, we glance around for Apollo, Dom, Leo — anyone. But there's no one.

We burst through the front doors and into the city. The pager vibrates uncontrollably, a horrible reminder of the subway's impending departure. Ethan gives me a panicked look, but I remain calm, determined to make it. I imagine myself back in New York, gearing up for a run. In my mind, the pager becomes Lieutenant Tillman's stopwatch — just another method of tracking our pace. I take myself there mentally and pick up my feet, bolstering as much upper body strength as possible to support half the girl's weight.

Ethan keeps up with me, and together, we rely on memory to carry us back to the station. Just as my shoulder starts to grow numb, I spot the opening in the ground and the warbled staircase leading down to the station. I point at it with my free hand and holler at Ethan to keep pushing. *We're almost there*, I tell myself. *Just a little further*.

Sprinting as fast as we can, we reach the edge of the stairs and descend into the station. I can still hear the whir of the subway below us, indicating it's still there. The girl's feet smack against every step, her body sagging further in our grasp, but we keep going. We spring from the last step and round the corner, expecting to find Lieutenant Kelley and the others, but they're gone.

We arrive just in time to see the subway peel out of the station, watching as it slithers around the corner and out of sight. Instantly, both our pagers stop buzzing, and the eerie silence lingering throughout the city returns.

Ethan and I release the girl and rest her against one of the pillars nearby. He turns to me with a white-hot ferocity in his eyes that terrifies me, but not nearly as much as the reality that's only now sinking in.

We missed it. We missed our only ride back to the city, leaving us here. Alone. A hundred miles from home with no other way of getting back. In a city rampant with The Truth.

Left to fend for ourselves.

Thirteen

Dusk falls over Philadelphia. We manage to find an old apartment building nearby that's suitable enough to hide out in. Ethan and I carry the girl up several flights of stairs until we reach the top floor. We figure the higher we are, the safer we'll be from anything lurking in the city tonight.

It takes a few tries before we agree on a room that's worth staying in. At the end of the hall, we find a small one-bedroom unit with a shabby couch and worn mattress, both of which are still intact. The windows along the back wall overlook the river. A chip in the glass lets in a thin stream of cool air, making the apartment frigid. But it's the best we've got.

By the time we reach the bedroom, my shoulder burns from carrying the girl for as long as we have. Ethan and I delicately lay her on the mattress. As we transfer her weight onto the bed, relief soothes my muscles. I use the hem of my shirt to wipe sweat from my forehead and take a minute to catch my breath.

I glance over at Ethan. His eyes are downcast as he removes his gloves. He balls them up and sets them on the table beside the bed, then buries his face in his hands. We've hardly said a word to each other since leaving the station — nothing more than what was necessary to navigate here, at least. Neither of us has acknowledged that we're stuck here, and that given we make it back to New York, the training officers will have our heads.

The girl lies still on the bed. By now, the blood has dried on her forehead, and the skin is already starting to bruise. She appears to be around our age, if not a couple years older. Her blonde hair is pulled back from her face, tucked against the pillow. She has a small build, and aside from the bruising, her skin is porcelain. Her chest rises and falls weakly, but it's steady. Enough to know she's still alive.

I start to approach Ethan, but he holds out a hand, keeping me at a distance.

"Don't," he says through gritted teeth.

"Ethan, I—"

"Just *don't*," he snarls. He lifts his face out of his hands, revealing bloodshot eyes that are full of fear. My stomach pinches with guilt. I'm the one who got us into this mess. But I'm determined to get us out.

In one swift motion, Ethan grabs my shoulder and ushers me out of the room. He closes the door gently behind us, careful not to disturb the girl.

We move to the center of the living room, as far away from the door as possible. Ethan closes his eyes and purses his lips, trying to gather his thoughts before he speaks.

But I can't stand the silence. I decide to talk first, which only makes things worse. "Ethan, let me just say—"

"No," he silences me. "You've said enough. Do you have any idea what you've gotten us into?"

I glance back and forth between him and the bedroom door. "We may have just saved someone's life."

"Well, we may as well have lost ours!" he yells. He holds a fist to his lips, trying to control his temper. Tears begin to pool in his eyes. I stand stiff, knowing nothing I say will help calm him.

"You're top of the ranks, John. You're supposed to be a *role model* for the rest of us," he hisses. "And what, you decide to throw it all away? For a girl who, for all we know, might not even wake up?"

"I didn't ask to be ranked number one, man," I say defensively.

"Oh, is that right?" he scoffs. "Looks like we both got something we didn't want then."

He paces around the room, moving in and out of the moonlight seeping in through the broken window.

"Look, we just need to wait here until the pagers go off again, then we'll be on the next train out of here," I say.

Ethan shakes his head. "If only it were that simple, John. And what do we do with her? Take her with us?"

"You seemed on board with that earlier."

He throws his hands up. "Because I didn't have a choice! You're out of your mind, John, if you think we can just waltz back into the facility with a half-dead girl and expect everyone to welcome her in with open arms. It's bad enough we weren't on that train, let alone if we show up with someone who wasn't supposed to be out here in the first place."

"But she was!" I interject. "That's the whole point. Don't you see? We've been told all this time we're the only ones left. But this defies that. We could bring her back, tell them about her, and maybe they'll go looking for others. And if there are others, think of what that could mean. Think of my father, Ethan."

"Maybe that's true, or maybe they won't want to go looking for others," Ethan says. "What if there's something wrong with her? I mean, did you ever consider that? We don't know what The Truth is, John. We don't know what it looks like, we don't know if she's bait, we don't know if—"

"I guarantee The Truth isn't a teenage girl," I mutter.

Ethan straightens his glare, ready to snap at me. But to my surprise, he doesn't. He pauses, then lowers his voice. "Look, John. Either way, this doesn't end well for us. By now, everyone is back in the barracks, probably talking about how stupid we are for missing the train. Lieutenant Kelley and Lieutenant Tillman are probably scrambling to figure out what to do and how they'll punish us *if* we ever make it back. Meanwhile, we're just sitting ducks, waiting for the pager to buzz and hoping we actually make it back this time — with or without the girl. We don't even—" he stops, covering his mouth with a shaky hand.

"We don't even know what we're up against," his voice breaks. He glances out the window at the darkened remnants of the city.

Anxiety burns in my chest. I know I've put us in a potentially dangerous situation, but I can't shake the feeling I had when I first saw the girl. I understand Ethan's concern — maybe this is a trap. Maybe she's bait for something much worse. But what if she's not? What if she's been out here, on her own, this whole time? And if that's the case, we have to help her. She deserves more than to be abandoned here.

"Okay, here's what we're going to do," I start. My mouth moves faster than my brain, and before I can keep up, I've committed to something I'm not entirely sure I'm ready for. "I'll run back to the station, trace the path, and double check it's doable in five minutes. And if it's not, we can move someplace closer before it gets too late. You stay here with the girl and take care of her. We have first-aid kits in our packs, right? Maybe there's something in there we could use to treat her wound."

Ethan's eyes grow wide. "I'm not staying here by myself with—"

"Ethan," I cut him off. "You have a gun. And you know how to use it, don't you?"

He crosses his arms, the realization dawning on him that he has the upper hand in this situation. "I guess so, yeah," is all he gives me.

"Then you'll be just fine," I tell him. "You can defend yourself, and ideally, I won't be gone more than ten minutes. Five minutes there, five minutes back. That's all it should take."

He seems to accept this. Kneeling down, I slide off my pack and pull it open. Inside, there's a small rectangular kit with a red label that reads FIRST AID. Opening it up, I find an adhesive bandage, a few cotton balls, and a small bottle of hydrogen peroxide. I hand the contents to Ethan, but he resists.

"Be my guest," he says. "You got us into this mess, you treat her. Then you can go, and I'll watch her."

I sigh, knowing he's right. I can't force him to be responsible for her. It's my job to take care of her, just like it's my job to get us out of here. All I can ask him to do is trust me.

Timidly, I push open the bedroom door with the first-aid contents in hand. The girl still lies in the same spot we left her. I tiptoe to the side of the bed and take a seat next to her. Carefully, I slide the cap off the bottle of hydrogen peroxide and dampen a cotton ball with it. It quickly soaks through, creating a soggy spot in the center. I dab it against her wound and watch the blood start to dissipate.

Once the wound is sterilized, I quietly holler for Ethan. He appears in the doorway with his arms crossed and eyes narrowed, judging me.

"Could you hand me the canteen out of the pack?" I ask. He obeys, but not without an annoyed huff.

He hands it to me, and I place it on the bedside table. In case she wakes up while I'm gone, I want to make sure she has something to drink. The table wobbles from the weight of the canteen, and I notice a dense crack splintering through the wood. It's not stable, but it'll hold.

I glance around the room for anything else I can use to clean the wound. Across from the bed, there's a set of double folding doors, slightly ajar to reveal a closet.

I cross the room and pull back the doors. To my surprise, there are still some clothes hanging inside. I rip a plain T-shirt off its hanger and fold it over a few times to form a small square. Then, I reach for the canteen and wet the shirt. I gently rub the damp fabric across her forehead, cleaning the hydrogen peroxide and grime, then apply an adhesive bandage to cover the gash.

A strand of hair falls out of place and curls against her chin. As I look down at her, my mind flashes back to the day in the ring with Apollo. Visions of a faceless figure rushing toward me. Blonde hair glinting in the sunlight, framing its face. The same way hers does now. I find myself staring too long at her eyes. Somehow, I know when they open, they'll be as blue as mine. Ethan catches me staring and scoffs. I flinch, suddenly remembering he's still there.

"Don't tell me you have a crush on her too," he scowls.

"No, it's not that. It's—" I stop myself. "I don't even know her. Right now, I'm just focused on making sure she's okay and getting us back home."

"Right," he says flatly. He turns to leave the room, but I linger a moment longer. *Where did you come from?* I think, brushing the hair back behind her ear. *How do I know you?*

I exit the bedroom and rejoin Ethan in the living room. The air seeping in through the window has turned the apartment into an ice box. Ethan sits on the ground with a dusty blanket wrapped around his body, clutching his knees to his chest. Without his gear on, he looks like a scared little boy. Cowered in the corner of the room, clutching his blanket to keep warm. Desperate to find his way home.

I suppose that's how I look too. Because deep down, I'm terrified.

I check the clip of my gun to ensure it's loaded. Moonlight gleams off a stack of copper bullets loaded to the brim. I shove it back in place and slide it into my holster.

"Five minutes there, five minutes back," I repeat to Ethan. "If I'm not back in that amount of time—"

"Don't even say that," he cuts me off. His eyes lift to mine, and all the anger they held before has fallen away. "I can't take that. You'll be back."

I smile softly at him. "I will be."

"Here," he says, extending his hand through the blanket. I can barely make out what he's holding. "Take this."

The cool metal rod of the flashlight lands in my palm. I click it on once, then turn it off again, checking that it still works.

"Thanks, man," I acknowledge. Ethan nods and pulls his hand back under the blanket to keep warm.

"I'll keep an eye on her, don't worry," he reassures me. And I trust him.

Turning away from him, I pull the front door open and step into the hallway. Instantly, I draw my gun and clutch it close to my body, along with the flashlight. My hands tremble from the cold, but I do my best to keep a steady grip.

Here goes nothing, I think.

Five minutes is all it should take, otherwise we'll have to find another place to camp out for the night. In double that time, I'll be back in the apartment with Ethan and the girl.

What could go wrong?

The hallway is illuminated by a red exit sign hanging over a door at the opposite end. The light is fickle, but it's enough to guide me there. I push through to the stairwell and slowly creep down the steps. I pay attention to every footstep, every sound and inadvertent thud my boots make. Turning on the flashlight, I shine it over the railing, checking to make sure the lower levels are clear. Once I'm sure, I continue down until I reach the ground floor.

I step out into the lobby of the apartment building. In the light of the flashlight, it's haunting. The old service counter is crawling with spiders that scatter when the light touches them. Vines spread across the walls. To my right, the elevator shaft is wide open, nothing more than a bottomless void carved into the wall. I hurry through the main entrance and out into the street, where the moon holds enough light for me to see without the flashlight. I tuck it away in my pocket and grip the gun with both hands, giving it more stability.

How Ethan and I got here is a blur, and I know it'll be even more difficult to navigate at night. But I have to try. I start to count in my head and take off down the path to the right. *One, two*, I count off, keeping track of how much time has elapsed.

I run alongside the river for about two blocks before veering right again. I jump over a heap of rubble blocking the path and squeeze between two buildings. My shadow dances along the walls in the moonlight, like a ghost passing through. Eventually, I come to the end of the alley and turn left. I notice an old convertible with its windshield shattered, its blue paint discolored from rust. The tires are blown out on all four sides and melted down to the asphalt. I make a mental note of it — *turn left out of the alley, past the blue convertible* — and continue running.

The moon falls behind a sheath of clouds, prompting me to pull out the flashlight. I stop for a moment to make sure I haven't lost count. *A minute 33, a minute 34*, I count off. My eyes examine every possible avenue for where to go next. The apartment building wasn't more than four blocks from the station, but it wasn't a straight shot either. I hang another right at the next intersection, where the buildings expand and the path widens.

I run for another block, then squeeze through another alley to my left. When I pop out on the other side, my flashlight finds an opening in the ground, leading down beneath the street. Right where I expected it to be. "Bingo," I say aloud.

I dart across the street to the top of the steps. *Two-38, two-39.* I hobble down the stairs, and when I reach the bottom, the stopwatch in my head clocks in at two minutes and forty-five seconds. I move the flashlight around to make sure it's the correct station. Between the graffitied cement pillars, the littered scraps, and the way the tunnel curves up ahead, everything matches up.

The flashlight starts to flicker. I slap it against my palm to keep it on, and thankfully, it works. It maintains the light for a while longer, but I decide it's probably best to conserve it for now.

Two minutes and forty-five seconds is all it takes. Just over half the amount of time we'd need to make it to the station. I linger on the platform for a moment longer in satisfaction before turning back toward the stairs.

As my foot strikes the first step, something crashes against the floor near the tunnel. My body freezes. I convince myself it was just me, and the noise must've echoed off the walls, making it sound distant. But then it happens again.

My legs spring into action. I take the steps two at a time, rushing upward until I'm back above ground. I spin around and face the opening with my gun aimed, waiting for something to emerge. But nothing does. The city grows eerily quiet again, but I know I heard something. I know I'm not alone.

I silently retreat back through the alley, walking backward with my gun pointed toward the station. I wait until it's out of view before turning around, then take off. I sprint as fast as I can, my arms slicing through the air. I fly through the intersection and pass the old convertible. As I do, I hear something shuffle behind me. Everything in me screams to keep moving, but I halt. I spin around and click on the flashlight, sending a beam of light through the convertible, shining beyond its busted windows.

There, on the other side of the street, is a blur of movement in the light. It takes me a moment to register what I'm seeing — and to determine if it's actually real or not. The outline of a person is visible for only a second before it moves out of the light. I shine the flashlight right, left, and all over the surrounding buildings, trying to find it again. But it's nowhere to be found.

But I know it was there. Watching me. Stalking me.

I click off the flashlight and break into a sprint again. Adrenaline propels me through the last two blocks. As soon as I reach the apartment, I barrel through the front entrance and straight to the stairwell. My body flies up the stairs in a panic. Even though I haven't bothered to look back, I get the chilling sense that whatever it is, it's right on my heels.

I sprint about halfway up before pausing on the landing. Noticing the silence in the stairwell, I wonder if I've managed to outrun it. I grip the railing and peer over the side, staring down into the shadowy void. For a moment, I think I'm in the clear. Then the door two levels below bursts open.

Something scurries up the stairs. Fast. Much faster than my legs could carry me. I hear it slam into the landing at the top of the first flight — but it doesn't stop there. I race up the remaining few flights until I reach the top level. Pushing through the exit door, I sprint down the hallway. The exit sign behind me flickers, casting a red glow down the hall, just bright enough for me to make out the apartment numbers. I count them until I'm no more than a few doors away from our hideout, desperate to make it there.

Behind me, the stairwell door creaks open, and I freeze. The exit sign flickers off, and the whole hallway goes dark. I flip around and raise my gun, but it's barely visible in my grip. Maybe if I can't see my pursuer, it can't see me either.

I tiptoe backward, careful not to give myself away. I keep the gun pointed ahead with both hands coiled tightly around the grip. The exit sign blinks weakly again with red light, but when it does, it reveals nothing but an empty hallway. The stairwell door is ajar, but there's no movement. No sign of anyone else but me.

I keep my right hand sturdy around the gun and, with my left, pull the flashlight out of my pocket. Clicking it on, the beam soars to the end of the hall, scanning the open doorway. I know it's here. I can feel its presence lingering in the hallway with me. But the light never catches it.

Holding my breath, I lift the beam toward the exit sign. It scans over the ceiling like a searchlight, revealing damp spots that swell and drip with moisture. I move the light closer to where I stand, keeping it pointed upward, until it's just about overtop of me.

The light lands on a gray heap of rotted flesh clinging to the ceiling, dangling above me. Its body is suspended upside down, its head twisted at an unnatural angle. Its blood-red lips expand as the creature lets out a horrible screech. Every nerve in my body rises to the surface of my skin. My body locks up in shock. Its bony fingers dig into the ceiling for support, sending thick blood oozing from its fingernails. Its bone structure is that of a human, but its features are so subhuman, so canine, I almost don't believe what I'm seeing.

I don't shoot. I run for my life.

I take off down the hall in the opposite direction. All the while I can hear the creature's turbulent breath heaving through its chest. Its nails scrape against the wall as it climbs down from the ceiling. In a horrible thud, its body lands against the floor, and it gallops on all fours — heading straight toward me.

"Ethan!" I scream. I'm close enough now to see our apartment number etched in the door. All I have to do is make it there — but it's gaining on me.

"Ethan, open the door!" I cry out again. I don't know if there's time for me to fumble with the knob. I don't know if I'm even going to make it. In a split second, I prepare myself for the possibility that I might have to fight this thing off.

My hands grab the doorknob and push with all my might. But it doesn't budge. I shake the door violently, throwing my shoulder against it. Trying to force it open. The exit sign flickers again, illuminating the hallway in a hellish glow. The creature is much closer now. But the door won't open.

I bang my palms desperately against it, praying that Ethan is still on the other side. Praying that I'm in the right place, and I didn't get it mixed up. I drive my shoulder into the door again and the wood splinters, but still, it doesn't give.

Gritting my teeth, I stop trying to break down the door and turn toward the creature. I lift my gun out in front of me. My hands tremble around the grip. I try to steady it for a clean shot, but the creature isn't charging in a straight line — it's jumping all over the hall, springing off the walls. There's no guarantee I'll make the shot.

There's no guarantee it won't kill me first.

As my finger sinks into the trigger, a hand drops on my shoulder, and I tumble sideways through an open doorway. I crash hard into the ground. The gun falls out of my hands and slides across the floor. Ethan stands over me and shoves the door shut, mere seconds before the creature would've leapt to strike me. He presses his palms flat against the door and twists a small lock on the knob. He whips around, his eyes wide with fear.

"What's going on out there?" he shouts.

I spring up from the ground and shove him hard. "Did you lock the door?"

He shrugs his shoulders. "Yeah, it was just a safety precaution! A force of habit!"

"One that almost got me killed!" I yell back.

As soon as the words leave my mouth, a loud thud crashes into the door from the other side. The door rattles violently against its frame. Ethan and I both jump back, hoping the door will hold. The locked knob twists and shakes. I glance at Ethan in terror, and he stares back at me the same.

"What is that?" he shouts over the noise. "What's out there?"

I start to open my mouth, but another voice answers for me — one I don't recognize at first.

"Monsters," a feminine voice says behind us.

Ethan and I jerk around. Standing in the doorway of the bedroom is the girl. She's wrapped in a sheet from the bed, tracing her fingers along the adhesive bandage on her forehead. Even through the darkness, her blue eyes glisten. They dart back and forth between Ethan and me, searching for any hint of familiarity.

The banging on the door slows to a soft, repetitive thud, as if the creature is beating its head against it over and over. Ethan and I aren't even fazed by it anymore — we're both focused on the girl, staring back at her in amazement. So many questions flood my mind, but one thing's certain: We saved her. And now, she's conscious.

The girl's eyes continue to shift between Ethan and me. She lowers her hands from her head and stuffs them in the pockets of her jeans.

"Where are we?" she croaks. "What happened to me?"

Fourteen

AFTER A WHILE, THE banging on the door ceases. Ethan and I explain everything to the girl — from finding her at the bottom of the stairwell to missing the subway to hiding out in the apartment. She tries to process everything, but it's clear she's exhausted. She barely says anything before returning to the bedroom, where she remains for the rest of the night.

Sunlight rises over the city the next morning and drives out the shadows. Ethan stretches awake on the couch with a loud yawn. Turning toward him, I notice his eyes are bloodshot. Even though he got the most sleep out of both of us, it clearly wasn't enough. He smiles weakly at me, and I smile back. We made it through the night. Now we just have to make it home.

We creep into the bedroom to check on the girl and find her half awake. Her body is still wrapped in the same sheet as before. The door creaks, giving us away, and her eyes blink open. She lifts herself up and scoots against the bed frame, staring back at us hesitantly.

"How'd you sleep?" I ask.

She continues to stare back, her eyes alert and untrusting. "Well enough."

"Good," I say. "We're only going to have a small window of time to make it to the train today, so we'll need to muster up all the energy we have."

She takes this in, weighing my words in silence. She slides to the edge of the bed and lowers her feet to the floor. Peeking through the cuffs of her jeans, I spot more bruising on her ankles. But she stands unbothered, brushing off the dust that clings to her clothes.

"In your city, are there others?" she asks curiously.

"Yes," I say, a little too enthusiastically. "Tons more."

Her face lights up. At the same time, a muffled hum begins to emanate from my pocket. I reach inside and pull out the pager, which is alive with green light. One quick glance confirms Ethan's is too, still clipped to his belt. My heart races, and a hopeful grin spreads across my face.

"Well," Ethan starts, "that's our cue."

We gather our belongings and head toward the door. I stick my head out and scan the hallway, checking for any signs of the creature. But it's empty.

I signal to Ethan and the girl that it's clear. Together, we jog down the hall and push through the stairwell door. I glance over the railing and don't spot anything below us. The creature must've moved on at some point in the night. When we reach the ground floor, we shuffle through the lobby and find it vacant too. We continue toward the front entrance and out into the morning. Sunlight beats down on us, harsh and unrelenting. The girl winces, throwing an arm over her face.

"The light," she mutters. "It's making my head ache."

I look over at Ethan. "We better move quickly," I whisper.

"You lead the way," he replies.

We follow the same path I mapped out for us last night. Ethan takes the rear, keeping watch behind us, while I lead at the front. We easily clear the first couple blocks, then veer into an alley. Visions of last night play through my head. Frantically, I look over my shoulder to make sure we're not being followed. But the city seems just the same as when we first arrived — an empty shell.

Once we've cleared the old convertible, we squeeze past a few more buildings before the station comes into view. To my relief, the pager continues to rattle against my belt, providing more comfort than stress. We descend the stairs and burrow beneath the city. When we hit the platform, the subway is there. I let out a victorious cheer, and Ethan hollers back in response. The girl stares at the train in awe.

I jump on first and offer a helping hand to the girl, and she takes it. Her fingers feel like ice against my warm palms. Ethan hops on behind her. Instantly, we both sag into the seats, relieved to be on board. Neither of us were certain we'd ever be sitting on this train again, but we're here now — and that's what matters.

The girl paces up and down the aisle, taking it all in. "This . . ." she mumbles. "This has been down here the entire time?"

"As far as we know, yeah," I confirm. "It operates on its own between New York and a couple other locations, like Philadelphia. It'll take us back to our city."

Her eyes sparkle as she observes every little detail. "Incredible," she exhales.

The doors automatically slide shut. The train lurches forward, knocking the girl off balance into a nearby seat. She grabs one of the standing poles to stabilize herself.

"Forgot to warn you about that part," Ethan murmurs before I can apologize. She lets out a friendly chuckle, pushing her hair back into place.

Within seconds, the station disappears. Soft blue lights illuminate the subway car, and the screen flashes between its various views.

"We did it, man," I say to Ethan. "We're safe now."

"Yeah, well, let's enjoy the feeling while it lasts. It won't exactly be a cheerful homecoming for us when we get back to the facility," he reminds me.

"What do you mean?" the girl intervenes. Glancing over at her, she's sitting upright in her seat, leaned forward. Paying attention to every word.

Ethan passes the baton to me, but I'm not sure what to say. I don't want her to think we're luring her into a potentially bad situation — even though we could be. We told her we were taking her somewhere safe, where there are others. Others just like her. Which is true, but there's still so much she doesn't know. It's up to me now to decide how much she needs to know and what can wait.

"Well," I start, "as you know, Ethan and I were separated from our unit. We were supposed to be back in New York yesterday, but we missed our ride back because—"

"Because you saved me," she interrupts. Her eyes don't move from mine, buzzing with an attentive intensity. "I remember."

"Yes," I gulp. "So when we get back, they're not exactly going to be happy to see us. I mean, they'll be happy we're alive. *Surely*," I let out a nervous laugh. "But we could face some serious consequences for getting ourselves stuck out here overnight."

Ethan's eyes burn into my profile. I know what he wants me to say, but I can't say it. I can't tell the girl she won't be welcome in the city. She's trusted us this far. We took her in, cared for her, and offered to take her to a place that's much better. It may not be where she belongs, but it's better than Philadelphia. I don't want to risk losing that trust because of what *might* happen when we get back.

"Isn't there something else we could face serious consequences for, John?" Ethan sneers. I glare back at him and rub my hands nervously.

You jerk, I think. "Um . . ." I clear my throat. "Yeah, uh, and we could face some consequences for bringing you back too, I guess."

The girl raises her brow. "And yet, you're doing it anyway?"

Ethan chuckles and kicks up his feet on the seat across from him, letting me take the full brunt of her questions. And sure, I'm the one who got us into this mess, but he still played a part. He willingly kept watch over her while I was gone, and he didn't stop her from getting on the train. And when we get back, he'll be there too, standing before Lieutenant Kelley and Lieutenant Tillman the same as me.

Lieutenant Kelley and Lieutenant Tillman. My stomach twists as I picture their faces, the look of pure, unbridled rage seared on them.

"Dude, could you please quit acting like you're not a part of this too?" I blurt out.

Ethan shifts in his seat. He lowers his feet and leans forward. "I'm not the one who's grand plan this is. I'm just along for the ride."

I throw up my hands. "Yeah, but don't you think if the roles were reversed, I would've gone along with it for you? I wasn't the only one who missed their ride back to the city. *You* did too, even if it was my fault. But do you seriously think the training officers will point a finger at me and not you too?"

He leans back in his seat, humbled. I look over at the girl, who's fully engrossed in our argument.

"She makes a good point, though," Ethan credits her. "We know there will be consequences, yet here we are, and here *she* is. So what exactly is y—" he stops himself. I watch his lips form the word *your*, but he never actually says it.

"... *our* plan?" he says instead.

My eyes lift to the screen in the upper corner. The line we're traveling down — the purple line — connects to a location deeper in Manhattan. From there, the red line continues to Battery Station, meaning we're not headed straight for the facility. We have another stop to buy us some time.

"We'll get off at the next stop," I say definitively. "We'll find a place to house her. Then you and I will go back to the facility, and we'll go from there."

Ethan thinks on this for a moment but quickly accepts it. In reality, there's no other option. The only other option would be to go straight to the facility with the girl, bypass the stop in between, and risk putting her life in danger. Ethan and I don't have to say anything to know that's *not* an option worth considering.

"Sounds like a plan, Johnny," Ethan holds up his thumb. "Wake me when we get there." He reclines back against his seat and turns to the side, facing away from me and the girl.

I turn back to her, and instantly our eyes meet. The corners of her mouth twitch into a hopeful grin, and relief washes over me. She's on board.

"What's your name, by the way?" I ask, catching her off guard. But her face softens as it comes to mind, almost like recalling a fond memory.

"Daphne," she says sweetly.

The subway barrels along the rails until we reach the edge of New York. My eyes follow the blinking dot on the screen until we pass under the Hudson. As the dot reappears on the other side, I shake Ethan awake. He swats me away defiantly, but I persist.

"We'll be there any minute now," I alert him. "We need to be ready."

Daphne sits quietly at the opposite end of the car. Her eyes scan the tunnel walls as they blur past us. Soon enough, the pager begins to vibrate again. I prop a knee against my seat and look out the window as the station comes into view — and it's familiar.

It's the same station we were taken to the night of the draft.

As soon as the subway slows to a stop, the doors open. We hop out onto the platform and take a moment to get our bearings, checking to make sure we didn't leave anything behind on the train. Being here takes me back to that first night — standing with the other draftees, taking everything in for the first time. Scared and unsure, but fully present. Glancing at Daphne, it's the same way she feels now.

"We must be on the civilian side of the city," I tell Ethan. His eyes survey the station, and he begins to recognize it too. "This is where they first took us the night we were drafted."

"Your pager went off too? Again?" he asks, his focus now shifted to the pager still flashing on my belt.

I nod. "It's gone off every time the subway arrives at a nearby station. It happened when we first got to Philadelphia and before we left, and again just now."

Ethan seems pleased with this. "So we'll find her a place, wait for the pager to buzz again, then ride back to the facility."

"That's the plan," I confirm.

We ascend out of the station as the subway roars to life. It rushes forward into the tunnel, surely headed to the facility. Once it vanishes, the pager stops buzzing, and the dull blinking red dot returns to the corner of the device.

At the top of the stairs, my whole body sighs with relief. The buildings around us look familiar. A few blocks ahead, I can see the peaks of The Market's white tents. It feels good to be back on our home turf. Even though we're not out of the woods yet, it's comforting to know we're no longer susceptible to The Truth. Looking up, I start to understand what Ethan meant about the sky feeling bigger in Philadelphia. Even though I can't see it, I know the Barrier is there — and I never thought I'd be so happy to be under it.

Ethan and I assess our surroundings, trying to pinpoint the best place to house Daphne. We come to an agreement that it needs to be somewhere within a five-minute radius of the station, for when we come back. Assuming we'll be able to.

"Should we bring her to your mom's house?" Ethan asks.

"No, it's too risky. Even though Mother would take care of her, it's better if this is . . ." my voice trails off. Daphne spins around in circles where she stands, captivated by the city. The damage is still evident, but it pales in comparison to Philadelphia. Here, the buildings are still mostly intact, especially on the civilian side. Watching her take it in for the first time makes me appreciate the city more. It may not be perfect, but it's ours. And it's home.

I lean in close to Ethan, making sure Daphne's out of earshot. "It's better if this is just our secret, for now," I whisper.

Ethan agrees. We lay low and stay close to the station. We jog about two blocks south, where the population is more scarce. Most of our community lives north of The Market, and very few people reside on the south side, nearest the military border. We crouch in an alleyway, avoiding a few pedestrians, and dart across the street once it's clear. Right on the edge of the community, we find a slender apartment building, similar to where we stayed in Philadelphia. The lower level is dark green while the upper levels are a scrappy shade of white, with arched windows overlooking the street at every level. A few of them are broken, but the top two levels appear to be in good shape.

There's a fire escape connected to the exterior of the building. It leads all the way to the top, with a landing at each level. The lowest landing is slightly disjointed, but it's slanted enough for us to climb onto it from the sidewalk. Jumping up, I grab the edge with both hands. Using all my upper body strength, I hoist myself into a pull-up and squirm onto the landing. The metal groans beneath my weight, but it holds.

"Give her a hand," I holler down at Ethan. He opens his palms and allows Daphne to step into them for support. She reaches her arms up to me, and as soon as Ethan hoists her up, I pull her onto the landing. She tumbles onto her chest and scrambles to her feet, cowering against the building's exterior wall. With both of us standing on it, the landing bends downward even further. I place my palm flat against the wall for support, trying to stay balanced.

"Go ahead and move up a level," I tell Daphne. "Just to make room for Ethan. But wait for us up there."

She doesn't hesitate. She moves against the building to the base of the first set of stairs. Gripping the railing, she climbs up to the next level and peers down, waiting for Ethan.

I extend a hand to Ethan, but he swats it away.

"Let's see if all those push-ups have paid off," he winks.

With a grunt, he grips both sides of the landing and pulls himself up. His forearms slam into the metal frame, and the whole platform shudders. It takes effort, but Ethan manages to wiggle his way onto the landing. Once he's up, he dusts off his hands and lets out a deep, satisfied breath.

"Piece of cake," he says, though his composure says otherwise.

"I never doubted you for a second," I affirm him.

Together, Ethan and I ascend the stairs to the next level. Once we're there, I slide in front of Daphne to take the lead. The further we go, the more secure the landings are, allowing us to move across them with ease. We climb up to the fifth level, where the building appears to be the most untouched. The stairs drop off once we reach the top landing, where there's a vertical ladder connected to the side of the building, leading to the roof.

Tall arched windows frame a pair of French doors, which open onto the landing. I press my palm to the cool glass, and to my surprise, the doors give way. They reveal a living room on the other side, fully furnished but seemingly vacant. Stepping into the room, I take a quick look around, then motion for Daphne and Ethan to come in.

"Anyone home?" Ethan calls out, but there's no response. He shrugs, and we agree this will work.

A cherry-red sofa is pressed against the wall to the left, with a round chestnut coffee table in the center of the room. In the corner, a spindly lamp stands between the couch and a stiff tan armchair. The walls are undecorated, and the floor is spotless. Every bristle of the carpet is perfectly aligned and untouched, as if it's never been walked on.

The room flows into a small kitchenette, with white appliances and pale cabinetry. A bar top juts into the living room, meshing the two spaces — much like the one in my own home — and two swiveling barstools are tucked beneath the overhanging counter. To the right, an open doorway leads into a small bedroom with a conjoined bathroom. A full-size bed rests against the wall, leaving space for one of the windows beside it, which fills the room with natural light. Salmon sheets are pulled tightly around the corners of the mattress, and a plaid quilt lays over it like a comforter.

"They must've blocked this off for community housing," Ethan guesses. "But it doesn't look like it's ever been lived in."

"Maybe it hasn't," I add. "Maybe they were saving it, in case they needed more space. Like some sort of community expansion."

Daphne wanders into the bedroom and disappears into the bathroom. A few seconds later, the sound of rushing water roars throughout the apartment, startling Ethan and me.

"Eeep!" Daphne exclaims. She rushes out of the room with a giddy smile lighting up her face. "There's running water here!"

Ethan and I exchange a look, but we don't dull the moment for her. "This should be good for you, for now," I say. "Go ahead and make yourself at home. Ethan and I will head back to the station and wait for the subway."

"When will you be back?" she asks. Her smile fades into a look of concern. Her words are piercing — there's no guarantee we *will* be back.

But deep down, I know there's a way. I'll find a way.

I wet my lips nervously. Lifting my eyes to her, I muster up as much optimism as I can. "Soon," I reply. "We'll come back as soon as we can."

It's not a definitive answer, but it's enough for her. Daphne disappears back into the bedroom while Ethan and I remain in the living room.

"What are we going to do, John?" Ethan mutters.

I don't look at him. I keep my head down, afraid if I meet his eyes, he'll see right through me. "I don't know," I exhale.

Ethan steps out onto the landing, and I follow after him. But before I'm fully out, I hear footsteps approaching quickly behind me.

"Wait!" Daphne calls out. My head spins around. One foot on the landing, one foot still inside the apartment, I look at her. In the light seeping in through the open door, her blue eyes gleam. Something about them sends my heart racing. Like I've gazed into them before, maybe in another life. But there's so much about her that still feels out of reach. So much I have to learn, and so much to keep coming back for.

"Thank you," she says, "for saving me."

"Don't thank me yet," I reply, blushing.

I step fully onto the landing and pull the doors shut behind me. Ethan and I climb back down the way we came. We jump onto the asphalt below, then take off toward the station. Once we arrive, it takes some time before the subway returns. As our pagers buzz, I consider the possibility of going home. Being on this side of the city, I could easily slip away to Mother and Liam. I could hide in my bedroom, close my eyes, and pretend none of this ever happened — the draft, Philadelphia, Daphne. I could pretend it was all a dream, and when I wake up, I'd be seventeen again. Still a year out from the draft, but safe from it. Safe from the monsters outside the Barrier, naive to their existence, and safe from Lieutenant Kelley's scorn waiting for me back at the facility.

But I can't. Even if I tried, they'd come for me. And the consequences of that would be worse than anything Ethan and I have coming for us.

But for a split second, as the subway pulls into the station, the thought crosses my mind.

Ethan and I board the train and take our seats. One look at the screen confirms we're headed back to the facility. I pull my knees up to my chest and rest my chin against them, trying to think through what comes next. What will we say when we get back? How do we explain ourselves, without giving Daphne away? How will I come back to her? I need more time, but the subway is unforgiving. Within minutes, it's pulling into Battery Station, and the vault door comes into view through the windows.

Lifting my head, I find Ethan staring at me. It's clear he's been watching me the entire ride.

"I'm sorry, John," he apologizes. "We made a pact to stick together, and I lost sight of that out there."

"No, you didn't," I assure him. "You stuck by me, even when you didn't want to. Even when it went against your better judgment. That's more than I could've asked for."

He smiles, and I can tell it means a lot to hear me say that.

"Plus, I'm the one who should apologize," I continue as the subway slows to a halt. "I shouldn't have dragged you into this. I shouldn't have even—"

My words fall flat. Because as soon as the doors open, Lieutenant Kelley steps onto the train. The sound of his heavy boots crashing against the floor startles me, pulling me out of the moment with Ethan. His eyes are wide and ablaze with rage. He rips Ethan and me from our seats, his fingers digging into our shoulders. I wince in discomfort, which only makes him press harder.

"You two," he snarls. "You're coming with me."

Fifteen

Lieutenant Kelley throws Ethan and me into the chamber. As soon as we step in, smoke spills out from the walls, covering us in a thick cloud. Within seconds, the smoke dissipates, and green light fills the room — much to our relief. Lieutenant Kelley mumbles something under his breath, then grabs our shoulders again, forcing us through the door to the lower level.

At first, I wonder if he's just taking us back to our barracks. Waiting to deal with us until the morning while he contemplates our fate overnight. But no. He ushers us into the elevator, which is already open and vacant. The capsule quickly ascends to the main level. As soon as the doors reopen, he forces us into the atrium and toward the stairs. We fumble our way up to the cafeteria. *Maybe it's time for dinner?* After all, when we reach the top of the stairs, the upper level is filled with draftees and soldiers, all sitting at their respective tables.

But Lieutenant Kelley doesn't lead us to the buffet. Instead, he pulls us in the opposite direction, heading toward an unknown area to the right — away from everyone else.

Drew rises from a table near the back of the room. Carson's head spins around, and his eyes grow wide in surprise as they meet mine. My heart sinks seeing the empty bench across from them, knowing we'd be seated there if things were different.

"Sit back down, soldier!" Lieutenant Kelley screams. Instantly, Drew glues himself back to his seat, but he keeps his head turned over his shoulder.

This catches Leo's attention. He's mid-bite when he sees us, and the color drains from his face, as if he's seen a ghost.

"Aren't you happy to see us, Lieutenant?" Ethan tries to lighten the tension.

Lieutenant Kelley's head snaps to the side, straightening Ethan with a look. "Shut up," he spits at him. "You're lucky I don't strangle you right here myself."

Ethan gulps and shrinks beneath his grip.

We come to a large steel door sunken into the wall. Lieutenant Kelley slides his all-access badge along a scanner, and a muted click unlocks the door. He pulls it open and shoves us through. We enter into a sleek corridor similar to the lower level — only this one is slightly curved, as if tracing the outline of the facility. Small porthole windows are carved into the wall. Views of the training lawn flicker through the glass as we pass by.

The hall ends with another steel door. Only this one doesn't come with a scanner. Instead, there's a black pad positioned on the door where the knob should be, and a covered slit at about eye level. Lieutenant Kelley releases his grip from my shoulder to knock. Temporary relief washes over me, but he instantly grabs me again the minute his fist leaves the frame.

The slit is pulled back from the other side, revealing a pair of beady eyes staring back at us. They glance from Ethan to Lieutenant Kelley to me, then disappear. There's a loud fumbling of a lock, then the door swings wide. Standing on the other side is General Conrad. Up close, his age is much more evident in his cracked skin and cheeks that droop slightly below his jawline. He lifts his snakelike eyes to Lieutenant Kelley and smiles, pleased.

"I can't believe you actually got them," he exhales, then lowers his eyes to Ethan and me. "And you two were stupid enough to come back."

General Conrad steps aside, motioning for us to come in. My body stiffens, too afraid to move, but Lieutenant Kelley insists. He releases Ethan and me with a flick of his wrists, sending us flying forward.

We enter a room that feels more like a museum than an office. Built-in bookshelves line the room on both sides like literary sentinels, filled with an array of books. The majority are emerald green or a muted shade of crimson. Their spines are embroidered with gold, making them feel antique. Along the back wall, a fireplace is carved into the stone wall, though I doubt it works. It's more for aesthetics, if anything. Hung above the mantle is a large hunting rifle, cradled by two iron hooks shaped like antlers. But most striking of all is the flagpole tucked in the corner. It scales the full height of the room, which is easily double the height of the corridor we entered from. Draped from its peak is an old American flag. Its red and white stripes are singed and pale. The stars that were once embroidered in the blue corner are gone — all except one, still intentionally etched into the fabric.

Across from the fireplace is a glass box suspended over the training lawn. From this perspective, the entire facility is visible. I can see all the way through to the other side, where the draftees and soldiers sit in the cafeteria. Beyond the facility wall, the Freedom Tower looms in the distance, towering over the city. The box juts out from the rest of the room like a balcony, giving the general a panoramic view over everything.

In front of the box is a sturdy wooden desk, shaped like a crescent. A padded, throne-like chair is pushed into the inner curve of the desk, its high back turned toward the glass. Faced toward it from the other side of the desk are two stiff-backed chairs. Lieutenant Tillman is already seated in one. He stands as we approach, leaving them open for Ethan and me. Lieutenant Kelley doesn't hesitate. He forces us down, and our tired bodies slam into the rigid seats. Once we're seated, he clasps his hands around the back of our heads, holding our gaze forward.

General Conrad sweeps around the desk with the authority of a man who owns the room. His fingers brush over the polished wood. My heart races wildly in my chest, threatening to break through my ribs. He sinks into his chair and lifts his eyes. His gaze could burn a hole right through me.

"Gentlemen," he addresses us. Lieutenant Kelley and Lieutenant Tillman linger a few feet behind us like shadows. "Thank you for meeting me here."

Not like we had a choice, I sneer in my head. But I don't say a word. Ethan sits stiff against the chair, frozen in fear. He doesn't dare to make any sort of sarcastic quip in response.

The general leans back in his chair and presses his fingertips together. "You do understand the severity of what you did, don't you?"

Neither of us speaks again. I hear the sound of shuffling behind us, and before I can think, Lieutenant Kelley's elbow delivers a blow to the side of my head.

"Speak when you're spoken to, soldier!" he screams in my ear. I cry out, rubbing the spot that's now tender with pain.

"Yes, s-sir," I stutter. "Yes, we do."

But General Conrad doesn't seem convinced.

"Not only did you risk your lives by failing to obey orders, you risked the lives of everyone on the mission," he says. "It was Lieutenant Kelley's responsibility to ensure you made it onto that train. And it was your responsibility to find him when your pagers went off. By not doing so, you caused him to have to wait on you until the very last minute, which could've resulted in everyone missing the subway too."

The general rises to his feet. He begins pacing around the desk in the same manner he paces across the stage in the Assembly Hall.

He continues. "Every second you spend outside the Barrier, you're vulnerable. You're vulnerable to things that are outside of our control. And every moment you delayed reporting back to Lieutenant Kelley left everyone else vulnerable as well. Do you have any idea how selfish that is?"

His voice swells at the end of his question, rising in ferocity. He slams his hand into the desk, and Ethan and I both jolt in our seats.

"Was it deliberate?" he asks. He leans over the desk, as close as he can get to us. His eyes glance back and forth, waiting for one of us to break.

"No, sir," I mutter, my eyes downcast. "It was an accident."

This strikes a nerve with him. "An accident," he repeats. He throws his hands up and begins pacing again. "Right. Let's just wipe the slate clean then. It was an accident, we forgive you, and we can all take your word that it won't happen again. No!"

The power in his voice glues me to my chair. My hands tremble against the armrests. Somewhere in the back of my mind, I wonder if we would've been better off in Philadelphia. I'm more afraid sitting here, in front of the general, than I was last night with that creature. At least I had a way to defend myself then. But here, we're General Conrad's chew toys.

"You were distracted," he accuses us. "There's no such thing as an accident in war. Your actions are either deliberate, or you're distracted. That's it. And any distraction will get you killed."

He slithers back into his chair. A malicious grin grows across his face, and he opens his palms to us.

"So, tell us," he says softly. It chills me how quickly he can switch from red-hot anger to instant composure. "What was so important that it distracted you from the mission?"

Out of the corner of my eye, I see Ethan's head twitch in my direction, subtle enough that the general doesn't notice. Panic bubbles up in my chest. There's a clear answer here, but we can't tell him. He can never know about Daphne. If he knew, they'd track her down before nightfall, and she'd either be shipped back to Philadelphia or killed.

"It was my fault, sir," comes out of Ethan's mouth before I can speak. My head snaps toward him, but he doesn't budge. He keeps his gaze fixed on the general, blocking me out. "John and I were searching for supplies. I wanted to go further, but he didn't. I pressured him, and he went with me. We were too far out by the time our pagers went off."

I'm stunned. General Conrad must see it on my face too, because his eyes remain narrowed at me the entire time Ethan is talking.

"Madoc," he addresses me. "Can you confirm that what Greene is saying is true?"

My bottom lip quivers. I don't want Ethan to go down for this, but I can't tell him the truth. I could alter the narrative and say I'm the one to blame, that I was the one who pressured Ethan, not the other way around. But I know if I were to deviate from his story now, the general would surely know we're lying.

I straighten myself in my chair and turn toward the general. With everything inside me screaming not to, my shoulders drop, and I say, "Yes, sir. He's telling the truth."

Lieutenant Kelley mutters something vulgar at Ethan, but I know he's strong enough to take it. General Conrad slowly reclines back in his chair, processing Ethan's excuse.

"Well, that settles it then," he declares. He lunges across the desk toward Ethan like a lion pouncing at its prey. Ethan flinches, gripping the armrests and leaning back as far as he can.

"Mark my words, Greene, if you ever disobey orders like that again, you'll end up just like your father," the general threatens. "I'll make sure of it."

Ethan's face sinks. General Conrad pulls back, his expression softening again. Everything in me wants to defend Ethan — especially after all he's done for me — but I don't move. I sit back and let him take the blame for it all.

"Did you at least manage to bring anything back?" General Conrad sneers.

Ethan nods and messes with his pocket. He pulls out the flashlight and drops it on the desk in front of the general.

"It still works," Ethan says, hopeful. "Could be of use."

General Conrad stretches out his fingers and takes the flashlight in his hand. He examines it for a moment, then tosses it across the room. I duck instinctively as it flies over my head. It crashes against the floor and rolls to a stop at the foot of the fireplace.

"Pathetic," he says. "Absolutely pathetic."

"General," Lieutenant Kelley speaks up, "I apologize for their lack of consideration toward the mission. I'm confident we trained them better than this." I feel his presence move closer, lingering over our heads. I can only imagine the type of punishment he's cooking up for us in his mind.

"You're not to blame," General Conrad assures him. "It was an experiment. When you first brought the idea to me, to send the top five draftees out on a supply run, I was initially against it. Draftees are selfish. They're only concerned with themselves. They have no concern for the greater world around them — not yet, at least. That's why they still have a long way to go before they're through with training. So this just proves me right. And now, we're all in agreement."

"I disagree, sir," I say. General Conrad's eyes whip across the room to me. He raises his brow, equal parts insulted and intrigued.

"Of course you do," he scoffs. "As I said before, you're selfish. Prideful. So prideful, in fact, that you must think you're right. I've seen many years of draftees come and go, Madoc, and you're all the same. You do well in the first quarter, rise to the top of the ranks, get all in your head, and suddenly you think you know what's best."

"I—"

Ethan places a gentle hand on my arm. He shakes his head, urging me to stop while I'm ahead. "Let it go, John," he whispers. "What's done is done. Just let it be."

But I can't. I don't want to reveal Daphne's whereabouts, but part of me wonders what he'd do if he knew we found *someone* outside the city. Not Daphne, but another survivor. What would he say?

Mae's words from before the draft cycle through my mind: *There's more to this than we all know. All it takes is one person asking the right questions for the whole system to break.* All along, we've been told everything outside the Barrier is dead and gone. That The Truth devastated it all. But there she was — bloodied, bruised, but alive. Maybe now's the time to start asking the right questions.

Maybe this is my chance.

"I don't think I know what's best," I clarify. "And we certainly weren't trying to jeopardize the mission for everyone else."

Every eye in the room is on me. Ethan clenches his fists until his knuckles are white. In the reflection of the glass in front of me, I see Lieutenant Kelley step forward. His arm is cocked, ready to smack the words right out of my mouth. But General Conrad raises a hand, ordering him to stand down. He wants to hear what I have to say.

I continue. "But you can't blame us for being a little curious. All our lives, we've lived under the Barrier. We'd never seen the outside world. So as soon as we got the opportunity, of course we ventured off a little bit. Of course we got turned around. Of course we stuck our noses somewhere they probably didn't belong. But you can't blame us for that. There's so much we don't know, and it was all right there, at our fingertips."

General Conrad chuckles. "Madoc," he starts. There's no intensity in his tone anymore, yet it's still condescending. Like a father gearing up to lecture his child. "There isn't anything more to know. You've been told everything, haven't you? There's nothing left beyond the Barrier. There's nothing waiting for you. Nothing for you to find. This," he extends his arms at both sides, "is all that's left. This is our future — *your* future. And it's your duty to protect it. Have you forgotten that?"

"But sir, have you ever considered the possibility that there could be others out there? We were out there all night and had a lot of time to think, and—"

"Ah," he interrupts. He taps his finger, then points it decisively at me. "I see what this is."

He rises from his seat and glides around the desk until he's at my side. He leans in, our faces inches from each other, trying to make me uncomfortable. Expecting me to shrink back from him.

But I don't.

"You really are your father's son, and you wouldn't even know it," he says. "Your father came to me many years ago with the same questions. Dangerous questions..." his voice trails off, as if recalling the memory. But then he snaps out of it. He slams his hand into the desk and leans in closer until he's all I can see.

"But let me make myself clear. There's no one else out there. And if you were truly loyal to the defense and safety of this city, you wouldn't even consider the possibility that there could be. So you have a decision to make — right here, right now. Are you loyal to the draft? Or are you going to feed lies? Lies that seem to have been passed down to you?"

Is that what my father did? I wonder.

Silence spreads throughout the room. General Conrad's stare is unwavering. He holds my gaze, expecting me to make the wrong decision. Ready to devour me when I do. But I'm not going to give him that satisfaction.

I smile politely at him and relax my shoulders. "My loyalty is here," I lie. "Thank you, General Conrad. Being outside the Barrier, I lost sight of it for a moment. But you're right. I apologize for even entertaining the idea."

General Conrad nods in contentment. "Very well," he says. "I'm glad to know you're a different man than your father."

His words pierce me, but I don't let him see it. "Of course, sir."

He withdraws and lifts his eyes to the training officers. "You're dismissed," he announces. "You may take them back to their barracks now."

Lieutenant Kelley grabs my arm and lifts me out of the chair. Lieutenant Tillman does the same for Ethan. They lead us toward the door and shove us back into the corridor. Glancing over my shoulder, I notice General Conrad turning toward the glass box, keeping a watchful eye over the facility.

Making sure everything continues to operate as he wants it to.

Once we're on the other side, the training officers throw Ethan and me against the wall. We've done our time with the general — now it's their turn to pick us apart.

"Did you manage to bring back your gear?" Lieutenant Kelley asks.

Ethan and I stare back at him, our faces riddled with guilt. "Most of it, sir," Ethan mumbles.

Lieutenant Kelley sighs in disappointment. "The helmets?"

I shake my head. "Back in Philadelphia, sir."

"Unbelievable," he mutters. "Hand over what you have."

We unclip our belts and lay them on the ground in front of us. I remove my handgun from the holster and pull the clip from the body, placing both pieces next to the belt. As I set them down, I notice the pager still clipped to the belt. I think about grabbing it, but with Lieutenant Kelley staring down my neck, there's no way I can. It'd be too obvious. As I straighten back against the wall, my eyes flicker past the badge dangling from Lieutenant Tillman's waist. It isn't until now that it hits me — the plan was flawed all along. Without the pager, there's no way for us to know when we could take the subway to see Daphne. And without an all-access badge, we'd have no way to access Battery Station.

I think of her alone in that vacant apartment building not far from where our two borders meet. Trapped under the Barrier, which she knows nothing about. All the while Ethan and I are held under lock and key. I have no idea what we're going to do. Even though General Conrad won't kill her, we might as well have done it ourselves.

"Greene," I hear Lieutenant Kelley say, "your pager?"

Looking down, I notice Ethan's pager isn't clipped to his belt. Turning toward him, I see him shaking his head. "I lost it, sir. It must've fallen off at some point along the way."

That's not true. I remember Ethan's pager going off when we got back to New York. He might've left it at Daphne's apartment, or maybe it really did fall off somewhere between here and there.

Either way, Lieutenant Kelley doesn't seem too concerned. He exhales heavily, exuding more of his disappointment.

Ethan's eyes quickly dart to mine. In a single glance, something passes between us. His pager didn't fall off. He didn't misplace it.

He's come to the same realization as me — and he has a plan.

The training officers gather our gear and escort us down to the lower level. They deliver us back to the barracks in silence. When we arrive, Lieutenant Tillman fumbles with his badge to scan open the door. But before he can, Ethan seems to trip. He falls forward clumsily, crashing into Lieutenant Tillman. All the gear nestled in his arm tumbles to the ground in a raucous outside the door. Lieutenant Tillman curses Ethan, and Ethan quickly crouches down to offer him help.

"Clumsy idiot," Lieutenant Kelley mutters.

"I'm sorry, sir," Ethan says apologetically as he gathers the gear. He hands it all back to Lieutenant Tillman dutifully, then stands. "My feet are tired. I must've tripped."

Lieutenant Tillman responds with a huff. While he's reorganizing the gear, Lieutenant Kelley lifts his own badge to the scanner to open the door. Pushing it open, he says, "Go. Get yourselves cleaned up. And don't think you're off the hook just yet."

"Yes, sir," we both reply with a salute.

Inside the barracks, every draftee jumps to their feet when they see us. A few seem to be showering — I can hear the faint sound of water running from the other side of the wall. Meanwhile, others are getting ready for bed.

But those who are already clean and prepped for bed rush toward us. Drew and Carson reach us first. Before they can ask, the questions are written all over their faces. They stare back at us baffled, unsure where to even start.

"How did you—" Drew blurts out.

"Are you—" Carson says at the same time.

"What did they—"

Ethan holds up his hand to silence them.

"Give us a second, okay?" Ethan begs. "Let us get cleaned up, then we'll explain everything."

"Oh, of course," Drew says.

"We're just really relieved to see you," Carson admits.

"We are too," I assure him.

The two of them drag themselves back to their bunks. Apollo scoffs from his bed. He pulls the sheets up to his chin and rolls onto his side, too tired to pester us.

As soon as Drew and Carson are out of range, Ethan turns to me. He places his hand against the frame of the bunk and leans in close.

"You think they bought it?" he whispers. A devious smile spreads across his face.

"You mean you didn't actually lose your pager?"

Ethan snickers. He digs his hand into his pocket, then exposes the corner of the small black device. Once he's sure I've seen it, he tucks it away again.

"You genius," I commend him. "Thank you for taking the fall back there, by the way."

He lowers his arm and rests his back against the bunk, standing at my side. "Someone had to. They were going to keep prying until one of us confessed, and you and I both know we couldn't do that. And plus, it's better that I take the fall than you."

"What makes you say that?"

He sighs. "You're on top, John. And they've already got their eyes on you because of your dad. I can afford to take the hit, but you can't. Besides, they're going to punish both of us. It may have been my idea in their eyes, but you were my accomplice. So don't thank me yet," he punches my arm playfully.

"Well, thank you anyway," I reply, and I mean it. "You didn't have to go along with any of this, but you did. And I really appreciate it."

He spins around and shrugs. "What are friends for, right?"

With a chuckle, he bends down and pulls a towel out of his drawer. He slings it over his shoulder and heads for the showers. He doesn't get more than a few feet from the bunk before something dawns on me. Ethan might have the pager, but without an all-access badge, we still can't get to Battery Station.

"Ethan, what about—" I call out to him, but I stop myself, realizing the whole room can hear me.

Ethan turns and retreats back. "What is it?"

"What about the door to the station?" I whisper. "Without an all-access badge, we can't get through."

"Ah!" Ethan exclaims. He digs into his pocket again, and before I can look down, he lifts a plain laminated badge in front of my face.

"I'm not *that* clumsy," he says, the same devious smile streaked across his face.

My eyes widen in concern, completely disregarding his sly success in getting the badge. "Ethan, Lieutenant Tillman is going to know. He's going to—"

"No, he's not," he cuts me off. "There's no way he'd ever know. He could've misplaced it, or it could've fallen off when he bent down to pick up the gear. The possibilities are endless. He'll request a new one, and he'll be too proud to admit he lost it."

Everything starts to fall into place. We have the pager. We have the badge. All we have to do now is slip in and out of the barracks unnoticed, and we could actually pull this off. If we're successful, we can get to Daphne and learn more about her. We can find out if there are others. And if we do it right, no one will ever know.

General Conrad may have been right about me being a different man than my father. There are many aspects of him that I'm not, but there are some things I could be. I want to believe my loyalty is here. I want to do well in the draft. I want answers about my father. Most importantly, I want to keep Mother and Liam safe.

But there's this deep longing to know more. If it's true that my father confronted General Conrad with questions about life outside the Barrier, maybe he was onto something. Maybe he acted on his curiosity, and they banished him for it.

There had to be a reason he was asking those questions. After all, I was only prompted to ask them because of Daphne.

Maybe it's foolish to think so, but if I'm right, she might be the key to finding out what really happened to him.

Sixteen

Lieutenant Kelley delivers our punishment in the form of a hundred push-ups. Before any other draftees are up, he drags us from our bunks and out to the front of the facility.

"Drop," he hisses at us. "And don't come up until you're finished."

Ethan and I push ourselves down and up against the concrete until sunlight spills over the horizon. Veins bulge from my neck with each movement, and my triceps burn. But I keep pressing down and forcing my body up, biting back the pain. Each time one of us falters, Lieutenant Kelley is quick to remind us we deserve this.

"This is what happens when you disobey orders under my watch," he growls.

With ten left to go, my whole body trembles. I take them one at a time. I exhale as I lower my body, then suck in a deep breath to inflate my body back up. Pushing myself into the final rep, I hinge my elbows and let my chest sink slowly. Just when I think I can't take it anymore, I let go. My chest smacks the ground, knocking the air from my lungs. I spin over onto my back and stare up at Lieutenant Kelley.

"How about another hundred?" he asks with a maniacal chuckle.

"You're cruel," I mutter breathlessly.

Lieutenant Kelley bends down and grabs a fistful of my shirt, pulling me right up to his face. "Then next time, how 'bout you follow my commands?"

"Yes, sir," I gulp.

He releases his grip, and I fall back against the concrete with a grunt.

Ethan groans next to me, still fighting through his last few reps. When he finishes, he peels himself off the ground and shakily stands to his feet. His face is flushed red, and his bottom lip quivers as if he might be sick.

He lurches forward and bends with his hands on his knees. "I'm fine," he huffs, trying to catch his breath. "Just give me a second. I'll be fine."

Footsteps approach from behind us, and I turn to see the rest of the draftees filing out of the facility. Some appear to still be waking up, but they're all instantly humored to see Ethan and me already outside, battered and covered in sweat. Lieutenant Tillman leads them toward us. As he passes, my eyes catch a new white badge dangling from his belt. Ethan seems to notice too, and he quickly smirks at me.

Lieutenant Tillman takes his place beside Lieutenant Kelley. He doesn't say anything about the badge. In fact, he doesn't even seem to notice Ethan or me. He stares over our heads at the rest of the group, just as he would any other day.

If he knew we had something to do with his badge, we would've answered for it this morning. I'm sure of it. But it seems he was easily able to replace it.

"Good morning, soldiers," Lieutenant Kelley greets us. Ethan and I scramble into formation with the others. I stand next to Leo, who looks me up and down, assessing my condition.

"What happened to you lads?" he asks.

"Don't miss your ride back to the city," I whisper.

He lets out a muffled laugh. "Noted."

Lieutenant Kelley continues. "Today marks the start of the second quarter of training. You all performed well during the first quarter, despite some setbacks." His eyes flash over to Ethan and me. "Now it's time to take it up a notch. We'll focus on the same three areas: strength, strategy, and skill. But your objective now is to hone your skills."

As the sun takes its place over the city, all I can think about is Daphne. I think about the light peeking through the window beside her bed. I think of her waking up in the city for the first time, not having to worry about monsters coming after her anymore.

Tonight will be the first time we attempt to see her. It's risky, given the training officers are keeping a close eye on us. But we'll go late, well after lights out — as long as the subway is still running at that hour. We'll wait until all the other draftees are asleep and make it back in enough time to still get a few hours of sleep. If all goes well, no one will know we were ever gone.

Lieutenant Kelley's words snap me out of my thoughts. "Forty-five minutes are on the clock this time. Go!"

My feet take off with the rest of the unit, sending me headfirst into the awakening city. Ethan trots next to me in agony, both of us quickly falling to the back of the group. Everyone else starts off strong. For now, we jog at a steady pace, waiting for our muscles to loosen and the ache to go away.

We pass by the Holland Tunnel and enter the straightaway toward the barricade. As we approach it, my eyes scan over the surrounding buildings. Daphne's apartment isn't visible from this side, but it's no more than a few blocks north of where we are. For a moment, I imagine slipping away from the group to go see her. *Maybe it'd be better to see her in the daytime*, I think. I could climb the barricade, slip onto the other side, see her for a few minutes, then sprint the last two miles to the facility. But no — there's no way I'd make it. But as we round the corner past the barricade, I don't stop myself from considering the possibility.

The draftees ahead of us start to spread out as their pace slows. Ethan and I use this to our advantage. Our exhaustion catches up to us, and my body grows weaker. But I pick up the pace and keep pushing on. The sooner we make it back, the sooner it'll all be over.

We ascend the path to the facility, and the training officers come into view. We finish the run a minute and a half past forty-five minutes, but we're not the only ones who seem to be lacking. Half the draftees are already back, including Drew and Leo, but the other half are trailing behind us, still making their way up the path.

As they finish, Lieutenant Tillman clicks his stopwatch and records our times on his tablet.

"That was weak," Lieutenant Kelley scolds. We stare back blankly, unfazed by his words, most of us just relieved to be finished running.

"Go," he orders. "Clean yourselves up and get some breakfast. And while you're at it, get it together. Because I expect more from you this afternoon."

"Yes, sir!" we shout.

Together, we march back into the facility and ride the elevator down to the lower level. When we reach our barracks, we take turns showering and head up for breakfast. Ethan and I wait on each other. Once we're dressed in our uniforms, we make our way to the cafeteria. Drew and Carson are already seated at our usual spot. Ethan and I carry our trays and slide onto the bench across from them.

"The prodigal draftees return!" Drew exclaims.

"You all really had everyone worried," Carson says.

Ethan rolls his eyes. "Oh, I'm sure Lieutenant Kelley was worried sick he wouldn't be able to whoop our butts himself."

"No, really," Carson continues. "There was a moment when the others got back and we realized you were missing. We weren't sure what happened. No one could tell us, and—"

"What *did* happen?" Drew interrupts.

Ethan and I keep our eyes glued to our trays. I worry Drew will see right through our cover story, but we stick to it anyway.

"We wandered off too far," Ethan says convincingly. "John didn't want to. He tried to get me to turn back, but I wanted to keep going."

"What did you do?" Drew presses more. "You know, after you realized you'd missed the train?"

"Celebrated," Ethan jokes. "Cheered from the rooftops. Contemplated starting a new life in Philadelphia, kissed our old lives goodbye, and—"

"We found a place to post up for the night," I cut him off. "We figured it'd be best to stay put and not venture any further from the station, after learning from our mistake the first time around." I glance at Ethan, playing along with his story. He nods in agreement.

I continue. "When the pager went off the next morning, we rode the train back to the city. By that time, Lieutenant Kelley was already waiting for us, ready to deliver our heads to General Conrad on a silver platter."

Drew's eyes widen. "Psh, yeah. Carson and I thought you were dead men when we saw him dragging you up here yesterday. I mean, there's no way that could've gone well."

"Not at all," I confirm. I slurp down the rest of my breakfast and wash it away with a sip of water.

Desperate to divert the conversation, I set my silverware against the tray and stand. "We better head back down," I suggest. "You remember what Lieutenant Kelley said: Time to *hone our skills* and whatnot."

This earns a laugh from them. The four of us return our trays and make our way to the training lawn. It feels good to be with them again. Part of me wants everything to go back to the way it was before Philadelphia. If it did, I'd stick with my group, go through the next quarter of training, maintain my rank, and continue flying under the radar. But now, there's an extra layer to everything. I have a responsibility to take care of Daphne — and that has to take precedence, at least for now.

Lieutenant Kelley and Lieutenant Tillman run us through a series of intense drills for strength training. They push us for the entirety of the afternoon until the sun begins its descent. Any weak spots from this morning are ironed out, and we work hard as a unit to perform at the level they expect from us. That evening, they dismiss us for dinner. I tuck a few pieces of food into my napkin and slide it into my pocket, saving some for Daphne. As Ethan and I head downstairs to turn in for the night, Lieutenant Kelley stops us.

"Well done today, men," he says. "Keep it up. And don't fall out of line again."

My stomach twists knowing tonight, we'll be breaking the rules yet again. But I don't give him any reason to suspect anything.

"Yes, sir," we nod.

While everyone settles in for the night, I grab Ethan to run through the plan. We talk quietly, our voices drowned out by the sounds of everyone shuffling around the barracks.

"When the pager goes off, I'll give you a tap, and then—"

Ethan stops me. "Actually, I've been thinking I might hang back tonight. It might be too dangerous for both of us to go. And plus, I could cover for you if things don't turn out well."

My heart sinks. I can't do this without him. I can't have him throwing in the towel now — not when we're only just getting started.

"Ethan, c'mon, man. You're not giving up on me now, are you?"

"No, no," Ethan whispers. "I just . . . it's easier for one to slip out than two, you know?"

I'm not buying it. I furrow my brows and hold my stare.

"Alright," he breaks. "I'm just really tired. But I still meant what I said. It'll be easier for you to slip out on your own."

He has a point, but I don't want to agree too quickly. I need Ethan to be a part of this, and quite frankly, I'd feel more comfortable with him there.

It may be simpler for me to go on my own, but what if I mess it up? What if I can't find my way back? I might need him as backup, but he's set in his decision.

"And besides, I think it'd mean more for you to go than me," he adds.

"What do you mean by that?"

He shrugs. "I don't know. You were the one to save her. I was skeptical the whole time. She'd probably feel more comfortable with you."

"Alright," I relent. "I'll go then, but I'll still give you a tap when I go. That way, you'll know when I leave and, I don't know, can be on the lookout for me."

Ethan gives me a pat on my shoulder, then keeps his hand there. "You can do this, John," he smiles. "If anyone can, it's you."

With that, he hurls himself up the ladder and plops onto the mattress. I appreciate his vote of confidence, but it doesn't stifle the doubts I have within myself. The lights in the barracks dim to darkness, and I roll into my bed with the pager clutched tightly in my fist. I turn over onto my side and tuck the device under my pillow. When it goes off, there won't be time to hesitate. I have to be ready.

I have to make it to her.

I'm stirred awake by the sound of the pager buzzing next to my face. Instantly, I sit upright and shove it into my pocket to muffle the noise. I swing my legs over the side of the bed and squat down next to my drawer. As I pull it out of the frame, I pause to look over my shoulder. From what I can tell, all the draftees are still asleep. The room is filled with snores and long, heavy breaths, making it easy to cover up any noise I'm making.

Carefully, I slide the drawer back into place and stuff my sheets with excess clothing. That way, if anyone wakes up or walks by my bunk, the heap under the covers will make them think I'm still there, tucked within the sheets. My hand pats my pocket, and I'm relieved to feel the thin outline of Lieutenant Tillman's badge still there.

I gently tap Ethan's arm to wake him. With a tired moan, he rolls toward me. Through the frame, I see his eyes slowly peel open. Half asleep but still conscious enough to notice me, he gives me a thumbs-up, then rolls back over. I take it he doesn't plan on staying up to be my lookout.

With the pager still vibrating in my pocket, I ease the barracks door open just enough to slip through. Once I'm on the other side, I press it shut, wincing as it clicks into place. The corridor is completely dark except for a trail of faint lights tracing the base of the walls. They outline the entire hallway, making the floor look like a runway, guiding me toward the vault door at the end.

I lightly jog down the hall, throwing a look over my shoulder every so often. When I reach the door, I slide the badge out of my pocket. Holding my breath, I brush it against the scanner. To my relief, it emits a muted beep — a sound that's much louder now, in the stillness, than it should be. The door unlocks, granting me passage to the other side.

I pause to glance over my shoulder one last time. The empty corridor behind me offers no reassurance. Taking a deep breath, I cross the threshold.

I hurry through the chamber and emerge onto the platform. The subway waits for me there, sitting with its doors wide open, welcoming me on board. *So far, so good*, I think. But I can't afford to waste any more time.

I hop onto the subway and fumble my way to the rear car. Glancing up at the screen, I notice the red line is the only path illuminated. I'm relieved to see it's headed where I need it to go.

As the subway roars to life, I take my seat and lean back against the window. In a matter of seconds, Battery Station fades out of view, and the train is sheathed in darkness.

It takes only a few minutes before it reaches the station. I jump to my feet when the bell chimes overhead, and the feminine voice welcomes me to the next stop. Through the window, the familiar platform starts to take shape. The subway slowly creeps to a halt. With a hiss, its doors disengage, and I hop off.

I jog the route to Daphne's apartment by memory. It doesn't take long to find the white mid-rise apartment building, with the dilapidated fire escape zigzagging across the front. Once I reach it, I hoist myself onto the lower landing. My muscles quiver, weakened by the absurd amount of push-ups from earlier today. With the last ounce of my strength, I tumble onto the landing, feeling it jolt beneath my weight.

Back on my feet, I ascend each set of steps leading to the top level. I crest the final set and pause in front of the windows that frame the exterior of Daphne's unit. Nerves start to bubble up inside me. I shouldn't be nervous. If anything, this is just a courtesy visit to make sure she's okay. But something more compels me.

Timidly, I push through the doors into the living room. My sneakers land softly against the carpet. Everything in the apartment is still. I hold my hands out at both sides, careful not to make any sudden noises that might alarm her.

"Daphne?" I call out in a whisper. The room is illuminated by a single strand of moonlight seeping in through the windows. Looking around, there's no sign of her. My heart sinks, thinking she might be gone. Holding onto hope, I tiptoe toward the bedroom door. As I push it open, I expect to find it empty too.

But that's not what happens.

Something rushes toward me in a blur, striking me on the forehead. I stumble back into the living room with my head in my hands, trying to collect myself. But before I can, a second blow hits me in the chin, knocking me backward.

I land on my back and cry out. When my vision refocuses, I see Daphne's silhouette lunge on top of me. In the darkness of the room, I can't make out her face, but her long hair hangs over her shoulder, tickling my skin. She wraps her hands firmly around my wrists and pins me down. Her knees dig into my thigh to hold me in place. I bite back against a small shudder of pain, but it escapes my lips in a whimper.

"John?" she says curiously. She releases me from her grip and stands, her body falling into the streak of moonlight cast into the room. I see her brush herself off and straighten her hair behind her ears.

"Yeah, yeah, it's me," I spit out. I struggle to my feet, using the bar top as leverage.

"I'm sorry," she apologizes. "I didn't know when to expect you, and it's late. And I didn't know who you were at first. And I—" she pauses for a moment as a thought forms in her mind. "Where's Ethan?"

"He decided not to join me this time," I say. She folds her arms across her chest and relaxes her shoulders.

"I see," she mutters. "Well, it took you long enough to come back for me."

"I'm sorry," I lift my hands in surrender. "I would've come sooner, but I couldn't. I—"

"Oh, right," she interrupts. "Because no one knows about me. And I'm not supposed to be here, otherwise there'd be major consequences," she curls her fingers into air quotes, recalling our conversation on the subway.

I can't help but chuckle at how ridiculous it all sounds, but it's true. "That's right," I confirm. "I brought you something to eat, though."

Reaching into my pocket, I pull out a few strips of jerky folded into my napkin, along with a protein bar I swiped from the buffet. Daphne takes them into her hand with a soft smile. Even though it's not much, I can tell she's grateful.

"So, where do you two hide out all day?" she asks, tearing off a bite of jerky.

"At a military base near the harbor. We're usually in training all day and are kept under pretty close watch. It's a miracle I even made it out of there tonight. You have no idea."

"Ah, yes. It's coming back to me now," she expresses. "You two are soldiers. Well, soldiers in training, I suppose. Though you really didn't dress the part this time."

Her eyes examine me up and down. Embarrassed, I glance down at my plain T-shirt and dark sweatpants that sag around my waist.

"Not a requirement to sleep in uniform," I shrug.

She purses her lips, then nods. "Fair enough."

A moment of silence passes between us. There's so much I want to ask, and so much I'm sure she wants to know too. But neither of us knows where to start. I stand awkwardly at the other end of the bar top while she finishes eating, watching her savor every bite.

"What were you doing out there?" I start. "In Philadelphia?"

Her eyes lower. She lifts her head and flattens her palms against the counter. "I can't remember. I've been trying to remember, but it's all fuzzy. It's like there's this gaping hole in my memory between before you and Ethan and after you and Ethan. And for the most part, all I can remember is the after." Her fingers rub the bandage still taped to her forehead. "I'm sure it'll all come back to me, though."

"Does it hurt?" I ask, pointing to her wound.

"It aches, but it isn't painful," she says. "When I think too hard, everything starts to feel heavy, like there's a huge weight pressing against my skull. But when I'm just resting, I hardly notice it."

"If you need anything for it, I'm sure Ethan and I could—"

"I'm fine, John," she interrupts sweetly. "Seriously. But I appreciate you checking."

We stand in the kitchen for a while longer, neither of us saying anything but remaining in each other's company. I feel a little hopeless knowing her memory is compromised, but I try not to let it discourage me. I didn't save her just to get answers. I brought her here so she'd be safe. To give her another shot — which is more than she would've had in Philadelphia. She may not feel totally comfortable here just yet, but I can see in the way she looks at me that she trusts me. And that's good for starters.

Nearly half an hour passes before the pager goes off again. I pull it out and clutch it in my hand, the green light flashing through my fingers.

"That's my cue," I tell her.

She doesn't put up a fight or stand in my way as I head toward the fire escape.

"When will I see you again?" she asks. I glance back at her from the doorway. She still hovers near the counter, hidden in the shadows of the apartment, only a sliver of her face visible in the moonlight.

"Tomorrow night," I promise. "You can count on it."

"So there's no need to tackle you next time, right?"

I shrug. "I could use the extra practice defending myself. After all, it's part of my training."

She lets out a laugh that quickly fades, then tucks a piece of hair behind her ear. "Look, John, I know you don't know much about me, and I feel like I don't know much about me either. And I don't know much about you or this place, for that matter. But I like it here. It feels safe. Even though I don't have a strong memory to confirm or deny it, I feel like that's something I haven't had in a while. Safety," she clarifies.

"You *are* safe," I assure her. "And you're safe with me. You may not know much else, but that's one thing you can know for sure."

She smiles, and it lights up everything inside me. But the relentless buzzing of the pager reminds me that my time is limited. I slip through the doors and down the fire escape. As soon as I reach the ground, I take off toward the station without missing a beat. When I get there, the subway is already waiting for me. I hop on and take my seat, double checking the screen that it's heading back to Battery Station. Soon after, it accelerates forward into the tunnel, carrying me away from her.

As the subway pulls back into Battery Station, I'm on high alert. I crouch down below the seats and peer through the base of the windows, making sure Lieutenant Kelley isn't waiting for me on the platform. But as it comes to a stop, I find the platform completely vacant. Hesitantly, I step off and approach the vault door. I press Lieutenant Tillman's badge to the scanner, and just as it did before, the door unlocks for me.

I step into the chamber, and I'm instantly met with a cloud of thick smoke. It dissipates almost as soon as it starts, and the room is filled with an affirming green light. The second door clicks unlocked. All I have to do is step through it, and I'll be safe inside the facility. Then it's just a matter of making it down the hall, sneaking into the barracks, and tucking myself in bed as if I've been there all along.

On the other side of the chamber door, the same trail of lights shines down the hallway, guiding my path. I hold my breath as I walk briskly toward the barracks. My heart races, expecting someone to emerge from the elevator or another room at any moment. But no one does. I make it all the way to the other end and scan the badge once more, granting me access to the barracks. The door clicks open, and I slide through without letting any light in.

I hesitate in front of the door and peer through the darkness to see if I've woken anyone up. But the chorus of snores and sluggish breaths carries on exactly as it did when I left, confirming everyone is still asleep.

I pull the contents out from beneath my sheets and stuff them back in my drawer. I bury the pager in my towel and bunch a few clothing items around it, just to ensure if it goes off again, its vibration will be inaudible. As soon as I'm finished, I slip out of my clothes and roll into bed. My whole body loosens as my head hits the pillow. *I did it*, I think — and there's nothing to stop me from doing it again.

As my eyes close, visions of Daphne form in my mind. Her body resting against the bar top. Her blue eyes glistening in the moonlight. Remembering the weight of her as Ethan and I carried her from the stairwell in Philadelphia, then feeling it again tonight as she tackled me to the ground. She's right — there's still so much I don't know about her. But there's something more than curiosity that keeps me wanting to go back. Some part of me that knows even if she never remembers anything, I'd keep going back for her. Every night.

Seventeen

It takes everything in me to wake up the next morning. I roll out of bed and drag myself to the shower. The cold water sprays against my face, snapping me out of my daze, but it doesn't last.

As soon as I'm dry, I waddle back to my bunk and slip on my uniform. Once I'm dressed, I collapse against the mattress. Sleep tugs at my eyes, and it feels impossible to resist. I fall in and out of sleep over and over again, jerking awake each time. It isn't until Ethan climbs down from his bunk that I'm fully awake.

"Oh good," he says as he springs off the ladder. "You made it back last night."

I sit up and drape my legs over the side of the bed. "Yeah, and so far, it seems like nobody noticed."

"How'd it go?" he asks, keeping his voice down.

"A lot smoother than I thought it would," I reply. I look past him and see a few draftees getting ready to head to breakfast. As they walk toward the door, I pause and don't say anything more until they're out of the room.

"Go ahead and shower," I prompt him. "I'll wait for you. We can talk more on our way up to breakfast."

"Roger that," Ethan says, patting the frame of the bunk.

I rest my eyes until Ethan's finished. By the time he's ready, we're some of the last ones left in the barracks, which works out in our favor. We leave the room and make our way toward the elevator. Once we're inside, the doors slide shut, closing us in.

"I think we pulled it off," I start, turning to him as the elevator lifts beneath us.

He raises a brow. "Well, of course we did. We're geniuses."

"I mean, everything was perfectly in place. The pager went off, the subway was there, it took me right to the station I needed to be at, and it was all the same on the way back."

The elevator doors open sooner than I want them to, and we step out into the atrium. A few soldiers shuffle past us, heading in different directions. We move out of their way and ascend the stairs to the upper level.

"I was right then," Ethan declares, lowering his voice now that we're in a common area. "It was easier for you to go alone than for me to come with you."

I shrug. "I guess so. She did ask about you, though."

"Psh," Ethan scoffs. "Nice of her to think of me, but I'm sure she was just fine without me there."

We move through the buffet line with ease, then carry our trays over to the table. Drew and Carson are already seated at our normal spot. Drew notices us and waves, inviting us over.

"I'm going back tonight," I tell Ethan.

"I think you should," he says. "Now let's shut up about it and pretend we don't have a hostage girl boarded up somewhere in the city."

"That's not what she—" I start, but we reach the table before I can finish.

As soon as we're seated, we occupy ourselves with our meals and make small talk with Drew and Carson, letting the morning pass by. When we're finished, we return our trays and head downstairs for training. Lieutenant Kelley and Lieutenant Tillman meet us in the atrium and direct us where to go.

"We'll be in the shooting range today," Lieutenant Kelley states. We nod submissively and move toward the elevator, riding it back down to the lower level.

The rest of the draftees file into the shooting range, followed by the training officers. The familiar dummies dangle loosely at the far end of each lane, their ceramic bodies menacing in the low light. As I stare at one, the view shifts in my mind to a vision of the hallway in Philadelphia. The subdued lights fade to near blackness, and the soft red glow of the exit sign flickers near the back of the lane. The dummy's limbs stiffen and contort as bones snap into place. Its white, powdered exterior melts into graying flesh. It rips itself from the chains that bind it and falls to the ground. Crawling on all fours, it races rapidly toward me — teeth bared, blood dripping from its lips, and nails digging into the sand. It reaches the divider that separates me from it, and when it does, it lunges over the top.

I flinch away in fear. Instantly, the scene shifts back to the shooting range, and the dummy hangs lifeless at the end of the lane. Lieutenant Kelley must've been talking because he glances at me with his mouth slightly ajar. It's clear I've interrupted him.

"Dozing off, Madoc?" he snaps at me.

I shake my head. "N-no, sir. Of course not."

Ethan elbows me subtly and leans in. "I know you stayed up late with your girl and all, but try not to give yourself away."

I nudge him away and refocus as Lieutenant Kelley picks up where he left off.

"As I was saying," he continues, "today we'll be working on agility. Rather than going in pairs or groups, you'll go one at a time, and you'll be handling all three lanes. For this exercise, the dummies won't be stationary. They'll be advancing toward you at different speeds. It's up to you to strike them down before they reach you. If they make it all the way to the end, the exercise will be over, and you'll have failed. Understood?"

"Yes, sir!" we shout.

Lieutenant Kelley draws a handgun from his holster and extends it to me. "Madoc, why don't you start us off? Since you could use a little help waking up this morning."

A few draftees snicker, spurred by insulting remarks from Apollo and his posse. Ethan pats my back as I take the gun into my hand.

"All the same rules apply," Lieutenant Kelley reminds me. "Keep an eye on all three targets, move swiftly, and don't let them reach the end."

"Yes, sir," I nod in understanding. I approach the center stall and wait for the dummy to make the first move. Wrapping my hand around the grip, I lift the gun to my chin and bend my knees, ready to strike.

A loud click releases the dummy from the back of the lane. It advances forward, sliding rapidly along a groove in the ceiling. It drags the dummy toward me at an alarming rate. Its body thrashes as it's jostled around, causing the chains to rattle violently.

I lock my first bullet into place and aim for the dummy's skull. My finger presses into the trigger, and the gun kicks back. The bullet tears through the center of the dummy's face. As soon as it makes contact, the dummy is yanked backward. It pauses for a brief moment, then begins advancing toward me again.

My feet slide to the right, moving over to the next stall. There, the dummy is moving much slower, but it's had enough time to get close by this point. My second bullet strikes the side of its head, amputating its ceramic ear. I quickly send another through its skull, and the dummy is yanked backward in the same manner as the other.

I dart across the room to the leftmost stall, where the dummy is only a few feet away from the divider. In a panic, I pull the trigger before aiming. The bullet sails through the dummy's gut, which doesn't stop it. It continues advancing toward me until I make the kill shot, then it retreats backward.

I shuffle side to side, occupying each stall and monitoring the distance of each dummy. Each time, I manage to hit the kill switch. The bullet soars through its skull, the dummy slides to the back of the lane, then lurches forward quicker than the time before. Sweat trickles off my forehead as I stride back and forth, keeping my knees bent and sturdy. For a moment, everything around me fades away. It's as if I'm the only one in the room. I send another bullet through the skull of the center dummy, then jump to the right and land another in the same spot. I hit the center dummy again on my way over to the left, not even giving it a chance to move forward more than a foot. I stop the leftmost dummy in its tracks, and after it withdraws to the back wall, it doesn't move again.

I jump over to the center stall and hesitate before hitting the dummy. Similarly, it glides to the back of the lane and stays there, singed with bullet holes. Quickly, I dart over to the rightmost stall one last time, but when I do, the dummy is too close. I step back clumsily as it crashes against the divider with a loud thud. The chains above it rattle, then rip it backward to its resting place. I lower the gun and sigh in defeat. The rest of the room comes back into focus, bringing with it the sound of Lieutenant Kelley's scorn.

"Close, Madoc," he sneers. "But not fast enough."

I hand over the gun and join the other draftees with my head hung. If only I hadn't lingered so long on the center target, I would've made it there in time. I know I could've been there, but I wasn't. I was too distracted.

Ethan tries to commend me on everything I did well, but I brush him off. It's easy to acknowledge that all I did was let one slip past me. And it's easier to accept that when it's a training exercise, but it's more than that now. I've seen the other side of the Barrier. I know what we're up against. In here, missing one shot is just a bruise to my ego. But out there, that would've cost me my life. I can't afford to make that mistake again.

The rest of the draftees cycle through the exercise. By the end, Apollo is the only one to hit every target and stop all the dummies from making it to the end. Many of the other draftees are worse off than me, but Apollo's performance is flawless. He's swift, observant, and quick to deliver the kill shot every time. He's sure of every shot he makes and never hesitates. As soon as he lands the final shot, he spins around and smirks. He lifts the barrel of the gun to his lips and blows. I roll my eyes as he hands it over to Lieutenant Tillman.

Training concludes for the day, and after dinner, we return to our barracks to shower before bed. I manage to stow a few leftovers from my meal into my drawer, saving them for Daphne. Everything we've done today feels far from my mind now — all I can think about is seeing her. I try to lie still in bed, but the anticipation makes me restless. Ethan passes by and pauses before climbing up to his bunk.

"You still have everything?" he asks.

I turn over and reveal the pager clutched in my fist, then tap the badge hidden in my pocket. "Good to go as soon as it goes off."

Ethan smiles. "Goodnight, man. Be careful out there."

He scrambles up to his bunk, and the frame shakes as he plops down. Soon enough, the lights in the barracks dim to nothing. It doesn't take long for the other draftees to fall asleep, but I lie wide awake in my bunk. Turning to the side, I set the pager next to my face, hypnotized by its red light blinking in the corner. Waiting for it to turn green.

Within the hour, the pager buzzes once against the mattress before I close it in my fist to muffle the sound. I tumble out of the bunk, retrieve the scraps from my drawer, and slip out the barracks door in one swift motion. I jog down the hallway and pass through the chamber. The subway surges out of the tunnel as soon as I hit the platform, slowing to a stop. When the doors slide open, I hop inside and take my seat. One glance at the screen confirms it's headed to Daphne's stop. So I rest my head against the window, close my eyes, and let it take me there.

As soon as the subway pulls into the station, I'm on my feet again. I step off and start down the familiar path to her apartment. The night air bites at my skin, sending shivers all over my body. Through the darkness, I manage to pinpoint her building. I pull myself onto the lower landing and scale the steps leading to her unit. At the top, I push against the double doors, which willingly open to let me inside.

Daphne jumps up from the couch. I freeze where I am, one foot in, the other still propped out on the landing, my heart skipping a beat when I see her. It's clear we've both spooked each other.

"One of these days, I'll get used to you coming in," she exhales, holding her hand to her chest.

I jump down onto the carpet and push the doors shut behind me. "It's okay," I assure her. "One of these days, maybe I'll be able to come through your front door rather than climbing in through the landing."

A gentle smile spreads across her face. She's wrapped in a wool blanket to keep warm, one she must've found in the apartment. Her hair is draped behind her, and her eyes look red and sunken.

"Have you been getting any sleep?" I ask.

She shakes her head. "Barely. I've been staying up, trying to remember. But it's all still so fuzzy."

"There's no pressure to remember anything right now," I assure her. "What you need is to get some sleep."

Daphne takes a seat back on the couch, pulling her legs up until her whole body is wrapped in the blanket. She offers me the spot next to her. "Come. Sit," she says sweetly, and I accept the invitation.

As I sit down, I pull out the jerky and dried fruit swaddled in my napkin. Daphne takes it with no objections. I mimic her body language, pulling my knees up to my chest, one cushion of space between us. We stay like this while she eats, neither of us sure what to say, but both of us aware our time together is limited.

"Tell me something real," she insists.

I furrow my brows. "What do you mean?"

"It feels like there's this void in my mind, like a massive blank space where a lifetime's worth of memories should be. At this point, I don't know what's real and what's not. So tell me something real."

I search my mind for something to give her. "Well . . ."

"Tell me about your training," she interjects. "You said you're in training all day. What are you training for?"

"For the end of the world, basically," I say nonchalantly, but it stuns her. I quickly backtrack and try to explain. "We were born here, in the city. And the city has always been a safe place. We're training so we can protect it, in case that ever changes."

"Very noble of you," she remarks. "Did you agree to this, or was it just luck of the draw?"

"Quite literally the opposite," I chuckle. "If anything, we're the *unlucky* ones. It's been required by law ever since I can remember. When we turn eighteen, we're drafted and trained for a specific term. Afterwards, we're given roles in the military to help protect the city."

"I see," she says, pondering this for a moment. "Is that what you want?"

"Do I want to be in the draft?" I ask, trying to clarify her question.

"Well, yes, but not exactly what I meant. Do you want to work for the military?"

"Not necessarily, but—"

"What *do* you want then?" she wonders. Her eyes beam at me from across the couch.

I drop my feet to the floor and run my hands over my scalp, thinking through her question. "No one's ever asked me what I want," I sigh.

Silence passes between us. Daphne lowers her eyes, then wiggles her way out of the blanket. She scoots closer with her hand outstretched toward me, but she stops herself. My stomach pinches — because I wish she wouldn't pull away.

"Well, I'm asking you now." She stomps her foot and lifts her chin to imitate taking a stance. "What do you want, John?"

I feel completely unable to answer her honestly. It's as if I'm hardwired to say one thing only: the draft. The military. The war to protect the city. My whole life has been about nothing but these things. All anyone's ever cared about is making sure the Barrier doesn't burst or The Truth doesn't get in. People have tried to move past the horrible things that put us here. My parents did. But somewhere in the back of their minds, their sole priority has been survival. Entertaining anything else seems foolish.

But in this moment, with Daphne, I'm reminded that her existence is a wrench in the narrative I've been told all my life. She's living proof that there's more out there than we know. So maybe it *could* matter what I want. Maybe there's even a world in which I could have it.

"I want . . ." I mutter. I search the depths of my heart for the things I desire most. The things I've denied myself of. The things I've seen other people have, but that I never could.

And as they come to mind, I tell her. "I want my family to be safe. I want my little brother to grow up to be strong and unafraid. I want things to be different for him than they were for me. Maybe the world could be different than this, and I'd want that. I'd want to know what it means to love someone or maybe have a family of my own. I'd want to live far away from here and visit places I've never seen before. But at the end of the day, even if nothing changed, I just want my life to mean something. Something more than the draft, more than just a rank, more than what my father left behind. But—"

"No, no," she holds her finger to my lips, stopping me. Heat rushes to my face. *I've said too much*, I panic. I feel vulnerable, and I don't like it. I stuff these things back into the recesses of my mind, regretting ever bringing them to the surface.

Daphne slowly removes her finger and keeps her gaze fixed on me. "No *buts*," she whispers. "You want your life to mean something. You want more than this. *That's* what you want. You don't have to justify it just because it feels impossible."

"But that's the thing," I say. "It *is* impossible. It's nice to think about, but until things actually change, this is my life. And in this life, I have to want to be a soldier. I have to want to protect the city. So that's what I'll do."

She doesn't push any further. She pulls herself back into the blanket but stays close to me. Her head falls against the couch, and her eyes flutter shut for a moment.

"What are you protecting the city from exactly?" she asks faintly.

"The Truth," I blurt out on instinct. Her brows scrunch together, and I realize she wouldn't know what I'm referring to. "I mean, the evil that's out there. Beyond the city. You know, like what we experienced the night we found you."

"The monsters," Daphne whispers, and I nod. All of a sudden, the pager comes to life. We both leap to our feet, spurred by its vibration. Looking over at Daphne, my heart aches. I don't want to leave her again. Not yet. But I know if I don't go soon, I'll miss my chance to get back to The Battery.

I turn to head toward the landing, but Daphne's voice stops me.

"That's the only thing I remember," she utters.

My head spins around, drowning out the buzz of the pager for a moment.

"You remember the monsters?"

She shakes her head. "That's the thing, John. There are certain things I remember, but they aren't memories. They're more like facts — truths that, once etched into your mind, never leave you, almost as if they're preloaded into my DNA."

"And The Truth," I say hurriedly, "I mean, the monsters. They feel real?"

Her eyes widen and look beyond me, out toward the city, searching for something in the night that's not there. The pager rattles against my hip, urging me to get going. But I need to hear what she has to say. I can feel her trying to piece together the words, but they're stunted by fear.

"Yes," she nods. "You call it The Truth, or monsters, but it's more than that."

She steps closer, clutching the blanket up to her chin. Then, her focus breaks. Her eyes turn toward me, and a wave of confidence rushes over her, driving out any fear that was there before. It's as if for the first time since I've known her, she's never been more sure of anything.

"The Truth, John, is a disease."

Eighteen

I have to tell Ethan.

It's the first thing on my mind when I wake up. But there never seems to be a good time to tell him. By the time I roll out of bed, Ethan has already gone to breakfast, along with the rest of the unit.

As I step into the cafeteria, I spot Ethan sitting with Drew and Carson. They welcome me over to the table, and I hardly say a word. Anything I want to say can't be said in front of them. For now, this needs to stay between Ethan and me. Even as we break away from them to return our trays, there are too many people around. I tug at Ethan's arm, trying to pull him from the crowd for a moment, but he resists.

"We need to get to training, Johnny," he says. "Time's ticking."

We file onto the training lawn with the rest of the draftees. Lieutenant Kelley and Lieutenant Tillman are already waiting by the combat ring. One by one, they pick us off to fight while the rest of us observe. But all I can think about is Daphne.

The Truth, John, is a disease. Her words play on a loop in my mind. It all makes sense now. The need for the Barrier. The way the creature in Philadelphia resembled the likeness of a human. Why didn't I think of it sooner?

But then again, I had no reason to. I've only been operating based on what I've been told. Even though we've kept the true identity of The Truth hidden, I always assumed it was an environmental threat. Or something extraterrestrial. I never considered it might be something *within* us.

"Madoc," Lieutenant Kelley's voice snaps me out of my thoughts. For a moment, I think he's caught me zoning out. But it's clear I'm up next.

"Patton," Lieutenant Tillman says next. "Both of you, in the ring."

Leo smirks at me as he steps out of line. Together, we enter the ring, taking our positions at opposite ends.

"Go easy on me, eh?" he hollers at me.

"Sure thing," I shrug.

I can't seem to focus. Every moment that I'm not paying attention, my mind wanders back to Daphne's living room, replaying her words. Leo's nothing but a blur to me. He bends his knees and slaps his hands together, but I couldn't be more disinterested. I almost miss it when Lieutenant Tillman commences the fight.

Leo lunges forward, but I remain frozen in place. When he reaches me, he dives into a tackle. At the last second, I jump out of the way, narrowly avoiding him. As I do, my foot juts out instinctively, catching his leg mid-strike. He trips, tumbling against the ground in a puff of dirt, but he's back on his feet in an instant. Before I can even catch my breath, he's hurtling toward me again.

With his fists balled, Leo tries to send an uppercut into my chin, but I intercept it, catching his fist squarely in my palm. The impact reverberates up my arm as I push back against his force. To my surprise, our strength is equal. Our muscles strain against each other, trying to keep the other at bay. Leo bares his teeth as he pushes harder while my bicep quivers, threatening to betray me.

But with Leo already exerting so much force, I realize I can use it against him. I let go. All his pent-up momentum propels him forward, causing him to teeter off balance. I sidestep out of the way and drive my fist into his gut. He grunts, doubling over slightly. But even while he's down, he anticipates my next move. Twisting to the side, he catches my fist before I can land another punch, then kicks his boot into my kneecap. My legs buckle, and I fall to my knees. Leo wastes no time — he shoves me backward and climbs on top of me, pinning me down with his forearm at my throat.

A vengeful grin spreads across his face. "Not so fast, mate," he winks.

I wrap my legs around his waist and flip, reversing our positions to give me the advantage. Leo hits the ground with a heavy thud. I push against his chest to create some distance and stumble back onto my feet. He remains sprawled on the dirt, temporarily dazed, while I retreat to the edge of the ring.

While he's down, my mind shifts back to Daphne. I think about how later tonight, I'll ride the subway to her apartment again. How her smile will light up the otherwise dark room. How her hair will fall against her shoulder just right.

I don't know what we are or where she stands, for that matter. To her, I'm just someone to keep her company. Someone she can feel safe with. But to me, she's more than that. I've never considered the possibility of falling for someone. But as I shared last night, it's something I want. Something that, in another life, I'd long for.

But it can't happen. Right now, I have to remain neutral, and she has to stay hidden. After all, there's still so much I don't know about her. Yet somehow, there's so much I feel like I already do. Something deep inside me feels tethered to her. Something I can't quite explain but can't ignore either.

But how do I know if she feels the same? How can I be sure it's not all in my head, and that when she's healed, she won't leave me?

"Focus, Madoc!" I hear Lieutenant Kelley yell over my shoulder.

These doubts temporarily blind me to what's happening right in front of me. I don't even see Leo coming until he knocks me cold against the ground.

I've given him too much time to recover. I squirm around, attempting to claw my way out from underneath him. But he blocks my path every time. He pins my arms down and holds his forearm to my throat a second time, hovering over me with a baffled look on his face.

"Second time I've had the kill shot on you, man," he says as his chest heaves. "You alright?"

I try to go for the same tactic as before. I attempt to coil my legs around him, but he presses his knee into my thigh, keeping all my limbs pinned down.

"I'm f-fine," I wince.

Leo loosens his grip just enough for me to break free. I spring to my feet, and within seconds, we're trading hits at one another. Leo swings wide, his fist slicing through the air above me as I duck out of the way. Seizing the opening, I send an uppercut into his chin. I feel his jaw crack against my knuckles, but he's impervious to the pain. He lunges again, knocking me back to the ground. His weight takes the breath from my lungs, but this time, I come back stronger. I plant my foot against his chest and send him flying backward. He lands against the dirt face-first and pushes off the ground, rising with a stamina that's unmatched.

I bend my knees to hold my ground. As soon as he's within reach, I fake him out with a faux punch to the left side and send a punch into his right cheek instead. His whole body rattles from the impact, but he shakes it off. When he looks back at me, his eyes sharpen, and his face grows stiff. Before I can react, his knuckle smashes into my eye. Pain explodes across my face, and I cry out. My vision tunnels as heat rushes to the point of impact. I cover my face, feeling my eye throb behind my fingers, but Leo persists. He tackles me to the ground for a third time. His forearm presses into my throat as he sighs deeply, as if he's disappointed.

"What's gotten into you?" he asks.

I let out a groan, my hand still clasped over my eye.

Leo's eyes dart across my face, assessing the damage. Lieutenant Tillman ends the fight there and awards Leo the victory.

Slowly, I lower my hand, and Leo's expression twists into both shock and guilt. It must look just as awful as it feels. He extends his hand to help me up, and I take it.

"Sorry about your eye, mate," he apologizes.

"No need," I whimper. "It's all part of the exercise, right?"

"Yeah, but . . ." his voice trails off.

My pulse races. I can't afford for Leo to sense even a hint of distraction or weakness. If he found out I was hiding something — or someone — I can't trust that he'd keep it to himself.

"You let me have that shot," he finishes his sentence.

"Or maybe I just didn't see it coming, and you're better than you think."

He smiles in appreciation and accepts this.

Once everyone's had a chance to go, we conclude training for the day. After dinner, we trudge back to the barracks to get ready for bed. Stepping out of the shower, I wrap a towel tightly around my waist and catch a glimpse of myself in the mirror. I stare in shock at the swollen black ring puffing beneath my eyelid. I rush up to the mirror to get a closer look. Putting a finger to the bruise, I wince sharply, the area still tender to touch. My whole eye aches every time it moves.

Ethan crosses into the bathroom behind me. His eyes meet mine in the mirror, and he steps back, startled by what he sees.

"Yikes!" he exclaims. "It gets worse every time I look at it."

"Don't be dramatic. It's not *that* bad." I stifle a shaky breath as a fresh wave of pain ripples across my face.

"Does it hurt?" he asks considerately.

"Yeah," I admit. "But don't tell Leo."

"Alright, Mr. Tough Guy," he chuckles, then heads for an open shower. I find some ointment in the bathroom and massage it gently over the wound. It cools my skin, relieving the fire burning behind my eye.

I walk out into the barracks. Draping the towel over the frame of the bed to dry, I pull on my sweatpants and slide a thin hoodie over my head. Rolling into the bottom bunk, I lay the side of my face lightly against the pillow, careful not to apply too much pressure. I pull the pager from my pocket and set it next to me, wishing the hours away until it buzzes.

As soon as it does, I slip out of the bunk and out the barracks door. Just as it has the past two nights, the subway waits for me at Battery Station, its doors already open to welcome me on board. The overhead lights lining the aisle beam at me, causing my eye to ache. For a moment, I understand how Daphne must've felt that morning in Philadelphia as the sun beat down on her head wound.

Once the subway pulls into the station, I hop off and blaze down the path to her apartment. I ascend the fire escape as if it's muscle memory now. When I reach the top, I press my palm against the doors. But before I can apply pressure, they're ripped open from the other side.

"Ha!" Daphne exclaims. Her eyes light up when she sees me. "I was expecting you this time."

I jump down from the landing and slip past her. I try to cover my face with my shoulder, hoping the dimness of the room will be enough to hide the black eye, but it doesn't work. Daphne grabs my arm and spins me around. My face catches in the moonlight, and her eyes widen in concern.

"John, what happened to you?"

I shake my arm out of her grip. "It's not a big deal, it's just—"

"No, you're hurt," she interrupts.

I manage to make my way into the kitchen. Resting my hands against the counter, I look up at her from across the room. "I got it from training. I took a pretty hard hit to the eye, but I'm alright."

She strides over to me, her level of concern unchanging. My stomach twists with embarrassment.

"Has this ever happened before?"

"No," I reply. "I can usually defend myself pretty well, but I—" the words catch in my throat. She raises her brow, waiting for me to finish. But I can't say what I want to say. I can't admit the only reason the punch got past me is because I was thinking about her.

"I guess I was just off my game today," I lie.

Her mouth sags into a frown. "Well, be more careful next time." She nudges my shoulder playfully and circles the bar top. My eyes never leave her.

"Is it worth it?" she asks. "Getting all bruised and beaten to defend your family?"

"It has to be," I shrug.

"Tell me about them," she says warmly. She leans against the counter, her hair brushing the granite. "Your family, I mean."

"There's not much to tell," I deflect, but that's not true. Images of my mother and Liam resurface in my mind. My eyes drift over to the windows looking out over the city. A few blocks north of here is all it'd be, and I'd be home with them. Knowing I'm on this side of the city but can't see them is torture, but that's not Daphne's burden to bear.

"Oh, come on," Daphne remarks. "Let's start with your mother. What's her name?"

"Lilian," I mutter.

She repeats it back to me. "Lilian. What's she like?"

My mind takes me back to the morning of my birthday. I think of how graceful she is. The smell of vanilla and eucalyptus that wafts through the house, following her everywhere she goes. The stretch lines around her lips that grow every time she smiles. How many times she'd smile at me and assure me everything would be okay — and how many times I refused to believe her.

"She's kind," I start. "Thoughtful. Gentle. She has a tough shell that's hard to crack, but life did that to her. She raised my brother and me almost entirely on her own. I'd imagine that changes a person a little."

Daphne's eyes gleam. "She sounds like an incredible woman," she says. "Tell me about your brother."

"Liam," I start with his name. "He's younger than me. Much younger, by nearly a decade. He's bold, a bit stubborn at times, but I guess he learned that from me. He clings to my mother and follows in her shadow most of the time."

"I bet he looks up to you."

I chuckle. "I'm not so sure I'm someone to look up to."

"Hmm," Daphne protests. "I disagree. After all, you did save me, a stranger, from a terrible place. And you took a black eye today for the sake of learning how to defend yourself and protect your family. I'd say that's pretty admirable."

"Well, thank you," I blush. It's encouraging to know that's how she sees me, even when I don't see it in myself.

"And your father?" she asks innocently. She doesn't know — *how could she?* — the weight her question holds. "Does he look up to him too?"

"I—" I stutter. I'm not quite sure how to say it, or how much I should say. "He isn't in our lives," is what I decide on.

Daphne's posture changes. Her face softens, and I feel my stomach twist again with embarrassment. I don't want her to feel sorry for me. But then again, I want her to know me — and sometimes the two go hand in hand.

"What happened to him?"

"He was an important man," I say. "Very involved in the draft. But the military banished him. As far as I know, he started digging around in places he shouldn't, and it cost him everything — his reputation, his family, and his place in the city."

Daphne's eyes swell with curiosity. I can tell she wants to know more but doesn't want to ask too much at the same time.

"So, you don't know where he is?"

I shake my head. "Not for certain. But I'm determined to find out."

"And how exactly do you plan on doing that?"

"I'm not sure yet," I admit. "But I'll find a way."

She remains silent for a moment, caught somewhere between caution and empathy. But before she can respond, I shift the focus away from me.

"Do you — *did* you — have a family?" I ask, even though I know she won't have an answer.

Her gaze sinks to the counter. I watch her eyes swim, treading through the depths of her mind, trying to conjure any memory of a long-lost family. But nothing surfaces.

"I-I don't remember," she stammers.

I quickly regret asking and hurry to change the topic. "Let's not focus on that right now. Let's go back to what you said last night — about what you *do* remember."

She lifts her eyes to me. "You mean the disease?"

Hearing her say the word again stuns me. I still haven't gotten used to it.

"Yes," I confirm. "Do you remember anything more about it? How do you know that's what it is?"

"Because I've seen it change someone," she answers.

My heartbeat quickens. From across the counter, her face twists into a look of horror, as if some awful, twisted memory is resurfacing.

Her bottom lip trembles until it drops open, and the words spill out. "Once one of the infected sinks its teeth into another person, that person begins to change. Slowly morphing into the worst possible version of themselves. It starts small. First, their skin grays. Then their hair falls out, and soon enough, their eyes roll into the back of their head until they're all white. It takes away their sanity, convincing them every other living thing around them is prey, and then it—"

She inhales sharply, startling me. Her eyes spread wide, and tears begin to pool in them, as if her next words are too painful to even speak.

"That's alright," I say in a panic, trying to steady her. "You can stop there. You don't have to say any more."

Her shoulders relax, but her eyes remain widened, unable to unsee the grisly details that have now been unearthed in her mind.

"But there's one more thing," she insists. "One more thing I remember."

I lean forward, patiently hanging onto every word. Trying to give her plenty of space to process the memories as they come to her. "What is it?" I ask.

"When you and Ethan found me in Philadelphia, I was headed somewhere. Somewhere safe," she clarifies. "To a place where I knew there'd be a solution to all of this."

"A solution?" I repeat back. "Like a cure?" I whisper the word as if it's something that shouldn't be said aloud.

She nods. "Yes, exactly."

"Do you remember where you were headed?"

But it's clear she doesn't. Not fully, at least. The details are fuzzy, but there's some level of knowledge that's still there. Just as she said last night, there are some things that can't be erased — they stick with you, whether you want them to or not.

"South," she guesses. "Or maybe it was north. I don't know. Someplace far from Philadelphia, at least. I remember feeling so desperate to get there."

The thought hits me that maybe she was headed here, to New York. Maybe somehow, she found out about the city, and she's been trying to get here all along. After all, the city is the only true safe haven.

But there's no cure here. If there were, wouldn't we have used it by now?

"Maybe it was here." I decide to test my theory. "You're safe here. Under—" I stop myself. Daphne doesn't know about the Barrier. If she did, it might help her feel more at ease. Or it might make her feel trapped. If she wasn't headed to New York, and there's some other place that may have a cure, I know she'd want to be there instead. But as long as she's here, under the Barrier, she can't get there.

I feel selfish for not telling her, but I'm scared if I do, I'll lose her. I want her to feel safe with me — with or without the Barrier. It might not be where she set out for, but that doesn't mean it isn't a good thing. It doesn't mean *we* aren't a good thing.

"Under my watch," I finish, quickly altering my words.

"Maybe . . ." she ponders, but she doesn't seem convinced.

The pager begins to buzz in my pocket, shattering the moment between us. I pull it out quickly and clasp it in my hand to muffle the sound. Daphne's gaze stays anchored to the counter, unfazed by the pager's beck and call, as if she's stuck in a trance. I can feel her fighting to cling to the memories as they come and go, each one crumbling out of her grasp.

As I make my way to the landing, she calls out to me, breaking through her thoughts.

"Wait, John!" she hollers

"Yes?" I say, turning my ear toward her.

"They really haven't told you about the disease? Or that there might be a cure?"

I shake my head. "No. Not one word of it."

She weighs my words carefully, and as much as I want to stick around, the insistent vibration of the pager urges me to go. I scramble down the fire escape and leap to the ground below. As I jog back to the station, her words echo in my mind. If it's true that a cure exists, why hasn't anyone told us?

Why wouldn't we want that? Not just for ourselves, but for the future of our nation?

But as I step onto the subway, I get a sinking feeling that if they wanted us to know about the cure, we would.

General Conrad said himself that my father questioned him about life outside the city. But maybe he took it a step further. Maybe he went looking for others. And when he did, he found the place Daphne spoke of. Another safe haven. A place where people don't hide behind strongholds or let fear dictate their means of survival. A place where they fight back and take matters into their own hands. Where they've found a cure.

If a place like that exists, it could threaten the sanctity of everything we've built here. Everything we've been told to believe.

And maybe that's just it. Maybe that's the truth they've been keeping from us all along. Not that a cure doesn't exist, but that one does — and they don't want to let it in.

Nineteen

By the end of the second quarter, my rank hardly matters. There have been too many distractions, too many things that have taken priority over training — well, one thing in particular.

I've grown used to spending my nights with Daphne. Every time the lights go out in the barracks, the cycle repeats. I wait for the pager to buzz, ride the subway to her apartment, and spend every moment with her until the pager calls me back. The closer I get to her, the more distant I feel from the draft. The ambition that once fueled me through every drill and exercise four weeks ago is now the same ambition that draws me to her each night. Any progress in training couldn't possibly compare to the progress I've made with her, and the way I feel when I'm with her.

When I'm with her, the world falls away. It's as if there's no Barrier, no war imminent on the other side, and no one depending on me — nobody but her. With her, I feel like a new version of myself, or maybe the version that was always there but buried beneath the weight of the draft. She pulls it out of me effortlessly, bringing me back to the core of who I am, not who I'm expected to be.

But reality is cruel. Every morning, as Lieutenant Kelley lays out our daily training regimen, I'm reminded that in order to be with her, I have to continue playing the part. As long as the Barrier stands, I have to be more — more than who she brings out of me, and more like the soldier the world needs me to be.

I'm reminded that if I become too indifferent to the draft, the whole thing could be ripped away from me. *She* could be ripped away from me.

After our second assessment, we file into the Assembly Hall. The room thrums with anticipation. The other draftees self-assess their own performances, making predictions on their ranks. Meanwhile I keep my head down and slide into the seat next to Ethan.

I don't have to speculate how I did or where my name might land. I know when the results are broadcasted onto the screen, I'll have fallen from the top. As General Conrad takes the stage, I wait for the whole room to find out too.

"Good evening," he greets us. "Draftees, congratulations on another successful quarter of training. You're officially halfway through your training, and halfway to becoming the soldiers you're destined to be."

Applause ripples throughout the room. General Conrad's eyes slither across our row. As they pass over me, my blood runs cold. To him, I'm no longer just a face in the crowd — I'm a threat. A potential trouble spot to look out for. I sink further into my seat, shrinking beneath his gaze.

Lieutenant Tillman and Lieutenant Kelley approach the stage with their tablets in hand. They pass the results to General Conrad, and he dutifully displays them on the screen behind him.

"As it stands, here are your ranks from quarter two of training," he announces.

1. APOLLO ANDRES
2. LEO PATTON
3. JOHN MADOC
4. ETHAN GREENE
5. DREW FITZGERALD

6. DANNY GUERRA
7. DOM D'ANGELO
8. LUCA ROSS
9. CARSON O'HAIR
10. RORY TAYLOR
11. JOEY CALLAHAN
12. ADRIAN HART

The room roars with applause. Despite my indifference, shame twists in my gut. I'm disappointed in myself for letting Apollo take the lead. I don't even have to look over at him to know he's pleased, though I'm not sure if he's more satisfied that he surpassed me or that he's top of the ranks.

Ethan nudges me. "Still got it, baby," he winks, flashing all five fingers at me. I let him have his moment, though I doubt Lieutenant Kelley will ever grant us special permissions again, despite our ranks.

Almost as quickly as it comes on, all my shame dissipates, replaced by a longing to see Daphne tonight. Our names fade out with the applause, and the screen behind General Conrad dims to a blank slate.

He clears his throat, then straightens his stare. "It's one thing to see the results on a screen, but another thing entirely to put the skills you've learned to the test. Remember, you aren't just training for a rank. You're training to become soldiers — strong, courageous men equipped to uphold the safety and preservation of this city. Each of you have dedicated your lives to that cause, and each of you have a responsibility to it. Obey, Preserve, Protect!"

"Obey, Preserve, Protect!" we chant as a congregation.

General Conrad grins with satisfaction. With that, he dismisses us from the Assembly Hall. Lieutenant Kelley and Lieutenant Tillman sidestep into the aisle, allowing us to pass through. Lieutenant Tillman leads the draftees up the ramp while Lieutenant Kelley hangs back. As Ethan and I reach the end of the row, he whispers harshly, "You two. I need to have a word with you."

Ethan and I exchange a nervous glance before replying with a dutiful, "Yes, sir." We step aside to let the others pass. Drew and Carson watch from over their shoulders, concern etched on their faces.

Anxiety boils in my chest. My first thought is Daphne. *He knows.* Somehow, he's found out about her, and he's put it together that Ethan and I have something to do with it. My heart pounds as I consider the possibility that they've already shipped her back to Philadelphia — or worse, they've hurt her.

But that's not the case. Instead, he holds out a firm finger and says, "Can I trust that the next time we go outside the Barrier, you two won't wander off again?"

"Uh, yes, sir," we respond with a hint of apprehension.

"Wait, why?" Ethan interjects. "Are we going on another supply run?"

"Yes," Lieutenant Kelley states. "Consider it an opportunity to redeem yourselves. The general was against it, but given your ranks, I convinced him you'd earned a second chance. Especially you, Greene."

Ethan smirks. After all, he deserves the recognition for improving his rank.

Lieutenant Kelley sharpens his tone. "This time, I don't want you going anywhere out of my sight. In fact, I don't want you doing anything without clearing it with me first. Do you understand?"

I try to contain the rush of nerves and excitement, but my face shows it all. Lieutenant Kelley narrows his eyes, threatening me with a look.

"I said, do you understand?" he shouts. His voice echoes throughout the now-empty auditorium.

"Yes, sir," we reply timidly.

"Good," he states. He turns to walk away, but I stop him.

"Sir!" I call out. "Are we going back to Philadelphia?"

He lets out a slow, exaggerated laugh as he pivots back around. "You'd like that wouldn't you? Since you two had such a nice extended vacation there." His laughter fades abruptly, and he hardens his stare. "No, we're going to Washington D.C."

Without another word, he ascends the ramp toward the exit, leaving us where we stand. My mind reels at the thrill of venturing beyond the Barrier again. This time, we're going someplace we've never been — a place where there could be others, like Daphne. A place that could bring us one step closer to the cure.

I have to be careful, though. Lieutenant Kelley will be right on our heels the entire time. But still, any place outside the Barrier holds another piece of the truth we've so meticulously fabricated here. I can't afford to reveal my intentions. Doing so would not only put my life at risk but Daphne's as well. But I can't let this opportunity pass me by. I have to stay vigilant and be observant.

Ethan turns toward me with the opposite reaction. His eyes widen with concern, clearly unsettled by the look on my face. Behind my eyes, he can tell I'm plotting something — something he has no desire to be a part of.

"No more surprises this time, please?" he pleads.

Setting my wishful thoughts aside, I rest a steady hand on his shoulder. "Don't worry," I reassure him. "No more surprises."

Twenty

Later that night, I take the subway to see Daphne. I jog to her apartment through the murky night. Clouds gather over the Barrier, holding back a storm. When I reach her building, I hoist myself onto the lower landing and race up the steps until I reach her unit. Pushing through the doors, I expect her to be right on the other side, waiting for me. But at first glance, the apartment looks vacant.

Hesitantly, I step down into the living room and close the doors behind me. There's no sign of her here or in the kitchen, but the bedroom door is open. Just as I'm walking through the doorway, she comes out at the same time.

Our bodies collide, and we both jump back, startled by each other. As soon as my mind registers it's her, my shoulders sag in relief. I smile at her, letting her know I'm happy to see her. But her reaction couldn't be more opposite. Her eyes harden, and her face contorts into a scowl, shattering my joy.

"Hi, uh—" I say nervously.

She brushes past me and storms into the kitchen. As she does, I notice a makeshift bag slung over her shoulder, crafted from the blanket she wrapped herself in the second night I came to visit her. I can tell it's weighed down by items stuffed inside of it.

With her back to me, I ask, "Are you going somewhere?"

She rummages through every kitchen drawer until she finds what she's looking for — a knife. She rips it out of the drawer and holds it in front of her face, examining it. I step back, worried she might snap and drive it into me.

But instead, she lets out a huff and deposits it into her bag.

"Whoa, whoa, whoa," I say, rushing toward her as soon as the knife is tucked away. But as I draw near, her palm stops me, keeping me at a distance.

"Stop," she demands. She keeps her chin down, but her eyes stare up at me menacingly, like any move I make might be fatal.

For a moment, I'm afraid of her. I'm afraid that Ethan was right all along — that we really don't know her or know if we can trust her. But I *do* know her. I've been with her every night for the past four weeks. If she was anything other than who she's presented herself to be, surely I would've seen it by now.

My mind scrambles, trying to pinpoint what could've tipped her off or changed to elicit this sort of response. But it doesn't make sense.

"Daphne, I don't understand—"

She slams the drawer shut with such force that I wince. She spins around, resting her back against the counter, and crosses her arms over her chest. Her eyes point back at me like daggers.

"Do you want to know what I did today?"

My heart sinks. Numerous possibilities come to mind, and none of them involve her staying in the apartment — and that terrifies me.

But I set aside any presumptions and let her speak. "What did you do today?" I prompt her.

"I decided to go out today," she answers. Her lips purse and her brow arches, as if to say she knows she shouldn't have, but she did it anyway. "All I wanted to do was go for a walk. I wanted to see more of the city, the city *you* brought me to. I wanted to know what it felt like to walk freely without having to look over my shoulder. I wanted—"

"Daphne, do you know what would've happened if you—"

She shakes a finger at me viciously, and I swallow my words. She grits her teeth to stifle a rush of emotion, but tears burst from her eyes. It breaks my heart to see her like this. To know the trust we've worked so hard to build may be dwindling. Whatever happened, it's given her a reason to see me as a threat. And if there's one thing Daphne is, it's stubborn — she won't back down that easily.

"I wasn't going to *speak* to anyone, John," she hisses at me. "I know you're so concerned about me running my mouth and someone finding you out."

"It's not about that," I defend myself. "It's not just about someone finding me out. This is all so much bigger than you realize." My words come out harsher than I intend, but they don't seem to affect her. The damage has already been done — nothing I say now could deepen the wound.

"Exactly!" she erupts, exasperated. "It *is* bigger than I realize, and that's just it. It should've been as simple as it sounds: All I wanted was to go for a walk. To feel safe again beyond these four walls. And the worst part is, I felt it. For a split second, I felt safe." Her voice breaks, and her lip starts to quiver. It takes everything in me not to reach for her and offer some measure of comfort. But I'm not what she needs right now. In her eyes, the last thing she wants is me.

She continues. "The feeling I've been chasing this whole time was right there, all around me. That is, until I hit some sort of invisible wall. It was as solid as the ground beneath me, but I couldn't see it. And yet, it was there, preventing me from going any further. And then I realized, I wasn't actually safe. Safety was just an illusion. And just like that, the feeling vanished." She puts her fingertips together, then releases them in a burst. "*Poof.* And all I was left with was panic."

She knows about the Barrier. All this time, I've kept it from her. At first, it was deliberate, but then it faded from my mind. I never wanted her to feel trapped here. I just wanted her to know she could trust me before revealing the truth.

But now, I see what I've done. By withholding the truth to gain her trust first, I've shattered it.

"So, I need you to tell me," her tone deepens, shaken with emotion. "Where am I? And what is this?"

I can't sugarcoat it. I have to tell her the whole truth. And I have to accept whatever the outcome is.

"The Barrier," I croak. "The invisible wall, it's called the Barrier. It encases Lower Manhattan from the top of the highest tower to the edge of the city. It's inescapable, but it protects us from The Truth."

"But the subway . . . how did you—" she asks, processing her question in real time.

"The subway is the only way in or out of the city," I explain. "It can pass beneath the Barrier underground and only connects to a few spots outside the city. But only the military has access to it. Only—" I pause. I cringe at my next words, knowing they'll make me look more like the bad guy. "Only men like Ethan and me have access to it."

Eight weeks ago, I didn't even know the subways existed. Eight weeks ago, I didn't want to be the man I am today. But now, here I am. I feel sick to my stomach. Standing before Daphne, I realize I'm no different than the men I've despised my whole life. The same men who cherry-pick the truth to further their own agenda, all the while convincing everyone their narrative is reliable.

The more I tell Daphne, the more I know I'm only pushing her away. But I need her to understand. As crazy as it sounds, I need her to buy into the truth, the same truth we've all bought into — because I need her.

Her eyes fall to the floor. She clutches the sling bag over her shoulder definitively. "I've heard enough," she says. "I'm going."

She attempts to move past me, but I grab her arm in desperation. "Daphne, no. Please."

Her eyes lock on mine with an incredulous look on her face. "What did you think was going to happen, John?" she asks. Her voice spikes, her anger piquing. "That I would just stay here and never venture out? I mean, were you ever going to tell me? Or were you just hoping I'd never find out?"

"I . . . I—" I stammer. "Of course I was going to tell you. But I was worried that if I did, this would happen."

She scoffs. "Well, I guess I proved you right then."

She tries to pry herself from my grip, but I stand firm. I need her to see this didn't all derive from selfish motives. Maybe it started out that way, but it's become so much more than that.

"Daphne, please just let me explain," I plead.

"No," she snaps. "You lied to me, John. You convinced me you were taking me somewhere safe, when in reality, you've been keeping me from somewhere safer all along."

"I didn't lie," I reply sharply. Heat rushes to my cheeks, and I feel my temper starting to escalate. "You *are* safe here. That's not a lie. The Barrier keeps us all safe. And without it, we'd be no different than you before Ethan and I found you."

"But am I really?" she questions. "You keep me in a fifth-story apartment on a street no one else lives on. You beg me not to go anywhere or near anyone else because you're worried someone might notice me. And if they did, and someone actually did find out about me, what would happen then, John? Would I be safe then?"

I don't respond because I know she's right. She wouldn't be safe, but I'd protect her. I'd do everything in my power to keep her safe.

My silence is enough of an answer. She shoves me aside and throws her hands in the air.

"See? I knew it!" she exclaims. She turns on her heels, inching closer toward the landing, but I intervene again.

"Daphne, please," I beg desperately. "You have to understand. Yes, I ask that you don't go anywhere else during the day or near anyone else *for right now*. But it doesn't mean that's how it'll be forever. I didn't think it all through before bringing you here. You were hurt. You were unconscious, for crying out loud. The only thing I knew was that here would be better than where you were. I know this isn't your final destination, but I just hoped it would be enough until we could figure out a better plan."

"But that's not how I see it," she says. "At least out there, in Philadelphia, I had a choice. I could fight. I could press on until I found safer ground. But here, you don't get to do anything on your own terms. You said it yourself: You can't even *think* for yourself." Her words pierce me. She throws everything I told her in confidence back in my face — all the things I long for and can't have because of the draft.

"You're all hiding," she accuses. "You're sitting ducks, hunkering down under this illusion of safety that you think will last forever. I thought you were training to become a soldier, John. Well, wake up — the war is here. It's happening outside the Barrier every single day. So why aren't you fighting back?"

"I will," I say defensively. "We *all* will, once the time is right. If the Barrier falls, then we—"

"That's the difference between you and me," Daphne interjects. "That, right there. The difference is, you wait for something to happen before you do anything about it. It's like the problem doesn't exist until it's staring you in the face, rearing its ugly head at you. I don't wait. I prepare for the worst and take action before anything happens to me. That way, I'm not shaken when trouble comes my way. And that's exactly what I'm doing now. I'm going."

She tries to step past me, but I jump in her path.

"Where would you go, Daphne?" I test her. "Where could you even go?"

She sighs. "Somewhere out there, there's a cure. There's a place where people are actively fighting back against this disease. Even if it's not protected by your Barrier, I have to believe I can be safe there too."

"And what if you're not?" I suggest. "What if you're wrong? Say you leave, and you find out there is no cure. There is no safe haven where someone has cracked the code. What if this is it? What if this is as safe as it gets?"

"That's a risk I'm willing to take," she bites back. "Because believe it or not, John, I'd rather live my life hoping for something greater than die with regret, wishing I would've listened sooner."

"What if we go together?" At this point, I'm stalling her. "I want to believe there's a cure. I want to find it and put an end to this just as much as you do. I've lived my whole life under the Barrier. And all my life, I've felt the exact same way you feel now — trapped, desperate to escape, afraid that if I don't go now, I may never get out. But it's not that easy for me right now."

"Well, it is for me," Daphne says without mercy.

She maneuvers around me and makes it to the doors. Pulling them back, she hops onto the landing, her silhouette glowing in the moonlight. Her eyes peer over the edge, scanning the fire escape leading to the ground below. To freedom.

I realize if I don't act now, I'm going to lose her.

"Remember the second night I came to see you?" I call out to her.

She hesitates. Her eyes don't meet mine, but she turns her ear toward me, willing to hear what I have to say.

"Tell me something real," I repeat the same words she said to me that night. "That's what you asked me to do. Daphne, I can't stand here and tell you I haven't done anything wrong. But you can't stand there and tell me the last few weeks haven't meant anything to you. That I don't mean anything to you."

Her blonde hair swirls in the wind, loose strands curling against her chin. For now, I have her full attention, so I lay everything out on the table. It may not change the outcome, but if she still chooses to walk away, at least she'll leave knowing how I feel. And I'll know I did everything I could.

"All my life, I've been told we were the last living people in the entire nation, and everything under the Barrier was all that's left. And then, for the first time in my life, I saw the other side. I went to Philadelphia, and I found you. And that has changed *everything* for me. Your existence has defied everything I've ever known. Sure, it may have been selfish to bring you here, but look at what it's led to. The more I've gotten to know you, I've felt hope. I've felt capable of becoming more than who *they* expect me to be. Because of what you've told me about the disease, about the cure, you've given me a greater responsibility — to my family, to the people of this city, and to you. And that's not something I take for granted. *That* is real."

Silence passes between us, but I cling to every second of it, hoping something will click and make her stay. She lowers her eyes, stuck between what her mind is already set on and what I've said.

"So I'm sorry for not being completely honest with you," I apologize. "And I'm sorry for holding you back. You're right, you have every right to go. To leave this city, to leave me, and find what you've been looking for. But please, if you can give me a chance to do what I have to do first, to finish what's left of the draft, then you won't have to go alone. Think of what we could do together. Together, we can find what else is out there. We can change the world."

With her eyes still downcast, Daphne steps down from the landing and back into the living room. My heart races, spurred by the fact that it might've worked. That something I said has bought us more time, and it's worth it to her to wait for me until we can work together.

She opens her mouth to respond, but before she can, the pager begins to buzz in my pocket, shattering the moment between us. Her gaze fixates on the green lights flashing through my sweatpants, but I keep my eyes on her, willing the pager to stop buzzing. Right now, nothing else matters but her.

"Aren't you going to go?" she asks in a whisper.

I don't move. I stay right where I stand and try to block out the noise. I know if I miss the subway, I may not have another way of getting back to the facility tonight. And if I'm not in my bunk tomorrow morning, it'll be the death of me.

But still, I can't leave her. Not like this. Part of me wants to throw it all away. To leave with her tonight and take the subway far from the city, far from any sort of consequence I could face.

But I can't. As long as I'm under their command, they'd come looking for me. And when they find me, they'd find Daphne too, and that would be the end of it. I can't give up now. I have to continue playing the part so we might actually have a shot at this.

"I just need to know that—" I mutter. My palms start to sweat, knowing at least a minute's worth of time has passed since the pager's first buzz.

"Go," Daphne interrupts me. "Just go, John."

The pager continues to vibrate against my leg, heightening my sense of urgency. But now that I've gotten through to her, I can't go. Not yet. I need to know she's not going anywhere.

"Go!" she screams, pointing her finger toward the landing.

"Daphne, I just need to know that you'll be here," I reply softly. "Just wait here, please. We can continue this tomorrow. We can figure this out together. Just don't go tonight, please."

She bites her lip, holding back a wave of emotion. "I told you, John. I don't wait for something to happen to me before I act. Now go! And don't bother coming back."

My heart sinks to the pit of my stomach. Any chance of her having considered what I said is gone. I give her one more moment to change her mind, but she doesn't. Reluctantly, I slip through the doors and rush down the fire escape. As soon as my feet hit the ground, I break. Tears fly out of my eyes as I sprint to the station. I make it with only a matter of seconds to spare before the doors slide shut, closing me in on the other side. The subway lurches forward and glides along the rails, carrying me back to the facility. Away from Daphne.

I don't sit in a seat. Instead, I collapse on the floor, balling my knees up to my chest. Rage swells within me. I hurl the pager down the aisle, hoping it breaks. Hating it for pulling me away from her. But it remains perfectly intact and rolls underneath a row of seats. The dull red light continues to blink in the corner of the device, a painful reminder that I'm still at its mercy.

I drop my head in my hands. I think back to when Ethan and I first found Daphne. She was all alone. She was hurt, defenseless, and in need of saving — at least that's how it seemed. Maybe Ethan was right. Maybe we should've just left her and wiped our hands clean of it. Then we wouldn't have missed the subway. We wouldn't have gotten ourselves stuck outside the city. We would've made it back with everyone else. I would've kept my focus on training, and none of this would've happened. I wouldn't feel so helpless right now, embarrassed that I even thought for a second she would wait for me. That after all this time, she'd feel the same way I do.

But we didn't. We took her in, cared for her, and because of it, I learned what it means to know her. And just as I've grown used to knowing her, I worry that this, what I feel right now, is what it feels like to lose her. As I picture her standing in the apartment — her back to the doors, her body framed by a halo of moonlight, her eyes lifting ever so slightly, giving me a glimmer of hope that I changed her mind — I'm afraid that might've been the last time I'll ever see her.

Twenty-One

The training officers storm into the barracks early the following morning. My eyes flutter awake, heavy with exhaustion. I peel myself out of bed and slide into my uniform. Lieutenant Tillman slams his palms against the frame of Apollo and Dom's bunk, jolting them awake. Ethan jumps down from the top bunk and begins dressing too, spurred by all the noise. By the time he's finished, we're the first two lined up.

Drew steps beside us with a grin stretched ear to ear. It's his first time beyond the Barrier, and the excitement is written all over his face. I wish I could share it with him, but I can't. Any anticipation I once had for the mission is smothered by the fear that Daphne won't be here when we get back.

Once we're all in line, Lieutenant Kelley orders us out while Lieutenant Tillman stays back with the rest of the draftees. We give Carson a friendly wave as we go. It feels wrong leaving him behind, but he doesn't seem too affected by it. He offers a soft smile before the door closes and we lose sight of him.

As we turn into the shooting range, I'm hit with déjà vu. Just like before, soldiers flood the room and run through our gear. I slip on the padded vest and secure the belt around my waist. It sags with the weight of the handgun tucked inside the holster. Next, I slide on the carbon fiber helmet. Once it's secure, I cover my hands with the thin protective gloves and snap the seams around my wrists.

"Try to bring it all back this time," says the soldier assisting me, giving my helmet an affirmative tap as he moves on to the next draftee.

Lieutenant Kelley comes down the line and hands each of us a pager. At first, I'm hesitant to take it, knowing Ethan's pager from Philadelphia is still in my possession. But he doesn't know that. Quickly, I take the pager from his hand and clip it to my hip.

Once everyone is prepped, we march down the hall and emerge onto Battery Station, where we're quickly met by another group of soldiers. They distribute our packs, equipped with a water canteen and first-aid kit. I sling the pack across my body and tighten the strap. I release it just in time for another soldier to hand me a different item. He drops three thick canisters into my palm, each one secured with a cap over the top. Without any explanation, he shuffles down the line to the next draftee.

I glance over at Lieutenant Kelley. He can tell something isn't clicking with me by the way I'm holding them.

"They're smoke flares," he shouts.

"What do we need these for?" Leo chimes in.

"It's not your job to ask questions, soldier!" Lieutenant Kelley screams. Leo recoils and stuffs the flares into a pocket in his vest.

I follow suit, deciding not to question it any further — or risk pushing Lieutenant Kelley over the edge.

The pager begins to buzz against my hip, and my heart leaps. I've grown used to attributing its vibration to getting to see Daphne. But it's not the same anymore. After today, who knows where she'll be. There's a chance that something I said might've kept her here. But just as the subway will carry us to D.C., it's possible it'll carry her somewhere far from here. Somewhere meant only for her.

The subway rushes into the station with a hot gust of wind. The smell of metal and grime fills the air as it screeches to a full stop. As soon as the doors open, Lieutenant Kelley prompts us to step on board. I take my seat in the furthest corner, and Ethan naturally claims the spot next to me. Drew files in after him, fumbling with his pager. He rotates it in his hand like it's some kind of treasure, amazed at how it works. Meanwhile I close my fist around mine to muffle the sound, resisting the urge to hurl it at the floor and grind it under my boot.

"Here we go again!" Ethan's perky voice startles me.

I groan, refusing to match his energy.

"Oh, c'mon." He elbows me with a playful grin. "Try not to fall in love again this time, okay?"

The doors snap shut, and the subway lurches forward. The initial force pins us to our seats, then eases to a steady pace.

"I didn't fall in love," I growl at him through gritted teeth.

He lifts his hands in surrender. "I'm just messing with you, buddy." But it strikes a nerve with me. He doesn't know that deep down, I *did* start to feel something for Daphne. And it was all ripped away last night.

The wound is too fresh for me to find humor in his words. "Well, it's not funny," I mutter. Ethan's eyes widen behind his visor, then look away. Leo glances up from across the aisle, and my stomach twists. I'm being too loud.

I feel out of control. Like a ticking bomb that could explode at any moment, with no regard to anyone in my vicinity. No one can know how I feel — not even Ethan, the person I trust most out of anyone. He has no idea what it was like with Daphne. He doesn't know about the disease. The cure. The possibility of another sanctuary outside the city.

It's all too much. Even the slightest look from Leo unleashes a wave of anxiety, and I'm not strong enough to hold it back. But I try my best. I take a deep breath and sink into my chair, resting my head against the window.

"Did something happen?" Ethan whispers.

I let out a harsh sigh, wishing he'd just drop it. But as I turn to him, his eyes swell with sympathy. Desperate to understand what's wrong and what he can do to fix it.

From my peripheral, I spot Lieutenant Kelley seated at the end of our row. His head is pointed down, his face hidden behind his helmet. But beneath it all, I know his ears are perked up, listening attentively.

"Not now, Ethan," I beg him, keeping my gaze fixed on Lieutenant Kelley. "We'll talk when we get there, alright?"

He nods in understanding. He turns away from me and jumps into a conversation with Drew. I lean my head back and gaze up at the screen, watching the dot blink along a new line — an orange line. As the screen zooms out, I can tell we're well beyond the Hudson now. And we'll only continue to go further until the city is hundreds of miles behind us.

Over two hours pass before the subway starts to decelerate. As it does, a wide platform opens up on the other side of the window. Lieutenant Kelley rises to his feet, gripping the standing poles for support.

"Everyone up!" he orders.

We jump to our feet, half of us asleep or close to it by the time the subway rolls into the station. I press myself against the back wall as we line up in the aisle. As soon as the train comes to a stop, the doors slide open, welcoming us to D.C.

We step onto a narrow strip that's nothing more than a wedge between the subway and a series of tangled rails that look inoperable. Rusted tracks veer off to dead ends, choked with weeds that curl around every groove. They blend in with the ground, like steel roots pushing up from the earth. As we file out, the platform opens into a larger space. The walls are adorned with limestone tiles, and the ceiling arches into a glass dome. It's cracked in places, allowing a cool breeze to slip through.

Moving forward, we descend a set of still escalators. Our boots clank against the aluminum steps. The sound ricochets off the walls, echoing into the dark tunnels behind us. I find myself nervously glancing over my shoulder, waiting for an infected to jump out. They're here — I know it. Lurking in the shadows. Waiting for the perfect moment to strike.

Part of me envies Drew and the others, who have nothing to fear. To them, everything outside the Barrier is a desolate wasteland. They've heard stories of The Truth, but they've never seen it for themselves. But at the same time, I pity them for not knowing. If they were ever separated from the rest of us, they'd have no idea what they were up against. They don't know there's a very present evil among us, even now as we move through the abandoned station. Any misstep, any wrong turn, and we could come face to face with it — and by that point, it'd be too late.

At the base of the escalators, the floor smooths into polished granite. We jog through a hollow corridor that spills onto a sweeping balcony overlooking a grand foyer. To my right, a curved staircase spirals between the two levels. Our level extends left and right, framing the space below like a mezzanine. Storefronts line the walkway, sealed behind barred metal gates. A few are warped, as if they were pried open in a desperate attempt to get in. Or get out.

Lieutenant Kelley leads us down the staircase to the lower level. As we descend, the ceiling stretches higher into an expanse of ornate marble, still just as spectacular now, even in the desolation. Small portholes are set deep within the stone, letting in pockets of light. Vines coil around towering limestone pillars. Our boots trample over shards of glass that have rained down from above. Every crackle sends a jolt of panic through my body. We're being too loud — and we're exposed. But we keep moving.

As we step out of the station, Washington D.C. unfolds around us. Similar to Philadelphia, the city is shrouded in a thick haze that completely devours the sun. A few rays struggle to break through, but they're snuffed out by the gray gloom. Even though it's hardly midday, the city appears to be stuck in an eternal dusk.

The courtyard in front of the station is littered with the remains of an abandoned encampment. Tents are scattered everywhere. Some are still intact, except for a few tears in the coverings, while others have collapsed entirely. Their assembly poles are thrown haphazardly across the lawn like discarded bones. The grass reaches past our ankles. Its wiry blades twist and snag at our boots. A few draftees get their feet caught in a weed and stumble. I keep my knees high and take slow, deliberate steps.

Once we reach the asphalt, we break into a jog. For at least a mile, we weave through streets cluttered with abandoned vehicles, bordered by hollowed-out buildings. Grand landmarks loom in the distance, tilting precariously on uneven terrain. Eventually, we reach another lawn enclosed by a wrought-iron fence. Near the center, the bars have been pulled apart, forming an opening just wide enough for us to slip through. Lieutenant Kelley orders Apollo through first while he hangs back. His head is on a swivel. His eyes dart left to right, his gun swinging in tandem with his gaze. He watches as each of us pass through, making sure we're all accounted for. Especially Ethan and me.

As soon as we're all on the other side, he takes one final look around, then follows after us.

The lawn stretches up to a white building set apart from the rest of the surrounding structures. It's much smaller in scale compared to the skyscrapers in New York, but it holds the same reverence as the Freedom Tower. A rounded two-tiered veranda juts out from the front, supported by six weathered pillars. The roof is edged by a sandstone wall that's barely still put together.

Still fluttering at its highest point is an American flag. Unlike the flag in General Conrad's office, this flag has retained all 50 stars. It sways in quiet defiance against the gloom that's taken over the city. As I gaze up at it, a chill runs down my spine. It's likely this flag is one of the last remaining symbols of our nation. Unlike the Freedom Tower, which stands only for our city, this flag stands for all things — everything before The Truth, and everything that's left.

Lieutenant Kelley leads us up the dual staircase to the first level of the veranda. Much like Daphne's apartment, the entrance is framed by massive arched windows at each corner, with French doors in the center. The glass is blown out, and one of the doors has been completely ripped from its hinges. Peering inside, I find it lying on the floor in a heap of broken stone and shattered glass.

Lieutenant Kelley pauses in front of the entrance. For the first time since we arrived, we stop moving. A grim stillness settles over everything, the kind that only comes in death. There's no distant hum of life, no muted breath, nothing stirring in the wind. It's as if all sound has been pulled from existence.

Then, all at once, Lieutenant Kelley's voice tears through the silence. "Welcome to your nation's capital," he announces. "This is the White House, the home of our former nation's president."

Another chill runs down my spine. I stare up at the hollow building in awe, gripped by it. It's stood through some of the greatest days in history — and even now, it still stands.

"The same rules apply: Only salvage items that are useful. Today, we're looking for documents, files, weapons, loose ammo. Anything that seems important, take it. Here — you can use these to collect your items."

He passes out the same tattered canvas sacks as before. Each of us takes one, and I fold mine tightly in my hand.

"Instead of waiting for your pagers to buzz, I'll decide when it's time to go," Lieutenant Kelley instructs. "It's over a mile's jog back to the station, so we need to make sure we're back before the train arrives. Understood?"

"Yes, sir!" we shout.

"Good," he states. "We'll split up into groups to make sure we cover as much ground as possible. Andres, you'll take Patton and Fitzgerald. Madoc and Greene, you'll be with me. No exceptions."

His eyes narrow at us through his visor. I don't need to see his face to know a wicked grin is spreading across it.

"Great, we get our own personal tour guide," Ethan mutters.

"He made it pretty clear that was going to be the case," I remind him.

"Yeah, but you still owe me an explanation. As long as we can get Sergeant Buzzkill off our backs."

I stifle a laugh and give Ethan a friendly knock on the arm.

"There's one more thing," Lieutenant Kelley says, drawing our attention back to him. "Before entering any room, remove the cap from one of your smoke flares and toss it in first. Wait for it to ignite, then as long as it's clear, you can proceed. This is an order. Fail to do this, and you'll be pulled from the mission. Is that clear?"

"Yes, sir!" we reply.

He holds two fingers to his eyes, then points them at Ethan and me. "You two aren't going anywhere out of my sight," he snarls.

Ethan and I take our place beside Lieutenant Kelley, while Apollo, Leo, and Drew huddle together. Once we're ready, we step forward in unison, crossing the threshold into the White House.

Inside, everything appears frozen in time. Except for a few shards of glass and debris kicked in from outside, the glossy tiled floors gleam, nearly untouched. Elegant crimson drapes brush the floor, framing the arched windows. A grand chandelier hangs in the center of the room, veiled in cobwebs. It's probably been decades since it last shone. Gold-framed portraits of past presidents line the walls. Their faces are blurred beneath a thick layer of dust that coats everything. Darkness swallows the room, and not even the feeble daylight from outside can pierce through it.

Lieutenant Kelley ushers Ethan and me down a hallway to our left, with Apollo and his group hunkering close behind. Through my visor, the only guide is the dull blinking light of Ethan's pager, reassuring me that he's still there. Apollo, Leo, and Drew slip into a vacant room. As soon as they vanish from sight, a sharp hiss cuts through the silence, startling me. Smoke plumes from the open doorway, indicating they've ignited a flare. Lieutenant Kelley turns toward another room across the hall, then stops.

Before we enter, he pulls a flare from his pocket and flicks off the cap. With a sweeping motion, he tosses it into the room. Instantly, the flare erupts into a cloud of neon-red smoke that fills the entire room. As it dissipates, it falls like rain on every surface, coating the furniture in a residual reddish glow that's visible, even in the darkness.

"Clear," Lieutenant Kelley mutters. He steps aside, allowing us to enter first.

The room is framed by crimson walls. Stately furniture lies overturned, scattered in disarray. Some pieces are even barricaded against doors leading to other rooms. Large ornate paintings cling precariously to the walls, hanging at odd angles. Strips of wallpaper curl away from the wall, exposing a stark white surface beneath, riddled with bullet holes. Entering the room feels like stepping into a crime scene. Something happened here — something terrible. And at first glance, it seems like nothing is worth salvaging.

"This room connects to two others," Lieutenant Kelley says. "You stay in this one — and do *not* venture any further until I say so. Understood?"

"Yes, sir," Ethan and I nod.

Once he's convinced, he slides past us. He sheaths his weapon and begins clearing a doorway. He removes the furniture like it weighs nothing, pushing it aside to blaze a path. As soon as it's clear, he disappears into one of the adjoined rooms.

Ethan and I split up. He tears through the furniture, turning up cushions, looking for anything that might be buried beneath. I move to a desk still resting against the back wall, just below the only exterior window. The first few drawers slide open with ease, all of which prove to be empty. But the bottom drawer won't budge. I plant my boot against the frame for leverage and yank with everything I've got. With a vicious crack, the wood splinters and releases the drawer. The force hurls me backward, and I slam into the wall, the drawer still clutched tightly in my hand.

Ethan's head jerks up. "You alright?" he hollers.

I grunt, lifting a thumb. He nods and ducks back down to continue his search.

Same as the rest, the drawer itself is empty. But wedged within the slot it once occupied are a stack of papers. I crawl closer and reach inside, pulling them out. I brush off the dust with my gloves and hold the first page up to my visor to get a better look. In the top-right corner, the black-and-white headshot of a man stares back at me. His first initial and last name are written in typeface beneath it, along with a line that reads: **SUBJECT DID NOT RESPOND TO ANTIDOTE. CAUSE OF DEATH: ELIMINATION.**

I swallow hard as I scan over the words a second time. I flip through page after page, each one bearing a different face. Mostly men, but some women. Dozens of them. All with the same line stamped beneath.

Near the end, one page breaks the pattern. Beneath the headshot, the name reads: **S. GREENE**

My breath catches. I glance at Ethan, who's still occupied across the room. *Is this . . .* I think. *No, it can't be.*

But directly below his name, the words confirm it. Instead of the same line, it reads: **SUBJECT DID NOT RESPOND TO ANTIDOTE. FOR MILITARY PURPOSES, CAUSE OF DEATH: HEART FAILURE. TRUE CAUSE OF DEATH IS UNDETERMINED.**

"What the . . ." I say aloud. My pulse hammers as the pieces fall into place in my mind. These weren't just casualties — they were test subjects for a cure. And if I'm right, Ethan's father was one of them. It wasn't a heart attack that killed him. The military might've covered it up that way, but it was something more. Something they didn't want anyone finding out about.

But nothing prepares me for the last page in the stack.

The final headshot is nearly a spitting image of myself, only a few years older. And beneath it, the name reads: **A. MADOC**

Father. It's been a decade since I've seen even a photograph of him. My chest tightens, burning with the ache he left behind. I brace myself for the same words written on every other page, sealing his fate. But this time, they're different: **SUBJECT RESPONDED TO ANTIDOTE. CURED.**

Footsteps thunder into the room. In a panic, I shove the papers back into the desk and jump to my feet.

Lieutenant Kelley reappears in the doorway. His eyes narrow with suspicion, expecting we're up to no good. "Anything?" he asks.

Ethan and I shake our heads, turning our palms up.

With a frown, he motions for us to exit the room. "Let's keep moving," he orders.

We venture further into the White House. The hallway grows darker the deeper we go. Behind us, another flare hisses to life, followed by Apollo's voice giving the all-clear to his group. Their footsteps shuffle from the hall into the room, then fade out of range.

"This one," Lieutenant Kelley points decisively to a room on our left. "Greene, you do the honors."

Ethan dutifully pulls a flare from his pocket. His fingers wrap around the cap, but before he can twist it free, Drew's voice stops him.

"Lieutenant!"

Lieutenant Kelley's head spins around. Glancing over my shoulder, I spot Drew a few rooms down, standing halfway out the door. He waves his hand frantically, trying to get our attention.

"I think we found something, but we need your help."

Lieutenant Kelley huffs, then drops his eyes to Ethan and me.

"Stay here," he barks at us. "If I come back and you two have moved even an inch, you're off the mission."

"Yes, sir," we reply.

Lieutenant Kelley draws his gun from his holster and jogs down the hallway. Once he reaches Drew, they disappear into the room, and everything grows silent again.

Ethan's hand clamps down on my shoulder. Without warning, he yanks me into a nearby room, causing me to stumble. I force my hand against the doorway, resisting his pull. But it doesn't work. I shove him back, and his grip loosens.

"What are you doing?" I hiss at him. I jab a finger into the side of my helmet to lift my visor.

Ethan raises a gloved finger to the mouthpiece of his helmet, silencing me. "Be quiet," he whispers. "Remember what Lieutenant Kelley said: If he comes back and we're gone, we're off the mission."

"Exactly," I snap back, as if it should be obvious. "Which is why we can't be in here. So knock it off, man."

But he doesn't. He tugs at my arm again. I try to wriggle myself free, but he persists. It isn't until I'm fully in the room that he lets go.

"Talk to me." He lifts his own visor, revealing his eyes. My heart sinks, knowing I looked into those same eyes on the page minutes ago.

"He's gone, so now we have a chance to talk," Ethan says. "It feels like it's been weeks since I've gotten a word out of you, dude, and something's clearly wrong. So talk to me."

Really? Here? I think, but I don't say it. There's so much he doesn't know. So much I've been holding back from him, and even more I've only just uncovered.

As much as I want to say now's not the right time, I remind myself where that got me with Daphne. I've already pushed her away. I don't want to do the same to Ethan.

"She's gone," I blurt out.

Ethan tilts his head. "Daphne? What do you mean she's gone?"

"She found out about the Barrier. It freaked her out, so she left."

"Wait," Ethan holds up a hand before I can say anything more. "She *found out* about the Barrier? You mean, you didn't tell her before?"

"I—" I stammer, starting to defend myself. But I've lost this fight once before. "No, I didn't," I sigh.

Ethan's eyes stretch wide. "Yikes, man. That's a pretty big piece of information to leave out."

I flail my arms in frustration. "That's not the point, Ethan. The point is, I didn't tell her, and she didn't feel like she could trust me anymore. And now she's gone."

"Well, where'd she go?" he asks.

"I don't know. But Ethan, I . . ." my voice trails off. I have to tell him now — about the disease. The cure. His father. My father. But we're pressed for time. Any minute now, Lieutenant Kelley will be back.

Out in the hallway, muffled voices start to grow louder, cutting through my thoughts. Ethan hears them too. His eyes shift past my shoulder, then back to me.

"Quick," he says. "You don't know where she went?"

I shake my head. "She threatened to leave. But I don't know if she actually did."

The voices get closer. Anxiety burns in my chest, urging me to leave the room. But Ethan keeps me here.

"Do you still have the pager?"

I nod. "Yes, and the badge."

"You have to check," he insists. "You have to be sure. Tonight, when we get back, see if she's still there, or if she's really gone. Maybe she didn't mean it. Or maybe she did, but she changed her mind, or her plan fell through. Either way, you have to—"

"Hold it!" Lieutenant Kelley's voice fills the hallway.

We both freeze. My heart sinks to my gut. I don't wait for Ethan to finish. I dart back out into the hallway, prepared to see a red-hot Lieutenant Kelley rearing his head.

But instead, as I step out of the room, someone rushes past me. Our bodies collide, knocking us both off balance. As I collect myself, I look up and lock eyes with a man.

This time, he's not on paper. Not trapped in a headshot.

He's here. Right in front of me.

His ice-blue eyes blink up at me through thin-framed glasses slipping down his nose — the same eyes I see when I look in the mirror. Shaggy blonde hair hangs unevenly past his ears, and unkempt facial hair covers his jaw and chin. The same tightness in my chest returns. Even though he was clean-shaven in the photo, I know it's him. Half a second must go by, but it's as if time stands still. "Fathe—" the word nearly slips out before it's choked out by gunfire.

Pow! I duck down as a bullet soars over my head. The man scrambles to his feet and vanishes into the shadows. Ethan pulls me back into the room and out of the line of fire. *Pow!* Another gunshot goes off, followed by Lieutenant Kelley's footsteps storming after him.

My heart races, threatening to burst from my chest. *Was that really him?*

"Get back here!" Lieutenant Kelley shouts. He sprints a few feet past our room before he stops. By now, the man is long gone. Through the doorway, I watch as Lieutenant Kelley lowers his weapon in defeat. Behind him,

Drew and the other draftees stand frozen in the hallway. Drew's helmet is off, clutched at his side. In the stunned silence, his eyes find mine, and he mouths something I can't quite make out.

Lieutenant Kelley slowly turns toward us. His eyes fall on Ethan and me, but they're distracted.

"Let's go," he orders. He marches down the hallway toward Drew, not bothering to reprimand us.

"We're leaving?" I ask. The question escapes my mouth before I can stop it.

Lieutenant Kelley rips his helmet from his head and spins around. He rushes toward me and jabs his finger into my chest. His eyes are full of rage, his mouth pooling with saliva. He looks deranged. I step back, but he moves forward, closing in on me until there's nowhere left for me to go.

"What did you think I meant when I said let's go?" he snarls.

I don't say anything. I know he's not looking for an answer, but he pauses as if giving me a chance to think of one.

"You're not entitled to any sort of explanation, Madoc. You obey my orders, and that's it!" he screams. "No questions, no backtalk. Just shut up and listen! Do you understand me?"

Veins bulge from his neck. His face flushes crimson, and his nose presses into mine, flattening me against the wall.

"Y-yes, sir," I stutter.

He doesn't let up. He holds his stare, then gives me one final jab before pulling away.

His nostrils flare, and with his eyes still fixed on me, he shouts, "Everyone, let's get going!"

Without hesitation, the other draftees flock down the hall in the same direction we entered in from.

Ethan takes my side, and together, we jog to catch up with the group. As soon as we reach the main foyer, Lieutenant Kelley does a quick headcount to make sure we're all accounted for.

"Leave everything," he commands. "It'll only slow us down. At this rate, we need to get back to the station as soon as possible."

"But—" Drew tries to debate, but Lieutenant Kelley silences him with a look.

"That's an order, soldier!" he yells.

Drew drops the items he carries at his feet. Anyone carrying anything follows suit. Their items clatter against the floor, joining the rest of the debris. It doesn't make sense, but Lieutenant Kelley is set in his decision. There's nothing we can do to change it.

We fly down the steps from the veranda, sprinting across the lawn until we reach the path. As we slip through the warped fence, I glance over my shoulder one last time. My eyes scan every busted window, every nook that offers a peek inside, watching for any signs of movement. Looking for my father. Knowing with every fiber of my being it was him. But he never shows.

When we arrive back at Battery Station, Lieutenant Tillman meets us on the platform. We hand over all our gear, along with the empty canvas sacks. A few draftees head inside, but I hang back. As I slip out of my vest, I keep my eyes fixed ahead but my ear turned toward Lieutenant Kelley, tuned in to every word he says.

"The mission was a failure," he mutters to Lieutenant Tillman.

"What would you have done?" Lieutenant Tillman asks. "He would've seen him, maybe even recognized him. And what about the others?"

Lieutenant Kelley shakes his head. "It was a flawed plan all along. General Conrad tried to warn me, but I insisted we try again."

"Don't worry," Lieutenant Tillman's voice softens. "We'll get him next time."

That's when it hits me. The smoke flares we'd ignite before entering every room. The way we left behind all the items we found as if they didn't matter. The pages hidden within the desk. My father's file — *cured*. The man in the White House. Lieutenant Kelley chasing after him. Lieutenant Tillman's words just now, the final piece completing the puzzle.

We were never going to D.C. to look for supplies. We were looking for my father.

Twenty-Two

My eyes blink open to the pager rattling against my palm. I close my fist around it and shove it under my pillow. It feels like seconds have passed since I first laid in bed. Looking around, the barracks are even quieter than they were before. By now, every draftee is fast asleep. I almost think about going back to sleep too, but I can't. I have to see if Daphne's still there — even though deep down, I'm afraid I'll find the apartment empty.

Carefully, I swing my feet over the side of the bunk and slide on a pair of worn sneakers. I gently pull a hoodie from my drawer and slip it on over my T-shirt. I throw the hood up, hiding my face. With the pager in hand and the badge in my pocket, I squeeze through the barracks door and out into the hall.

Once the door clicks back into place, I pause. I listen for any noises, keeping an eye out for any soldiers who may still be shuffling about. But I'm met only by the sound of my own breathing. I jog down the hall and through the chamber. On the other side, the platform is bare, and the subway waits for me. I feel a hint of nostalgia from all the times I've made this journey alone. No one sees me when I go to visit Daphne. It's just me and the subway, a shared secret between us.

I hop inside and tuck myself in the corner of the rear car. As soon as the doors slide shut, the subway lurches forward and barrels through the tunnels, carrying me beneath the city.

As I ride along the rails, I prepare for the possibility that she's gone. She's had too many opportunities to slip away, too many for me to expect she'd still be there. But even if she is, will she welcome me in? Or will she put up her guard? I tell myself not to hope, but it's impossible not to. My chest aches to see her again. To hear her say she's changed her mind. That she'll wait for me to finish the draft, and then we can leave together. To search for others. To find my father. To a place where we can be safe — together. I picture her midnight blue eyes fixed on mine. Her blonde hair bathed in moonlight. If I could just get one more glimpse of her, even if it was my last, it'd be enough. At least then, I'd have some closure.

But I can't expect that.

Despite my fears, I follow the path to her apartment under the pale glow of the moon. When I get there, I pull myself onto the landing and dart up the fire escape. All sense of reality is gone — hope burns through my chest, lighting a fire beneath my feet, propelling me up to her level. As I stand in front of the doors, I gulp, then step inside.

At first glance, the apartment is vacant. The wool blanket is thrown haphazardly on the couch. The knife she pulled out of the kitchen drawer sits on the countertop, next to a drawer that's still slightly ajar. My heart races. *She's not here.* But no, just because it seems that way doesn't mean it's true.

I tiptoe into the bedroom, thinking maybe I'll find her there. She might not have expected me to come back tonight. After all, she told me not to. Maybe she's asleep. But as I round the corner, my heart sinks.

The bedroom is empty too. The bed is perfectly made, the conjoined bathroom is nothing but a shadow, and the closet is wiped clean. Before, there had been a few clothes hanging inside. Now everything is gone.

I drop to my knees. The reality hits me like a bullet. Tears bite at the corners of my eyes, but I don't let them out. It's all my fault. I should've told her about the Barrier. I should've given her the choice to stay or go. We were wrong to bring her here. She never belonged here. She never could — not as long as the draft still exists and the Barrier still stands. I knew it all along, but selfishly, I held onto the hope that after all was said and done, we could build something together. Just like my parents did. For the first time in my life, I imagined what that could be like. But now, it's been ripped away from me. I feel foolish for even entertaining the idea.

There's nothing more I can do. There's no telling where she went or where she could be now. But even through my regret, there's a peace stirring. At least I know now — and I did all I could.

I pick myself off the ground and trudge back to the fire escape. As I step onto the landing, something catches my attention. A faint sound, almost like a whimper, carried on the wind. It almost sounds like it's coming from behind me, but it isn't. The only thing behind me is the vacant apartment.

There, bolted to the exterior wall, is the vertical ladder leading to the roof. The noise drifts past me again, this time more prominent. Everything in me tells me if it's coming from anywhere, it has to be up there.

The pager hasn't gone off. There's no reason to head back to the station just yet. Without anything more than a hunch, I decide to investigate. I grip the chipped rungs of the ladder and lean back, testing my weight. To my relief, it holds. I scramble up it until my hands find the flat-top gravel roof. As I pull my body over the edge, I brush myself off and lift my eyes — and what I see stuns me.

Sitting at the opposite end of the roof, gazing out into the night, is Daphne. In the distance, the Freedom Tower dominates over the sleeping city. Nearly six stories up, the view is jaw-dropping. But all I see is her.

I approach her timidly, afraid that any sudden move could send her over the edge. My feet slide quietly against the gravel in sweeping motions. Daphne lets out a harsh sob. She doesn't think anyone can hear her. She doesn't know I'm here now. When I'm no more than a few feet away, I reveal myself.

"You didn't leave," I say calmly.

Her body jolts slightly. My reflexes kick in, and I dive to grab her arm. She grips the ledge with her other hand to stabilize herself. I feel her arm loosen in my grip as her eyes meet mine, recognizing me. A smile breaks across her tear-streaked face.

"You came back," she exhales.

I let go of her arm and take a seat next to her. My feet swing over the edge, dangling over the darkened street below. Vertigo swells in my brain. I scoot back until the height isn't noticeable anymore, making the certainly fatal fall feel more distant.

Daphne turns her head away from me. I can tell she's ashamed, but all I can think is she's *here*. Despite everything, she stayed. I don't know what it means yet, but I'm grateful for it.

"Daphne, I—"

"No," she interjects. "You don't have to say anything. You didn't even have to come back. You shouldn't have, really."

"Of course I did," I scoff. "How could I not? I couldn't accept that you'd leave that easily. I had to know, one way or another."

She sniffles and tucks her hair behind her ear, revealing her face. Tears glisten on her cheeks. Her eyes are puffy, evidence of hours spent crying, and the tip of her nose is bright scarlet from the cold. How long has she been up here? How long has she sat here alone, never expecting anyone to find her?

"Nothing about this is easy," she sighs.

"Look," I start softly. "I should've given you a choice. You deserved to know exactly where you were — every detail. And you deserved to have a say in whether you stayed or went. I didn't want you to go, but I never gave you the chance to tell me if you even wanted to. I would've understood it if you did. Even now, I went to the apartment. It was empty. I thought for sure you'd left, and it nearly broke me. But I would've come to terms with it eventually."

"But it's so much more than that," she cries.

"You didn't have to stay," I assure her, though I'm not sure I mean it. Knowing she's here now, that she *did* stay, I don't know if I could handle her leaving now.

"It's not even about that anymore," she shakes her head. "It's you, John." Her breath shudders as she inhales sharply.

"Oh," I let out. I'm not entirely sure what she means. It grieves me to see her in so much pain. But it's clear whatever she's wrestling with is deeper than what's on the surface. I try not to pry. I give her plenty of space to say what she needs to say, when she's ready to say it.

Her eyes flutter closed, then she sighs. "Yes, I was frustrated about the Barrier. It felt wrong for a place like this to exist. It felt—" she stops, trying to find the right words. "It felt unfair. That there could be a place spared from all the fear and evil, things the rest of the world is consumed by. That someone like you would take me in and risk everything to give me a taste of that. It's not fair. Is it?"

She throws her hands up and lets out an incredulous laugh.

"I'm . . . not sure," I admit.

She squeezes her eyes shut. A single tear rolls down her cheek and clings to the edge of her chin, then falls into the dark abyss below us.

"This," she lets out, motioning to the two of us. "You and me. It's not fair that we can't exist here. We can build a force field around an entire city, survive a nationwide apocalypse, but you and me? That's what feels impossible."

Her head falls in her hands, and she groans.

"You must think I sound crazy."

"No," I reply. "Not at all. The only thing that's crazy is believing we don't have a chance."

She lowers her hands and extends them toward the city sprawled before us. "Don't you see? This world is built against us, John. People like us don't get to—" the word lingers on the tip of her tongue, but she never says it. "We don't get to have each other."

"But I believe we can," I argue. "We can leave the city, leave it all behind, and search for the cure. We can start over. We can build a whole new life somewhere. Either way, as long as we're together, that's what matters. All I have to do is finish the draft, then I can be free."

Daphne shakes her head. "That isn't freedom, John. As long as we exist here, in this world, you have to play by their rules. They may color it with promises of a role in the military or having a purpose, but in the end, none of it is actually yours. You're just furthering their agenda. And even if we could leave, we'd always be on the run. Constantly looking over our shoulders for soldiers who'd surely come after us. Either way, they'd still have the power, and that's not freedom. That's control."

Her words feel like a punch to the gut. But she's right. The odds are stacked against us. Either way, we lose. I either become a slave to the draft or a fugitive, risking Daphne's life in either scenario. In a world like this, the most impossible thing you can have is love. Hopeful, nonsensical love, with the person you want to be with. Sure, there may be other girls in our community, but I want *her*. Anywhere else and I could have her, but not here.

Daphne notices me starting to come to terms with the situation. "Like I said, it's not fair," she repeats.

Part of me wonders if this is how my father felt. If after every attempt at trying to replicate a normal life here, under the Barrier, he realized it wasn't possible. I wonder if he felt like a bird in a cage, desperate to break free, but confined by his destiny. Maybe that's what finally drove him away. Maybe it had nothing to do with the cure after all, but a feeling he was chasing —

one that was deemed dangerous and disloyal to the military. Maybe he was searching for a place to feel whole again. Maybe he's still searching.

But still, I want to believe that love could triumph over it all. In a world that's consumed by evil, love has to be stronger. It was there in my mother's eyes as she held me one last time on my birthday. It was there every time Liam looked at me, even as I pushed him aside. It was there that night in Philadelphia, when Ethan refused to let me consider the possibility of not making it back alive. It's here now, in the space between Daphne and me, present in every stolen glance. That *has* to be more.

"It really is beautiful, though, isn't it?" Daphne acknowledges, snapping me out of my thoughts.

She holds out her finger, tracing the decrepit skyline all the way to the Freedom Tower.

"The city," she clarifies.

I stare out at the vast cityscape. Crippled skyscrapers stretch toward the sky, merging with the darkness. The Freedom Tower looms over it all, illuminated by the moonlight like a beacon. Somehow, seeing it all from this height moves me.

"It is," I agree. "It's tragic, but it's beautiful."

"I came up here to see it," Daphne says. "Even though I felt like I couldn't go out again, I just wanted to see it. I've been staring at the tower for hours, trying to understand how it all works. Looking at it, you'd never know the Barrier was there. And every time I convince myself it's not, I remember the way it felt . . ." her voice trails off. She lowers her eyes, scanning the surface of her palms, as if recalling the feeling.

"There's only one time you can actually see it," I tell her. My eyes lift to the antenna, tracing the imaginary curve down from its tip to the edge of the city. "There's a moment every morning as the sun comes up, when the first light hits the rim of the Barrier. For that split second, it's visible. And there's this glow that covers everything, almost like an iridescent ray of light. But as soon as it happens, it's gone. That's the only time you'd ever know it's there."

Her eyes widen in wonder. I can almost see the scene taking shape in her mind as she imagines what it'd be like. If I could, I'd sit with her until the morning light, just to witness her seeing it for the first time. To watch the iridescent glow cover the whole city instead of only seeing a sliver of it from my bedroom window. But I know before the moon has risen any higher in the sky, the pager will buzz, and I'll have to leave her.

"Why did you save me, John?" Daphne asks.

Her question catches me off guard. "What do you mean?"

"In Philadelphia, when you and Ethan found me. You had every reason to turn back and leave me there, but you didn't. You stayed. Why?"

There are so many things I could say, most of which she already knows. The most obvious reason being the pure shock I felt at finding another person outside the Barrier. Another being that she was wounded, and I couldn't just leave her there to die. But deep down, I remember the first time I saw her. There was something familiar about her. Something instinctive, as if my heart had always known her, even if my mind had somehow forgotten. From the moment I saw her, I knew I couldn't leave her. I didn't know what we were going to do, but I knew that much.

"Why did I save you?" I repeat her question. "Because everything around me told me not to. Saving you went against every protocol I've ever been told to follow. Even Ethan begged me to leave you. He only saw the danger in it, but I saw so much more. Despite everything around me screaming not to, I wanted to save you. I wanted you to have a chance at life, because you deserve one. I believe everyone does. I might not have had a chance at anything beyond the draft, but in that moment, you did. And I wanted that for you. No one told me to do it, no one forced me into thinking it was right, but I knew. I took one look at you, and I knew if I didn't save you, I'd regret it every day for the rest of my life."

Her body is fully turned toward me now. Her eyes fix on mine, just as I hoped they would again. I could stare into those eyes for a lifetime. Tears swell in the banks of her eyelids. She holds them back, but one word could send them into motion.

I keep going. "And now, I'm so glad I did. I never imagined all you'd mean to me once I got to know you. I get through each day because I know the night brings you. When I thought you'd left, I didn't know what to do. It felt like I'd lost my way, like I'd maybe never find it again. But here you are. Just like that day in Philadelphia, I stayed for you, and you stayed for me. That *means* something, Daphne. I don't care what anyone else thinks. I don't care that the world may never give us a chance to be all we could be. Every day, we get to make the choice to be something more. So make that choice with me. Tonight. Choose me, Daphne."

Everything else fades away. The city, the Barrier, the limitations that make our reality impossible. There's no telling what tomorrow will bring. Or what happens once the pager beckons me back to the facility. But right now, we have this moment. Together.

Daphne moves closer, so close that our shoulders touch. "Do you really believe we have a chance?" she asks, hopeful.

I lean in until our foreheads meet. Nerves bubble in my stomach. Her breath quickens, and I can tell she's nervous too. But neither of us resists.

"I do," I say. "Because a world without you isn't one worth living in."

Electric heat rushes to my face and ignites my senses. Our noses brush together, our lips barely an inch apart. My heart drums against my chest, and I worry she can feel it. But I can feel hers too, pulsating with the same momentum as mine. Wanting the same thing as me.

"Me neither," she whispers.

The corners of her lips curl into a smile. All at once, I feel the weight of her crash into me as she closes the gap between us.

I barely make it to the station in time to catch the subway back to the facility. When it pulls into Battery Station, I clutch the pager and badge in my hand and hop off. I pass through the chamber and let the smoke circulate around me. Green light fills the room, and the door to the lower level clicks open.

As I step through, my heart sinks. Halfway down the hall is a person standing with their head hung. Their features aren't visible in the low light, but I can make out the outline of their body. My pulse spikes. I think about moving backward into the station before they notice me, but I don't. I stand frozen at the other end of the hall, waiting for them to make the first move.

The figure lifts its head. It moves into the light, and Ethan's face comes into focus. My heart steadies, but the panic doesn't leave me. I rush toward him and don't stop until I'm right in front of him.

Keeping my voice low, I whisper harshly, "What are you doing out here?"

He doesn't reply. Getting a closer look, there's a grayish tint to his skin that looks sickly in the dull lighting. His bottom lip trembles as if he's trying to say something, but he can't formulate the words. His green eyes don't meet mine. They look past me, fixated on what's behind me.

"I can't control it, John," he croaks. His voice doesn't sound like his own. I glance over my shoulder, worried that something may be lurking behind me with the way his gaze is fixed there. But all I see is the vault door, still open from when I came in.

"What are you talking about?" I ask. I try to grab his arm, but he pushes me aside. His strength nearly knocks me off my feet.

"Ethan," I plead. My own voice starts to tremble. The longer we're out here, the more likely someone could overhear us. Panic bubbles in my throat until it boils over. I'm desperate now. I'm worried I won't be able to coax him back to the barracks in the state he's in — and there's no telling what he'll do next.

"You don't look well," I whisper. "Whatever's going on, we can get Lieutenant Kelley and tell him—"

Before I can finish, Ethan swipes the pager and badge from my hand and shoves me to the ground. My body collapses with a loud thud that echoes down the hall. In the tension of the moment, it sounds like a bomb detonating. Ethan sprints toward the open door. I bite my tongue to stifle the urge to call after him. My mind scrambles. I don't know which to be more concerned about — someone hearing us, or the fact that he's headed straight for the subway.

I take off after him in a frenzy. My hands slice viciously at my sides, trying to keep up with him. But he's too fast. His speed is almost inhuman. I sprint through the chamber as he's already crossing over onto the station. I hear the subway doors hiss, threatening to close. For a moment, I think he's not going to make it in time.

But to my horror, he does.

I spring onto the platform just in time to see the doors slide shut, sealing Ethan on the other side. He stares at me menacingly through the window, holding the pager and badge like they're his prize. In an instant, the subway roars to life. It lets out a mechanical huff, then surges forward. There's no time to act, nothing I can do to stop it. All I can do is watch.

I stand frozen in disbelief as it disappears into the gaping mouth of the tunnel, carrying a deranged Ethan and my only key to seeing Daphne again somewhere far away from here.

Twenty-Three

What just happened?

I pace down the hallway, trying to wrap my mind around it all. Ethan can be impulsive, but he's not reckless. He'd never just take off like that. Where would he go, anyway? If he's not in his bunk tomorrow morning, he knows he'll face Lieutenant Kelley's wrath. We've been through it once before, and there's no doubt it'll be even more brutal the second time around.

But he didn't seem well. He wasn't in his right mind. *I can't control it, John.* Those were his words to me. They replay over and over in my mind, but I don't know what to make of them. What couldn't he control?

Without any answer, I slip through the barracks door. I glance at Ethan's bunk on my way down to mine, thinking for a second it might've been some crazy dream. But his sheets are ripped back, thrown into a messy heap at the foot of his bed, and he isn't there — confirming it was all real.

I bury myself underneath the sheets. My body trembles with worry for him. Afraid that he'll end up somewhere he doesn't belong, or that he won't be able to find his way back. And if he can't, what then? He has the pager and the badge. Without them, there's no way for me to see Daphne. My heart sinks imagining her sitting in her apartment alone, waiting for me to show up each night, but I never do.

Eventually, the dark room lulls me to sleep. All my anxious thoughts drift away as I close my eyes. But just as I feel myself slipping away, I'm rattled awake. With my eyes still shut, I hear the barracks door pop open, followed by footsteps shuffling into the room. As I open my eyes, the door closes, taking away the light seeping in from the hall before I can see who it is. Darkness fills the room again, hiding the intruder in the shadows. Whoever it is, they linger close to the door, no more than a few feet from my bunk.

I assume it's Ethan. It has to be. If it were one of the training officers, they wouldn't wait this long before spurring us awake. I can hear their breathing — and it's heavy. Each sharp inhale sends a chill down my spine, and every exhale feels choked, almost as if there's something blocking their windpipe. I turn my head against my pillow and see their silhouette, but nothing else is distinguishable.

Then the intruder moves. Darkness envelops them as they wade deeper into the barracks. Their breathing grows quieter, more distant. Tension starts to build up inside me. If it's Ethan, I want so badly to jump out of bed and pull him back to our bunk before he's caught. Whatever he's up to, it's risky. Another draftee could easily wake up. They could see him. They could—

An agonizing scream stops me dead in my thoughts. Instantly, my blood runs cold. Mattresses creak and sheets rustle around the room. Several draftees are awake now, startled by the scream. A second scream sounds, followed by a wet ripping noise so distinct, it makes my stomach twist.

Another draftee screams out of pure fear.

"What the—" another draftee yelps, but he's cut short by a third scream. It's much more prolonged now, held out until it turns into a cry.

Footsteps clatter toward my bunk. I push myself back into the corner until I hit the wall. My pulse hammers, afraid the source of all this pain is headed straight toward me. But in the thin strip of light seeping in beneath the barracks door, I see another draftee come into view. His hand slams into the light switch beside the door, and in one horrible moment, the room bursts with fluorescent light.

Several draftees are up and out of their bunks. Some sprint toward the door, while others are too stunned to move. Danny tugs at the handle, trying to escape, but the door resists. It comes out of its frame, then slams back into place, as if someone is holding it shut from the other side, keeping us trapped inside.

Another scream rips through the chaos, yanking my gaze across the room. Dom D'Angelo's body thrashes on the top bunk diagonal from me. Thick blood spills down onto the stone floor and splatters on the wall next to him. His head is wrenched back at an unnatural angle, held by another hand clutching his chin, one that doesn't belong to him. My skin tingles as I watch the color drain from his eyes. They roll into his skull until only the whites are visible.

He falls lifeless against the mattress. As he does, it reveals the thing holding him — something so terrifying, my breath seizes in my throat.

Hovering over his body is an infected. Fresh blood drips from its lips. Its back is arched, the vertebrae poking through its rotting flesh. It wears a tattered gray rag of a shirt that's soaked with blood. Its gray skin is covered in yellowish pores that look contagious, giving it a sickly look. It lifts its head for a moment, then lowers it again. Its teeth rip through a cavity in Dom's chest while its fingers tear at his throat. Thin white hairs poke out from its scalp, but for the most part, it's entirely hairless.

Carson vomits, and I think I might be sick myself. Panic surges through me. I've never seen it so up close before. In Philadelphia, it was hidden in the shadows, lurking just out of sight. But here, the lighting of the barracks highlights every horrific detail.

"Get off of him!" I hear Apollo's voice shout. My eyes snap to the right, and I see Apollo standing with his palm still pressed against the light switch. Other draftees join Danny in trying to pull at the door handle, but it doesn't give. My eyes flick up at Leo, who sits perched on the top bunk directly across from Dom. He meets my gaze, and the look on his face says everything. One wrong move, and the infected may notice him and come for him next. But if he doesn't do anything, he's just sitting bait.

It doesn't go well for him either way — and he knows it.

Apollo rushes toward the infected and slams his fist into the frame of the bunk. The infected's head shoots up, chunks of flesh still wedged in its teeth. Its white eyes stretch wide. For the first time, genuine fear spreads across Apollo's face. All the chivalry he had before is gone. He sprints back toward the door and away from the infected just in time for it to pounce.

It hurls itself from the bunk and slams onto the floor below. As Apollo runs, his shoulder knocks against Leo's bunk, causing it to rattle. Leo lets out a sharp, panicked gasp that seems to slice through all the other noise. The infected must notice too, because it stops. Apollo no longer holds its interest. Instead, its ears twitch, and its eyes turn upward, locking on its new target. Leo.

The infected springs from the floor up to his bunk in a single motion. Leo scrambles to the edge, desperate to escape, but it pins him down before he has the chance.

Everything blurs. It all happens too fast, and my mind blocks out most of the grisly details. The infected bares its corroded teeth and tears into Leo's shoulder. His scream sharpens, rising in pitch. My stomach twists. He kicks and squirms against the mattress, using every ounce of his strength to try and throw it off him. But his struggle only fuels the infected's frenzy.

He screams against the pain, begging for help. Nobody moves. Not me. Not any of us. None of us wanting it to notice us next. None of us capable of fighting it off.

None of us wanting to touch it.

Leo manages to kick the infected off before it can do any more damage. It dives in for a second bite, but Leo's quicker. He shoves his foot into its chest and sends it hurtling to the floor. The impact makes me wince — a sickening crunch of bone against hard stone.

But it doesn't seem to injure it. In an instant, it scrambles on all fours and vanishes into the bottom bunk, where Rory sits curled in a ball. He lets out an ear-splitting scream. The infected sinks its teeth into his neck, and his scream warps into something much worse — a garbled, choking squelch. Blood spews from his neck. He collapses against the mattress, staining the sheets red almost immediately. His eyes roll upward until they're solid white, just like Dom's did.

Just like how the infected's look.

Apollo darts out of the way as the infected lifts its head to peer around the room. The draftees nearest the door press themselves into the corner, trying to stay as far away from it as possible. Leo clutches his shoulder in pain. Blood oozes from between his fingers, but he stays silent. He digs his teeth into his lower lip to stifle a cry, worried the infected might hear him again.

In the silence, there's a shared moment where none of us are sure what happens next. A moment where every single draftee wrestles with the possibility that we might not make it out of this alive.

But something must set it off. The infected peels itself off Rory's lifeless body and leaps through the frame of the bunk toward Apollo. He dodges it, stumbling aside as the infected crashes to the floor in a twisted heap. Apollo stands with his back to me. He tiptoes backward, inching closer to my bunk, anticipating its next move. The minute it lifts off the ground, he dives.

The infected barrels forward, reaching for Apollo, but it misses him.

Instead, it slams into the wall next to me.

Then falls against my mattress.

Into the bunk with me.

My whole body stiffens. I hold my breath, trying not to give myself away — but every subtle shift I make beneath the sheets is magnified. The infected crawls onto all fours, no more than three or four feet away from where I sit. I think about darting out of the bunk, but there's nowhere to go. I wouldn't be fast enough. It'd chase me around the barracks until either I relent, or it finds another draftee to mutilate. I curl myself into a ball in the corner, where the frame of the bunk meets the wall, trying to make myself as small as possible. Hoping maybe if I shrink back far enough, I'll disappear.

The infected stares at me straight-on. Blue and red veins bulge from its glossy white eyes, almost as if they're being stretched from the inside out. Its teeth jut out from bloodied gums and grind against each other. Its skeletal hands claw at the sheets, pulling them out of my grasp and exposing my limbs.

My breath quickens. I can't control it. Panic overtakes all my senses, and everything feels involuntary. The infected's head twitches from the sound of my breathing. It senses me. It knows I'm here. There's no escaping it now.

I can't breathe. I can't focus. My vision fractures, and every time I blink, the infected is closer. All I can smell is the stench of its decomposed flesh, like burnt plastic fused with something far worse. Its breath is hot on my face, thick with rot and the sickly sweet hint of blood. My hands tremble as I pull my knees tight to my chest. There's nothing I can do. No one comes to my rescue. They can't — otherwise they risk their own lives. Everyone watches in horror, waiting to see what happens.

Waiting for it to strike again.

I squeeze my eyes shut and clamp my hands over my ears to avoid hearing the sound of my own mutilation. My mouth falls open. All the fear bubbling up inside me spills out in one raw, existential scream. But the scream doesn't feel like mine. It feels separate — like it belongs to someone else. As if I'm no longer in my own body but outside of it, a spectator to my own demise.

The infected matches my tone, unleashing a vile screech that sends every hair on my body straight up. I feel it press into the mattress, the inches between us sagging beneath its weight.

I brace myself to feel that same weight crash against me. To feel its jaws tear through my flesh.

But it never happens.

A gunshot rips through the room and shatters the infected's skull. With my eyes still shut, I feel hot blood and brain matter spray against my face. I continue to scream. I don't come up for air. The ringing of the gun matches my pitch, the two sounds fusing together. I scream until my throat dries up and there's nothing left but a raspy whimper.

A hand comes down on my shoulder, silencing me. All the noise of the room rushes back in at once. Slowly, I peel my hands from my ears and open my eyes.

The infected's body lies in a mangled heap at the foot of my bed. Its blood soaks through the mattress, and its arms hang limp at its sides, draping over the edge.

Time catches up with my body, and I spring into action. I leap from the bunk and make a run for the door, but a firm hand presses against my chest, stopping me. My eyes lift to see Lieutenant Kelley staring back at me. Beside him, Lieutenant Tillman stands with a gun outstretched, still smoking from the kill shot it delivered just moments ago. He lowers it cautiously, waiting to see if the infected will spring back to life. Once he's sure it's dead, he deposits it into his holster and moves toward the adjacent bunk, where Leo sits whimpering.

Lieutenant Kelley drops his arm, and I crash into him with all my momentum. To my surprise, he doesn't push me away. Pulling back, I notice his bottom lip trembling. His eyes scan the room, looking at the carnage in horror.

He's afraid, and that makes me even more terrified.

"All of you, out of the room!" he shouts. "Now!"

The draftees cowering nearest the door sprint into the hall on command. Apollo follows closely behind them. Drew and Carson sweep across the barracks, and Drew grabs my arm, ushering me out of the room.

"C'mon," he whispers. "That was a close call, John."

I follow them out in a daze. My feet feel heavy. They drag against the floor while Drew supports my weight, carrying us both as far away from the barracks as possible.

"Where's Ethan?" Carson hollers over his shoulder.

Both of their eyes turn to me, but I don't look up. I stare solemnly at the ground, unable to gather my thoughts. Unable to wipe the image of the infected staring at me from my mind.

"I . . . I don't . . ." I mumble.

"I'm sure he'll catch up to us," Drew says. He grips my arm tighter and pulls me down the hall.

The vault door at the end is wide open. Red light pours from the passing chamber. Lifting my head, I notice a handful of soldiers waiting there, motioning for us to come toward them. Rather than their normal gear, each of them wears a hazmat suit, covering their bodies and faces in airtight protective gear.

"Keep moving!" they shout, and we quicken our pace.

The first batch of draftees pass through the chamber and onto the platform. The subway is stalled in the station, and I notice a few other soldiers inspecting the contents inside.

What did you do, Ethan? I think, picturing him on the subway just hours earlier, staring back at me through the window. I don't want to believe it, but I can't help but think he had something to do with this. I peer ahead to see if maybe he's already on the platform, but I don't see him.

As we pass through the chamber, three gunshots sound behind us, echoing down the hallway. I slam my feet into the ground to keep Drew from pulling me any further. My head spins around, turning toward the barracks at the other end of the hall. Something in my gut tells me one of them was for Leo. My heart sinks with grief. Once the infected sunk its teeth into him, I knew the damage would be irreversible. It'd only be a matter of time before the disease took over him, and he became just like it.

"Move, Madoc!" a soldier yells. Drew propels me forward, yanking me through the chamber. We spill onto the platform, and the soldier behind us closes the vault door.

We hunker in the center of the platform. Some draftees are barely clothed, pulled from their beds in the middle of their sleep. Some are stained with blood splatter from their peers, who are now either dead or diseased. Regardless, we all stare back at the soldiers like scared children, desperate for their help. We cling to each other for comfort, none of us able to comprehend what just happened.

A soldier steps forward to address us. "We'll take you in through the contamination chamber one by one," he announces, his voice muffled by his suit. "If it lights up green, you're safe to move forward. If it lights up red, you will be shot on the spot."

My stomach lurches. A few draftees whimper in fear. The vault door leading into the chamber stares back at us like a reaper of death. There's no guarantee we'll all make it through to the other side alive. Many of us were close to it — I was close. The infected was right in front of me, breathing its contaminants onto my face. All of us are reluctant to step forward.

But we don't have a choice.

The first draftee is ripped from the group at random and escorted into the chamber. He tries to pry his way out of the soldiers' grasp, desperate for one more minute before it all happens, but they overpower him. The vault door closes behind him with a thunderous echo, sealing his fate on the other side.

One by one, we're picked off and taken into the chamber until only Drew and I remain. The soldiers give us no indication of whether any other draftees have passed or failed, but I hold onto the hope that they're all waiting on the other side. Drew keeps his arm slung around my shoulder until the soldiers take him away. Before they carry him off, he turns to me.

"It didn't touch you," he mutters. "I watched the entire thing. It didn't touch you. You'll be okay."

I try to find comfort in his words, but they pass right through me. The soldiers force him into the chamber and seal the vault door shut, leaving me alone on the platform.

Within the same minute, the soldiers come back for me. They tug at my arm and pull me toward the door. My heart races violently in my chest. Even though Drew assured me the infected didn't touch me, I worry that something will set it off. As we approach the chamber, visions of the infected perched at the edge of my bed play through my mind. I inhaled its vile scent. I felt its blood graze my cheek as the bullet ripped through its skull. It was only inches from my face. It might not have touched me, but it was *right there* — ready to devour me in an instant.

The soldiers shove me into the chamber. Inside, another soldier waits wearing a full-body hazmat suit, just like the others. He stands with his back to the door leading into the facility and his arms crossed. In his hand, he's holding a handgun. His finger hovers over the trigger, ready to pull it the moment the lights turn red.

As the door closes behind me, I squeeze my eyes shut. I drown out the hum of the chamber and try to hold fast to Drew's words. I imagine the smoke unfurling from both sides, covering me in a suffocating mist. Green light will fill the room as it always does, and when I reach the other side, Drew will be standing there, ready to tell me he told me so. Maybe Ethan will be there too, and this will all have been some big misunderstanding. Some nightmare that I can finally wake up from.

I hold onto that hope as the smoke envelops me, praying the inside of the chamber won't be the last thing I see alive.

Twenty-Four

Bright green light swirls around me. The smoke is whisked away, sucked out of the chamber through the ventilation system. The soldier blocking the facility door steps aside, allowing me to pass through. Relief washes over me, drowning all the anxiety I had before. I feel a slight shove against my shoulder and stumble forward into the hallway.

But it's vacant. Not a single other draftee is anywhere in sight. My heart plummets to the pit of my stomach. *Did no one else make it through?* But that's impossible. Out of everyone, it was closest to me. It didn't touch anyone else or breathe on anyone — except for me. Dread squeezes the air from my lungs, making it difficult to breathe. I can't be the only one who survived. I can't live with that. Without the other draftees, what does that make me? What about the rest of the draft?

"Move it," a soldier barks at me. Another push against my shoulder sends me further into the empty hall. "The general wants everyone in the Assembly Hall."

He continues to shove me forward until we're in front of the doors leading into the Assembly Hall. He pulls his badge from its clip and slides it against the scanner. The door clicks open, and together, we step through.

As soon as we're inside, I find the draftees seated on the leftmost side of the auditorium — all seven of them. Scanning the row, I easily spot Carson and Drew, but I don't see Ethan. A lump forms in my throat, but I stifle my emotions and keep moving forward until I reach them.

The soldier shoves me into an empty seat beside Drew. He smiles softly at me and gives me a pat on the leg. We both let out a sigh, grateful to be reunited with each other.

"I told you you'd be okay," he reminds me.

My lips break into a grin. "I had a feeling you were going to say that."

My eyes move past him, looking at each draftee's face. I know I won't find Ethan, but now I'm looking for Leo. Despite the sinking feeling that one of the gunshots back in the hallway was for him, I hold onto the hope that he's here somewhere. Or maybe he hasn't joined us yet.

"Is this all of us?" I ask no one in particular, though Drew seems to be the only one listening. "Leo?"

Drew shakes his head. "This is everyone, John. Leo . . . that thing . . . it *bit* him."

I slowly recoil back against my chair and hang my head. The lump swells in my throat, threatening to erupt in a burst of emotion, but I can't let it. Not here. Leo was the only one who managed to get the infected off him, but it wasn't enough. As soon as it sunk its teeth into him, it was too late — the disease contaminated his bloodstream within seconds.

But his injuries weren't fatal. If we had a cure, we could've saved him. There's so much more we could've done for him. Killing him at point-blank range should've been the last resort. But instead, it was the first, the only way for them to ensure the disease didn't spread. My stomach twists, but it's more than sadness. It's resentment. Pure, agonizing resentment — and I feel it bloom into rage as General Conrad takes the stage.

Silence falls over the room. General Conrad walks solemnly to the center with his head tucked against his chest. He slowly lifts his eyes and surveys the room. His eyes sweep across every soldier seated before him. When he reaches our row, his skin pales, as if sobered by the reality that only eight draftees remain in total.

"Gentlemen," he starts. His voice booms off the walls of the auditorium. "This facility has always been a safe place. There's never been a moment when I have questioned that. There's never been a reason for anyone to think otherwise — until tonight."

He begins pacing across the stage, trudging from side to side.

"Tonight, a great evil was brought into our facility, throwing off our sense of safety. It took the lives of three of our draftees and would've taken many more, if we hadn't stopped it."

His words confirm Leo didn't make it. My body sinks further into my chair, held down by the weight of losing him. Images of him clinging to his shoulder play through my mind. Blood gushing between his fingers as he tried to close the wound. His eyes watching as we fled, wishing he could go with us, but knowing he couldn't. Tears well in my eyes. One blink sends a few trickling down my cheek.

General Conrad continues. "This evil is something we've known about for a long time. It's something you've known about too, but only by one name — The Truth. In nearly two decades, it has never once crossed the line under the Barrier. But now that it has, it's time you know the truth. It's time you know what you're up against."

The lights in the room shift in a dizzying whirl. They dim until there's nothing more than a single spotlight on General Conrad. The rest of us are sunken into the shadows.

I grip the armrests of my chair so tightly, I think they might pop off. He's about to tell everyone about the disease — and even though I know what's coming, I'm not prepared for them to find out.

"As you know, The Truth is a violent entity that tore through our nation nearly two decades ago," he explains. "You've been told very little about it as a way of preventing paranoia. For as long as you've lived under the Barrier, you've never had a reason to fear. Your whole lives," he signals to us draftees, "you've been safe here. And because of that, the true identity of The Truth hardly seemed to matter. All that mattered is that you were protected."

He pauses for a moment, carefully pondering his next words, then says, "Those who were here before the Barrier and live under it now came here for a fresh start. They survived an unimaginable tragedy, and all anyone wanted was to forget it and start over. They wanted to find a way to press on, to forge a better future for themselves and their families. So, we called it The Truth, because that's precisely what it is.

"But the truth catches up to us all in time. We can't deny it forever. It's buried somewhere within all of us, and it's bound to come out at some point. What happened here tonight is a reminder that The Truth is still out there. And I'm afraid tonight won't be the last time it strikes."

General Conrad stops pacing. He stiffens at the center of the stage. His chin lifts, his shoulders sag, and his whole body relaxes, as if settling in.

Time stands still for those few seconds. My pulse hammers. Any minute now, the veil that's hidden us from The Truth's identity will be removed. Once he says the words, there's no going back. Everyone will know.

"The Truth," he begins, and I finish his sentence in my head before he can, "is a disease."

Several draftees gasp. Many soldiers around the room even look shocked. Did they not know? Have we really kept The Truth a secret from the men who risk their lives to protect our city?

"And a powerful one at that," he rambles on. "The disease enters a human host through blood contact, like a scratch or a bite. Once inside, it rots their brain from the inside out. It doesn't kill the host — it slowly drives them insane. But it has the ability to severely alter a person's appearance. Their skin will gray. Their bones will wither and contort in horrifying ways. Over time, they'll rip out every hair on their head. Their eyesight will perish, along with their sense of smell, but their hearing will enhance. This is what makes The Truth so dangerous. It can't see you, it can't smell you, but it can hear you. Every breath you take, every slight twitch, it hears it all — and it will send it into a killing spree."

I glance over at the other draftees, watching them take it in for the first time. Drew's jaw drops open. Even Carson perches on the edge of his seat, leaning in to absorb every word. It all makes sense now — the glossy white eyes, the decaying skin. How it'd drain the life from every draftee it touched. How every scratch or bite was surely fatal, even for Leo.

Part of me feels guilty for not telling them. Maybe if they'd known, they would've been prepared. Maybe if Ethan knew, he wouldn't have left and possibly lured the infected here unintentionally. I think back to all the times I almost told him. Or the times I wanted to, but it never felt right, or he was too distracted to hear me.

But no. I can't blame myself for this. No matter what, nothing could've saved Leo and the other draftees from what happened tonight. The truth is, someone let that thing into the facility. They unleashed it into our barracks. They knew exactly what it'd do and that we'd be at our most vulnerable. That's not my fault.

After all, I was almost a victim. I knew the truth, and still, I was completely defenseless. Just like everyone else.

General Conrad continues, cutting through my thoughts. "The origin of the disease is still unknown. As you know, it began in the west and spread east, but no one could say for certain how it started. But once it did, it spread like wildfire, devouring everything in its path. Because of this, there's no known cure either."

That's a lie. My ears perk up. Everything I uncovered in D.C. proves that a cure exists. That it was being tested, and my father may have cracked the code. But General Conrad would be the first to shut down any conspiracies about my father.

Is what he's built here so precious to him that it's worth denying the cure? And at what cost — our lives? Lives that could've been saved tonight?

"Our best hope at survival is to remain under the Barrier," he says. "Here, we can ward it off. We can protect ourselves. We can build up an army strong enough to wipe it from the face of the planet once and for all. As long as we're here, in the city, we have the upper hand. We have the power. We have freedom."

That's not freedom. Daphne's words play through my mind. She's right, and it's never been more evident to me now. The general doesn't want freedom. He wants control. As long as the Barrier stands, he has full authority. The city yields to his every request, even to the point of risking the lives of our men to fight his battles. He doesn't want to preserve our nation. If he did, he wouldn't have banished my father. He would've used him for the cure, because *that's* ultimately how we'll defeat The Truth.

But no, he wants to preserve The Truth. He depends on it. The sicker the world is, the more powerful he becomes.

The room erupts in applause, but I don't join in. Everyone buys into General Conrad's words, believing the same lie I've believed all this time — that obedience to him, and to the draft, will lead to victory.

But not anymore. I've seen what The Truth is capable of. If left unrestrained, it will kill and keep on killing until every living thing is dead. We're not strong enough to destroy it. Fighting back would be a suicide mission. Even if we enlist our men, assemble an army, and go to war against it, it won't be enough. The Truth will come back. It always does — and there's only one way to stop it.

Someone has to take a stand. Someone has to find the cure, unleash it, and purify our nation.

Once the applause subsides, General Conrad begins pacing again. "But that still leaves one thing we have to address." He taps his finger against his lip, keeping his other hand tucked behind his back. "You see, each of us has a duty to protect our nation. It's ingrained in our pledge here. It's at the core of everything we do. The draft exists to protect all of humanity, and that's not just extended to those outside the facility — it includes each and every one of you. As long as we're united, your duty should be to protect one another so we can protect this city together."

His words feel like a sharp turn in a different direction. Protecting each other and the city is something we all know. It's a message we've been branded with since day one. We haven't forgotten that. If anything, our awareness of it has been heightened by everything that happened tonight.

So why is he saying this now?

His voice rises, and his next words echo the same choice he presented to me the day we returned from Philadelphia. "There comes a moment in every soldier's time here where he has to decide who he's obedient to. Will you serve your nation with dignity, or will you go your own way? Will you follow the rules, which have been put in place solely for your protection? Or will curiosity get the best of you? So long as you're in this facility, you have access to more than you've ever had access to in your lives. We trust you with it because we trust that you'll make the right decisions. We trust that you'll stay in line, obey your commanding officers, and do as we've trained you to do. But it's come to my attention that we're not all aligned in that."

My heart skips a beat. Does he know about Daphne? Does he know I've been using stolen gear to see her every night? Instantly, my mind thinks it's personal. But from the corner of the stage, something catches my attention. Lieutenant Kelley and Lieutenant Tillman step into the light. Held between them is a hostage. Their head is covered with a sack. Their wrists are bound by handcuffs, and their ankles bound with chains. They writhe viciously, fighting against their restraints. They guide the hostage to the center of the stage and position them right next to General Conrad.

"I asked myself, how did one of the infected manage to get into our barracks tonight? How could something like this happen? And the answer is right here: It's because one of your own lost sight of his duty and broke our trust."

No. My gut wrenches. Before they can even remove the sack, I already know who it is — and I think I might be sick.

Ethan's face slips out from behind the sack. His clothes are tattered and nearly ripped to shreds, revealing a diagonal gash across his midsection. Blood oozes from the cut as his lungs expand to breathe. His scalp is dripping with sweat, and his green eyes have faded to gray, like storm clouds. His spine bends as he tries to break free, but his restraints don't budge. Every time he moves, I wince, worried that one wrong move might snap his wrists.

"Is that . . ." I hear Drew say, but I don't respond. My ears tune him out, and my eyes remain glued forward, locked on Ethan.

A wicked smile spreads across General Conrad's face. Red-hot adrenaline courses through my veins, puffing out of my ears like smoke. My whole body trembles uncontrollably.

"Ethan Greene slipped out of his barracks last night and took the subway to an undisclosed location outside the Barrier," General Conrad announces. He reaches down and fishes into Ethan's pocket, sending him into a fit. His body convulses. His teeth grind against a thick piece of fabric tied around his head and stuffed in his mouth. He lets out a muffled groan as General Conrad pulls two small items from his pocket. Quickly, his agitation turns to weeping. Tears pour down his face, and a sob escapes his throat.

In General Conrad's hands, he displays the badge we stole from Lieutenant Tillman and the pager we kept from Philadelphia. In that moment, I know I'll never see Daphne again. Wrestling with that reality, all the while seeing Ethan tied up in front of everyone like a spectacle, is too much to bear.

"He used an all-access badge, stolen from one of his training officers, and a pager kept from a supply run to accomplish this," General Conrad reveals. He holds up the evidence for everyone to see.

No, I think again. *No, no, no.*

"Stealing from a training officer and hoarding gear that doesn't belong to you..." General Conrad says softly, clicking his tongue as he turns toward Ethan. "We don't take that lightly around here."

More tears spill from his eyes. His lips quiver, and he lets out another groan. I can tell he's trying to say something, but nothing more than a pitiful yelp comes out.

"Are you pleased with yourself?" General Conrad screams. "Are you proud of what you've accomplished? You held the door while it tore your friends to shreds! Their blood is on *your* hands!"

Ethan weeps desperately now. His knees buckle, and he falls to the stage floor in a heap. Instinctively, I rise out of my chair, but Drew is quick to yank me back down. The whole time, my eyes never leave the stage.

"Soldiers," General Conrad's tone shifts to address his audience. "The point I'm trying to make is this: This is what happens when loyalty is betrayed. Contempt born in secrecy is a recipe for disaster. It pushes you to steal, to scheme, and to commit heinous, unthinkable acts. It blinds you to the consequences. It doesn't matter who's affected or who gets hurt along the way. In the end, all you care about is your own selfish interventions, no matter the cost."

Before I can think, General Conrad draws a handgun from his holster. He presses the mouth of the gun to Ethan's skull, causing him to shift off balance. He falls on his side against the floor. Lieutenant Kelley steps forward and pulls him back onto his knees.

No.

"This is what happens when you fall out of line!" General Conrad howls. His whole face flushes red, and his eyes bulge out of his head. Ethan lowers his head and lets out a low, defeated sob. It's clear he's given up. He has no more fight left in him.

"This is what happens when you forget who you're obedient to. There's a system in place for a reason, a system designed for unity and protection. This is what happens when you decide to go your own way. People die, and you die alone."

No.

Ethan's eyes lift slowly and find mine in the crowd. In that moment, I feel everything he feels. All the regret, the guilt, the humiliation — all of it. The wit and innocence that once distinguished Ethan from everyone else is gone. Now, he's nothing but flesh and bone. *I can't control it, John.* His words cycle through my mind. Something happened to him. This wasn't like him. None of this was his own doing. He's not well. I can see it in his eyes, but there's no stopping General Conrad.

And Ethan knows it too.

Bang! A gunshot echoes throughout the room. I feel my body lift up. Someone grabs at my arm again, most likely Drew, trying to pull me down. But I resist. My ears ring, and my hands ball into fists at my sides. My mouth opens, but no sound comes out. Nothing that I can hear. All I hear is ringing. A vibration tears through my throat, and I see General Conrad's head whip around. I can't hear myself, but I'm screaming. I know I am. But it's all consumed by a shrill, flatlined ringing.

"No!" I cry out. My mind blocks out Ethan's body lying dead at the general's feet. Out of the corner of my eye, Lieutenant Kelley and Lieutenant Tillman spring into action. But I keep my eyes on General Conrad.

"Liar!" I scream at the top of my lungs. "You did this, not him! It was you!"

The ringing in my ears subsides just enough for me to hear General Conrad's final words. It's as if everyone else falls away, and his words are meant only for me. "As I said before, every soldier has a decision to make. Don't make the wrong one."

All the rage bubbling inside me explodes. I can't stop screaming. My throat burns, but I don't stop. I *can't* stop. A hand wraps around my arm, then another takes hold of the other, and soon enough, I'm being dragged down the aisle with my legs sprawled on the floor in front of me. My eyes shift to the blood splattered across the stage floor where Ethan once laid. Lieutenant Kelley and Lieutenant Tillman remove his body, dragging him away to dispose of like he's waste. Like he isn't one of us.

Like he isn't my best friend.

General Conrad's words haunt me. *This is what happens when you decide to go your own way.* It was so easy for him to pull that trigger. The minute he determined Ethan was against us, he put an end to him. There was no room for mercy, no chance for an explanation. Nothing he could've said or done to stop it. The general requires one of two things — obedience or death. You're either with him, or you're against him. And if you're against him, he'll stop at nothing until you're dead.

The draftees and I are forced back to our barracks. As we enter the room, I notice the beds of the three draftees we lost have been stripped. One painful glance reveals Ethan's has been stripped too. The floors and walls have been scrubbed clean of any blood. The room is sterile again, as if nothing happened here. As if the slate is wiped clean — and that nearly sends me into another fit of rage.

Before I can collect myself, someone shoves me hard. I collapse against the frame of my bunk. My head slams into it, and I let out a sharp yelp. Lifting a hand to my temple, I can already feel the skin starting to bruise.

Turning around, I see Apollo glaring back at me. He grabs the collar of my shirt in his fist and pins me against the bunk. His eyes swell with tears, but he never lets them out. Doing so would be weak, and Apollo would rather die than be seen as weak.

"Did you know about this?" he questions me. "Did you and your little buddy have this whole thing planned?"

Drew intervenes. He rushes up behind Apollo and tries to pull him off me.

"C'mon, man!" Drew exclaims. "Let him off the hook! He just lost Ethan."

Apollo spins around. "I lost someone too!" he fires back at Drew fiercely, his voice breaking. "He got Dom killed, and none of this would've happened if it weren't for him!"

He turns back to me now, barely maintaining his composure. "*You* are responsible for this!" he accuses me. "Just by being his friend, this is *your* fault!"

Something snaps in me. I launch myself at Apollo and shove him to the ground. Almost as soon as he falls, he tries to scramble to his feet, but I pin him down. I drive my fist into his jaw, and Apollo lets out a groan. I don't let up. I rear my fist to deliver another blow, but Drew catches my hand in midair.

"John!" he shouts. "What good will this do?"

His words stun me. I soften my composure and slowly lower my fist. Apollo quivers beneath me, bracing for impact.

I push back against his chest and rise to my feet. Drew stands between us, holding his arms out in case one of us tries to pounce again.

"We *all* lost somebody here!" Drew emphasizes. "Every single one of us. It doesn't matter if they were your best friend or not. They were one of us. It could've been any one of us who lost their lives tonight. And how do you respond? By assigning blame and coming at each other's throats? You should be grateful to even be alive right now!"

Apollo and I both stand dumbfounded. Every eye in the room is on Drew. His voice softens, and he turns toward me, placing a steady hand on my shoulder.

"Look, I know how much Ethan meant to you," he says gently. Turning to Apollo, he says, "And I know how much Dom meant to you. But this is no way to honor them."

He's right. Apollo grits his teeth. With a sigh, he walks away and disappears into the bathroom.

Drew turns to me again for consolation, but I don't want his sympathy. I hold out my hand to keep him away. All my emotions catch up to me at once. The weight of it crushes me. I sink down against my mattress and bury my face in my pillow. I curl into the corner of the bunk and fold into myself, as if by making myself smaller, the pain might feel smaller too. But it's no use. The pain overtakes me, and I sob hard. I turn my back to the rest of the room, wishing no one could hear me. Knowing everyone can.

We all lost someone tonight, but this is more than that. This isn't just grief. Everything I've ever held onto has been ripped from my hands, sending me into a spiral. But this isn't the freefall. It's the cold, bone-shattering ground at the bottom. I don't know how to go on from here. I don't know if I want to.

I wait for the top bunk to creak from Ethan's weight, just as it has every night since we arrived here. But it never comes.

Twenty-Five

Waking up the next morning feels impossible. My eyes slowly blink open. They're dried out and puffy from hours spent crying. I don't remember falling asleep, but at some point, I must've drifted off. The barracks are still dark, and most of the other draftees seem to be sleeping. As I glance around the room, panic sets in. The last time it was this dark and this quiet, an infected was lurking in the shadows. My eyes try to adjust, but they can't, not fully at least. All I see is darkness.

I slip out of bed and trudge into the bathroom. As soon as my feet hit the tile, the automatic lights come on. I step into the shower. I rest my arm against the wall and my head against my arm, letting the water trickle down my spine. All my emotions come rushing in again. My body trembles as I let out a sob. I worry the others will hear me, but the sound of the shower running is enough to muffle the noise. Over and over again, I relive the events from last night, like a nightmare I'll never wake up from. Every time I close my eyes, I see the infected's eyes staring back at me. Its teeth tearing into Leo's shoulder. General Conrad removing the sack from Ethan's head. The bullet ripping through his skull. The general's eyes glaring at me, warning me if I venture down the same path, I'll be next.

The sound of the shower seems to escalate. Its deafening roar fills my ears, drowning out everything else. The water crashes against my skull like a gushing waterfall. My hand flies to the faucet. I twist it violently to stop it, and even though the water ceases, the roar lingers. I feel it everywhere

— in my ears, in my head, reverberating through my bones. My lungs heave frantically, desperate for air. It's as if the walls of the shower start to cave in, slowly inching closer until they press against my body. A phantom hand tightens around my throat. I claw at it, desperate for air, but the grip tightens, squeezing my windpipe.

I fall to the floor and hug my knees to my chest. My nails dig into my flesh, drawing blood that drips down my leg. Eventually, the roar subsides, and the soft silence of the empty bathroom returns. I gasp for air, and it fills my lungs. My breathing steadies, my heart rate stabilizes, and suddenly, it all feels manageable again.

I quiver on the cold floor as my body recalibrates. I've never been so afraid. Before the draft, there was fear — fear of the unknown, of losing touch with the rest of my life, of being thrown into something I had no control over. But this fear is greater than that. I'm afraid of myself. I'm afraid of what happens when I'm all that's left. Going on without Ethan or Daphne feels impossible. Without them, all I'm left with is the draft, The Truth, and myself.

I don't know if I can do this alone. I don't know how.

After some time, I pick myself off the ground and rush out of the bathroom. I dress in my uniform and slide back in bed. One by one, other draftees start to wake up. I lay in my bunk until they're all dressed and gone, wanting to head up to breakfast alone. But Drew and Carson linger. They wait until the room clears, then lean into the bunk, hovering over me.

"Come with us, John," Drew says, offering a hand. "We won't leave you behind."

My hardened resolve softens, and I take his hand. Once I'm up, Carson slings his arm around my shoulder, and together, the three of us head to breakfast.

When we're finished eating, we follow the crowd outside to meet with our training officers. As we push through the main doors, my stomach twists at the thought of seeing them again. They may not have been the ones to pull the trigger, but they delivered Ethan to General Conrad. They dragged his lifeless body from the stage. They knew what would happen, and they allowed it. They're just as responsible.

Lieutenant Kelley and Lieutenant Tillman wait for us near the trees. They stand poised with their shoulders back and hands clasped behind their backs. They nod at each of us as we gather in front of them, but I don't meet their gaze. I keep my head down and fall in line between Drew and Carson.

"Good morning, soldiers," Lieutenant Kelley greets us. "We understand that with recent events, we've been out of our normal rhythm. Training may be the last thing on your minds right now. But it may be just what you need to help you focus on other things. We can't let these things hold us back. In the war against The Truth, there will always be setbacks. These things are meant to test us, not deter us. So the best thing we can do is keep pressing forward."

He pauses for a moment to let his words settle, hoping his pep talk will take root within us. But it feels shallow — empty words strung together to smooth over the cracks and push past what happened.

"With that said, today marks the official start of your third quarter of training," Lieutenant Kelley continues. "We'll begin today with a run. This time, you'll have an hour to complete it. Take your time, but be diligent. Don't slack off. Instead, use this as an opportunity to get back on track. The sooner we unite together again, the stronger we'll be."

Lieutenant Tillman clicks his stopwatch. As soon as the time starts, we break into a jog down the wooded path and disappear into the city.

The morning sun rises over the Barrier. Its rays poke through the buildings towering over us, warming my skin. Drew and Carson hold my pace with Apollo just a few strides ahead, leading the pack on his own.

As I run, I gaze out at the city — the only place I've known my whole life. A place that used to feel like home. But it's tainted now. The safety it once promised has turned sour. I don't feel safe anymore. I feel trapped. As long as I'm here, General Conrad has control over me. There's no escaping him. There's no hope for a cure, no chance at a future beyond the city. He holds the fate of humanity in the palm of his hand, and as long as I'm here, I'm nothing more than a pawn in his game.

But if the cure really worked on my father, then I have to go back for him. I have to believe we both want the same thing — to bring the cure to the city. To free everyone from The Truth. If that's what he intended all along, then I have no choice. I have to finish what he started.

Finish what your father started. Mae's words echo through my mind, and suddenly, it all makes sense. She knew. Somehow, she knew they were testing a cure — and she knew my father had something to do with it. But she couldn't speak of it, not openly. It was too dangerous. She knew if word got out, she'd be killed or banished from the city, just like he was.

Yet still, she believed in him. She knew the cure was our only hope. Without it, we're all slaves to General Conrad. But with the cure, our future is boundless. That's why she urged me to finish what he started. To do what he couldn't do. To free us from this, once and for all.

Glancing over at Drew and Carson, I realize how clueless they are. They may know about the disease now, but they don't know about the cure. They only know what they've been told — that a cure doesn't exist.

If Mae wanted it, would they want it too? We've lived our entire lives under the Barrier, held under the notion that the world beyond the city is hopeless. They've been fed the same lie that our only option is to fight the war to survive. If they knew things could be different, wouldn't they want that? Would they be willing to risk everything, just like my father did? Just like I intend to?

Drew catches me staring for too long and furrows his brows. I didn't realize how long I'd spaced out, lost in my thoughts.

"You look like you're plotting to kill us, John," Drew chuckles.

"Please do," Carson exhales. "Put me out of my misery. Anything to get this run over with as soon as possible."

"Sorry," I let out a nervous laugh, turning away from them.

But as soon as I do, my head spins back around. If I were them, I'd want to know. Even if I said no in the end, I'd want the choice to be mine. So I take a chance, hoping they'd want the same.

"It's just . . ." I mutter. I struggle to find the right words. It's the same struggle I felt with Ethan. How do you tell someone something that's certain to turn their whole world upside down? Even more, how do you convince them it's true?

But I can't make the same mistake I made with Ethan. Instead of waiting for the right words to come, I pose the question and leave the rest in their hands.

"What would you do if you could get out of here?"

Drew's brows scrunch together. "You mean, out of the city?"

I nod. "Yes. If there were no Barrier, no disease, nothing holding you back, what would you do? Would you leave?"

Carson lets out a deep laugh. "Don't tease me, man. I can't even imagine anything different."

"Me neither," Drew says. "It sounds great in theory, but it's not possible. Where's this coming from, anyway?"

Before I respond, I consider my options. If I tell them what I know, they might not believe me. They might think I'm being delusional, that my mind is jaded from the grief of losing Ethan, and I'm clinging to a false hope.

Or maybe, they'll believe me, and the delusions of a better world — a *cured* world — will become a real possibility in their minds. I have to believe we're not all so brainwashed that we can't fathom the chance at something more than this. I have to trust that deep down, they want it. Of course they want it — they just don't know how.

My next words come out before I'm ready to say them. "I think my father may have found a cure. And I think that man in D.C. was him."

Drew and Carson stare back at me as if I've lost my mind. My heart sinks. This was a mistake. I shouldn't have brought them into this, but there's no going back now.

"I'm sorry, *what* man?" Carson asks. "You guys found someone?"

"No," Drew is quick to deny. "Well, yes. But—"

"You saw him yourself," I interject. "Remember, Drew? When Lieutenant Kelley chased after him, you mouthed something to me. What were you trying to say?"

Drew's face turns pale. He swallows his pride, then says, "Hideout. That's what I was trying to tell you. We were searching a room and found a hatch hidden under the rug. We figured it could be worth investigating, so we asked Lieutenant Kelley for help. As soon as we pulled it open, the man came running out, as if he'd been hiding in there."

I stifle a smile to keep it from showing. All this time, he's been hiding in D.C. under the military's radar. And that's exactly where I'll go to find him.

Carson stares at us, dumbfounded. "And you think this man was your father, John?"

How much do I tell them? But I have to tell them everything. No more secrets. No more hiding.

"Yes," I blurt out. "When we were there, I found papers. Old files on test subjects for an antidote. One of them was my father's. All the others were people who didn't respond to the cure. But my father's . . . his was different. It said he was cured."

Drew's eyes widen, but he's still holding back. Fear keeps him in doubt, too afraid to accept what this could mean.

I keep going. "Before the draft, a woman at The Market told me my father was banished. All along, I thought maybe he'd done something wrong. But now, I see he was trying to do the right thing. People died trying to develop a cure. Gave themselves up as test subjects. The military covered it up, but my father was cured. He must've brought it to the military and they didn't want it. So they banished him to shut him up. If there's any chance at finding the cure, it starts with my father. In D.C."

Drew sighs in frustration. Carson jogs silently, trying to discern what to believe. Up ahead, the Hudson Tunnel comes into view. We round the corner and start down the next straightaway, putting the tunnel at our backs. Apollo's pace slows as he tires. He's much closer to us now. I worry if he gets any closer, he'll overhear us, and that won't go well.

"So let's say you're right, and your father *did* find a cure," Drew reasons. "Why wouldn't the military want it?"

"That's the thing," I start. But before I can elaborate, he adds onto his question.

"I mean, it seems like a no-brainer. If there were a cure, wouldn't they want us to have it? We're trying to stop The Truth. What better way to do that than with a cure?"

"Exactly!" I exclaim. "They don't want a cure because as long as there's no cure, the military thrives. General Conrad has built up an empire here. Without a cure, we need the Barrier. And as long as we're under the Barrier, he has the power. If a cure existed, the Barrier could come down, and he'd be no better than the rest of us."

"That's absurd," Drew scoffs. "If that's true, I mean, then that's absurd. There's no way we can stand against The Truth forever. The odds are stacked against us — and that's never been more clear to me than last night. A few hundred soldiers aren't going to end a nationwide epidemic."

Something clicks in my mind. The draft has always existed in the event the Barrier falls. All my life, I've wondered why we'd create a faulty shield. If we went to the extreme of encasing an entire city in a force field, why not make it impenetrable? Why turn to a group of young soldiers instead?

"That's it," I let out. "The draft isn't a war tactic against The Truth. It might've started out that way, but it's turned into something much more now. Like you said, there's no way we can stand against The Truth forever. What if we're not training to fight it? What if all along, we've been training to fight against a cure? To keep it out?"

I feel mildly insane for even considering that possibility, but one look at Drew and Carson confirms they're thinking it too. All the gears click into place. Why else would they have sent us after my father? They don't want a cure — they want to preserve the city, Barrier and all, and they want us to defend it.

And they want to keep my father out.

"What are you three talking about?" Apollo's voice cuts in. My head jerks around, and I see him running in step alongside us.

My heart races. I don't know how long he's been there or how much he's heard. I shouldn't have said anything — not here, at least. But where else? I couldn't have said any of this in the barracks. Not at breakfast, with the other draftees and soldiers lurking nearby. Now seemed like the only time, while we're miles from the facility, deep in the city.

None of us say anything, which only heightens Apollo's curiosity.

"Are you deaf?" he hollers. "I said, what are you talking about?"

Drew and Carson's eyes fall on me, relying on me to cover our tracks.

"It's none of your business, Apollo," I snarl at him.

He chuckles deviously. "Whatever it is, knock it off. Your buddy already got several of our guys killed because he was delusional. I don't need you planting any more delusions in peoples' heads."

My hands clench into fists, and I grit my teeth. "When are you going to stop blaming me for what happened?"

"When you stop giving me a reason to believe you're the one to blame," he says. "The apple doesn't fall far from the tree, Madoc. And a bad tree produces bad fruit. I never trusted you, and I still don't, especially now."

I resist the urge to shove him onto the asphalt right here, right now. Drew settles me with a look, and to my surprise, Carson steps up to my defense.

"Speak for yourself, Andres," he snaps. "John hasn't done anything wrong. From day one, he's done nothing but stay out of your way. You're the one who's always picking a fight. So if there's anyone who shouldn't be trusted, it's you."

"Shut it, O'Hair," Apollo barks back. "You're just as delusional. Both of you." He moves his finger between Carson and Drew. "Happens, apparently, the longer you stick around a Madoc."

"Well, then you better not stick around, in case you become delusional too," Carson widens his eyes and twiddles his fingers.

Apollo fires off a string of obscenities and takes off ahead of us, burning all his anger into the final sprint of the run.

As soon as he's out of earshot, I turn to Drew and Carson, lowering my voice to a whisper.

"How much do you think he heard?" I ask.

Carson shakes his head. "Enough to make an assumption, maybe. But probably not enough to use against us."

Drew sticks his hand out, silencing us. "Either way, we've said enough as it is. Let's just finish the run, okay? We can talk more about this later, when it's safe."

We put it all behind us and continue down the last straightaway. We pass through the outer wall and under the shade of the trees, ascending the path toward the facility. Before the training officers come back into view, Drew runs right beside me. I'm so focused on the finish line, I almost miss it when he says, "We're on your side, John. Whatever happens, we're with you. Just know that."

Relief washes over me as we break through the trees. One nod from Lieutenant Tillman indicates we've made it back in time. Apollo stands near the corner of the courtyard. He glares at us as we approach him, his eyes untrusting.

As more draftees make it back, I smile at Drew. I don't say anything, but I don't have to. Any worries I had about letting him and Carson in on the truth have faded. His words affirm it was the right decision. It feels good to know I have them, and that all along, they've been here — and they're not going anywhere.

For the first time since Ethan's murder, I don't feel panicked. I don't feel sad or alone. I feel safe again. Most of all, I feel hope.

Twenty-Six

Our run begins early the next morning. The training officers barge into the barracks well before dawn and force us out of bed. I groan and roll out of my bunk, my body still aching from yesterday's run. The rest of the draftees are just as sluggish, most of them still struggling to adjust back to training.

A few in particular haven't been sleeping through the night. The past few nights, it's become almost routine for a draftee to wake up screaming from a night terror. Like clockwork, the whole barracks will spring to life, and someone will sprint across the room to turn on the lights. As the light breaks through, the draftee will be sitting upright in his bed, drenched with sweat. His eyes will dart around the room, searching for some unseen terror, thinking it's real.

But it never is. It's all in his head every time.

Drew and Carson join me for breakfast. We eat in silence and slowly come to life, holding out for the slight boost of energy our meals provide. We don't say a word about the cure or my father. Once we're finished, we return our trays and head outside to meet our training officers.

"Forty-five minutes are on the clock this time," Lieutenant Kelley declares as we gather outside the facility. "Don't be slow."

With that, we take off down the path. Our arms droop at our sides, and our feet lazily scuff along the asphalt. The city buildings are still blanketed by the shadows of the morning — all except the Freedom Tower, which gleams on its own, even without sunlight. In the gloom, the path is hazy. It takes at least a quarter of a mile before my eyes fully adjust.

Drew, Carson, and I allow the other draftees to pass us, taking up the rear. We'll make up the time later on. But these runs are the only chance we get to discuss our plan. My eyes follow Apollo as he darts past us. He throws a smug look over his shoulder, all too satisfied to be taking the lead but still holding some suspicion.

Once he's out of range, Carson yawns and slaps his face, trying to wake up. Drew's eyes are heavy, but his mind reels with questions.

"What would we need to get out of the city?" he asks.

"We'd need an all-access badge to get onto Battery Station," I say. "Also a pager to alert us when the subway arrives and departs. That way, we know when it's time to go and when to be back." *If we plan on coming back*, I add in my head but don't say it.

"I see you've given this some thought already," Drew chuckles.

"Yeah, I mean—" I stop myself. I realize I haven't told them about Daphne. They don't know about us finding her, or that she was the one to set most of these thoughts into motion. She's arguably one of the most important pieces of the puzzle, but I hold back for now. I've already given them a lot to process. I don't want to risk them backing out.

"That's how Ethan did it, at least," I finish. Drew furrows his brows, and I scramble to cover up any suspicion. "Just based on the gear the general collected from him. I pieced it together myself from there, but it makes sense."

"How did he even get an all-access badge?" Drew ponders. "The pager I can understand. He could've kept it from any one of our supply runs. But the badge . . . that's a mystery."

I bite my tongue to resist telling him the truth, that Ethan swiped that badge from Lieutenant Tillman after our visit to the general's office. That he took it from my own hand the night he left the facility.

"Beats me," I lie. "But you're right. Getting the badge will be the hardest part."

"Even then, how would we do it?" Carson chimes in. "Say we get the badge and the pager. Then what? We just sneak out of the barracks, take the subway to D.C., and hope for the best? Hope we find your father? All before wake-up call the next morning?"

Drew and I both nod as if the answer should be obvious, which makes me grin. It's comforting to know that Drew is all in. Out of the two of them, I expected him to be the most skeptical.

"I don't know," Carson hesitates. "Seems risky."

"You can't back out now, bro," Drew throws a light punch at his arm. "The details are . . . a bit loose right now. But we'll figure it out. And plus, at least we have a starting point. We'll start in D.C., because we know that's where John saw his father." He turns to me, and with all the confidence in the world, he says, "If there's a better plan, John will come up with it. He'll tell us."

I nod affirmatively. But deep down, I know there isn't a better plan. Our best bet is to do exactly as he's said — get to D.C., find my father, and let the rest fall into place.

We quicken our pace to catch up with the rest of the group. For now, any further ideas about how we'll make it to D.C. become secondary to training. We complete the first stretch, the tunnel coming into view on our left, and round the corner. By now, the other draftees are no more than a few strides ahead of us. Once we reach them, we join in and match their pace.

As we pass by the tunnel, something catches my eye. In its gaping mouth, I spot movement. Nothing more than a slight twitch in the shadows, offsetting the otherwise still darkness. At first, I think it's just my eyes playing a trick on me. Maybe I'm delirious. After all, I'm running on little-to-no sleep. But as I glance over my shoulder, it moves again.

I stop running and stare into the mouth of the tunnel. Drew's head spins around, and while still running, he calls out, "What are you doing, John?"

I keep my eyes fixed ahead, trying to pinpoint what I'm seeing.

"Go on," I holler back. "I'll catch up."

He doesn't put up a fight. He and Carson continue to run until they vanish further into the city. I stand alone in the center of the street, gazing into the tunnel. Timidly, I approach the fence that separates me from it. With little hesitation, I hoist myself up and scale the fence. Once I reach the top, I swing my legs over and jump down. I fall from nearly twice my height before my feet slam into the asphalt, jolting my body.

As I turn around, the darkness moves again. I still can't make out what's causing it. Each flicker is quick and subtle, but it draws me in. I move closer toward the opening. Water droplets fall from the ceiling and smack the ground, sending a rippling echo down the hollow shaft.

The sunlight only reaches so far down here before there's only darkness. The deeper I go, the shadows seem to pull back, revealing more of the tunnel in segments. Graffiti covers the walls, and debris crackles under my boots. Looking over my shoulder, the path is far from sight now. I know with each second I spend here, I'm losing time I need to finish the run. But I can't shake the feeling that something about this isn't right. There's something down here — something that isn't supposed to be here.

Up ahead, the movement starts to morph into the outline of a head, followed by the body connected to it. The closer I move toward it, the more it takes shape. It appears to be human — all its limbs are where they should be. Even though I can only make out its silhouette, I can tell that much.

I take another step forward, and in an instant, my eyes adjust. My blood runs cold. I inhale sharply and freeze where I stand. Thin wiry hairs poke out of a balding scalp. Its gray skin blends with the darkness, as if cut from the shadows. Its skeletal arms hang loosely at its sides, decaying flesh barely clinging to the bone. Even from several feet away, I know what it is.

The infected's head twitches and tilts forward, then falls back again. It repeats this movement over and over, stuck in a perpetual mechanical nod. But every time its head comes forward, it's met by some sort of invisible shield that restrains it from coming any closer.

Holding my breath, I take one more step. I cringe as my boots crunch against loose pebbles in the concrete, worried that even the slightest sound might send it into a frenzy. As I approach it, a faint buzz tickles my ears. It reminds me of the pager, only this sound is much more intense. I swat at my ears, trying to get it to stop, but it only intensifies. It rises to a shrill, piercing whine that makes me grit my teeth. The frequency sets alight every nerve in my body, like nails on a chalkboard. A sound so unbearable, it makes me want to tear myself apart just to make it stop.

I get close enough that I'm sure the infected will sense me. Even though it can't see me, it might feel my breath or hear me shudder as I step closer. Without warning, its head comes crashing forward again. I jerk back, but the same invisible barrier intervenes. As its head makes contact with it, it sends a ripple through the air between us. The infected shakes it off, leans back, then the cycle repeats again.

Its head collides with the obstruction much more aggressively this time. The ripple multiplies, sending small sparks of blue electricity crawling up through the concrete overlaying the tunnel. The impact throws the infected off balance, and it stumbles back a few feet — which only aggravates it. It lets out a heinous screech that fills the tunnel. I slam my palms over my ears and crouch down, cowering in the shadows, afraid it might break through whatever separates it from me.

But it never does.

My stomach twists from being this close to it again. But beneath the unease, there's a thrill to it. It's like standing in front of a pane of glass, staring eye-to-eye with a vicious animal that, in its natural habitat, would rip me apart in seconds. I step forward until I'm so close, I could almost reach out and touch it. Its head flies forward again, triggering another electric current that crackles through the space between us.

I lift a trembling hand, and my palm finds something as sure and solid as a wall but entirely invisible. The infected's head crashes down, striking the spot where my palm rests, but I don't feel anything. Nothing but a slight vibration from where it made impact.

The buzzing hum is everywhere now. All around me. With my palm still outstretched in front of me, I realize what this is.

It's the Barrier.

I lift my other palm and place it against the Barrier wall. As the infected falls forward again, I don't flinch. I stare back in amazement. I've never been so close to the Barrier before. I've never felt it against my hands. Now I understand what Daphne meant, and how it must've felt for her to discover this.

My hands slide over the surface, amazed by its complete transparency. It makes it seem like there's nothing between us at all. The infected is as clear as my own reflection, but as soon as its head strikes again, the reflection blurs and glitches.

Without meaning to, I let out a chuckle. It slips out of my mouth, muffled by the hum. Adrenaline courses through my veins. In this moment, I have the higher ground. The infected can't get to me. It will never be able to get to me, as long as the Barrier stands.

It's profound, really. All my life, I've known we were protected by the Barrier. It's designed to keep The Truth out. It's designed for moments like *this*. Seeing it in action is mesmerizing. Even though the infected is inches from where I stand, I'm completely safe — so long as I'm on the other side.

The sound of my laughter permeates through the Barrier's hum. It must reach the other side, because the infected's head twitches and its ears perk up, breaking its cycle. It presses its face into the Barrier, but this time, it doesn't lean back. It holds its ghastly face against the surface, perplexed by the noise. Listening intently for it again.

Something about the infected's face sends a chill down my spine. As I stare back at it, I feel the slightest hint of familiarity. Like I've seen it before — like a nightmare come to life.

The few hairs that pepper its scalp shine with a hint of gold, like they were once blonde. Behind the smoke in its eyes, I see a tinge of blue. It's faint, but it's there, just a slight pop of color. As we stare back at each other, its forehead lines up perfectly with mine. Its shoulders sag the same way mine do. I lower my hands and let them fall at my sides, and to my horror, my fingertips align with the infected's on the other side.

A deep sense of agony comes over me. The last time I saw something bearing this much resemblance to me was in the first assessment. At the time, I didn't know what it was. I convinced myself it was in my head or a cruel twist of the simulation. But now, it's standing before me — and it's real.

All its features are consistent with mine. All the color is squeezed from its flesh, but it's still *my* flesh. The same cracks and freckles that pattern my skin. The same ears that stick out from my head. The same nose that's flattened into my face.

The same scowl I've worn for eighteen years.

I jump back and move away from it. It remains glued against the Barrier wall, staring back at me with hollow eyes, like a horrifying reflection etched into the surface. I don't understand it, but I can't shake the feeling that it's *me*. Or some sort of sick, twisted depiction of me. A version of myself that only exists beyond the Barrier, where The Truth has taken over me.

Slowly, I walk backward toward the mouth of the tunnel, keeping my eyes locked on it the entire time. It twitches again, and I freeze. Even though the Barrier is there, panic shoots across my chest. It unleashes a deep, guttural growl, then lets out another ear-splitting screech. The bones in its hands crack and bend, and veins throb against its neck. In a flash, it turns away from the Barrier and sprints down the shaft on the other side, retreating into the shadows. I watch in horror as the darkness envelops it, and the last glimpse of it fades out of sight.

As soon as it's gone, I sprint out of the tunnel. I launch myself up and over the fence and crash against the asphalt on the other side. I bend over and let out a dry heave. I think I might be sick. But as much as I gag, nothing comes out. My heart threatens to burst from my chest. Flattening my hands on my head, I fight to steady my breath, but the panic has already set in. I can't stop it now. All I can do is ride it out.

It's not that I'm afraid of what I saw. It's not even that I'm afraid the Barrier might break. It's the horrible reality that The Truth has made its way here. For nearly two decades, we've managed to keep it away. But now, it knows where we are. The infected doesn't understand it can't break through the Barrier wall, but it wants to.

It might not be able to now, but it's not to say it never will. And the worst part is, if the Barrier were to fall, one day, it'll come back, and its head will fall all the way through. There will be no more invisible wall, nothing holding it back. Nothing to keep it from charging straight into the city.

It knows how to get in. And there's nothing we can do to stop it when it does.

Twenty-Seven

As the first week since Ethan's murder nears its end, I catch myself staring at his empty bunk. No matter how hard I try, I can't look away. It's hard to believe so much time has passed. It feels cruel to think at one point, I couldn't imagine one day without him. Now the normalcy of him being gone gnaws at me. As I stare at the bare mattress, I try to picture him lying there. I've almost forgotten what it was like to see him there. Worst of all, I can hardly remember what he looked like. The details blur, and any time I think of him, all I see is his last moment. That, of all things, remains sharp. And out of all my memories of him, that's the one I wish I could forget.

Once we're ready, Drew, Carson, and I head up to breakfast together. We seat ourselves at our normal table and pick at our meals until we've had our fill.

"I don't know how much more of this stuff I can take," Carson groans. He swallows reluctantly against a spoonful of mushy oatmeal and makes a face. "I think I'd rather starve."

"Well, it's not like you graduate from it after we finish our term. This stuff's forever . . ." Drew takes another bite, and with his mouth full, finishes by saying, "unfortunately."

I tune out their conversation. My mind drifts elsewhere. I think back to the morning of my birthday. Everything was simpler then. Even with the draft impending, there was nothing real to worry about. Nothing compared to all there is to worry about now. There was no awareness of what The Truth is, no plot to leave the city, no lingering feeling that everything could slip away at any moment. And now, even with the hope that my father is out there, everything feels hopeless.

For a moment, I contemplate giving up, surrendering any plans to chase after my father and the cure. Besides Drew and Carson, no one else knows. Nobody else would be let down. Forfeiting any chance to do something about it wouldn't result in anything other than mild disappointment from Drew and Carson.

But I know that's not true. They may not know it, but finding a cure would ultimately set the whole city free. It would give people a fighting chance against The Truth, instead of relying on the military. It'd give Mother closure, potentially even reuniting her with Father, and it'd give Liam a second chance — a chance at the life I never had. It'd give Daphne and me a future. *Daphne*. As her name crosses my mind, my heart sinks. It's been nearly a week since I saw her last. She doesn't know about Ethan. She doesn't know about any of this — about the plan to pursue the cure or that Drew and Carson are in on it.

But why does it all have to depend on me? Why couldn't it have been someone else? It'd be so much easier to give it all up. To throw my arms up and wipe my hands clean of it. I could just—

A gentle tapping noise against the glass behind me slices through my thoughts. I flinch, startled by the sound. My eyes lift to Drew and Carson seated across from me. Both of them are staring over my shoulder with their mouths slightly ajar.

I grip the edge of the table and spin around. All I see is the grand window overlooking the training lawn. I scan the glass for any sign of impact, sure that something hit it.

Then I see it. A small droplet of water hits the glass again. It streaks down the pane, leaving a thin trail. The cafeteria falls silent. Looking around, all eyes are on that singular drop. No one makes a sound. We all stare stunned at the window, waiting to see if another will follow.

Another droplet falls, followed by another — faster this time. Suddenly, a rush of water crashes down against the window and over the lawn outside. It fills the entire facility with a great roar. Everyone jumps up from their tables. The window smears, and a dark cloud drifts over the facility, dimming the whole upper level.

"Everyone move back!" someone shouts. But there's nowhere to go. Turning around, I see the water raining down outside the front of the facility too. It seems to pour over the entire city, blurring the buildings. The Freedom Tower fades from view, disappearing into the gray mist. From where we stand, it's almost as if we're in the eye of a storm — peaceful and dry inside, but outside, it's chaos.

I turn back toward the window, watching the water smack against it but never hit me. It ricochets off the glass and trickles down its surface. Just like rain does when it falls against the Barrier.

Rain. That's what this is — and somehow, it's penetrated through the Barrier. But that's impossible. All this time, the Barrier has kept us safe from any weather event. I've never felt rain before. I've never seen it the way I do now. It'd come down against the Barrier, but it'd never meet the ground.

But now, the Barrier isn't stopping it. The rain seeps right through. And if something as small as a raindrop can get through, I can only imagine what else can too.

Over my shoulder, I see Lieutenant Kelley and Lieutenant Tillman sprint up the staircase. On the far side of the cafeteria, the doors leading to the general's office swing open, and General Conrad himself steps out. All the color drains from his face as he watches the rain fall. His precious Barrier is wilting. His plan is failing before his eyes. It won't be long before The Truth is here, and the city will no longer be his.

"Draftees, get to your barracks now!" Lieutenant Kelley roars from over my shoulder.

In the shuffle of everything, my mind recalls the infected I saw just a few days ago. A sick, warped version of my own flesh and bone staring back at me from the other side of the Barrier. Then, it couldn't break through. But now . . .

I envision the infected hitting its head against the Barrier wall. Only this time, there's no ripple of electricity. No invisible wall to keep it at bay. Its head pokes through, its nostrils flare, and it opens its decaying mouth. It lets out a screech that reaches every corner of the city. My stomach twists. It *will* come back. I'm sure of it. And if one can get through, more will follow — if they're not here already.

My eyes fix on Lieutenant Kelley. He's barking orders, but I have to tell him. He needs to know what I saw. We need to be prepared.

"Lieutenant," I mutter.

Lieutenant Kelley's eyes flash wildly at me. "Madoc, what did I just tell you to do?"

"Just listen to me, please. I know—"

"Save it!" he screams at me. "I don't want to hear your excuse. Now get back to your barracks. That's an order."

"I saw one of them," I blurt out. "In the Holland Tunnel. I know we're not supposed to go past the fence, but I did. It was there, on the other side of the Barrier."

His tough exterior hardens even more. But behind it, I can tell he's panicked. This has never happened before. It's what he's been training for — what we've *all* been training for. But now that it's happening, we don't know what to do.

"You did what?" he starts, but he shakes his head. There's no time to reprimand me for straying off course. There are more important matters at hand, and Lieutenant Kelley knows it. "Never mind that. What did you just say?"

"It was right there," I repeat. "It was beating its head against the Barrier, like it was trying to break through. But it couldn't, at least not at the time. But—" I don't even have to finish my sentence for him to know what I'm about to say.

The realization dawns on him. He steps back but keeps his gaze locked on me. Raw fear floods his eyes. Before either of us can say anything more, I'm swept away in the rush of draftees and soldiers. Everyone's boots hitting the ground mixed with the onslaught of rain outside is ear-splitting. My breath quickens, and my heart races. I feel the panic setting in again. I can't stop it. My vision tunnels. I'm whisked through the crowd, but I don't actually comprehend where I'm going. I feel someone tug at my arm and turn to see Carson's face. He mouths something. I think he's urging me to keep moving, but I can't hear him. I can't focus. Everything feels so fragile — like at any moment, my whole world could shatter, along with the Barrier.

Within seconds, I'm forced into the elevator. I stand wedged between Drew, Carson, and other soldiers I don't know. The elevator doors slowly shut and trap all the noise on the other side.

As silence settles back in, my heart slows, and my vision refocuses. I gasp for air, clutching my chest as my lungs heave. A few soldiers throw a look over their shoulders. Drew leans in, turning to me with sympathy.

"You okay?" he whispers.

I nod subtly, slightly embarrassed. Before long, the elevator doors open to the lower level, and we spill out into the hallway. The soldiers break away from us and retreat toward the other end of the hall while we head to our barracks. The sound of their footsteps echoes down the corridor until they're too distant to be heard, leaving everything quiet for a brief moment. The air is still, almost peaceful. But the moment we push through the barracks door, that peace is shattered.

Chaos ensues inside the barracks. The other draftees are already back by the time we arrive. Apollo and Danny yell at each other while the others pace back and forth, trying to wrap their minds around what's happening. As soon as we step in, Drew pulls Carson and me aside, shoving us into the corner near my bunk.

"What do we do now?" he whispers.

I settle my mind and close my eyes. Taking a deep breath, I think through what this means for us. If rain somehow managed to get through the Barrier, it means the Barrier is weak. It won't be long before the infected are here, and we'll be sent off to fight. And that means we have to be ready. All of us.

"We're going to war," I reply. "I'm certain of it."

Carson takes a step back. But Drew remains steady.

I realize now would be the worst time to tell them about Daphne. But between standing on the brink of war and desperately needing to find a way out of the city, she's all I can think about. I imagine her in her apartment, listening to the rain pour against her windows, peppering the landing outside. She knows what this means too. She knows the Barrier is impenetrable, and she'll be waiting for me, expecting me to take action.

But I know Drew and Carson can handle it. If they're going to be in this with me, they need to know. If I don't tell them now, there may never be a better opportunity to tell them later. This might be all we have left before it's too late.

"There's a girl," I spit out. "Ethan and I found her in Philadelphia. That's why we missed the subway that day. We brought her back into the city, and she's been staying in an apartment just over the barricade."

Now Drew loses his composure. Carson lets out a nervous laugh that catches Apollo's attention. Drew clasps his hand over his forehead in disbelief.

"Oh, great," Drew grits his teeth. "That would've been a really great detail to include in your grand plan, John."

"It doesn't change anything," I say quickly. "Her name is Daphne. If we can get to her, we can take the subway from the station near her apartment to D.C. All four of us."

"No, it *does* change things," he argues. "Because now we have to go on a whole rescue mission before we can figure out the rest of the plan. It's already so risky, man. This just increases our chances of getting caught or something going wrong."

"We're not going anywhere without her," I stand my ground. "I had the badge and pager before Ethan did. I was using it to see her at night, while everyone else was asleep. Ethan only had it because he—" My words catch in my throat. I think back to the night Ethan swiped the items from my hand, but it's too painful to remember. How it all happened doesn't seem that important now. What matters is we've found a way before, and we'll do it again.

"Anyway," I continue, "what I'm trying to say is we can do this. I don't know how it'll all go down, but I need you to trust me. We just need to ride this out, and when the opportunity comes, we need to be ready to take it. No hesitations."

I stare back at them, hopeful. Carson nibbles at his bottom lip. His eyes flicker back and forth between Drew and me, waiting to see if Drew budges.

Drew places his hands on his hips and lets out a sigh. "It's risky," he repeats again, "but if we manage to pull it off, it's worth the risk."

Carson releases a breath he was holding. "Phew," he exhales. "I was hoping we weren't going to have to leave you behind." He extends his hand out in front of him, hovering it over the space between us. "I'm in."

Drew places his hand over Carson's, and I set mine on top. My eyes flicker to the left, glancing once more at Ethan's empty bunk. I know if he were here now, he'd be in on this too.

We have to do this. If for nothing else, for him.

We discreetly lift our hands in unison, uniting us as a team. As we break away, I catch Apollo staring at us. My eyes lock on his, and nerves bubble up from my stomach. But his eyes don't hold the suspicion and distrust they usually do. They seem hopeful. Eager. Almost as if he wants in on whatever I have with Drew and Carson but can't break through some part of himself to do it.

The training officers burst into the barracks. We all freeze. They march to the center of the room in silence. Lieutenant Kelley takes a deep breath before addressing us.

"The general wants everyone in the Assembly Hall," he declares.

We collect ourselves and follow them out into the hall. Both doors to the Assembly Hall are open by the time we arrive. We march through them and down the aisle to our normal row. Several soldiers are already seated around us. Once we're in our seats, the training officers convene with a group of soldiers across the aisle. I hear them talking amongst themselves, but I can't make out their words. I lean out of the row, trying to tune in to their conversation, but Lieutenant Kelley catches me. He throws me a menacing glare, and I straighten myself in my seat.

Only a few minutes pass before the lights dim. A weak spotlight falls on the center of the stage, and out of the shadows, General Conrad steps into it. He keeps his head tucked low, his hands stiff behind his back, and stops as soon as he's in the center. As he lifts his eyes, there's a somberness to his stare.

But I quickly realize his grim demeanor is actually something much more powerful. It's not melancholy — it's vengeance. Like a sitting bomb that has yet to be detonated. And it terrifies me.

"Soldiers," he bellows, his voice thundering throughout the auditorium. "Thank you all for gathering here on such short notice. I regret to inform you that we're in the midst of something unprecedented. What happened this morning was . . ." his voice trails off, but it comes back just as firm once he finds the words, "uncalled for. It took us all by surprise. But we're choosing not to let it shake us. Instead, we're choosing to take it as a call to arms."

Voices murmur throughout the room before they're hushed.

"Our Barrier is getting weaker," he confirms. "For nearly two decades, we've anticipated this. We've awaited the day the Barrier would no longer be able to sustain us. We don't know what it's capable of keeping out anymore, but we do know this: The Truth is closing in on us. It won't be long until we have no choice but to put up our defenses. So we're choosing to get ahead of it. We're choosing to act now — before it gets to us."

Adrenaline surges through my body. This is it. This is the moment we've all been preparing for. The moment that gives purpose to the draft. The moment we thought would never come. The moment we have to fight back.

A crude chuckle rises in my throat. Now that the moment has arrived, it's almost laughable. It won't be the general's war I'll be fighting. All along, I've been training for the wrong fight. There's something much greater at stake now. General Conrad's words may be a battle cry for everyone else. But to Drew, Carson, and me, they're something else entirely. They're a signal. A call to action — not for his war, but for what we know is right. For what we know will ultimately set this city, and everyone in it, free.

"Tonight is the night all your training comes to a head," the general declares. "Tonight, we'll march into the city and defend its borders dutifully. Tonight will go down in history as the moment we took a stand against The Truth. The moment we proved that nothing can overtake our city. We are our nation's only hope, and it's up to us to protect and preserve what's left of it."

His voice rises and fills the room. Soldiers begin to stir in their seats, but I remain completely still. *There's another way*, I think. Fighting back against The Truth is certain suicide. It's taken over our entire nation before, and it won't be long before it takes the city too. The cure is our only hope. My father knew it, and I know it now. Without it, we have no way forward. We have no chance.

"The Truth has sent us into exile once before," General Conrad shouts. "It has burned our nation's pride to the ground. But now, it's time for us to rise from the ashes and prove that The Truth no longer has any hold on us! It has no power here!"

The more he riles up the crowd, the more it feeds his ego. He has the power to sway an entire army, and to him, it's intoxicating. If it were true that The Truth didn't have a hold on us, there'd be no need for the Barrier. As long as it stands, we're trapped. Hunkered down in fear. Naive to any imminent threat because of the false sense of security we've built around ourselves.

"Arise, soldiers!" he commands. Everyone in the room stands to their feet, but I remain seated. Drew and Carson succumb to peer pressure and stand with the rest of the draftees. They nervously glance down at me, expecting me to stand with them. But I don't. I stay glued to my seat, my eyes pointed straight ahead at the general, seeing through every lie he feeds the crowd.

"This city will not be handed over to The Truth," he continues, amping up his audience more with each word. "This is what we were made for. This is what *you* — each of you — were made for. Let us defend our nation with honor and integrity! Obey, Preserve, Protect!"

"Obey, Preserve, Protect!" everyone chants in response.

I refuse to fan the general's flame. I refuse to settle for anything less than a cure for The Truth. This city may be my home, but beyond its borders, there's a world crying out for salvation — for someone to willingly take a stand for something bigger. Something more. That person could've been my father. But if not him, it has to be me. Choosing to answer that call takes more courage than any charge the general could lead. And I won't keep fighting his battles while the world suffers for it. I won't fall captive under his rule any longer.

As the crowd erupts in triumphant applause, the general's eyes fall on me. He narrows his gaze, a scowl deepening on his face. But I remain still. I don't stand. I don't recite the pledge. I glare back at him with an unwavering stare of my own, making sure he sees me.

Making sure he knows in the end, I won't stand with him.

Twenty-Eight

That night, we gather in the shooting range. Lieutenant Kelley and Lieutenant Tillman strap us with gear, the same kind we've worn on every supply run before now. Night has fallen outside the facility, and even though we're below ground, the lower level of The Battery feels more grim than ever before.

Soldiers shuffle in and out of the room. They tear weapons from the lockers behind us until every single one is practically emptied. From there, they disappear back into the hall and are dispatched to different parts of the facility. As for the draftees, there's only one place we'll be tonight: on the front lines.

Lieutenant Kelley hands me a gun much larger than any weapon I've ever practiced on. I sling the strap over my shoulder, its weight dragging me down like an anchor. "Use both hands," Lieutenant Kelley orders. Though my hands tremble, I tighten my grip and pull it to my side. He moves to the helmet next, sliding it over my head. The padding devours the noise of the room until all I can hear is my own breathing.

"All clear," Lieutenant Kelley declares once I'm fitted in my gear. He slaps his palm against the top of my helmet and orders me to wait out in the hall.

One by one, we line up with our backs to the wall. Drew and Carson file out after me, taking their place beside me. We stand in silence, letting the reality of what's about to happen sink in. My mind spirals, trying to keep up with it all. There's no telling what we're walking into. By now, The Truth could've already infiltrated the city. It could be crawling with infectious monsters, and we'd never know it until they were staring us in the face. Either way, I have to devise a plan. I have to be ready for the moment we can slip away — and I have to be willing to fight to get there.

"Any ideas, John?" Drew mutters through his helmet.

I shake my head. "I don't know . . ." But I have to think of something. Before more draftees can join us in the hall, I turn to Drew and Carson. Without thinking it through, I rattle off what comes to my mind as soon as it does.

"Here's what we'll do," I start. "When the time's right, we'll break away and head for the barricade. There are only two ways to get to Daphne: the subway, or climbing over the barricade. It's likely we won't be able to get out of the facility that easily, so we'll wait until we're in the city, then we'll go to the barricade." My eyes narrow at them through my visor, and I sharpen my tone. "But we have to be ready. I don't know when we'll be able to break away, but on my command, we go. We get Daphne, and we get out of the city."

"Whatever you say, boss," Carson replies.

Drew's eyes crease with the hint of a smile hidden behind his helmet. "We'll be ready," he assures me. "Whatever it takes."

The rest of the draftees file out of the room. After the last of them, the training officers appear in the doorway. They step in front of us, staring through their visors.

"It's time," Lieutenant Kelley says, causing my stomach to twist. "Follow us."

I half-expect him to lead us to Battery Station. But instead, we head for the elevator. Once it arrives, we gather inside, and the doors quickly close us in. The elevator whirs, carrying us to the main level. When the doors open again, I'm struck by what I see.

The atrium is packed with soldiers standing in organized rows, facing the front doors. The grand emblem of the Freedom Tower is no longer visible, buried beneath a sea of black uniforms. Each of them clutches a weapon similar to my own at their side. They don't move. They stand as firm and rigid as statues. For a moment, it takes my breath away. Nearly the entire military stands before us, a force forged over nearly two decades. Everything we've built here hangs in the balance of this war. We could gain so much, or we could lose it all tonight. And despite Drew, Carson, and I choosing our own path, I can't help but pity the soldiers around us. Some won't live to see the morning. Others may become diseased, with no hope of a cure, helplessly letting the disease drive them insane. And there will be parts of the city that, once The Truth enters, may never recover. No matter what happens tonight, by the time the sun creeps over the Hudson tomorrow morning, the city — as we've known it — won't be the same.

The training officers usher us through rows of soldiers until we're standing at the front. Peering out through the doors, black clouds swirl over the city. The Freedom Tower's antenna is alight with electric-blue energy, fighting to hold the Barrier in place. A hush falls over the room, and we wait for someone to make the first move.

Lieutenant Kelley pushes through the doors. On cue, the rest of the military comes to life. They march forward, and together, we spill out of the facility. There's no going back now. No changing what's already been done. All we can do is move forward, straight into battle.

We pass through the outer wall and emerge into the city. Glancing to the side, I notice there are still two soldiers posted on either side of the wall. While we march on, they stay back, destined to protect the facility. We advance down the familiar path we're used to running every morning. So far, everything seems intact. The fence still borders the path, protecting us from anything lurking on the other side. As we walk, my head is on a swivel.

Every rustle in the wind, every shadow cast from the towering buildings nearby, I mistake for an infected waiting to strike.

A slight mist sprays against my visor. Small droplets of rain fall against my shoulder pads and roll down my arms. The rain continues to squeeze through the Barrier, but it's less intense now — but every bit as exhilarating as it was this morning. The further we go, it dawns on me we're not just marching aimlessly down the path. We're headed toward a specific destination. One destination in particular.

The Holland Tunnel.

Lieutenant Kelley must've listened when I told him about the infected I saw there. I clutch my weapon close to my chest as the gaping mouth of the tunnel comes into view. At the fork in the road, there's a second group of soldiers waiting for us, much smaller than ours. They pull back the fence blocking the tunnel, allowing us to pass through. As soon as we do, they fall into formation at our sides. The ground beneath us tilts into a decline, propelling us toward the tunnel. We're not standing guard — we're going into it.

Soon, the city disappears behind us, and everything fades to black. Our gear blends with the darkness, making us seem invisible. The sound of our boots echoes off the walls of the tunnel. I take slow, deep breaths, trying to maintain my composure. But being able to hear myself breathe only heightens the panic boiling in my chest.

We march deep into the tunnel, then halt. In the silence, the hum of the Barrier fills my ears, piercing through my helmet. It swells with each second that passes until it consumes everything. I notice a few soldiers fidgeting with their helmets, visibly on edge from the sound. At the front of the line, Lieutenant Kelley unclips a flashlight from his belt. He slaps the metal tube against his palm, and with a sharp flicker, a burst of light flares from its tip. The light skims across the tunnel floor. He holds it steady at his feet. It's feeble, but it's enough to reveal a white laminated badge clipped at his hip.

And directly next to it, a small square device that can only be one thing — a pager.

My eyes widen. I'm so close I could reach out and swipe them both before he'd even notice. But before I can, Lieutenant Kelley lifts the light in one slow, heart-stopping motion, until it's pointed directly ahead.

My breath catches. There, bathed in the harsh light behind a rippling wall of energy, are the sickly faces of a dozen infected. They stand pressed against the Barrier wall, no more than a foot from where we stand on the other side. Lieutenant Kelley's hand trembles, trying to keep a steady grip on the flashlight. Every single soldier and draftee alike holds their breath. We know that any sudden movement could give us away. From the depths of the tunnel, more white eyes emerge from the darkness. More infected press in, swarming the tunnel as far as the light reaches. They trudge toward the Barrier in slow, disjointed movements. Their heads twitch, limbs jerking with unnatural tics. Their ears flare, as if drawn in by something. But what?

And then it hits me. The hum. It's loud enough to permeate through all my protective gear. They can hear it too — and it's luring them in.

"The Barrier . . ." I mumble under my breath.

Carefully, I step out of line to get to Lieutenant Kelley. Someone grabs my arm, and I turn to see Apollo's eyes glaring at me through his visor.

"What are you doing, Madoc?" he hisses at me.

"It's the Barrier," I whisper back. "It's drawing them in. Don't you hear it?"

He pauses for a moment to listen. The hum swells again, rattling my bones. As it does, the infected move at a more accelerated rate.

Apollo releases me and motions for me to keep going. I push past another draftee and gently place a hand on Lieutenant Kelley's shoulder, careful not to startle him.

His head jerks around. With the flashlight still held out in front of him, he says, "Madoc! Get back in line!"

"Lieutenant, the sound of the Barrier is drawing them in," I tell him. "If the Barrier is really as weak as it seems, it won't hold them. They'll pass right through."

His face softens, but almost as soon as it does, it scrunches into a scowl. "I said, get back in line," he orders.

"Just listen to me," I plead with him. "We can't be in the tunnel when they break through. We have to move out. Surround the tunnel, wait for them to come out, then strike. We'll have more room if we spread out in the city. Here, we're as good as dead."

With his free hand, Lieutenant Kelley grabs my shoulder pad and pulls me so close that our visors touch. "You don't get to make the demands around here. I don't care what you think or how afraid you might be, this is the plan. Now get back in line!" he growls.

He releases me, and I throw my hands up in surrender. But before I can move, a horrible screech fills the tunnel — and my blood runs cold.

My head snaps around just in time to see the hand of one of the infected reaching through the Barrier wall. The lining of the wall stretches like a transparent film, wrapping around the infected's arm as it forces its way through. It quickly swipes at Lieutenant Kelley's flashlight. It clatters to the ground and rolls deep into the tunnel, its beam spinning wildly, casting dizzying streaks of light along the walls.

Another screech sounds, followed by a dozen more. The infected pushes its face through the Barrier once it's sure it can get through. The force of the wall peels back its skin, revealing bone and muscle underneath. My stomach lurches. In the same moment, it claws at Lieutenant Tillman and slashes his shoulder. He fumbles for his weapon, but the infected is quicker. It lunges, seizing him and driving its nails through the fabric of his uniform.

Lieutenant Tillman lets out a raw scream that cuts through the air like an agonized battle cry.

And that's all it takes before the rest of the infected erupt into a frenzy. My heart races. I don't think. I don't hesitate. Before too many can break through, I swipe the pager from Lieutenant Kelley's belt but miss the badge. I reach back for it, but as I do, an infected leaps onto him. He pulls the trigger on his weapon as he falls. The gun jerks upward, sending an array of bullets into the ceiling of the tunnel. The entire tunnel shudders. My head spins around, and I find Drew and Carson in the line. Perched with their weapons drawn. Ready to fight. I tear the helmet from my head so that my full face is visible.

Locking eyes with them, I mouth the word, "Now."

I shove past Apollo and the other draftees until I reach them, then the three of us retreat toward the mouth of the tunnel. Behind us, I hear Lieutenant Kelley let out a piercing wail as the infected tears into his flesh. More gunshots sound off, shaking the ground beneath us. Looking over my shoulder, I see hundreds of infected piling over one another, barreling through the Barrier wall. The soldiers stand firm, firing back at them, their gunfire lighting up the tunnel with each bullet they send into motion.

"Keep going!" I holler at Drew and Carson. I shove my palms into their backs to propel them forward. Lieutenant Tillman and Lieutenant Kelley are gone. There's no more authority out here. Behind us is a bloodbath. Everyone in the tunnel will be killed or infected within minutes. We can't stay here. We have to keep running.

We have to get out of the city, I think. *We have to get to Daphne.*

Drew, Carson, and I emerge from the tunnel and sprint down the straightaway toward the barricade. We run for half a mile before we pause. I pull them aside, keeping my eye on the mouth of the tunnel in the distance.

Drew and Carson remove their helmets and toss them to the ground. Both of their hands tremble. Tears well up in Carson's eyes. It's clear they're both shaken up.

"It's over," Carson says through staggered breaths. "It's really all over now, isn't it?"

"No," I say definitively. "It's not over. This is only the beginning. It's up to us now to make it out of the city and make everything right."

My words don't seem to land with him. Carson shakes his head in denial, letting his emotions take over. I glance at Drew desperately, hoping to find the same steadiness he had before. He grits his teeth, at odds with his own mind, and takes a deep breath.

"What about a pager?" he asks, switching gears. "Or a badge? Did we happen to get any of that?"

I fumble for the pager in my pocket and pull it out. "I swiped a pager from Lieutenant Kelley's belt. I tried to get the badge but—" I stop, picturing the infected lunging at him. Sinking its teeth into his neck. My whole body shivers.

"We can just stay on the subway then," Drew reasons. "We don't need to go back to the facility, right? If we do, we'd need a badge. But if not, we can just stay on the subway."

"Our weapons might not last us for too long," I say. "But if we can't reload at the facility, then they'll have to do."

Drew forces a smile, but it's clear he's hesitant. Carson paces back and forth, dragging his hands down his face.

I have to think of something. I have to find a way to convince them it'll be alright. I got us into this, and now it's up to me to get us out alive.

"Look," I start, lowering my voice. "I'm sorry I dragged you into this. But remember, you wanted this too. We could've easily been killed back there, but we weren't. We made it out. That has to count for something."

Drew's eyes lift to mine. "Do you really think we can survive this?"

"Of course we can," I say. "Trust me."

I extend my hand out, trying to mimic the gesture Carson made in the barracks just earlier today. Drew places his hand over mine, but Carson hesitates. His eyes flicker nervously between Drew and me. I can tell he's at war with himself. He's unsure if he's strong enough to go on, or if he's brave enough to follow through with this. But I know he is. I believe in him. I need him to believe in himself too.

"Carson, we're not going anywhere without you," I tell him. "I refuse to leave you here. I'm not losing another one. Not after Ethan."

He lets out a sigh. His hand drops on top of Drew's, and we lift our hands in unison. "Alright," he says. "You lead the way."

My lips break into a smile. I sling my arm around his shoulder and give him a firm pat on the chest. Together, the three of us stare back at the tunnel. Light occasionally flickers from within it, followed by the distant, muffled crack of gunfire. Then, the ground trembles beneath us. The mouth of the tunnel explodes in a blinding white light. The concrete slabs that held it in place give way, crumbling into the Hudson, severing it completely from the city. We flinch, staring back in horror as it falls apart.

For a long, breathless moment, nothing moves. No soldiers. No infected. Stillness falls over the city, and it seems like no one made it out. Even with all the draftees and soldiers inside, we might've managed to keep the infected from making it out of the tunnel, drowning them in the Hudson.

But as soon as that hope creeps in, two figures begin to take shape, rising from the wreckage. They ascend the broken slab of asphalt where the tunnel and the city used to connect. As they step into the moonlight, their bodies twist, and they let out a monstrous howl — confirming they aren't survivors. They're infected.

"Okay," I say quickly. "We've run this path many times before. Daphne's apartment is just over the barricade. All we have to do is make it there, climb over the barricade, and get to the other side before the infected get to us. Once we're there, we'll be safe — for now."

Drew and Carson nod. They've already come to terms with the fact we have no other choice. We take off down the path in the opposite direction of the infected. Another distant screech sounds behind us — this time, more powerful. There may be more that escaped, and they're only just now coming to the surface.

Our boots burn against the asphalt as we run. The edge of the barricade starts to come into view, only a few hundred feet ahead of us. *I'm coming, Daphne*, I say in my head. *I'm coming.*

As soon as we reach the barricade, I urge Drew and Carson to climb over the fence. "Go, go, go!" I holler, keeping my eyes turned in the direction of the infected. Once they're on the other side, I grip the chain-link fence and begin to pull myself up. My feet barely lift off the ground when I hear the sound of someone shouting. A *human* shout. I jerk my head around, scanning the city to pinpoint the sound. Breaking over the horizon of the path is a soldier. His gear distinguishes him, but his helmet is still on, masking his face. His arms flail frantically over his head as he runs toward me. I jump down from the fence and draw my weapon. Drew and Carson scream at me to keep climbing, to leave him behind, but I don't.

The soldier stops several feet away and falls to his knees. He removes his helmet, revealing his identity, and my jaw drops. Somehow, Apollo stares back at me helplessly. His whole body quivers, his eyes pleading for mercy. I slowly lower my gun but keep a firm grip on it. There's no telling if he's been scratched or bitten — maybe it just hasn't taken effect yet.

"I'm safe," Apollo gasps. "Madoc, please. Where are you all going?"

"We're getting out of here," I say.

"Let me come with you."

I narrow my eyes, unsure if I should trust him. As long as I've known him, he's held my father's reputation over my head. He's deemed me a threat because of who my father is. If he knew what we're doing — that we're going to find him and finish what he started — what would he think? Would he still want to come with us then?

Apollo's eyes swim back and forth. He notices Drew and Carson on the other side of the fence, clinging to it. Waiting to see what I do.

"Please, just . . ." Apollo's voice drifts off. I can tell he's wracking his brain to come up with a reason I should trust him. He lowers his hand into his pocket. As he does, I lift my weapon, aiming for his skull. Prepared to pull the trigger as soon as he snaps.

But instead, he pulls a badge from his pocket, just like the one Lieutenant Kelley wore. He holds it out in front of him as a peace offering.

"See?" he says. "I overheard you all talking in the barracks. I saw you grab the pager before . . . before everything went down. I just thought that—" he stops again. His voice breaks. He's too stunned to keep going. Too traumatized from what he witnessed in the tunnel.

"Everyone's d-dead," he stutters. "Please. Just let me go with you."

I don't give in that easily. I keep my gun aimed at him. As much as I want the badge, I don't want him to jeopardize the mission. We're so close. One wrong move, and he could ruin it.

"I know we've had our differences," Apollo starts. He rises to his feet and holds his arms up, keeping the badge tucked between his fingers. "But it doesn't matter now. None of it matters anymore. Please, if you have a plan, just let me come with you. Let me make it up to you."

Behind him, several infected begin to take shape. They crawl and writhe their way through the city — and they're gaining on us. There's no time. He either comes with us, or we leave him here to die.

I glance over at Drew and Carson, hoping they'll give me some sort of confirmation. From behind the fence, Carson opens his mouth and repeats the same words I said to him. "We can't lose another one," he whispers.

"Fine," I give in. Turning back to Apollo, I lower my weapon and extend my hand, welcoming him in. "But you need to do exactly as I say. No questions asked."

Apollo nods in understanding. He approaches me and hands me the badge. I slip it into my pocket beside the pager and hoist him onto the fence. He begins to climb, and once he's over, I follow after him.

As soon as my feet touch down on the other side, I lift my gaze to them. And it hits me — we might be all that's left. Beyond the barricade, there's a city full of people sleeping, oblivious to the nightmare unfolding on the other side. People like Daphne. Like Mother and Liam. All our families. The Barrier is defenseless against The Truth. Now it's up to us to stop it. To protect them.

To put an end to this — once and for all.

Twenty-Nine

We scramble over the barricade before the infected notice us. We peer down at them from the top of the heap, watching as they scatter throughout the city. They holler into the night, their grotesque, raspy voices echoing off the skyscrapers. Carefully, we slide down the rubble and land safely on the other side. Here, the city is much quieter. We dust ourselves off, and Drew, Carson, and Apollo wait for me to give them further instructions.

There's so much Apollo doesn't know, but there's hardly time to catch him up to speed. The best I can do is fill him in as we go — beginning with Daphne.

"Where are we going?" he asks.

Drew and Carson throw me a look, eager to hear how I explain this to him.

"There's someone else we need to get," I say without elaborating.

Apollo scrunches his brows. "Everyone else was back in the tunnel," he argues. "There might be a few more back at the facility. But we're going the opposite way. The facility is—"

"There's a girl," I cut him off. Apollo's eyes widen. "Ethan and I found her back in Philadelphia and brought her here. She's in an apartment on this side of the city, where it's safe."

Apollo shakes his head in disbelief. "Didn't realize you were such a lady's man, Madoc."

I roll my eyes. "Yeah, well I'm full of surprises. C'mon, we don't have much time."

We take off in the direction of Daphne's apartment. Every so often, I tuck my hand into my pocket to feel for the pager, just in case it buzzes. Until then, we have to find her and make it to the station, all before it goes off.

The mid-rise apartment building and dilapidated fire escape come into view. We sprint up to the base of it, and when we get there, I coach them through how to get up.

"Just hoist yourself onto the landing," I explain. "Take the fire escape all the way up. She's on the top level."

"Done this before, Madoc?" Apollo questions.

"More than you know," I admit.

I hop onto the landing first, then turn to extend a hand to Drew. He willingly takes it, and I pull him up. Once he's on the landing, I motion for him to continue up the stairs to make room for Carson and Apollo. Carson comes next, followed by Apollo last. I offer my hand to him, but he refuses.

"I can do it myself," he sneers. Leave it to Apollo to cling stubbornly to his ego.

Once we're all up, I squeeze to the front and lead them to the top floor. As soon as we're there, I push through the double doors. The apartment is completely dark. Storm clouds gather outside, only adding to the dimness of the room. So much time has passed since I last stepped foot in here — and that time has taken so much. My heart longs for Daphne to be here. To see her eyes light up. To pull her close and tell her everything that's happened, and that it's time for us to go. To feel her lips on mine again.

But the apartment seems vacant. Nothing stirs. Drew, Carson, and Apollo glance around the room, waiting for something to happen, but nothing does.

"Daphne?" I call out, but I'm met with silence.

"Do you think he made her up?" I hear Apollo mutter behind my back. I throw him a look, and he mouths an apology back at me.

Now I'm frantic. I burst through the bedroom door to find the sheets pulled up, the bed neatly made, seemingly in the same condition as the night I found her on the roof. My last night with her. *The roof.* If she's not here, maybe she's there. Watching down from the edge of the building. From her view, she might've seen the tunnel explode. Does she know I'm coming for her? Would she wait for me? I hold onto the hope that she'll be there and push past Drew, Carson, and Apollo toward the landing.

"Are we leaving?" Drew hollers after me.

"No," I say without turning my head. "Stay here. I'll be right back."

I hurry up the frail ladder bolted to the building. As my hands grip the edge, I expect to see her sitting right where I left her last. Her blonde hair drenched in moonlight. Her eyes scanning the ground below — searching for me.

But as I peer over the other side, the only thing I see is the gravel roof. There's no sign of her. No indication that she's been here. My heart sinks to my stomach. Maybe she's already gone. After all, it's been days. We had one moment — one spectacular moment — and then nothing. For all she knows, something might've happened to me. She could've heard the explosion, seen the infected, and taken the opportunity to get out of the city while she could. And I can't blame her for that. If I were in her position, I would've done the same.

I climb back down the ladder and step into the apartment. I hang my head and pace back and forth, trying to think of what to say to them. Trying to come to terms with it all.

"She's not here?" Drew asks.

I shake my head viciously, sliding my hands over my scalp. "I don't know where she could've gone. I don't know where she is."

"And you're *sure* she's real?" Apollo asks again. This time, he's met with a look from both Drew and me. He lets out a chuckle, but no one finds humor in his words. "Okay," he relents. "So what now? We just sit tight and wait for her to show up?"

I don't know, I think. Part of me wants to say yes. But we can't. Not while the rest of the city is crawling with infected. It won't be long before they reach this part of the city, and by that time, we need to be far from here. We need to be on our way to D.C. so we can bring back the cure.

It takes every ounce of strength to say what needs to be said, but it doesn't stop the words from crushing me as they come out.

"We have to go on without her," I sigh. "We have no choice."

Drew tries to offer sympathy, but I push him away. All three of them stare back at me, trying to understand what they can do. They're relying on me. They need me to be strong. They're too afraid to go back to where we came from but still afraid to go forward. Right now, I'm the only hope they have — even when I feel hopeless myself.

I have to be strong enough to do this without Daphne. Just as I found her before, I'll find her again. No matter what it takes. We're both after the same things: a cure, a safe place to call our own. I have to believe if we keep moving toward that, our paths will cross again.

We file out of the apartment and down the fire escape. As soon as our feet hit the asphalt, Drew, Carson, and Apollo turn to me, waiting for me to reveal the next part of the plan.

"There's a subway station just a few blocks from here," I tell them. "Now that we have the badge, thanks to Apollo," I tip my head at him, "we can reload at the facility and take the subway out of the city."

"And where exactly do we plan on going?" Apollo asks.

"D.C.," I say. "That man in the White House was my father, and I think he found a cure. So that's where we'll start."

To my surprise, Apollo doesn't argue or question my motives. He nods submissively, sticking to what we agreed on — do what I say, no questions asked.

I lead them away from Daphne's apartment and trace the path to the station. Beyond the barricade, the grisly shrieks of the infected pierce through the night. We run in silence, but in that silence, I run through the plan in my mind. The subway will take us first to the facility, then we'll hunker down until it takes us to D.C. We can stock up on ammunition, supplies, anything to sustain us for some time. If there are any soldiers left, we can rally more troops. Maybe others will want to come too.

But no. The general might be there. Even if others have survived, he won't let them leave. And if he sees us, he'll do everything in his power to prevent us from leaving too.

We have to be quick. In and out in five minutes — as long as it takes for the pager to buzz and the subway to depart again. We can't stay at the facility. We won't be safe there. The Battery is General Conrad's domain, and as long as we're there, he's still in control.

As we round the last corner, the ramp leading down into the station comes into view. I point at it to alert Drew, Carson, and Apollo, ushering them toward it. We quicken our pace and sprint as fast as we can until we reach it.

"John!" I hear my name from somewhere behind me — soft, almost like a whisper in the back of my mind. But sure enough to make me stop in my tracks.

I start to turn around, but Apollo grabs my arm to pull me forward.

"C'mon, man!" he shouts. But I shake him off.

"John!" I hear it again. This time, it's louder. I spin in circles, trying to pinpoint where it's coming from. I don't see anything. But I *hear* it.

Drew and Carson stop running too. Apollo stands at the edge of the station, holding his arms out at his sides.

"What's the hold up?" he hollers.

Drew steps forward. "John, what is it?" he asks. But I can't give him an answer.

"You guys go," I say to them. "I'll meet you down there. The pager hasn't gone off yet, so we still have some time." Turning to Drew, I finish with, "Keep an eye out. And if anything happens, go on without me."

But Drew doesn't budge that easily.

"Now you're talking nonsense," he laughs. "There's no way we're going without you. This is *your* father we're talking about, dude. You're the glue that holds this whole operation together."

I shake my head. "This is bigger than just me. If anything happens, find the cure. Bring it back to the city. And if nothing happens, then I'll be down there with you in a minute. You'll have nothing to worry about then."

He resists, but I place both hands on his shoulders. "Drew," I say. "Trust me. I won't be long."

"John!" There it is again. Drew's ears twitch, and for a moment, I think he's heard it too. But he doesn't stick around to investigate. He throws one last nervous glance in my direction, then ushers Carson and Apollo down the ramp into the station.

I spin around, listening intently for my name again. "John!" Instantly, my eyes turn right to where it's coming from. Nearly two blocks ahead, standing at the edge of an alleyway between two buildings, is Daphne. She waves her arms to get my attention. As soon as I notice her, a smile breaks across her face.

I don't hesitate. I take off in a sprint toward her, desperate to get to her.

I'm nearly ten feet from her, then five, then I'm closing the gap. But before I can reach her, my body crashes into something unseen. I'm thrown off my feet. My body flies backward, crashing against the asphalt. Daphne lets out a sharp gasp. I choke up air and dust, the force knocking the wind out of me. I shake my head to steady my vision until Daphne comes into view again.

She hasn't moved. She stays locked on the edge of the alley, her eyes filled with concern. But she doesn't move any closer toward me.

I stare back in a daze, trying to understand what just happened. I press my palms against the asphalt and push myself upright. Brushing off my hands, I jog toward her — this time, at a slower pace. Once I'm close enough, the same thing happens. My body collides against a wall. I fall backward, slamming into the ground again. Daphne holds her palms up parallel to her face. But something about her stance is wrong. Her arms hover stiffly beside her face, and she leans forward — so far, I think she might teeter off balance. But she doesn't. She holds steady, almost as if she's resting against something. Something invisible.

And that's when it hits me.

I spring to my feet and creep up to where she stands. Her eyes swim across my face, watching me put the pieces together. I hold out my palm and wait to make contact with it. My fingers graze along a surface as solid as brick, but as transparent as glass. I ball my hand into a fist and slam it into the wall, and just as I expect, a streak of blue electricity materializes in front of my eyes. It slithers above us, curving upward in the shape of a dome. In the shape of the Barrier.

But how? Somehow, it's there, and she's on the other side of it. It shouldn't be here. The Barrier extends nearly a mile north of here, all the way to my community. To the home I grew up in. It's impossible that it'd touch down here, unless — unless the Barrier is shrinking.

"Daphne!" I call out to her. I curl my fingers into a fist again and beat against the Barrier wall. Electric currents ripple across its surface, blurring her image on the other side. I can see her so clearly. It's as if I'm staring through a window, nothing more than a millimeter of glass between us. So close I should be able to touch her. So close that, by now, she should be wrapped in my arms. And yet, I can't get to her — and that makes me feel so far from her.

"John, listen to me," she says calmly.

I bang my fist into the wall again. "How is this even possible?" I shout.

"John, please, if you can just—"

"I'll find a way to break through it," I interrupt her. I can't focus on a word she says, not until she's here with me, on the other side. My hands tear and claw at it, trying to rip through a weak spot. Why isn't it weak anymore? Why would it be sturdy now? She should be able to pass right through it, just like the infected did.

"You can't," I hear her say. But I've *seen* it with my own eyes. Dozens of infected forced their way through tonight, right in front of my eyes.

"No," I snap back. "There has to be a way. If I could only—"

"There's no way, John. I need you to listen to me."

"C'mon!" I slam my palms flat against the wall. Tears burst from my eyes. My heart rattles inside my chest with each spark of electricity. I refuse to give up. I need to get to her like I need air to breathe, and I'll stop at nothing until I do.

"You can't get through to me," Daphne says, her voice breaking. "I don't know how, but you can't. And you have to stop trying."

"I won't," I stand my ground. "I'm not leaving you." My lips quiver, and my own voice starts to tremble.

"John, please—"

"This isn't fair!" I scream. "I'm not leaving you!"

"You have to," she shouts back. "You don't have a choice!"

"Why can't I get to you? Why can't I just—"

"Because none of this is real, John!" she yells over my voice.

Her words stop me before I can send another blow into the Barrier. I furrow my brows, unsure if I heard her correctly. "What did you just say?"

She lowers her hands and starts to sob. I press mine firm against the wall, trying to get as close to her as I can. No matter how hard I try, it's no use. I can't get to her. I can't console her. All I can do is stand helplessly on the other side, watching her fall apart.

"None of this is real," she weeps. "This is all in your head."

"What are you talking about?" my tone sharpens, starting to get defensive now. "If this is some sort of coping mechanism, Daphne, for not being able to break through the Barrier, it's not making any sense."

"*This* is all your coping mechanism, John," she says. She flails her arms, signaling to the city around us. "All of this. It's all in your mind. You're not actually here right now. You're out there, in real life, fighting for a chance to live. Fighting for your life back. And that's why I need you to listen to me."

I step back from the wall. I don't understand what she means. None of it makes sense. I feel her starting to give up, coming to terms with the fact that we're separated. And that kills me. Whatever she's talking about, I need her to let it go. I need her to try harder. I need her to need me like I need her.

"I'm right here," I plead with her. "Daphne, I'm right in front of you. *I'm* real. You and me? *That's* real. The Barrier? *That's* real." I beat my fist into the wall, and it ripples, proving its existence. But Daphne doesn't budge.

"But it's not," she pushes back. "You might not realize it. In fact, there's a part of your subconscious that's been manipulated to block out the truth. But this, John, it's all in your head. It's a simulation. You were put here as a test, but all along, there's only ever been one outcome. And that outcome is you dying here. Dying to your own mental illness and inability to cope with loss. To cope with what *really* happened, out there, in your real life."

Anger surges through my body. I grit my teeth, trying not to lash out at her. Why is she making this up? And why now? Is she trying to keep me from getting to her? But just as it all boils over, a sense of awareness washes over me, simmering my rage.

Something shifts. Visions flood my mind — memories I never knew I had, or that I'd forgotten. Memories of sitting in a sterile lab. Harsh overhead lights beating down on me. A woman's voice I don't recognize, somewhat sweet at first but turned sour. Lying against a metal table. Being pulled back into a dark machine. Feeling the fabric of my own being slip away, dissolving me from consciousness, only to wake up to the iridescent glow of the Barrier shimmering across my bedroom wall. In the room I thought was mine. In the house I thought was mine.

It all felt so familiar. So *real*. Now, I realize it was all fabricated.

I feel my legs buckle, and I drop to my knees. My heart threatens to tear itself from my chest. The panic I've grown familiar with sets in. I'm trapped here. This whole time, I've been trapped inside my own mind. Living out a life I believed to be my own. So distant from reality, yet so tethered to this one at the same time. My fingers claw at my cheeks, trying to pull the very skin from my bones. I want out. I feel my own consciousness trying to separate from my body, but like a magnet, I'm pulled back in. Something stronger is holding me here, like a cosmic hand wrapped around my throat, keeping me from breaking free.

"How . . ." is all I manage to croak out. Daphne lowers herself to my level and presses her face against the Barrier wall.

"There's no way you could've known," she says delicately. "Your memories were wiped before you entered the simulation — except for people you knew and the place you grew up in. Your consciousness then created illusions of those people. People like your mother, your brother, even your friends—"

"Ethan," I exhale.

"Yes, Ethan," Daphne confirms. "Like in a dream, they *feel* real. They're nearly exact replicas of the real thing. But they're not quite who they are in your reality."

Some part of me longs to think that if what Daphne's saying is true, Ethan could still be out there. In my reality, he could still be alive. But it all felt so real — the crushing weight of losing him, the bullet tearing through his skull. It was all right there in front of me, and I felt every bit of it. I *lived* it. Yet it was all an illusion.

"How do you know all of this?" I manage. My chest tightens. I try hard to steady my breath, but there's no use in fighting it.

"Because . . ." her voice trails off. She hangs her head, and when she lifts it again, tears gush from her eyes. "Because I'm a part of it too, John."

This will only sting for a moment, then you won't feel any pain. My mind spirals back to that day in the ring with Apollo. Only this time, the vision isn't hazy. It's crystal clear.

Daphne rushes toward me, her blonde hair slipping out of a ponytail, curling against her chin. A white lab coat is draped over her shoulders. She forces a needle into the crease of my elbow, her blue eyes blurring as the simulation takes over. It was *her* voice — her voice saying those words to me. Telling me not to worry. Telling me I'd be okay.

All my grief fades away for a moment. I lean back from the Barrier and stare at her, stunned. This whole time, she's been in on it. She put me here. What I felt for her could've been a ploy to weaken me. How is she here? How can I trust what's real and what's not anymore? How can I trust her?

"You?" I hiss at her. "You did this?"

"No, no," she stammers. "I mean, not exactly." She puts her face in her hands and lets out a disheartened huff. "At first, I was brought into this to be a distraction. You were excelling in training. You were getting stronger, and therefore strengthening your mind in the process. The system wasn't designed for you to succeed. It was designed to weaken you, isolate you, and tear down your mind. I was meant to pull you off course, to distract you from your training, and set you back on the path they intended for you to go down all along."

"I can't believe this," I scoff. I lift myself off the ground and turn my back to her. Everything feels like it's caving in on me. Everything I've held onto this whole time has been a lie. Daphne was the one thing keeping me sane. I felt like I could trust her. In a world that was built against me, she was my refuge. I loved her. I can't believe I *let* myself love her, or some version of her. A version that only exists here. Am I supposed to believe it was all just for a distraction?

"John, please," she begs. "You have to understand. Everything has changed."

I turn toward her and hold out an accusatory finger. "How can I trust anything you say anymore?"

"Because I wasn't put here to fall in love with you," she whimpers. "That wasn't part of the plan."

My face softens. I lower my finger and stare back at her. Her composure breaks, and she sobs again.

"That was real?"

She nods. "Somehow, I fell in love with you, John. I don't even know how it happened. You just—" she stops, choking back tears. "You captivated me. The system is designed for people who are too far gone. Whose grief has gotten the best of them, and who have no fight left in them. But you, John, you were willing to fight. And you were kind. Compassionate. Selfless. Deep down, I knew there was still hope left in you. I knew it the first night I saw you, after you chose to save me. Then again when you said you wanted your life to mean more than just the draft. Then again on the roof, the night we kissed. There's more fight left in you, John. And that's a *good* thing."

I drop my head against the wall. Tears stream down my face. I want to be near her now more than ever. If the way I feel for her is strong enough to throw off the system, why isn't it strong enough to tear down the Barrier between us?

"Your love," she continues, "*our* love. It's changed everything. It weakened the Barrier. It set everything that's transpired since the night we kissed into motion. And now, it's given you a shot at getting out of here. And that's why I need you to listen to me."

I lift my eyes to hers, clinging to every word she says.

"You can't go to D.C.," she states firmly. "That's what they want you to do. By continuing to chase after your father, you're weakening your mind. Out there, you lost your father. In real life. You never got over his death. It ruined you, so much so that you ended up here. And continuing to chase any possibility of him still being alive means you can't let him go. Because the truth is, he's not in D.C. He's not waiting for you anywhere in this simulation. You've seen illusions of him, but he's gone — in here *and* out there."

My heart surges, but not because it's not what I want to hear. Because I know she's right. I can feel the years of denial weighing on my chest. That much carried through to the simulation, incapable of being erased. All the time spent holding onto the hope that he'd still be out there. Even now, with Drew, Carson, and Apollo waiting for me at the station, I'm choosing to believe there's still a way to get to him. Daphne's right — I have to let him go. But once I do, what happens then? Where do I go from here?

"I'm so sorry, John," Daphne consoles me. "It's a horrible grief that you never should've had to carry on your own. But you're stronger than it. You're strong enough to get yourself out of this. And that's why you can't go to D.C. You have to go to the tower instead."

"What?" I blurt out. The city is failing all around us. The Barrier is closing in, the infected are swarming the streets. How could the tower change any of that?

"The tower is the veil between your consciousness and reality," Daphne explains. "It's the one thing that connects the two worlds. That's why the Barrier stems from it, and why it's in perfect condition compared to everything else. You have to go to the tower and break the force field. You have to shut it down."

A laugh bubbles up in my throat. What she's asking me to do is impossible. There's no way I could make it to the tower, not with the city crawling with dozens of infected. What would I say to Drew, Carson, and Apollo? Would I just abandon them? But they quickly fall from my mind. I have to remember they're merely an illusion. What happens here and what happens to them doesn't have any real effect on them in reality.

But what about the people controlling the simulation from the outside? Anything I say or do could tip them off. I can't reveal my plan. I can't trust that Drew, Carson, and Apollo aren't being controlled by them too. Maybe that's why they went along with my plan so easily. It was never about the cure or finding my father — it was about making sure I stayed on the path to my own demise.

I'm the only one who can do this. And I have to do it alone.

"But what about you?" I ask. "If I manage to break the Barrier and make it out of this, what happens to you? Where does that leave us?"

Tears trickle down her face. I know what she's going to say before the words form on her lips, and it breaks me. It can't be true. I can't accept it.

"I don't know," she sobs. "What we had in here, John, it was *real*. But you were the one who allowed me to feel it. You have the power now. You've had it all along, you just didn't know it. You have to do this on your own. You have to get yourself out. You're the only one who can set yourself free from your own mind."

I bang my fist against the Barrier in defeat. My body collapses forward, sliding against it. If only I could hold her one more time. Just to feel her touch, now that I might never feel it again. As painful as it is, I know she's right. She can't go where I'm going. It terrifies me to go alone, but I have to believe I have the power to do this. To change this for myself.

I have to want it — even if it means I can't have her.

"John," Daphne whispers sweetly. "I love you."

I crumble against the Barrier wall. Our foreheads meet from opposite sides, but they never touch. "I love you too," I say back to her. "I don't know how to go on without you."

"You'll find a way," she assures me. "Now go. You don't have much time."

My palms press into the wall, and she places hers in the same spot. For a moment, I think I can feel her warmth, but it's only the electric current radiating through the Barrier.

"If there's a chance you're out there, and we both make it out of this, I'll find you," I tell her. "If there's a way, I will."

Electricity fizzles between our fingers as her palms squeeze against the wall. "And if you're right, I'll be waiting for you."

I stay with her against the Barrier until our time is up. The pager begins to buzz in my pocket, pulling me away from her for the last time. I stumble backward and watch her as I go, taking in her every detail. Burning her existence into my memory. I turn away for just a moment, just to get my footing, but when I look back, she's gone. All I have to hold onto is the memory of her — but I guess that's all she ever was. Just a product of the simulation. Something that felt real but was never actually mine.

Through all my sorrow, a vengeance stirs within me. A vengeance to fight back against the people who put me here. Who stripped away my humanity and took Daphne away from me. As my feet teeter on the edge of the station, I gaze up at the Freedom Tower burning against the black sky in the distance. Bolts of blue electricity swirl among the clouds and travel down the curve of the dome. My eyes lock in on the point where the tip of the antenna and the Barrier meet. As impossible as it seems, I know what I have to do. They've taken everything from me, and I'll use all I have left to make sure they never take from anyone ever again.

I will get to the tower, and I will shut down the simulation. They may want me dead, but Daphne was right — there's more fight left in me. And I won't go down without a fight.

Thirty

I RUSH DOWN THE ramp into the station as the subway screeches to a stop. Drew's eyes widen the moment he sees me. He rises to his feet and approaches me. Next to the rails, Apollo sits with his knees pulled close to his chest. As soon as the doors open, he stands without a word and boards the train. Carson hesitates with one foot in, the other still on the station, waiting to make sure Drew and I make it on board.

"What was that all about?" Drew asks. He grabs my arm and ushers me toward the subway in a gesture that's meant to feel friendly. But I can't help feeling like it's manufactured, now that I know the truth. As if now that I'm here, he's seeing to it that I get on the subway and don't try to stray off course.

"I thought I saw someone," I say candidly. "I thought it could be Daphne, or maybe another survivor."

He raises his brow. "Well, did you? Was anyone there?"

"No," I lie. Pain sears across my chest. I replay my last moments with Daphne, then envision the moment I turned to find her gone. "No one was there."

Drew gives me a firm pat on the back. Once I'm within a few feet of the subway, Carson extends his hand, motioning for me to hop on board.

"Let's get going then," he urges.

We step onto the train and take our seats next to Apollo, who's already made himself comfortable. One quick glance up at the screen confirms we're headed for Battery Station. As it zooms out, I notice a faded orange line connecting Battery Station to a distant location. I remember back to our supply run and recognize it as the line to D.C. The plan is seamless — and if it were still my plan, we'd be right on track. But it's not anymore. Not for me, at least.

The subway doors slide shut, and we launch forward into the tunnel. It'll only be a matter of minutes before we're back at the facility. As we glide along the rails, I can't shake the image of the infected swarming the streets above us. Down here, it's quiet. Almost peaceful. But up above, the city is unraveling.

I lean against the window and close my eyes, wracking my brain for how I'm going to get to the tower. I'll need some sort of excuse to break away again, but Drew won't let me go that easily. Not this time. However I do it, it needs to be quick. Impulsive. Something so sudden, it doesn't give them the chance to follow after me.

Without coming to any conclusion, the pager begins to buzz again in my palm, signaling our arrival. I peer out the window and see Battery Station come into view. In the corner of the room, the vault door leading into the facility is wide open. An eerie red glow spills out of the chamber, indicating something sick has passed through. *They're here*, I think. *They've infiltrated the facility.*

Drew, Carson, and Apollo know it too. As soon as the doors open, we all hesitate to step off the train. We remain in our seats, glancing back at each other, no one brave enough to make the first move.

"Okay," I exhale. "We have five minutes. There's no telling how many are inside. There could be one, or there could be dozens. Either way, when the pager buzzes, we need to make our way back to the station immediately. The subway *cannot* leave without us." I pause, glancing over my shoulder at the red glow emanating from the doorway, and a chill runs down my spine. "We don't want to get stuck here."

I stow the pager in my pocket and take the lead. With our weapons drawn, we step off the subway and move toward the door. Drew watches to our right, Carson to our left, and Apollo faces backward, in case any infected are lurking in the tunnels behind us.

I step through the vault door and squint against the harshness of the light. From where I stand, I can see straight through to the lower level. The entire hallway is flooded with red light. Though it's hard to tell, I can make out streaks of a deeper shade of red splattered across the walls. Halfway down the hall, where one of the doors to the Assembly Hall should be, a pair of black boots jut out from the wall. The body they're connected to is hidden from view. Every so often, the boots twitch involuntarily, as if something on the other side is toying with them.

Pressing a firm finger to my lips, I signal for Drew, Carson, and Apollo to move forward in silence. We step into the crimson hallway, our silhouettes bleeding red from the light. Curiosity kicks in, pulling me toward the corpse. Blood pools around its ankles — and it looks fresh. As we draw closer, unease sets over me. Instinct takes over. I throw out an arm, stopping the others from going any further.

I crane my neck forward just enough to peer through the doorway. But before I see it, the sound fills my ears — a horrible squelching of teeth gnawing at wet flesh. On the other side, an infected is crouched in one of the aisles of the Assembly Hall, digging through a raw cavity in a soldier's throat. My stomach turns over. I pull back from the opening and turn toward the others. My eyes widen, and I shake my head.

"Don't move," I mouth at them. All three of them nod, their weapons still clutched tightly in hand.

I lean into the doorway again, making sure the infected is distracted. Once I'm sure, I motion for Drew, Carson, and Apollo to retreat backward toward the shooting range. There, we can get more ammunition and make a swift escape back to the station. As soon as we're in front of the door, I remove Lieutenant Kelley's badge from my pocket. Before I scan it, I pause, lifting my gaze to them.

"As soon as I do this, the infected will hear it," I whisper. "We need to be ready. We need to move *fast* as soon as that door unlocks."

"Roger that," Drew says. The three of them gather around me, ready to press into the door.

I slide the badge along the smooth face of the scanner. A small green light flickers three times, each pulse accompanied by a beeping tone. The lock clicks out of place — a sound that, in the silent tension, echoes throughout the entire hall. The sounds of flesh being torn apart suddenly stop, followed by a low canine growl.

"Move!" I shout.

We push through the door right as the infected lunges into the hallway. As we heave it shut, I catch a glimpse of the infected hurtling toward us, its limbs clawing at the walls, blood drooling in thick strands from its lips. We barely miss it as the door clicks into place, sealing us safely inside the shooting range. A sickening thud reverberates through the door as the infected's body slams against the other side. It quickly turns into a persistent dull knocking, reminiscent of the infected that stalked me in Philadelphia.

We all take a moment to catch our breath. My shoulders sag in relief, and Drew lets out a nervous laugh. I don't even flinch as the infected continues pounding against the door.

"That was a close one," Apollo exhales.

"No kidding," I reply.

Scanning the room, my eyes fall on the weapons lockers lining the wall. I rush over and use the badge to unlock a few. The doors pop open, and their ammunition cubbies slide out from below.

Drew, Carson, and Apollo gather around. "Make sure you have enough ammo to last for a while," I instruct them.

They don't waste any time. The three of them begin digging through stashes of ammunition, heaving handfuls of copper bullets into their pockets. As they do, I direct my attention to a locker in the far-right corner. I swipe the badge again, and it clicks open. In the dim lighting, steel hooks gleam on the other side, clutching a set of hand grenades. With a sideways glance to make sure they don't notice me, I reach for one. My heart races. It feels risky, but it might be my only shot at destroying the Barrier. No bullet is capable of doing what I need it to do. The tip of the antenna links to the dome, and one explosion detonated from within the antenna should be enough to sever the tie.

My fingers coil around the rugged shell of the grenade as I pull it from the rack. Quickly, I deposit it into my pocket and set the locker back in place.

"What's that for?" Drew says from behind me.

My stomach flips. I turn slightly, but I don't meet his eyes.

"Just in case," I say grimly. "You never know when it might come in handy."

I can feel his eyes burning into my profile. He may be suspicious of my need for the grenade, but surely he's not onto my plan. I've given him no reason to question my loyalty to the mission. But with every word he says, I can't help but think it's not coming from him. It's coming from *them*, the ones outside the simulation, controlling him to keep a close eye on me. To make sure I stick to the plan.

The pager's vibration cuts through the tension. I spin around just as Apollo and Carson finish gathering the ammunition they need. The infected continues to beat against the door outside, its hoarse voice groaning through the metal.

"Alright," I say. "This is it. As far as we know, there's only one infected outside." Another thud sounds right on cue, as if the infected can comprehend my words. "*Right* outside. Once we get past it, we'll head straight for the station. We don't have long, but we should have all the time we need."

Apollo and Carson nod dutifully. Drew's eyes narrow at me. My pulse hammers, and my palms start to sweat. I become increasingly worried that he's onto me. But I set that aside and straighten my shoulders, standing with authority to show unwavering dedication to the mission.

"As soon as we open this door, we need to be ready," I continue. "Apollo, will you—"

"Already one step ahead of you," he interrupts me. A click of his gun indicates he has a bullet locked in place, ready for the kill shot.

"Perfect," I give him a thumbs-up. "Carson and Drew, we'll stay back. Wait until it's clear."

The three of us huddle behind Apollo while he steps forward. I toss him the badge, and he takes it. As soon as he swipes it along the scanner, the door clicks out of place. The infected topples inside onto the stone floor. We all jump back, and the sound of our shuffling is enough to send it into a frenzy. It leaps to its feet and lets out an ear-splitting shriek that chills my blood. Just as it springs into action, Apollo lifts his weapon, aims, and sends a bullet straight through its skull.

The impact sends the infected flying backward. It lands on its back, its body sprawled in the threshold between the hall and the shooting range. Blood pools around its head and mixes with the other carnage outside. Apollo turns toward us with a devilish grin, the mouth of his gun still smoking.

"Nailed it," he brags.

The pager continues to vibrate insistently against my hip. "Let's move," I order them, not sparing any time to sing Apollo's praises. "We're running out of time."

We file out of the shooting range and jog toward the station. The vault door is still wide open. As we're about to pass through, a soft melodic ding resonates from somewhere behind us. I slow my pace and cock my head. The sound is familiar, like I've heard it countless times before.

And then, I realize. The elevator.

All at once, the elevator doors slide open, and dozens of infected spill out. They tumble over each other in a tangled knot of rotted flesh and bone. One by one, they drag themselves free from the heap, clawing over one another, their limbs intertwined and twitching. Once they get to their feet, they lurch forward — headed toward us. *Fast.*

"Run!" Drew shrieks.

I spin around on my heels and bolt after Drew, Carson, and Apollo. We sprint through the chamber and burst onto the platform, where the subway waits for us. The doors are open, yearning for us to make it on board. Behind us, the infected continue to pursue us in a writhing, relentless flood, like a herd of rabid animals. They erupt into a nightmarish symphony of agonized moans and dry, guttural screams, filling the lower level with the worst noise I've ever heard.

Drew and Carson leap onto the train, followed by Apollo. The moment they're safely inside, Drew turns back toward me. He extends a hand out of the car, ready to grab mine and pull me on board. All the while the pager vibrates wildly in my pocket, warning me that any second now, the doors could slam shut, and the subway will leave — with or without me.

This is it, I tell myself. *This is my chance.*

I dig my heels into the platform and come to a screeching halt. As soon as I do, the subway doors disengage and begin to close.

"John!" Drew screams. "What are you doing? Run!"

But I don't move. I stand firm on the platform until the doors meet. Drew pulls his hand back inside to keep from getting trapped in the doors. Carson and Apollo press their faces against the windows on the other side, their eyes wide with horror.

With a shudder, I swallow my fear and turn to face the infected. They barrel toward me with their teeth bared, their hollow eyes blazing with bloodlust. It'll be seconds before they're upon me. The subway releases a hiss, followed by a rush of hot air whipping at my back. The train shoots forward into the tunnel, carrying Drew, Carson, and Apollo away from here — and leaving me to face the infected alone.

I can do this, I think.

If I'm going to get to the tower, this is the way forward. Through the infected. Directly into the fight.

I close my eyes. In my mind, I transport myself back to the shooting range, gearing up for a training session. I imagine I'm perched at the end of the lane, staring at the distant, lifeless dummy dangling at the opposite end. That's all this is. It's the same concept — regardless of what's on the other end of the gun. Simulated or not, every hour spent training, preparing for a moment like this, *that* was real. And it's that confidence that will get me to the tower alive.

I suck in a deep breath, and as I exhale, a scream tears through my mouth. I slam my finger into the trigger and step forward, moving toward the infected as bullets fire out of my weapon. The bullets rain down on them, each one finding its mark in an infected's skull. Slowly chipping away at the horrific mass. One by one, they drop like flies. Blood spews in all directions, spraying against my face, tainting my flesh. They howl with rage, their bodies convulsing as bullets rip through them, preventing them from getting to me.

I keep advancing forward until I'm down to just one. With my finger still pressed against the trigger, the gun stalls, and the trigger stiffens. My scream falters into a whimper. Quickly, I slide the clip out of place and stare down into the empty shaft. *No*, I panic. *Not now*. I fumble for more bullets in my pocket, but there's not enough time.

The last infected is on me before I can reload.

I fall backward against the floor. My gun spins out of my hand and down the hall, just out of reach. The infected's sickly hands press into my shoulders, pinning me down. Its contagious saliva drips onto my uniform. I stare into its gaping mouth — gray teeth chattering, pores oozing from its gums, blood-red tongue wetting dry lips, hungry for a bite.

It shrieks in my face, the sound splintering my ears. A scream escapes me out of pure fear. I can't let it get to me. I don't want to die — but it's closing in. Before it can strike, I kick my foot against its chest, sending it flying backward. It yelps, the sound ripping through the air as it soars. I flip onto my stomach and crawl down the hall, reaching for my gun. As soon as my fingers find the cool metal, the infected is on me again. But in the same instant, I roll on top of it, clutching my weapon in hand. I force its spine into the floor, hearing a crack that makes my skin tingle. It unleashes a vile roar, its limbs clawing at its sides, desperate to sink into flesh.

I drive the butt of the gun into its skull. The skin cracks, and its white eyes appear temporarily dazed. But it quickly shakes it off, returning to the same crazed state as before.

I do it again. And again. And again. A primal yell slips out, and as I scream, I beat the infected's head to a pulp until it's nothing more than blood and brain matter smeared against the floor. Its white eyes slant, its limbs fall limp at its sides, and the hallway grows silent again.

My scream morphs into a maniacal laugh. Slowly, I lower the weapon with trembling hands. Glancing around the hall, the lifeless bodies of dozens of infected clog the doorway to the station ahead of me. Beneath me, the infected is flattened into the floor. And behind me, the path is clear. I almost can't believe it. I'm *alive*.

I lift myself off the ground and make a run for the elevator. With my gun slung over my shoulder, I retrieve the badge from my pocket and scan it. As soon as the doors open, I hurl myself inside.

The elevator doors slide shut, and the pod lifts, carrying me to the main level of the facility. I dig my hand into my pocket and pull out a handful of copper bullets. With the elevator still in motion, I reload my clip to make sure I'm prepared. There's no telling what waits for me in the atrium, or in the city. But I've already come this far. I have to keep going.

As the doors part to reveal the atrium, I brace myself for the worst. Expecting another flurry of infected to be waiting to devour me on the other side. But to my surprise, the atrium is deserted. The gold emblem etched into the stone glistens in the pale moonlight streaming in from outside. My footsteps echo throughout the vacant foyer. Am I the only one here? The only one who's left?

Timidly, I push through the doors and out into the bitter night. A sharp wind gushes past me, sending a shiver down my spine. My eyes lift to the Freedom Tower, fixating on the antenna. Envisioning the moment the grenade falls through it and the Barrier erupts in a burst of light. The thought lures me in, carrying me down the familiar path that spans between the facility and the city. As I pass through the outer wall, I notice the soldiers who once stood watch are gone. There's no one here — no one left to defend the facility, leaving it susceptible to The Truth.

I quicken my pace and jog toward the tower. The grenade rattles against my hip, clipped at my belt. I keep a firm grip on my gun, in case any infected dart out in my path.

Once I'm close enough, I scale the fence bordering the path and hop onto the other side. The tower is no more than a few blocks from where I am, but it's a maze of decrepit buildings and infectious monsters between here and there. When I'm ready, I take a deep breath and let the city swallow me whole.

I make it through the first block before the path veers. I jump into a nearby alleyway, forging a shortcut to a path that's a straight shot to the tower. As I hunker in the shadows, a figure jumps in front of me at the end of the alley. Both of us pause — the figure facing forward, not noticing me at first — then it turns. Its fingers curl at its side, and its spine bends backward. With a gut-wrenching screech, it takes off down the alley in a mad dash.

Bad idea, I think, kicking myself for trying to take an easier path. I pick up my feet and sprint in the opposite direction. I can follow the fence to the tower, then weave between a few buildings, and I'll be there. Either way, it'll get me there. It's just more technical.

But before I reach the other end of the alley, a group of infected intercept my path. My feet slide against the rubble, and my breath catches. The infected behind me continues to howl into the night, closing in on me. But several more stand in front of me. They sense me. Their ears twitch, and their heads snap to the side.

I'm outnumbered. I'm trapped.

What now?

I spin around and lift my weapon, making the split-second decision that it'll be easier to strike down the one than multiple. My finger slams into the trigger, and a bullet rips through the infected's forehead, stopping it in its tracks.

This excites the others. Their bodies contort, and they break into a sprint, chasing the sound of my gunshot. I don't fight back. The more I shoot, the more infected will be drawn in. It's a never-ending cycle. Instead, I make a run for it, charging forward with my arms slicing at my sides, desperate to break out of the alley.

The moment I do, I round the corner. I keep running. The tower looms right before my eyes, rising against the night sky like an insurmountable steel giant. It takes my breath away — but I keep going. I can't afford to stop. The infected gain on me. Their claws scrape at my heels, their vicious jaws snapping at the nape of my neck. *One more block*. The street widens into a vast concrete arboretum, with the tower poised at its center. I zigzag my way through, trying to throw the infected off my path. But with every move I make, they move in sync.

My feet hit the path leading to the Freedom Tower. Multiple glass doors frame the front entrance, with a sleek glass overhang shading the entryway. Faint white letters line the edge and read: ONE WORLD TRADE CENTER. I pound my hand against the first door I see and, to my relief, it opens. I fly through it and spill into a stunning modern atrium.

Large white beams stretch from floor to ceiling like pipes inside an instrument. They tilt inward to form an A-frame shape and converge at a narrow glass slit in the ceiling. From where I stand, a staircase descends to a lower balcony, which branches into others spiraling down to a foyer several feet below. The marble floors shine under the moonlight spilling in from the skylight above.

But I don't have time to admire it. The infected aren't far behind. More have gathered now, lured by the commotion I've caused. They press against the main doors until the glass shatters. Their flesh tears against the jagged edges, and blood pours out onto the polished floor. They collapse in a heap and pick themselves up, scrambling toward me in a frenzy.

I hurl myself down the first staircase and swing around the balcony. Momentum threatens to pull me off balance, but I grip the railing to steady myself. Behind me, the infected tumble down the stairs like an avalanche. Several of them fling themselves over the railing, crashing onto the foyer below, trying to intercept my path. I scramble down the next staircase and emerge onto a mid-level mezzanine. My eyes dart frantically from side to side, looking for an escape. But there's no time. More infected crawl down the stairs. Others are already on my level, closing in fast.

Then I see it. Sunken into a pillar in the wall is an elevator. I make a run for it, praying that it still works. Knowing if it doesn't, I won't make it. I'll have nowhere left to run. The simulation will end, and they'll have gotten their way. I'll be dead.

My palm slams into the arrow pointing up in a desperate attempt, and a soft hum cues the elevator doors to open. "Yes!" I cry out. I jump into the empty pod, squeezing myself into the corner. I turn around and aim my weapon. Through the opening, I fire off several rounds that manage to choke out a few infected. The elevator doors slowly begin to slide shut. As they do, I deliver a final bullet into an infected's skull, watching as they disappear — for maybe the last time.

At first, the elevator doesn't move. But the doors remain shut. I panic, worried that I've trapped myself in here. Maybe I've made the wrong call. But as my eyes glance over the button panel, I realize I haven't selected my floor. Scanning the options, I skim over the numbers until I reach the very last one: *104*. I jab my finger into the button, and the elevator comes to life. It lifts off, accelerating at a pace that makes my ears pop, carrying me to the top floor.

Above the panel, the numbers begin to climb, ticking upward as the elevator soars past each level. The weight of everything crashes down on me. My knees buckle, and I sink to the floor. The moment I hit the ground, I break. Tears spill from my eyes. My whole body convulses in an uncontrollable sob. It's all too much — the exhaustion. The weight of what's at stake. The fear that coils around my throat. Every near miss with the infected. The ache of loss for people who never even existed. Not here, at least.

Daphne. Ethan. Mother. Liam. I cry for them. For what they meant. For what the simulation allowed me to feel for them. I long for them in real life, but I don't know where they are. I don't know *who* they are. My memory is clouded by the system, by who I've known them to be here. The more I think of it, I'm not even sure I know who I am outside of this.

For a moment, I question whether it's worth it. To destroy the Barrier and shut it all down. Am I better off here? Here, where I've gained so much. Where I've grown stronger and managed to overcome a world that's stacked against me. Where I've loved, and I've lost. Where I've become more than I ever thought I was capable of.

Out there, in the real world, will it carry over? Will the things I've experienced here go with me, even after the simulation ends?

They have to. Surely, they will. Some things transcend realities. Strength, courage, love, hope — those are the things that bleed through, that aren't confined to just one existence. The very things that let me push past the limits of this world and take control. The things that allowed me to love Daphne, and for her to love me in return.

It has to mean more. A melodic hum sounds overhead, and my eyes lift to the screen above the panel. The pixelated number *104* flashes back at me. I've made it — and now it's time to put it all to the test. To see if love truly has the power to triumph over it all. To set me free.

The elevator opens to a narrow empty hallway. I step forward, and a series of overhead lights flicker on. I walk past closed doors on both sides of the hall, each one labeled with a number etched into a nameplate. My head stays on a swivel, looking around in every direction, waiting for more infected to emerge.

But I'm completely alone. The whole floor is desolate. The only noise is the sound of my boots trotting along the floor.

I march down the hall, guided by a red exit sign illuminated above a door. Painted across the surface of the door in bold lettering are the words: ROOF ACCESS. I press my hands into the latch and push through. On the other side, a stairwell spirals in both directions, with only two flights leading upward. I ascend them until I hit a dead end. Much like in Philadelphia, there's a vertical ladder bolted to the wall, leading to a hatch in the ceiling. Taking a deep breath, I sling my gun behind my back and grab ahold of the rungs. I hoist myself up and pound my fist into the hatch, sending it flying open, and the midnight air rushes in.

I break through the opening and out onto the roof of the Freedom Tower. The wind whips at me, threatening to throw me off balance. From this high, the view is spectacular. The river hugs the edge of the city, and buildings sweep across the peninsula for miles. I can even make out the faint outline of the Statue of Liberty's torch rising out of the Hudson.

Above me, a massive three-tiered structure pulses with kinetic energy. Within it, a towering cylinder rises from the rooftop, jutting through the center, reaching skyward. This must be the antenna.

At the base of the spire, a cage of metal bars encircles the rod, encasing it like a ribcage around a vital organ. Within the cage, black rungs cling to the body of the antenna, forming a ladder. Moving my eyes upward, I trace the ladder until it vanishes into the storm clouds circling above the tower, buzzing with blue electricity. The wind howls across the roof, blowing the cage door open to reveal the first set of rungs. Its hinges creak — as if beckoning me forward. Inviting me to climb.

I step into the cage and grip the rungs, gritting my teeth against the ice-cold metal that bites my palms. My stomach lurches. Even with the cage surrounding me, closing me in, the reality of what I'm about to do terrifies me. Vertigo rushes to my head. One wrong move, one faulty rung, and I could plummet, entering a merciless freefall that would surely kill me before I ever hit the ground.

But I can't back down now. I can't hold onto fear. Fear will keep me here, a prisoner inside my own mind. But courage will get me out.

I don't look down. I keep my eyes pointed up and grab each rung, one after the next, feeling myself lift off the ground as the roof below grows distant.

The ladder passes through three circular platforms, each one offering the chance for me to hop off. But I keep going. I ascend until the ladder finishes at a fourth and final platform. I swing myself from the last rung and onto the grated metal floor. Beneath my feet, the rooftop glares back at me from a hundred feet below, its surface hard and unforgiving. Beyond that, the city sprawls nearly two thousand feet below. My hands tremble. I grip the railing that encircles the platform until my knuckles are white, anchoring myself to it, trying to steady myself. But it's impossible. The antenna sways in the harsh wind, teetering in both directions.

Looking around, I search for a place to plant the grenade. Somewhere that's sure to sever its connection to the Barrier. But there's nothing. Nothing but the dark metal platform coiled around the spire and a second set of black rungs stretching even higher. Only this time, there's no cage. No enclosure to shield me from the fall. The rungs are exposed, bolted directly to the antenna's exterior, offering no refuge to anyone who dares to make the climb.

My whole body tenses. *It's not real*, I remind myself. *There's nothing to be afraid of*. I don't have a choice. Either I climb, or I give up. There's no other option.

I reach for the first rung with a shaking hand, but something stops me. A voice.

"Not so fast," it says.

My head jerks around, scanning the platform for any sign of life. *Is there someone up here?* That's impossible. Maybe it's coming from somewhere deep in my mind. From the other side.

But no. General Conrad appears on the other side of the platform, dragging his hand along the railing. A menacing scowl forms on his face as soon as our eyes meet.

"How are you—"

"What do you think you're doing?" he cuts me off.

I feel like I should be asking him the same question. But it's evident he's here to stop me. Somehow, he knew. Or he was brought here. He knew exactly where I'd be and exactly what I planned to do. And he's not going to let me get away with it.

"I'm going to shut it down," I say, certain he knows the truth. Convinced at this point he's not the man he was in the simulation. He's just a vessel for someone else on the other side.

"No, you're not," he argues.

"And what makes you so sure?"

He lets out a maniacal laugh that seems to echo throughout the atmosphere. "Because you're a coward, John. You're not capable of this. You'll never succeed."

"No," I say. "It's *you* who won't succeed. You're not in control. You've created this world — this whole system — to make you think you had control. But you don't. Not anymore." I'm not speaking to General Conrad. I'm speaking to the ones who put me in here. The ones who would do anything to keep me in it.

"No, John," he mocks me. "*You* created this world. You built the Barrier from the walls in your own mind to block out the truth. You're the one who's sick. You're the one with a disease. You built this world to keep the darkness out because you're too afraid to come to terms with it. And you'll die with it."

"I refuse to accept that," I say definitively. "I'm strong enough to handle this now. And I'm strong enough to get out."

General Conrad chuckles, as if he doesn't believe me. "Well, then you're going to have to get through me first."

He lurches forward. His feet hammer against the platform, causing it to shudder. I let go of the rung and bolt in the opposite direction, but there's nowhere to run. Nowhere to hide. We can dance around the platform all we want, but in the end, there's no escape.

General Conrad gains on me quickly. He closes in, advancing toward me in slow, calculated movements, like a predator narrowing in on its prey. My back presses against the thin railing, my upper body hovering over the freefall below. There's no time to think. No time to fight back. I have to act now.

His hands reach for my throat, but I duck beneath his arms. As I do, I wrap my arms around his torso and tackle him to the ground. The whole platform tremors, the metal groaning underneath us. I rear back and send my fist into his jaw. His head snaps to the side, and his mouth pools with blood. He shoves me backward, his strength overpowering mine. I stumble back, circling the platform's edge to create distance between us. He rises slowly, wiping the blood from his lips. His movements reminiscent of an infected — sluggish, limbs hanging loosely at his sides, but persistent. Eyes fixed on the kill.

"You can fight it all you want, Madoc," he bellows. Thunder rumbles overhead, but his voice is louder. "But you'll never escape yourself. You'll never break free."

My gun taps my elbow, still slung over my back. The general closes in. A few more feet, and I'll be within his reach. And it'll be too late.

"That's where you're wrong," I shout back at him. "You don't control me anymore. You don't get to decide my fate. I'm not obedient to you."

As the last words leave my mouth, I reach for my gun and chamber a round into place. General Conrad swipes at me, but this time, I'm faster. My finger slams against the trigger, and a bullet tears through his chest. His eyes widen in shock, and he staggers backward. Blood gushes from his wound, slipping through the grates in the metal at his feet. He wavers a few steps back, then he falls limp against the railing, teeters off balance, and plummets into the pitch-black night.

I don't waste any time. I sling the gun over my back and race toward the rungs fastened to the antenna. There's nothing to fear anymore. No one standing in my way. I unclip the grenade from my belt and clamp it between my teeth. With both hands free, I hoist myself onto the first rung. I continue up until I'm hovering several feet above the platform. The wind swirls around me, but my grip holds steady. I climb relentlessly until the antenna narrows to a point, like a harpoon piercing the dark clouds above me.

The rungs come to an end at a small opening in the rod that gushes with visible energy, forming a brilliant electric-blue current. It shoots upward into the turret that crowns the antenna. There, the Barrier reveals itself. Its energy fizzles and cascades downward in the shape of a dome, falling toward the rim of the city. As it falls, it fades until it blends seamlessly with the night sky. I've never seen anything like it before.

Clutching the top rung, I stare down into the opening. It pulses with energy as far down as I can see, spiraling all the way to the roof of the tower, where I first began my ascent. I rip the grenade from my mouth and don't hesitate. I pull the lever. In seconds, I know it'll detonate. And when it does, it'll take the entire city with it — the world I carved out of my own grief. A physical manifestation of my worst fears and deepest wounds. The parts of me I've tried to deny or run from. The things that make me who I am. But here, I don't have any hope of overcoming them. Here, I'm not meant to.

But out there, I can. And it starts here, right now, with this.

I force the grenade into the opening. A surge of electricity burns through my palm, setting every nerve in my body ablaze. A scream tears through me as I grit my teeth, but I know any pain I feel now is temporary to the relief that's coming on the other side.

I inhale, breathing in the last of the city. Before I can exhale, the Barrier explodes in a burst of white light, wiping the war, the city, and everything in it from existence.

And for the first time in my life, I don't feel empty. I don't feel afraid. I don't feel trapped.

I feel free.

END OF BOOK ONE

Acknowledgements

You did it — you made it to the end! I can only imagine all that you're feeling right now. Are you confused? Sad? Angry? Relieved? All would be acceptable ways to feel after finishing this book.

If there's one thing I want you to know, it's this: It was always going to end this way. All along, it was always going to be in John's head. There's no other way it could've ended because of all that's at stake beyond the simulation. There's a much larger story at play, one you'll learn more about in Book Two.

First, I want to thank God. Thank you for the gift of writing. Thank you for prompting me with this story all those years ago and for giving me the perseverance to see it through. Thank you that you are sovereign, and that you make all things work together for good. Thank you for sending Jesus as a sacrifice for our sins, to break through the barriers of this world and provide the only way for us to be reconciled to you.

To my wife, Courtney: Thank you for your unwavering support through all the time (and money) I poured into this. You never failed to encourage me, dream with me, and give me the space I needed to craft this story to its fullest potential. I love you more than any words I could string together on this page.

To my sister, Tiffany: You've read every version of this story — all the versions I wish would never see the light of day, and the one that finally made it across the finish line. You inspired my love of reading at a young age, and your feedback has been invaluable ever since the very first draft. Thank you for believing in this story and helping it become what it is today.

To my parents, Melanie and Rob: Thank you for your love and support throughout the entire process. You also read an earlier draft of this story, and you believed in me, even when I didn't believe in myself. To my dad, who reviewed a publishing contract with me when I was only fifteen. To my mom, who always let me share every detail and gave me the confidence to believe I could do this. Your unconditional love and guidance have carried me through every pivotal moment of my life, which ultimately shaped the heart of this story.

To my grandparents, aunts, and uncles: Thank you for reading an earlier draft and for your constant excitement about the finished product.

To my friends growing up: Thank you for taking an interest in this story as I toted it around school. You always said you'd see my name in bookstores one day, and now, I hope you're right.

To Lyndsey, my cover designer: Thank you for bringing the cover of this story to life in a way I never could've imagined. It's everything I dreamed it would be.

To Megan Records, my developmental editor: Thank you for your constructive feedback and industry expertise. You helped me crack the code when I felt like I had nothing left to give — and helped me trim nearly 30,000 words!

To Alexandra, Madison, Michael, and Tiffany, my beta readers: Thank you for investing your time and energy into this project. I always looked forward to receiving your texts and live reactions to parts you were reading.

To Ben, Faye, Scott, Kayla, Austin, Christopher, and my nephews, Griffin and Noah: Thank you for your encouragement and support. I'm honored to call each of you my family.

To my work team: Thank you for your endless support and for always letting me pause work to talk about my book.

To Sparrow, our goldendoodle: I'm sorry for all the times I could've taken you to the dog park but chose to write instead. I promise to make it up to you with all the toys, treats, walks, and field days you could ever want.

And last, but certainly not least, to my readers: This story is ultimately for you. I'm eternally grateful to everyone who chooses to pick up this book, whether you know me personally or not. I hope you feel even a fraction of the passion and heart that went into this book, and I hope it sticks with you long after the final page.

www.ingramcontent.com/pod-product-compliance
Lightning Source LLC
LaVergne TN
LVHW091659070526
838199LV00050B/2211